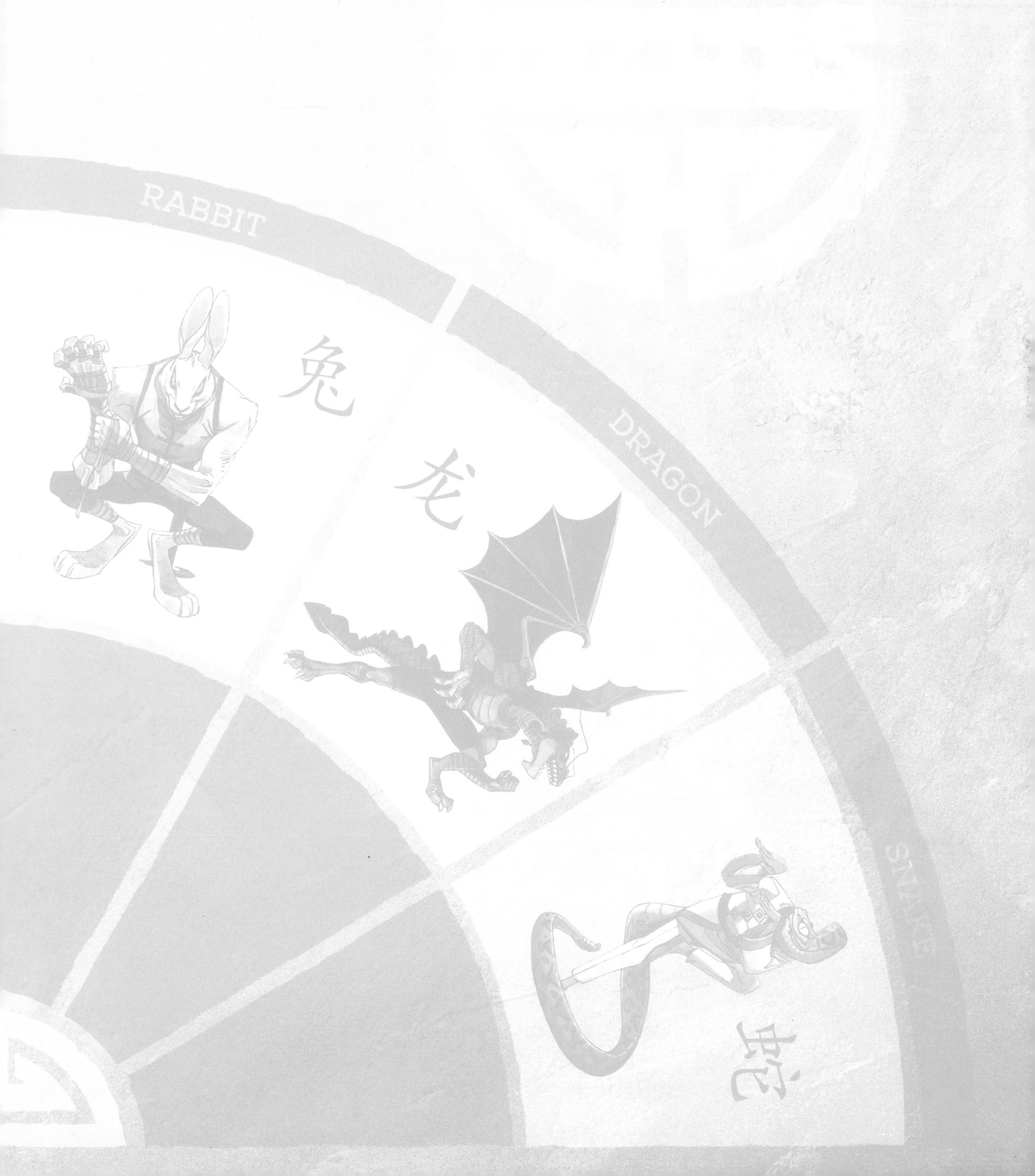
RABBIT
兔
DRAGON
龙
SNAKE
蛇

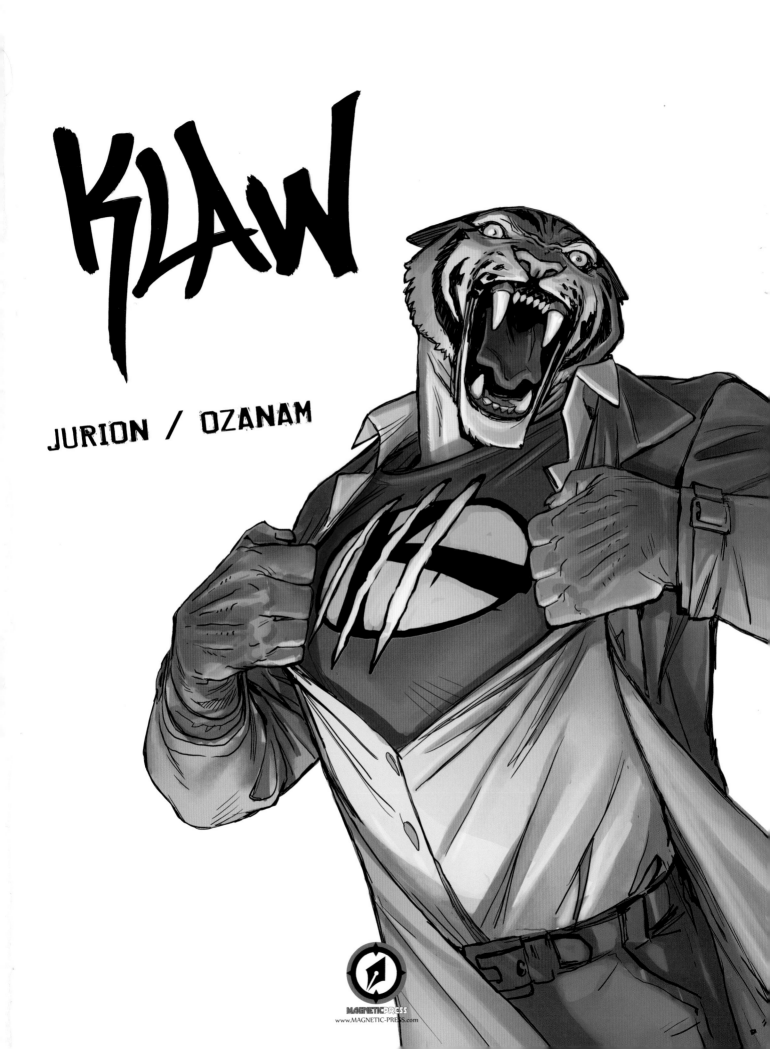

KLAW

JURION / OZANAM

www.MAGNETIC-PRESS.com

KLAW

THE FIRST CYCLE

Written by
OZANAM

Illustrated by
JOËL JURION

Colored by
YOANN GUILLÉ

Translated by
MIKE KENNEDY

Lettering and Design by
NEUROBELLUM PRODUCTIONS

MAGNETIC PRESS
Mike Kennedy, *President/Publisher*
Wes Harris, *Vice President*
David Dissanayake, *PR & Marketing*
4910 N. Winthrop Ave #3S
Chicago, IL 60640
WWW.MAGNETIC-PRESS.COM

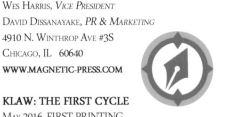

KLAW: THE FIRST CYCLE
May 2016. FIRST PRINTING
ISBN: 978-1-942367-20-8

First published in France in 2011 by Lombard. www.lelombard.com

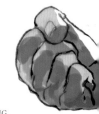

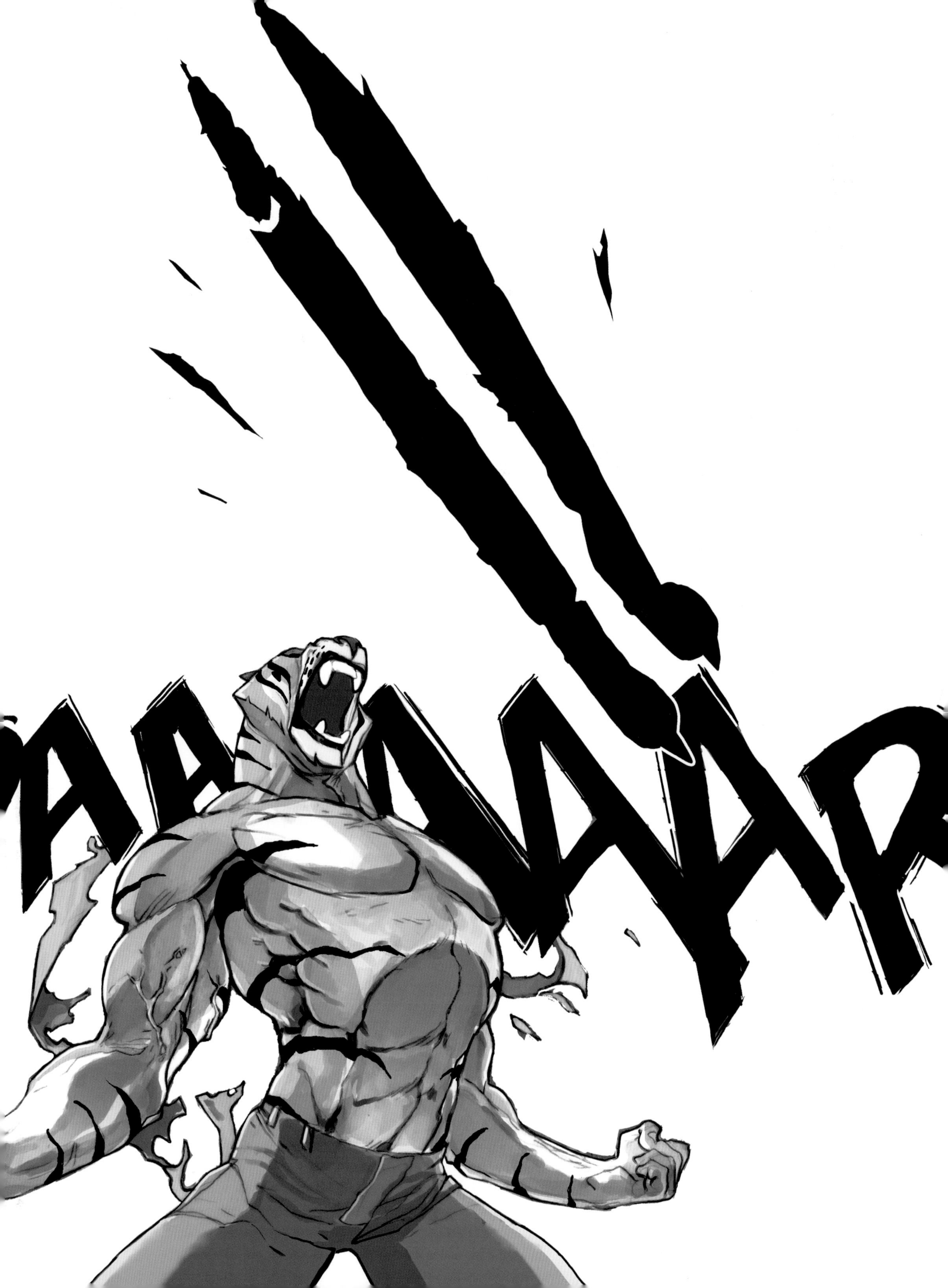
AAAAAR

PART ONE: AWAKENING

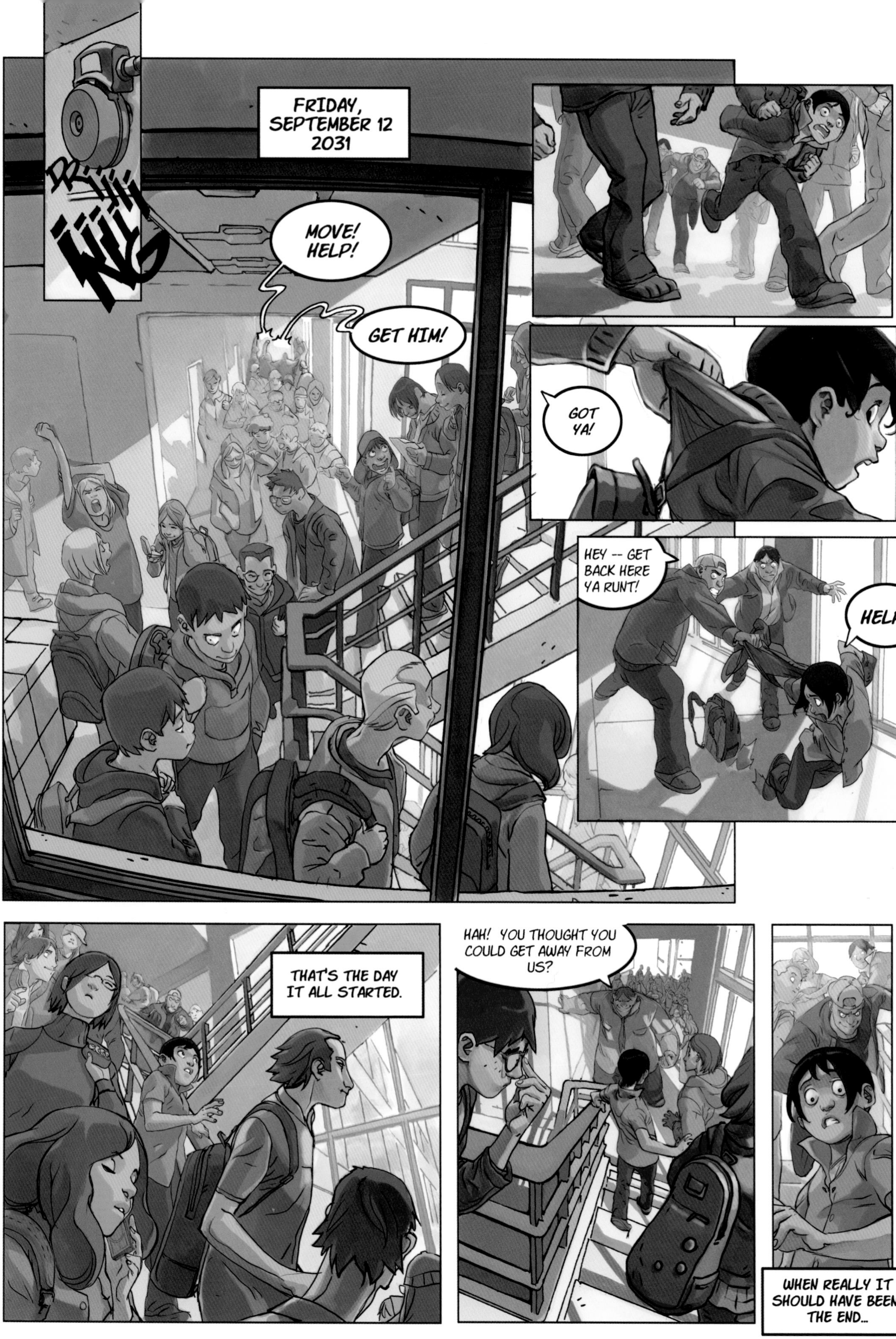
FRIDAY, SEPTEMBER 12 2031
DRIIIIIING
MOVE! HELP!
GET HIM!
GOT YA!
HEY -- GET BACK HERE YA RUNT!
HELP!
THAT'S THE DAY IT ALL STARTED.
HAH! YOU THOUGHT YOU COULD GET AWAY FROM US?
WHEN REALLY IT SHOULD HAVE BEEN THE END...

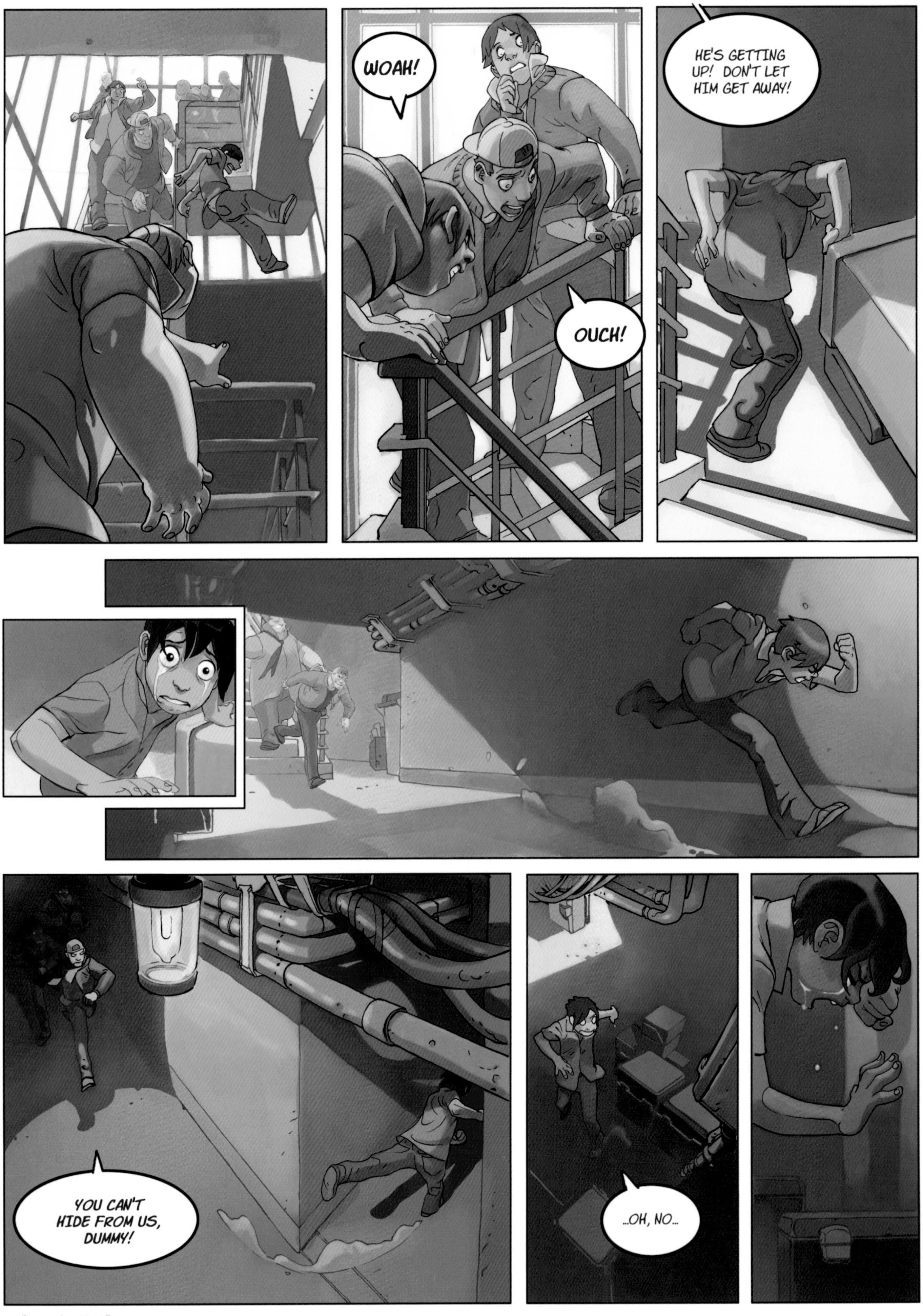
WOAH!
OUCH!
HE'S GETTING UP! DON'T LET HIM GET AWAY!
YOU CAN'T HIDE FROM US, DUMMY!
...OH, NO...

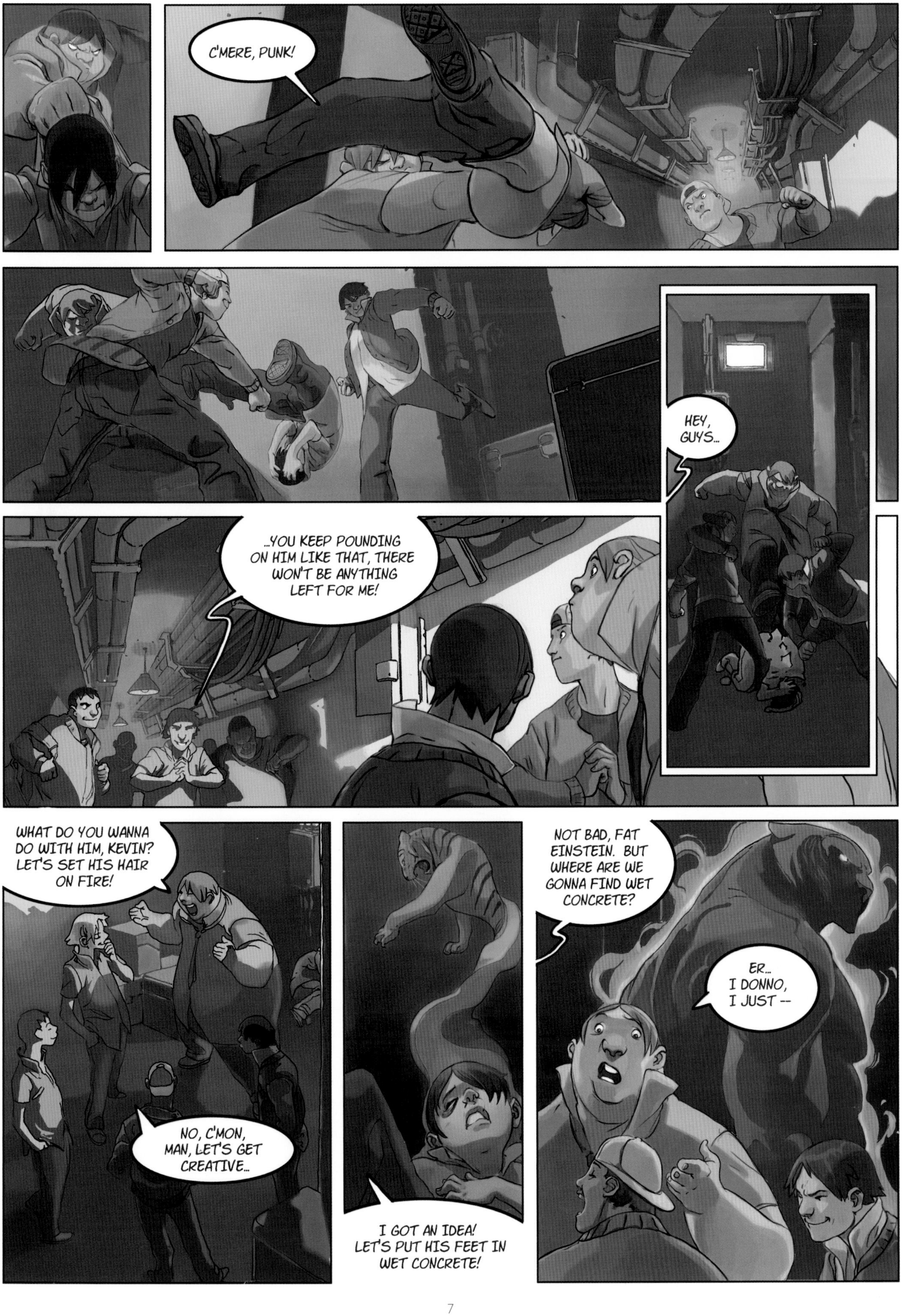
C'MERE, PUNK!
HEY, GUYS...
...YOU KEEP POUNDING ON HIM LIKE THAT, THERE WON'T BE ANYTHING LEFT FOR ME!
WHAT DO YOU WANNA DO WITH HIM, KEVIN? LET'S SET HIS HAIR ON FIRE!
NO, C'MON, MAN, LET'S GET CREATIVE...
I GOT AN IDEA! LET'S PUT HIS FEET IN WET CONCRETE!
NOT BAD, FAT EINSTEIN. BUT WHERE ARE WE GONNA FIND WET CONCRETE?
ER... I DONNO, I JUST --

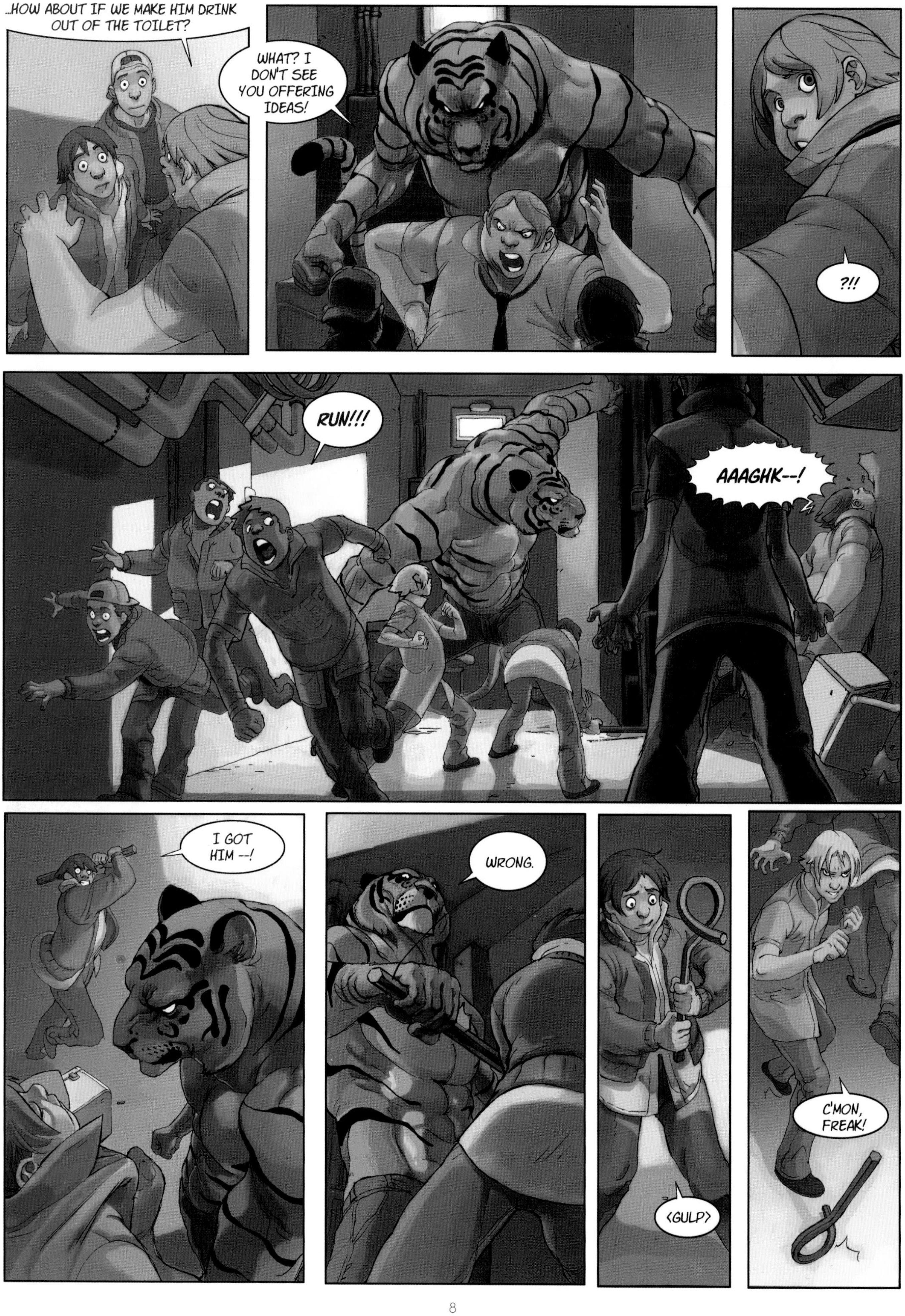
...HOW ABOUT IF WE MAKE HIM DRINK OUT OF THE TOILET?
WHAT? I DON'T SEE YOU OFFERING IDEAS!
?!!
RUN!!!
AAAGHK--!
I GOT HIM --!
WRONG.
<GULP>
C'MON, FREAK!

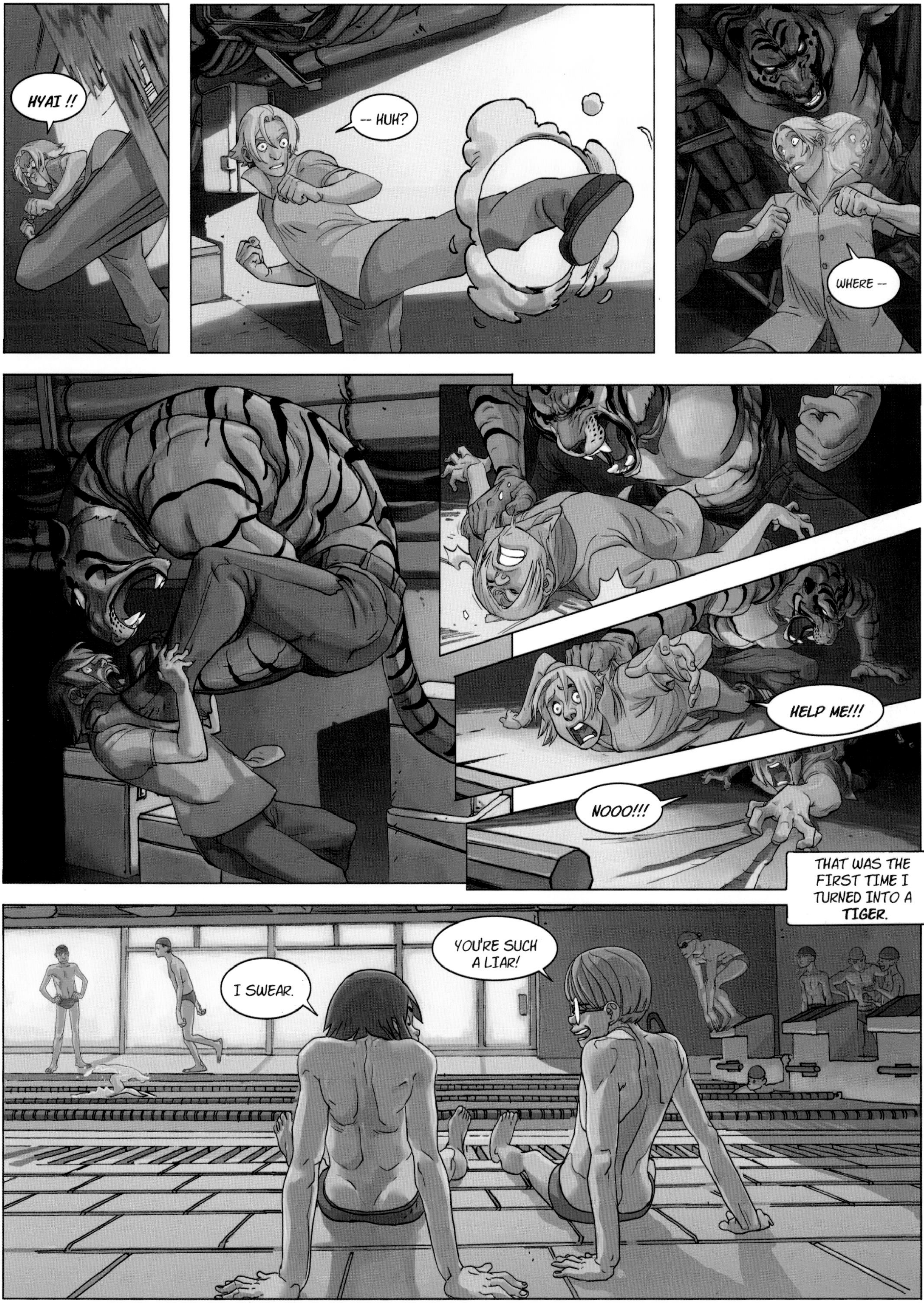
HYAI !!
-- HUH?
WHERE --
HELP ME!!!
NOOO!!!
THAT WAS THE FIRST TIME I TURNED INTO A TIGER.
YOU'RE SUCH A LIAR!
I SWEAR.

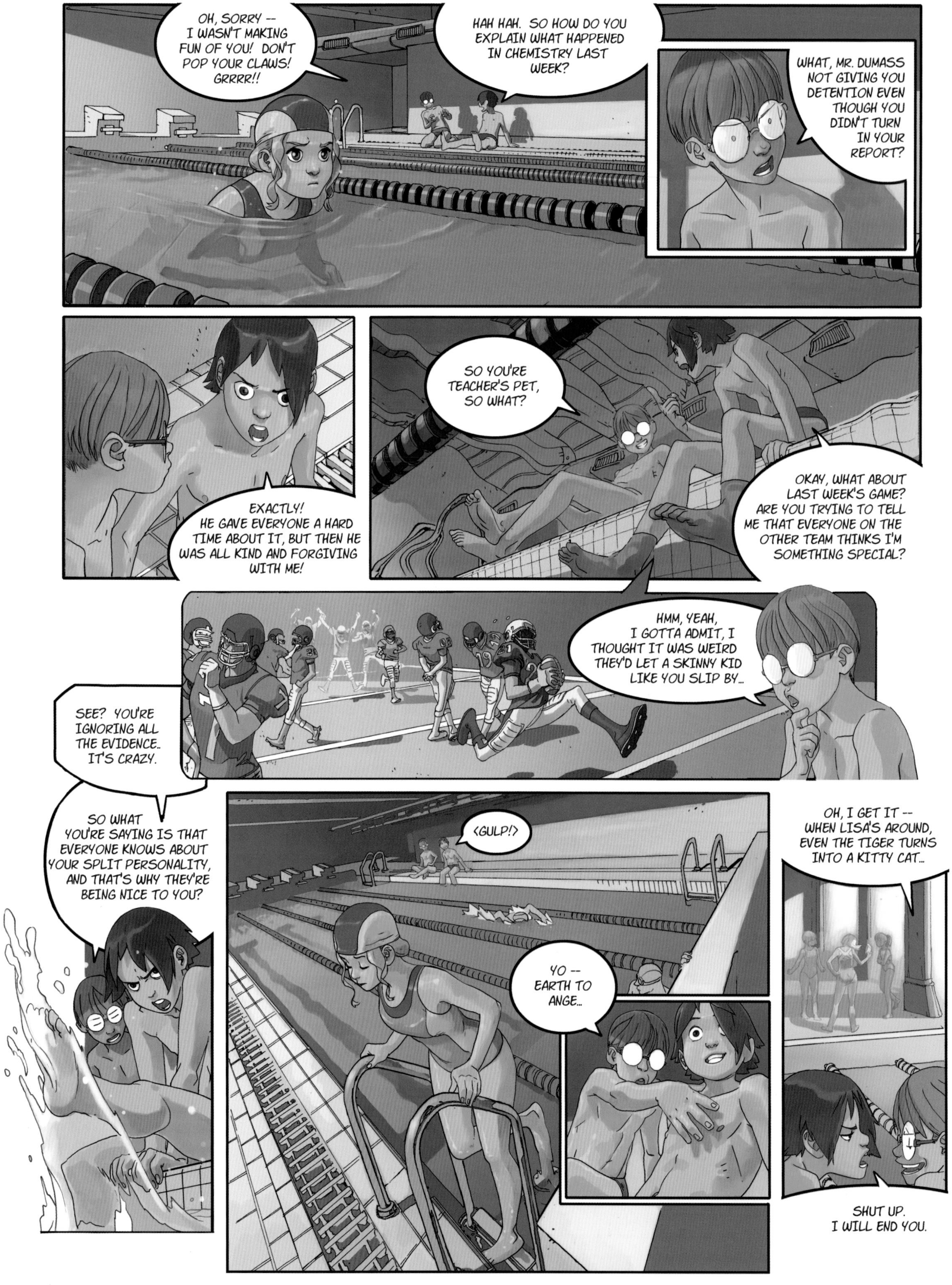
OH, SORRY -- I WASN'T MAKING FUN OF YOU! DON'T POP YOUR CLAWS! GRRRR!!
HAH HAH. SO HOW DO YOU EXPLAIN WHAT HAPPENED IN CHEMISTRY LAST WEEK?
WHAT, MR. DUMASS NOT GIVING YOU DETENTION EVEN THOUGH YOU DIDN'T TURN IN YOUR REPORT?
EXACTLY! HE GAVE EVERYONE A HARD TIME ABOUT IT, BUT THEN HE WAS ALL KIND AND FORGIVING WITH ME!
SO YOU'RE TEACHER'S PET, SO WHAT?
OKAY, WHAT ABOUT LAST WEEK'S GAME? ARE YOU TRYING TO TELL ME THAT EVERYONE ON THE OTHER TEAM THINKS I'M SOMETHING SPECIAL?
HMM, YEAH, I GOTTA ADMIT, I THOUGHT IT WAS WEIRD THEY'D LET A SKINNY KID LIKE YOU SLIP BY...
SEE? YOU'RE IGNORING ALL THE EVIDENCE.. IT'S CRAZY.
SO WHAT YOU'RE SAYING IS THAT EVERYONE KNOWS ABOUT YOUR SPLIT PERSONALITY, AND THAT'S WHY THEY'RE BEING NICE TO YOU?
<GULP!>
YO -- EARTH TO ANGE...
OH, I GET IT -- WHEN LISA'S AROUND, EVEN THE TIGER TURNS INTO A KITTY CAT...
SHUT UP. I WILL END YOU.

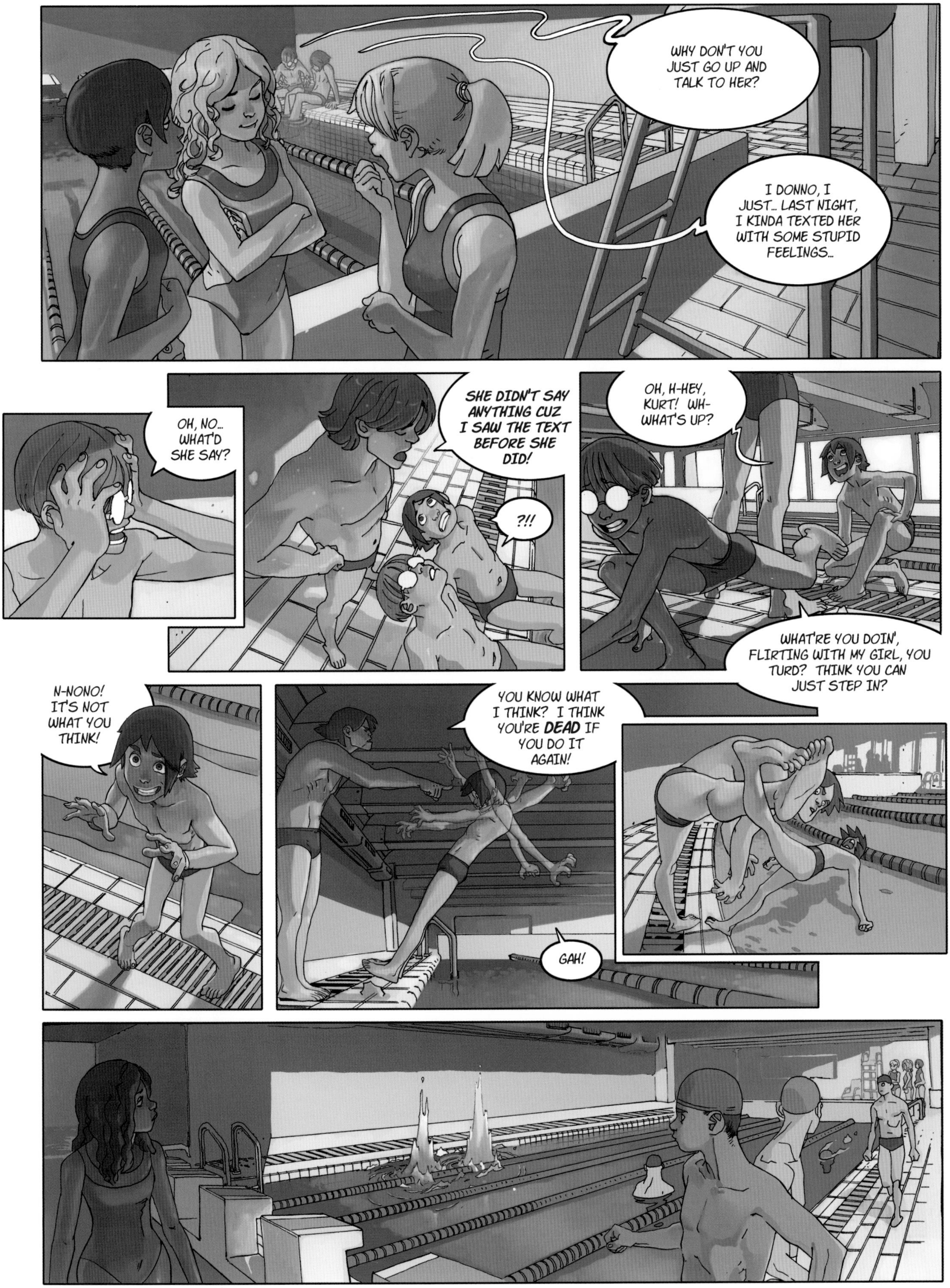

WHY DON'T YOU JUST GO UP AND TALK TO HER?
I DONNO, I JUST... LAST NIGHT, I KINDA TEXTED HER WITH SOME STUPID FEELINGS...
OH, NO... WHAT'D SHE SAY?
SHE DIDN'T SAY ANYTHING CUZ I SAW THE TEXT BEFORE SHE DID!
?!!
OH, H-HEY, KURT! WH-WHAT'S UP?
WHAT'RE YOU DOIN', FLIRTING WITH MY GIRL, YOU TURD? THINK YOU CAN JUST STEP IN?
N-NONO! IT'S NOT WHAT YOU THINK!
YOU KNOW WHAT I THINK? I THINK YOU'RE DEAD IF YOU DO IT AGAIN!
GAH!

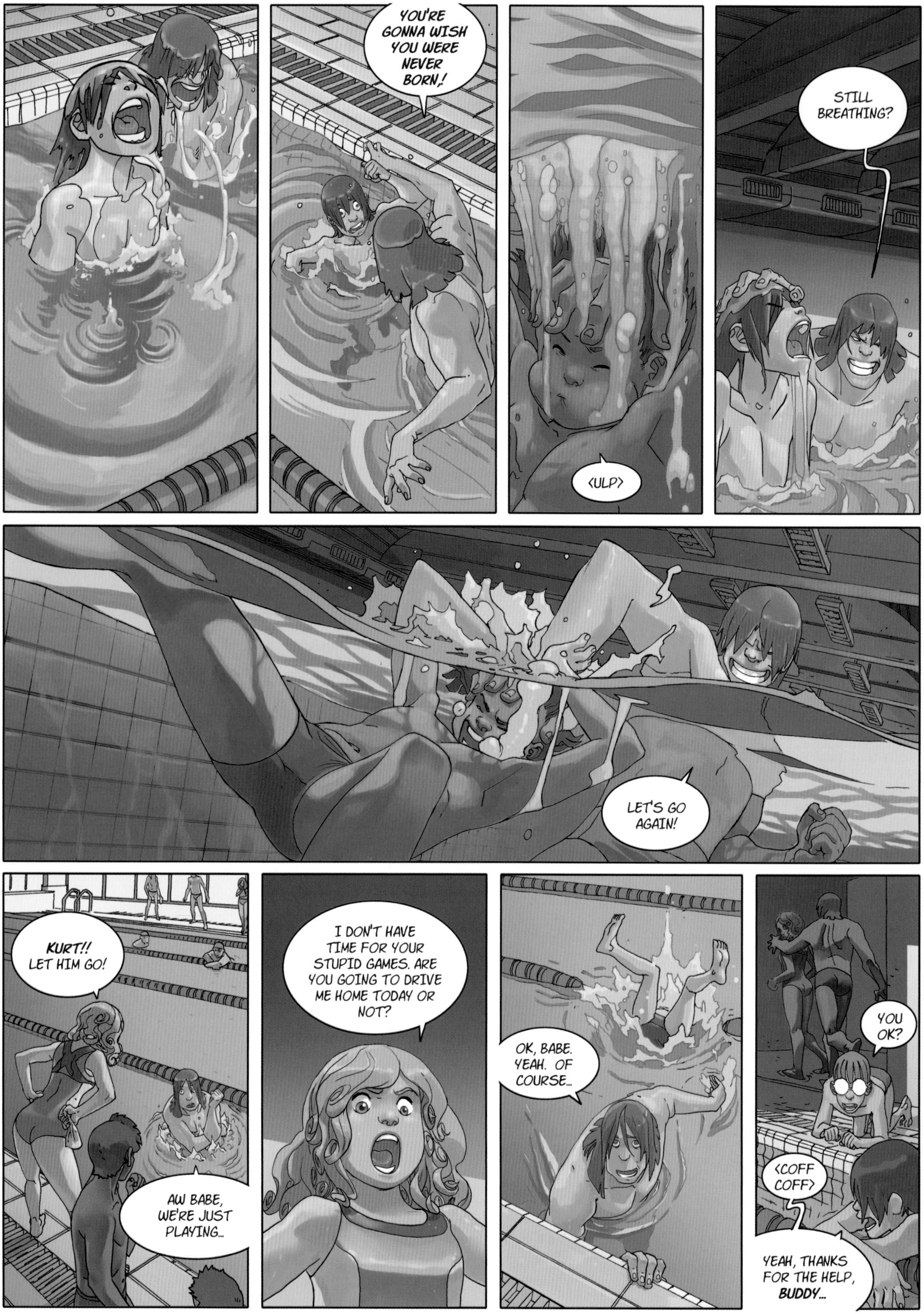
YOU'RE GONNA WISH YOU WERE NEVER BORN,!
<ULP>
STILL BREATHING?
LET'S GO AGAIN!
KURT!! LET HIM GO!
AW BABE, WE'RE JUST PLAYING...
I DON'T HAVE TIME FOR YOUR STUPID GAMES. ARE YOU GOING TO DRIVE ME HOME TODAY OR NOT?
OK, BABE. YEAH. OF COURSE...
YOU OK?
<COFF COFF>
YEAH, THANKS FOR THE HELP, **BUDDY**...

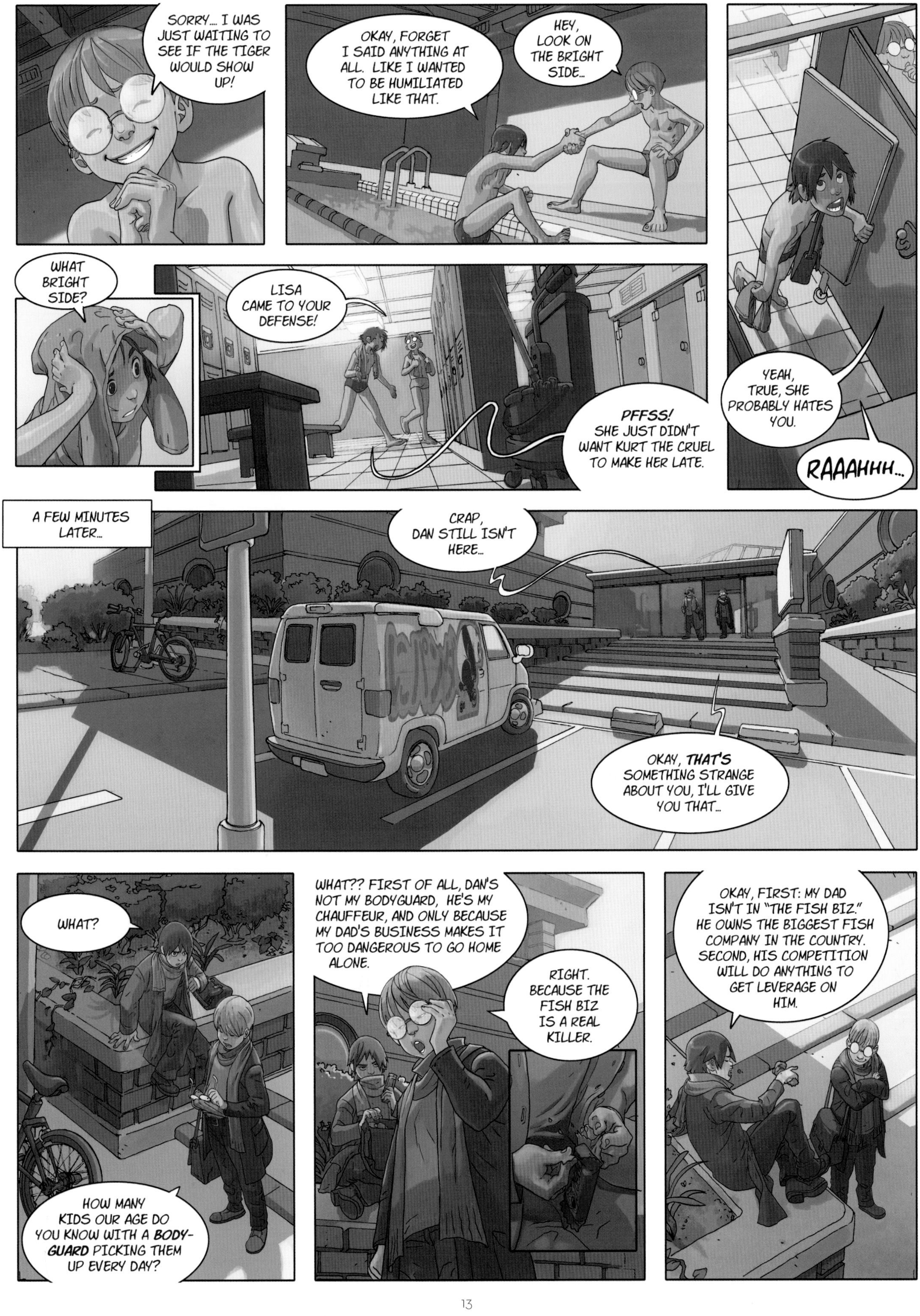
SORRY.... I WAS JUST WAITING TO SEE IF THE TIGER WOULD SHOW UP!
OKAY, FORGET I SAID ANYTHING AT ALL. LIKE I WANTED TO BE HUMILIATED LIKE THAT.
HEY, LOOK ON THE BRIGHT SIDE...
WHAT BRIGHT SIDE?
LISA CAME TO YOUR DEFENSE!
PFFSS! SHE JUST DIDN'T WANT KURT THE CRUEL TO MAKE HER LATE.
YEAH, TRUE, SHE PROBABLY HATES YOU.
RAAAHHH...
A FEW MINUTES LATER...
CRAP, DAN STILL ISN'T HERE...
OKAY, THAT'S SOMETHING STRANGE ABOUT YOU, I'LL GIVE YOU THAT...
WHAT?
HOW MANY KIDS OUR AGE DO YOU KNOW WITH A BODY-GUARD PICKING THEM UP EVERY DAY?
WHAT?? FIRST OF ALL, DAN'S NOT MY BODYGUARD, HE'S MY CHAUFFEUR, AND ONLY BECAUSE MY DAD'S BUSINESS MAKES IT TOO DANGEROUS TO GO HOME ALONE.
RIGHT. BECAUSE THE FISH BIZ IS A REAL KILLER.
OKAY, FIRST: MY DAD ISN'T IN "THE FISH BIZ." HE OWNS THE BIGGEST FISH COMPANY IN THE COUNTRY. SECOND, HIS COMPETITION WILL DO ANYTHING TO GET LEVERAGE ON HIM.

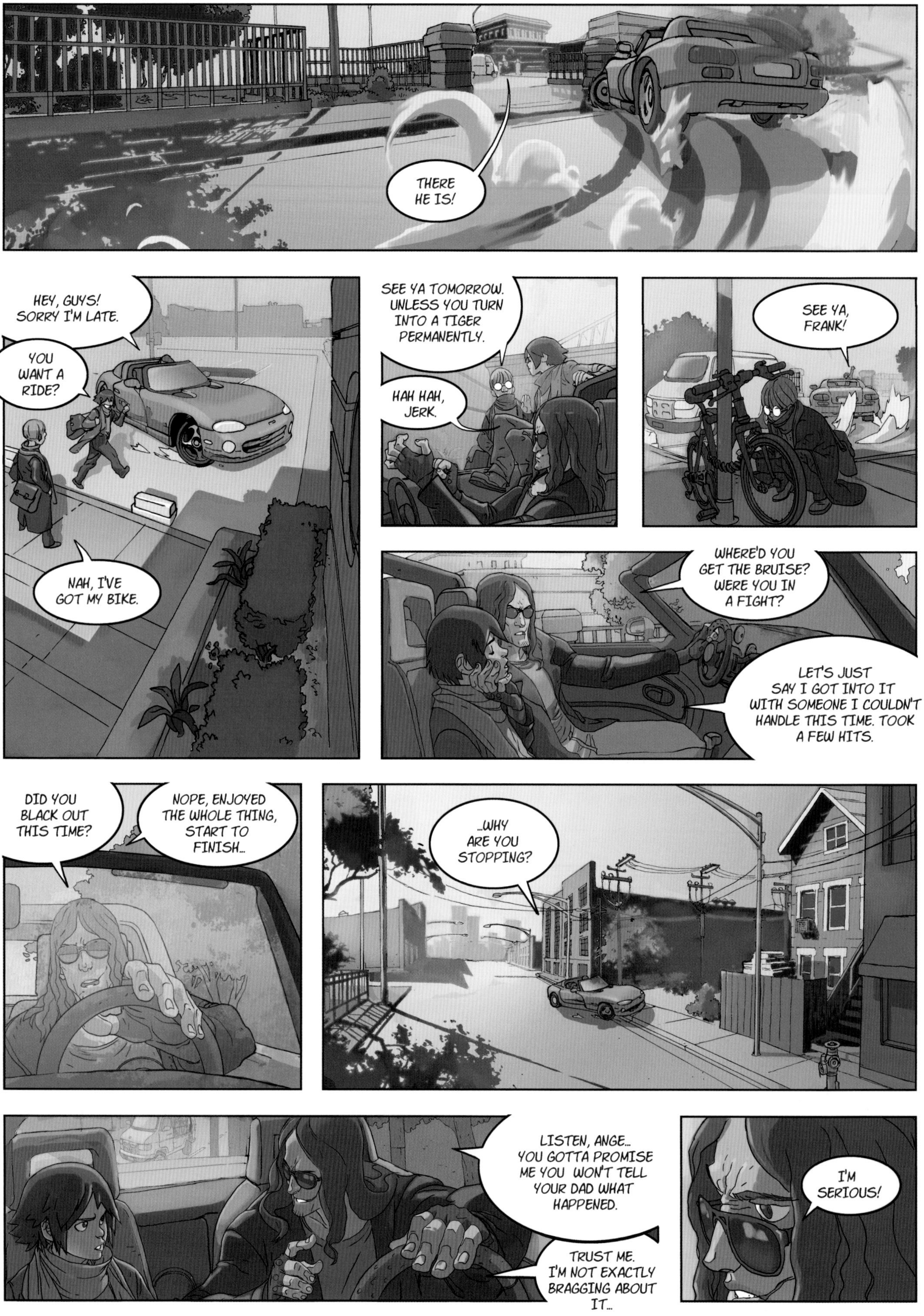
THERE HE IS!
HEY, GUYS! SORRY I'M LATE.
YOU WANT A RIDE?
NAH, I'VE GOT MY BIKE.
SEE YA TOMORROW. UNLESS YOU TURN INTO A TIGER PERMANENTLY.
HAH HAH, JERK.
SEE YA, FRANK!
WHERE'D YOU GET THE BRUISE? WERE YOU IN A FIGHT?
LET'S JUST SAY I GOT INTO IT WITH SOMEONE I COULDN'T HANDLE THIS TIME. TOOK A FEW HITS.
DID YOU BLACK OUT THIS TIME?
NOPE, ENJOYED THE WHOLE THING, START TO FINISH...
...WHY ARE YOU STOPPING?
LISTEN, ANGE... YOU GOTTA PROMISE ME YOU WON'T TELL YOUR DAD WHAT HAPPENED.
TRUST ME. I'M NOT EXACTLY BRAGGING ABOUT IT...
I'M SERIOUS!

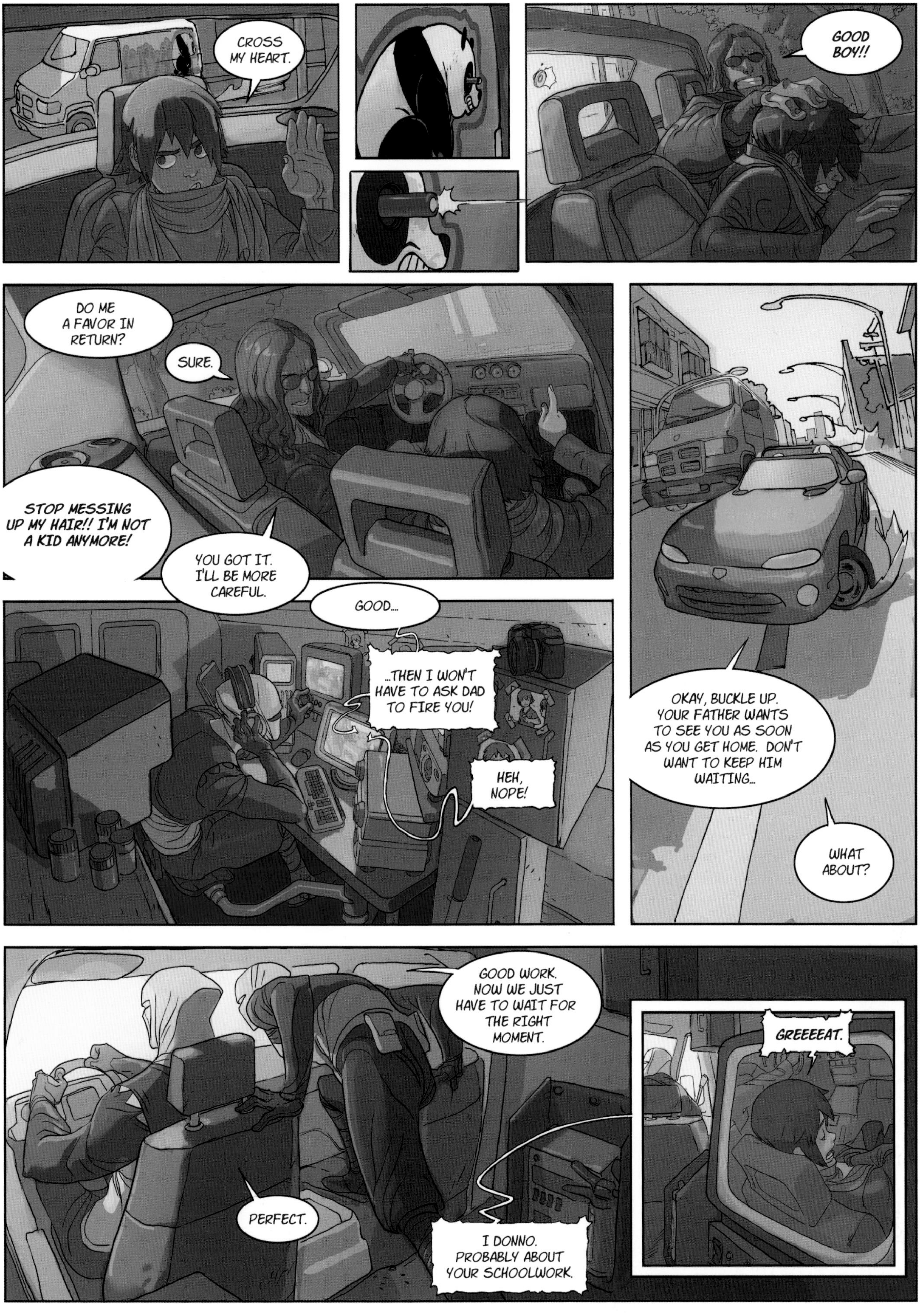

CROSS MY HEART.
GOOD BOY!!
DO ME A FAVOR IN RETURN?
SURE.
STOP MESSING UP MY HAIR!! I'M NOT A KID ANYMORE!
YOU GOT IT. I'LL BE MORE CAREFUL.
GOOD...
...THEN I WON'T HAVE TO ASK DAD TO FIRE YOU!
HEH, NOPE!
OKAY, BUCKLE UP. YOUR FATHER WANTS TO SEE YOU AS SOON AS YOU GET HOME. DON'T WANT TO KEEP HIM WAITING...
WHAT ABOUT?
GOOD WORK. NOW WE JUST HAVE TO WAIT FOR THE RIGHT MOMENT.
PERFECT.
I DONNO. PROBABLY ABOUT YOUR SCHOOLWORK.
GREEEEAT.

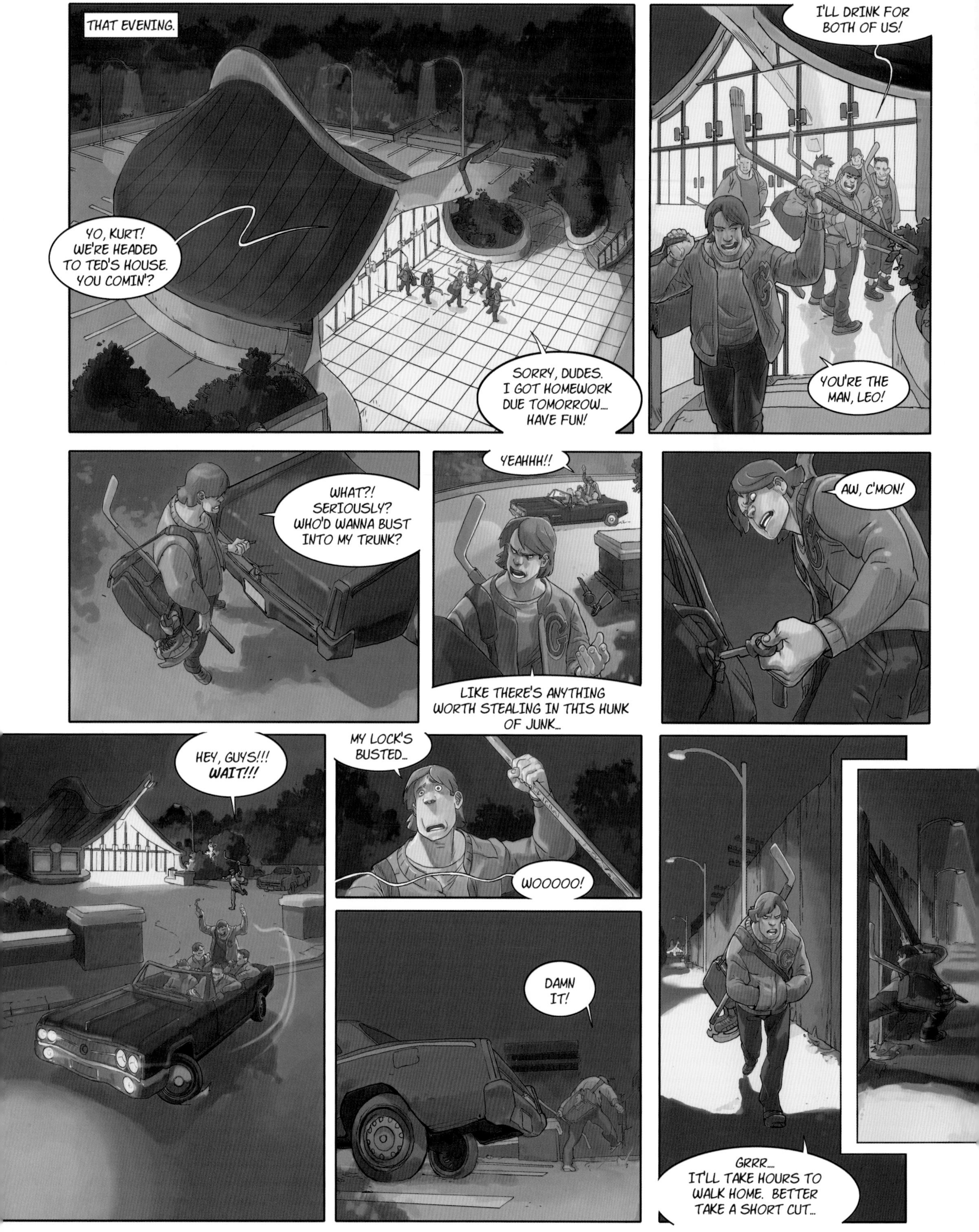

THAT EVENING.
YO, KURT! WE'RE HEADED TO TED'S HOUSE. YOU COMIN'?
SORRY, DUDES. I GOT HOMEWORK DUE TOMORROW... HAVE FUN!
I'LL DRINK FOR BOTH OF US!
YOU'RE THE MAN, LEO!
WHAT?! SERIOUSLY? WHO'D WANNA BUST INTO MY TRUNK?
YEAHHH!!
LIKE THERE'S ANYTHING WORTH STEALING IN THIS HUNK OF JUNK...
AW, C'MON!
HEY, GUYS!!! WAIT!!!
MY LOCK'S BUSTED...
WOOOOO!
DAMN IT!
GRRR.... IT'LL TAKE HOURS TO WALK HOME. BETTER TAKE A SHORT CUT...

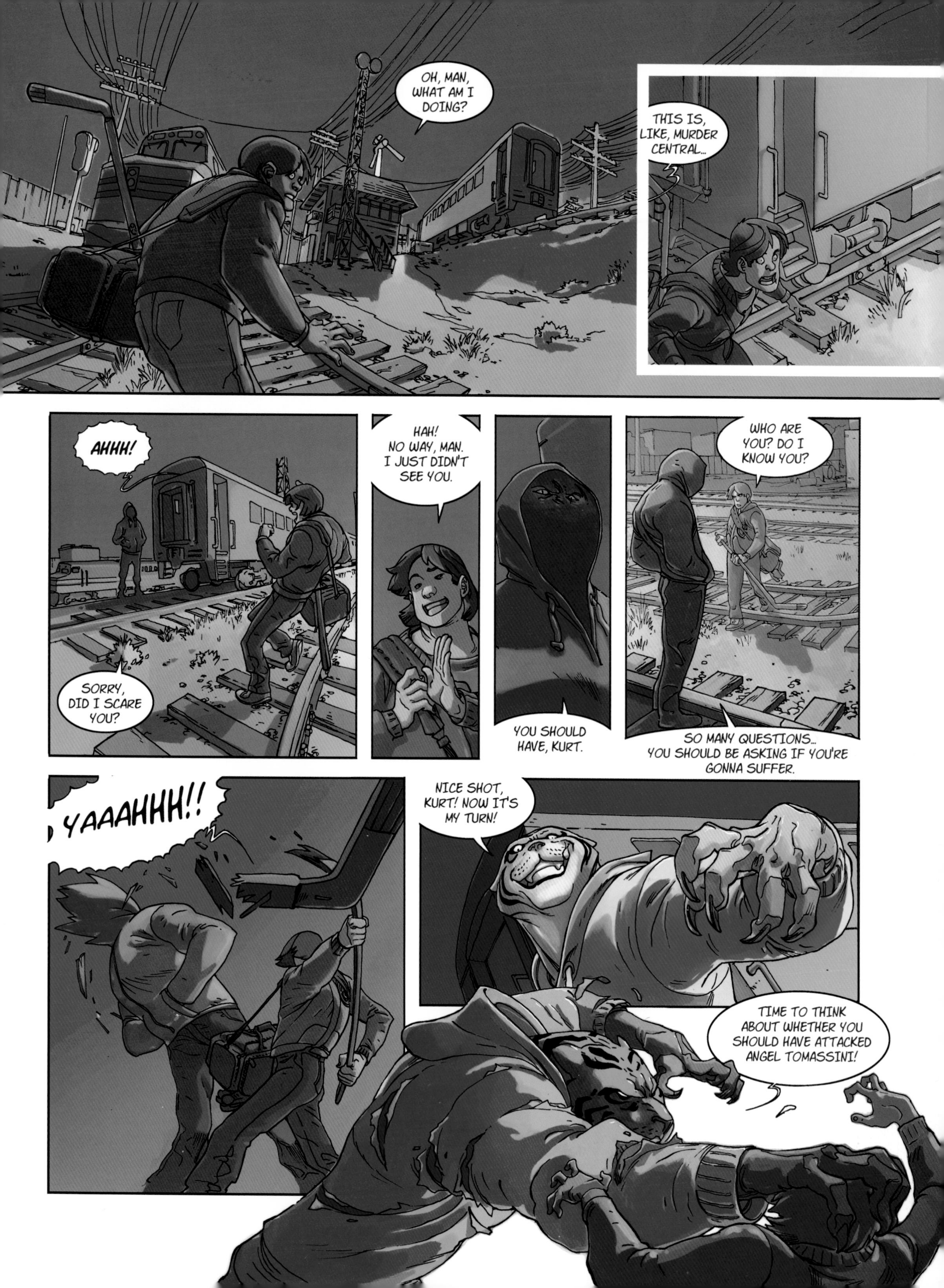

OH, MAN, WHAT AM I DOING?
THIS IS, LIKE, MURDER CENTRAL...
AHHH!
SORRY, DID I SCARE YOU?
HAH! NO WAY, MAN. I JUST DIDN'T SEE YOU.
YOU SHOULD HAVE, KURT.
WHO ARE YOU? DO I KNOW YOU?
SO MANY QUESTIONS... YOU SHOULD BE ASKING IF YOU'RE GONNA SUFFER.
YAAAHHH!!
NICE SHOT, KURT! NOW IT'S MY TURN!
TIME TO THINK ABOUT WHETHER YOU SHOULD HAVE ATTACKED ANGEL TOMASSINI!

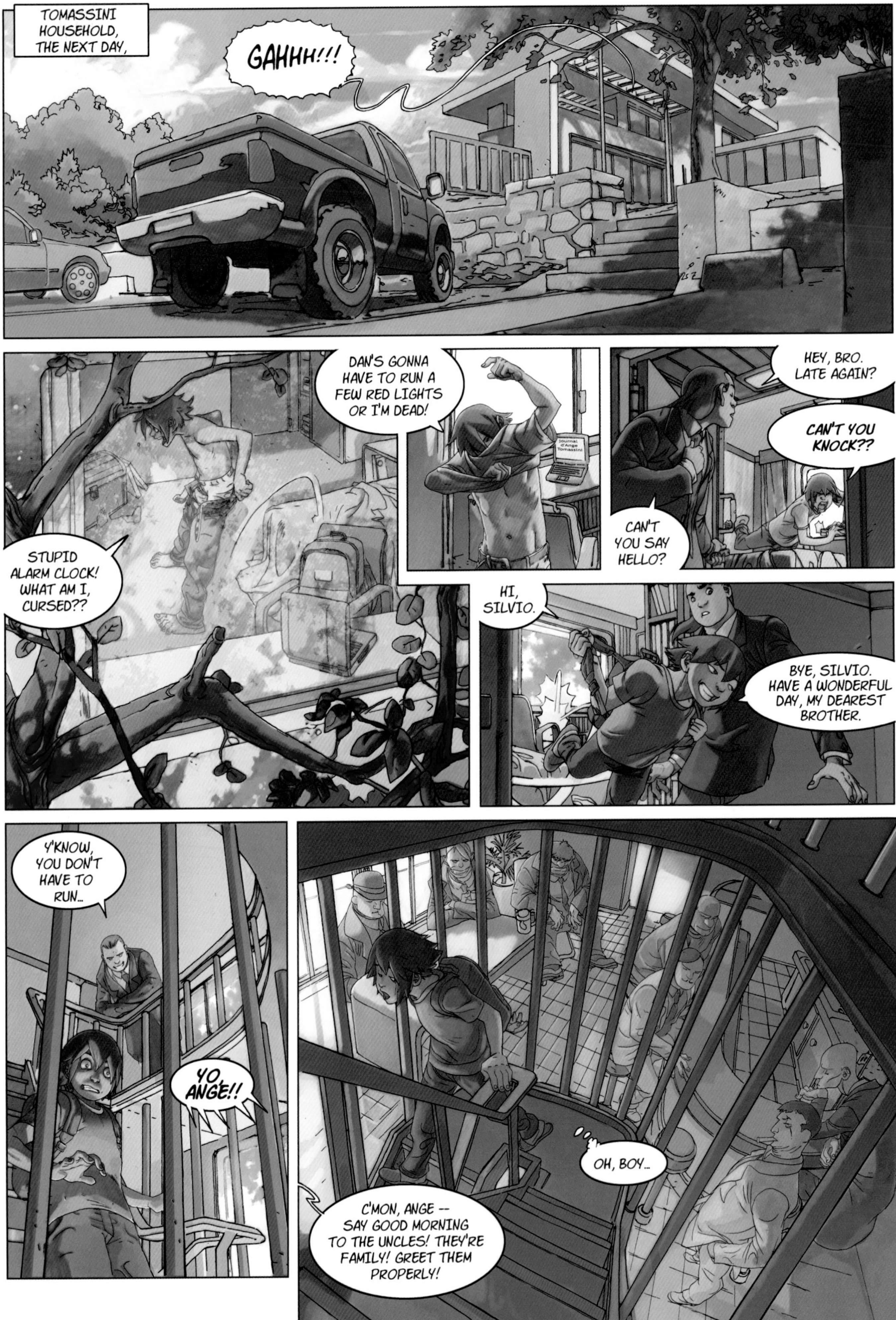
TOMASSINI HOUSEHOLD, THE NEXT DAY,
GAHHH!!!
STUPID ALARM CLOCK! WHAT AM I, CURSED??
DAN'S GONNA HAVE TO RUN A FEW RED LIGHTS OR I'M DEAD!
Journal d'Ange Tomassini
HEY, BRO. LATE AGAIN?
CAN'T YOU KNOCK??
CAN'T YOU SAY HELLO?
HI, SILVIO.
BYE, SILVIO. HAVE A WONDERFUL DAY, MY DEAREST BROTHER.
Y'KNOW, YOU DON'T HAVE TO RUN...
YO, ANGE!!
OH, BOY...
C'MON, ANGE -- SAY GOOD MORNING TO THE UNCLES! THEY'RE FAMILY! GREET THEM PROPERLY!

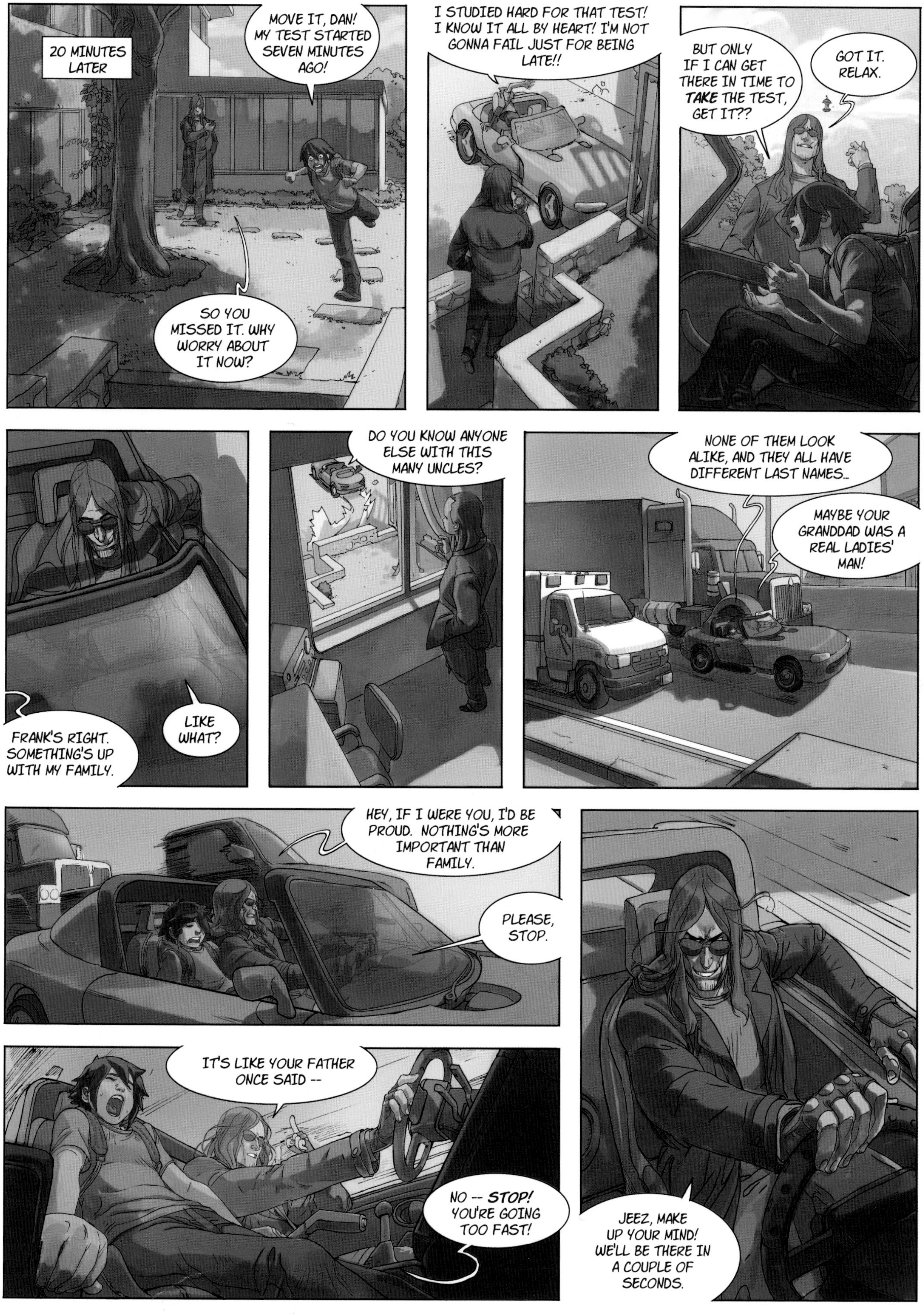
20 MINUTES LATER
MOVE IT, DAN! MY TEST STARTED SEVEN MINUTES AGO!
SO YOU MISSED IT. WHY WORRY ABOUT IT NOW?
I STUDIED HARD FOR THAT TEST! I KNOW IT ALL BY HEART! I'M NOT GONNA FAIL JUST FOR BEING LATE!!
BUT ONLY IF I CAN GET THERE IN TIME TO TAKE THE TEST, GET IT??
GOT IT. RELAX.
FRANK'S RIGHT. SOMETHING'S UP WITH MY FAMILY.
LIKE WHAT?
DO YOU KNOW ANYONE ELSE WITH THIS MANY UNCLES?
NONE OF THEM LOOK ALIKE, AND THEY ALL HAVE DIFFERENT LAST NAMES...
MAYBE YOUR GRANDDAD WAS A REAL LADIES' MAN!
HEY, IF I WERE YOU, I'D BE PROUD. NOTHING'S MORE IMPORTANT THAN FAMILY.
PLEASE, STOP.
IT'S LIKE YOUR FATHER ONCE SAID --
NO -- STOP! YOU'RE GOING TOO FAST!
JEEZ, MAKE UP YOUR MIND! WE'LL BE THERE IN A COUPLE OF SECONDS.

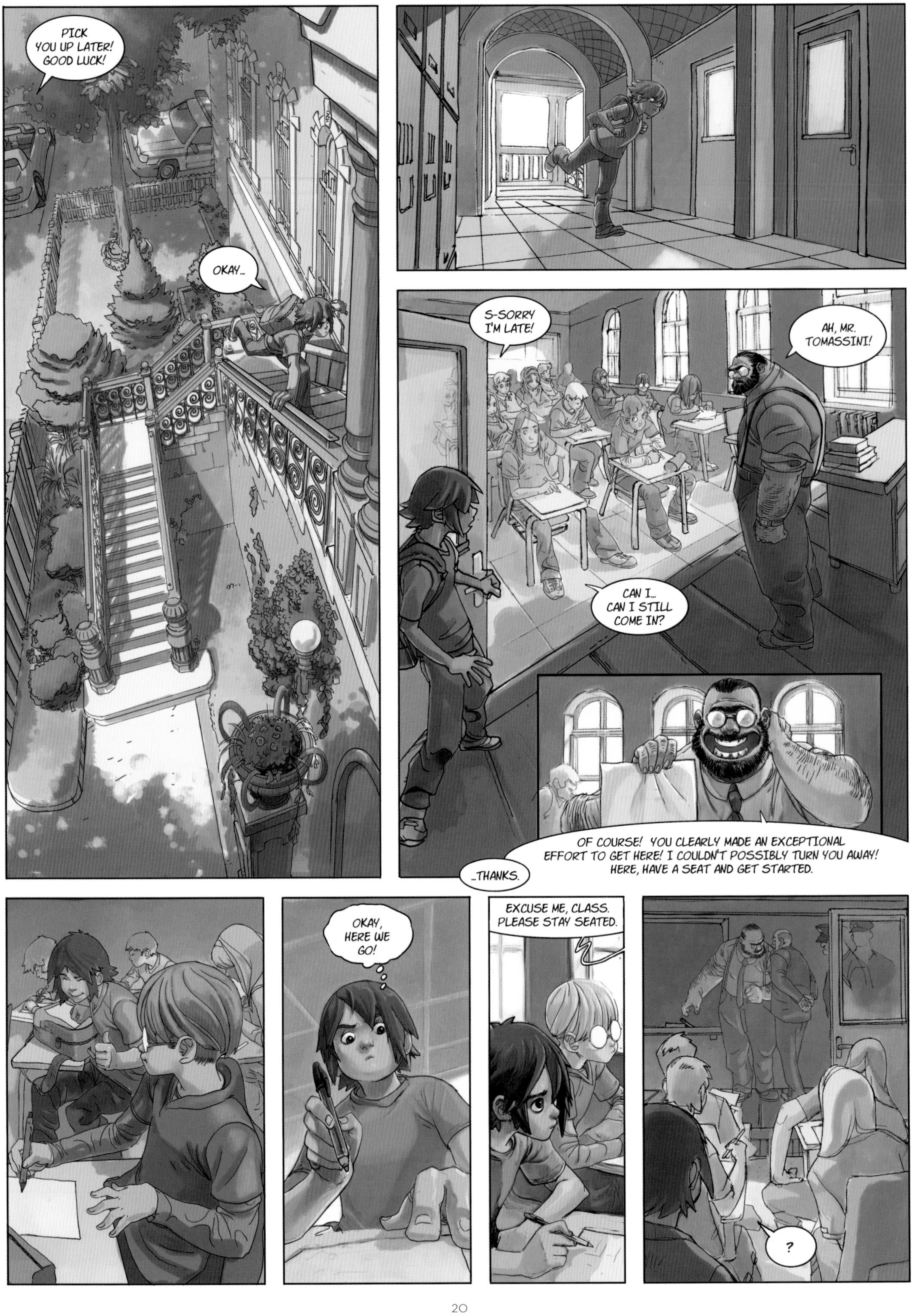

PICK YOU UP LATER! GOOD LUCK!
OKAY...
S-SORRY I'M LATE!
AH, MR. TOMASSINI!
CAN I... CAN I STILL COME IN?
OF COURSE! YOU CLEARLY MADE AN EXCEPTIONAL EFFORT TO GET HERE! I COULDN'T POSSIBLY TURN YOU AWAY! HERE, HAVE A SEAT AND GET STARTED.
...THANKS.
OKAY, HERE WE GO!
EXCUSE ME, CLASS. PLEASE STAY SEATED.
?

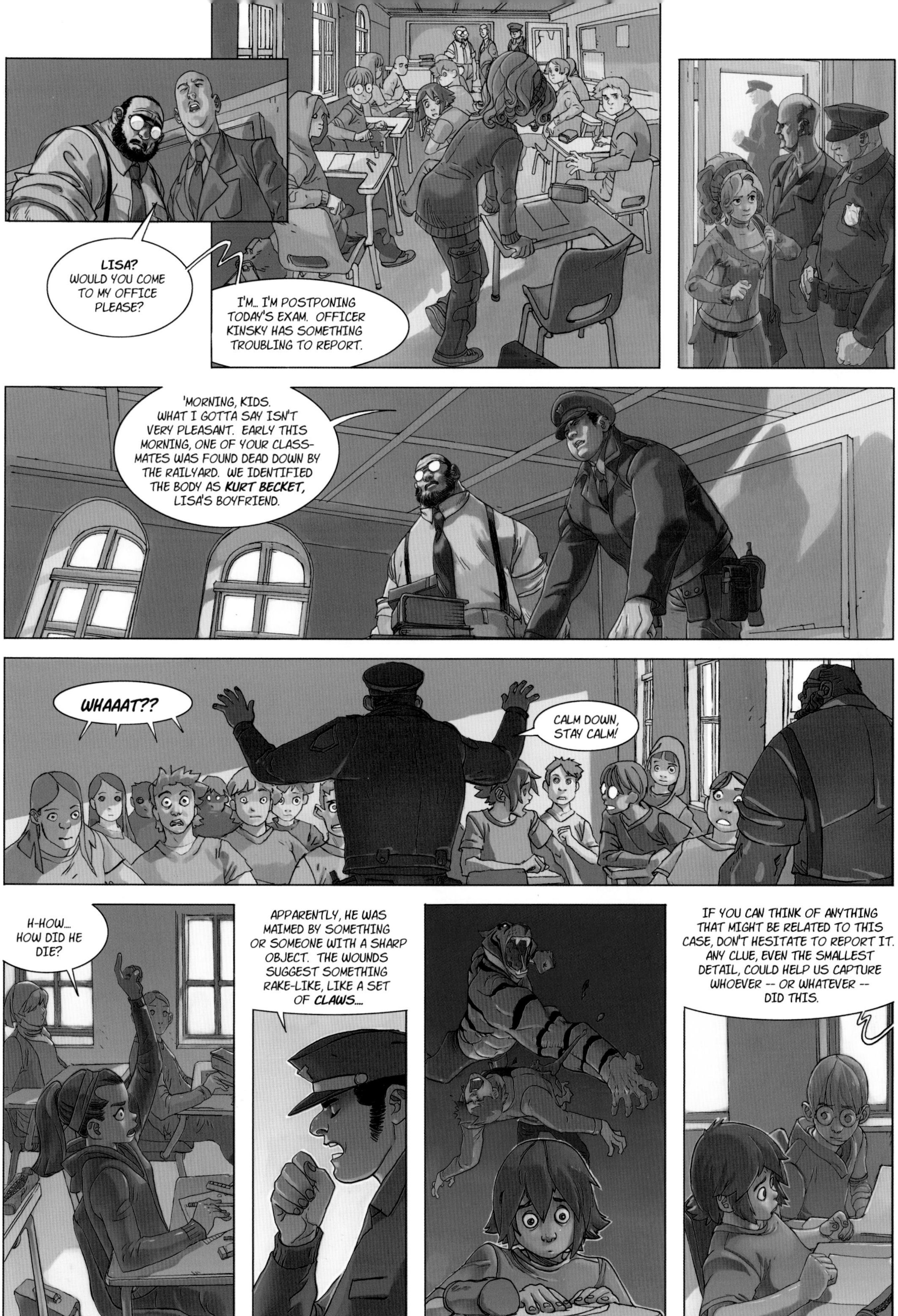
LISA? WOULD YOU COME TO MY OFFICE PLEASE?
I'M... I'M POSTPONING TODAY'S EXAM. OFFICER KINSKY HAS SOMETHING TROUBLING TO REPORT.
'MORNING, KIDS. WHAT I GOTTA SAY ISN'T VERY PLEASANT. EARLY THIS MORNING, ONE OF YOUR CLASSMATES WAS FOUND DEAD DOWN BY THE RAILYARD. WE IDENTIFIED THE BODY AS KURT BECKET, LISA'S BOYFRIEND.
WHAAAT??
CALM DOWN, STAY CALM!
H-HOW... HOW DID HE DIE?
APPARENTLY, HE WAS MAIMED BY SOMETHING OR SOMEONE WITH A SHARP OBJECT. THE WOUNDS SUGGEST SOMETHING RAKE-LIKE, LIKE A SET OF CLAWS....
IF YOU CAN THINK OF ANYTHING THAT MIGHT BE RELATED TO THIS CASE, DON'T HESITATE TO REPORT IT. ANY CLUE, EVEN THE SMALLEST DETAIL, COULD HELP US CAPTURE WHOEVER -- OR WHATEVER -- DID THIS.

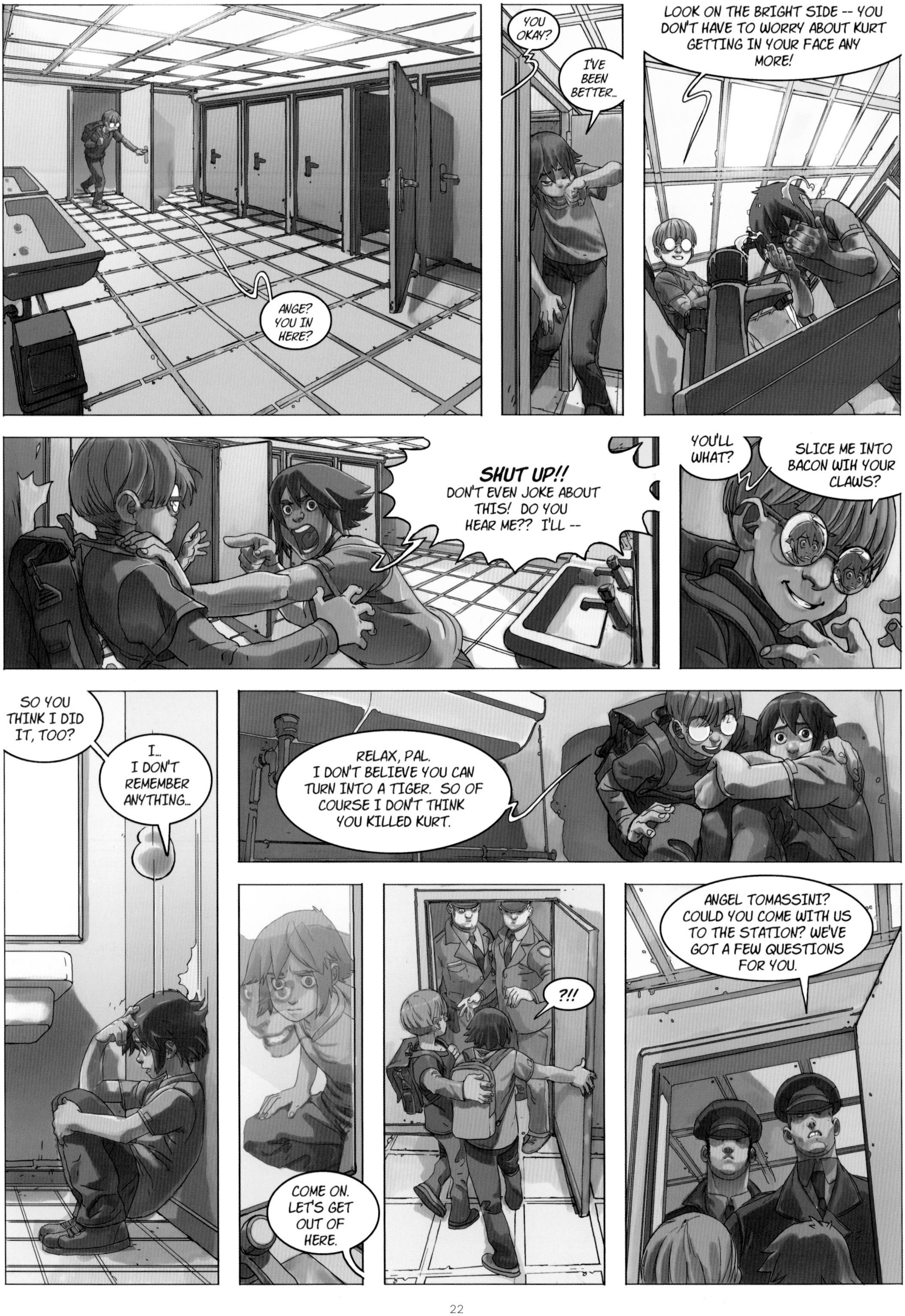
ANGE? YOU IN HERE?
YOU OKAY?
I'VE BEEN BETTER...
LOOK ON THE BRIGHT SIDE -- YOU DON'T HAVE TO WORRY ABOUT KURT GETTING IN YOUR FACE ANY MORE!
SHUT UP!! DON'T EVEN JOKE ABOUT THIS! DO YOU HEAR ME?? I'LL --
YOU'LL WHAT?
SLICE ME INTO BACON WIH YOUR CLAWS?
SO YOU THINK I DID IT, TOO?
I... I DON'T REMEMBER ANYTHING...
RELAX, PAL. I DON'T BELIEVE YOU CAN TURN INTO A TIGER. SO OF COURSE I DON'T THINK YOU KILLED KURT.
COME ON. LET'S GET OUT OF HERE.
?!!
ANGEL TOMASSINI? COULD YOU COME WITH US TO THE STATION? WE'VE GOT A FEW QUESTIONS FOR YOU.

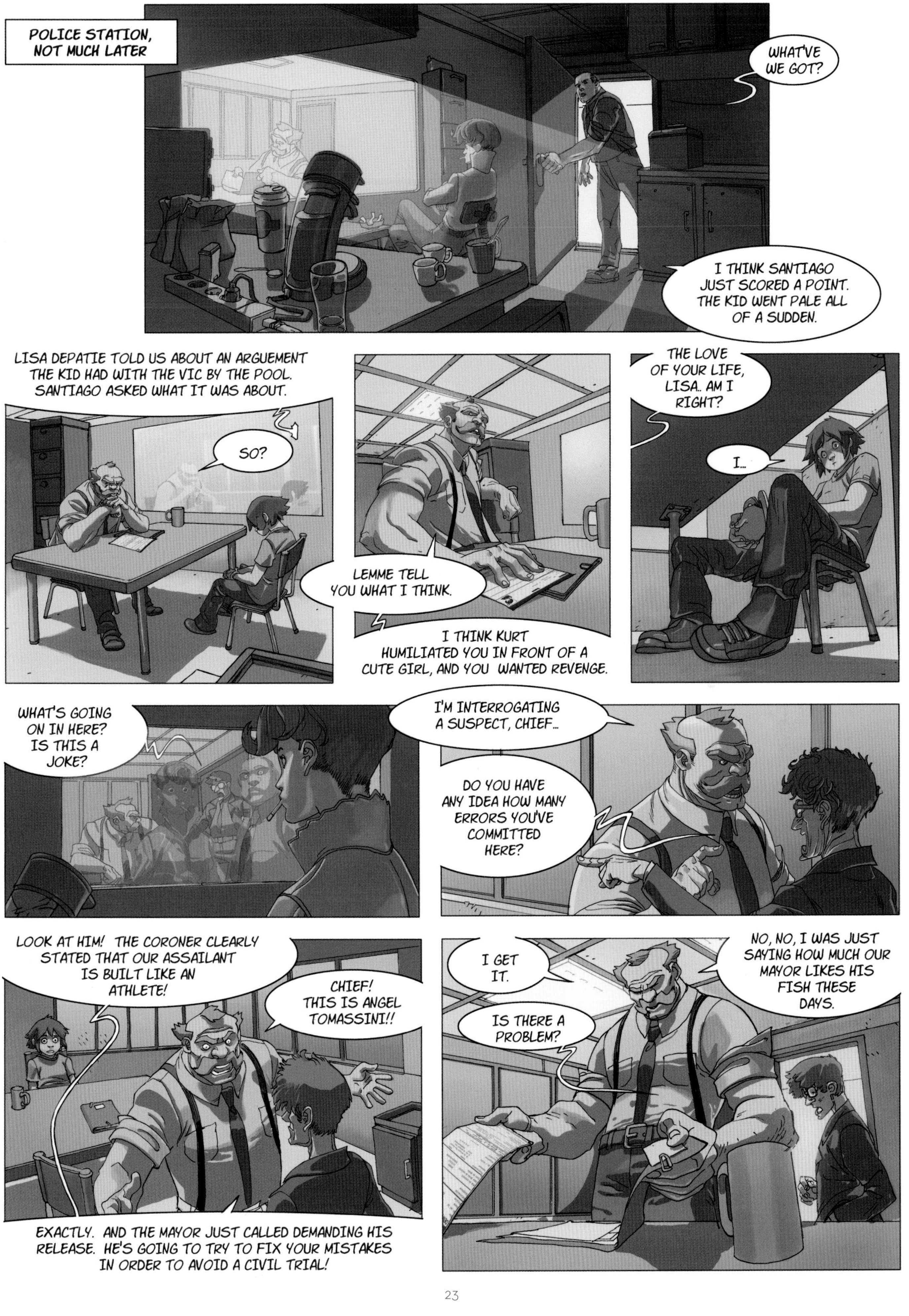
POLICE STATION, NOT MUCH LATER
WHAT'VE WE GOT?
I THINK SANTIAGO JUST SCORED A POINT. THE KID WENT PALE ALL OF A SUDDEN.
LISA DEPATIE TOLD US ABOUT AN ARGUEMENT THE KID HAD WITH THE VIC BY THE POOL. SANTIAGO ASKED WHAT IT WAS ABOUT.
SO?
LEMME TELL YOU WHAT I THINK.
I THINK KURT HUMILIATED YOU IN FRONT OF A CUTE GIRL, AND YOU WANTED REVENGE.
THE LOVE OF YOUR LIFE, LISA.. AM I RIGHT?
I...
WHAT'S GOING ON IN HERE? IS THIS A JOKE?
I'M INTERROGATING A SUSPECT, CHIEF...
DO YOU HAVE ANY IDEA HOW MANY ERRORS YOU'VE COMMITTED HERE?
LOOK AT HIM! THE CORONER CLEARLY STATED THAT OUR ASSAILANT IS BUILT LIKE AN ATHLETE!
CHIEF! THIS IS ANGEL TOMASSINI!!
EXACTLY. AND THE MAYOR JUST CALLED DEMANDING HIS RELEASE. HE'S GOING TO TRY TO FIX YOUR MISTAKES IN ORDER TO AVOID A CIVIL TRIAL!
I GET IT.
IS THERE A PROBLEM?
NO, NO, I WAS JUST SAYING HOW MUCH OUR MAYOR LIKES HIS FISH THESE DAYS.

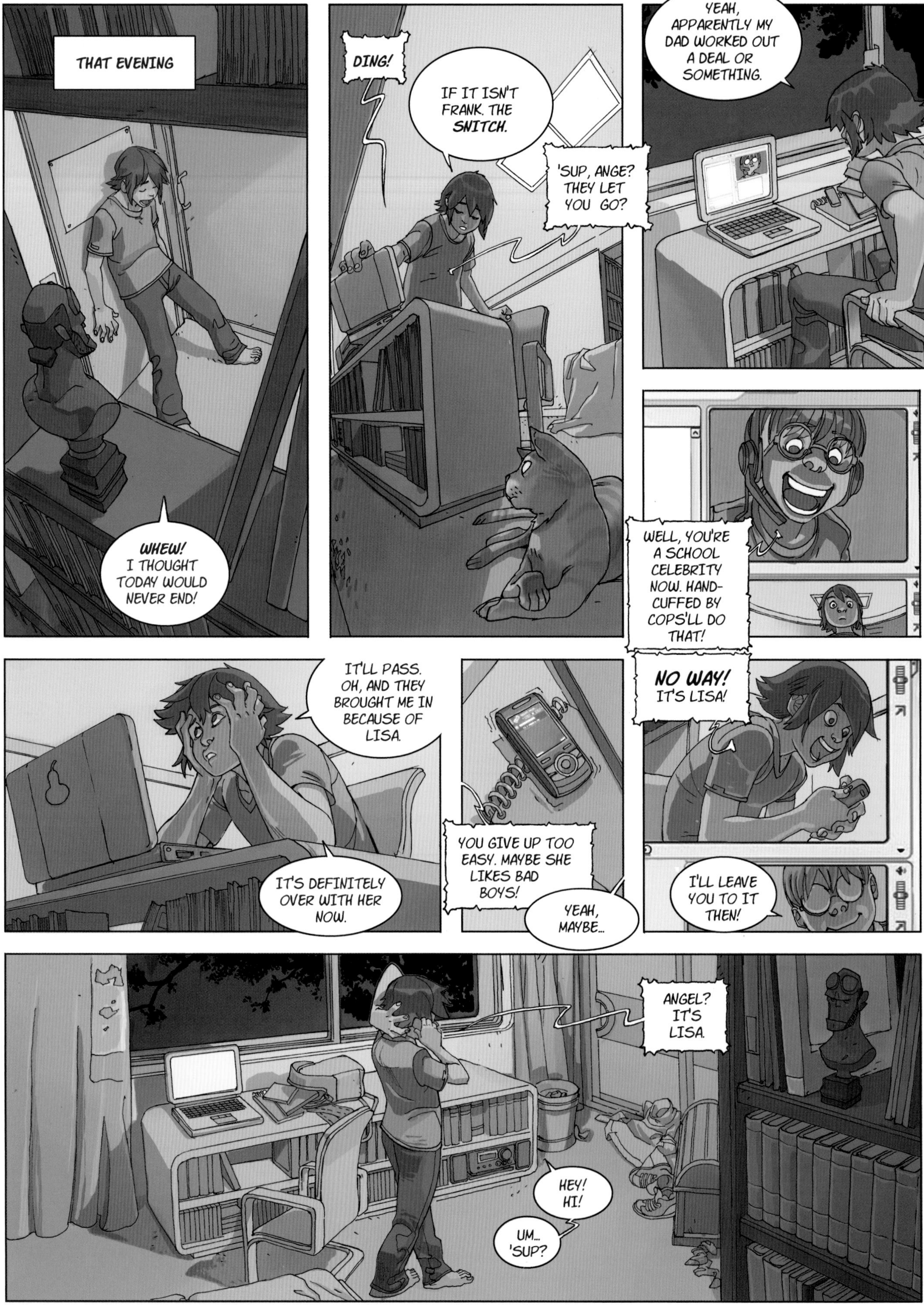
THAT EVENING
WHEW! I THOUGHT TODAY WOULD NEVER END!
DING!
IF IT ISN'T FRANK. THE SWITCH.
'SUP, ANGE? THEY LET YOU GO?
YEAH, APPARENTLY MY DAD WORKED OUT A DEAL OR SOMETHING.
WELL, YOU'RE A SCHOOL CELEBRITY NOW. HAND-CUFFED BY COPS'LL DO THAT!
IT'LL PASS. OH, AND THEY BROUGHT ME IN BECAUSE OF LISA.
IT'S DEFINITELY OVER WITH HER NOW.
YOU GIVE UP TOO EASY. MAYBE SHE LIKES BAD BOYS!
YEAH, MAYBE...
NO WAY! IT'S LISA!
I'LL LEAVE YOU TO IT THEN!
ANGEL? IT'S LISA.
HEY! HI!
UM... 'SUP?

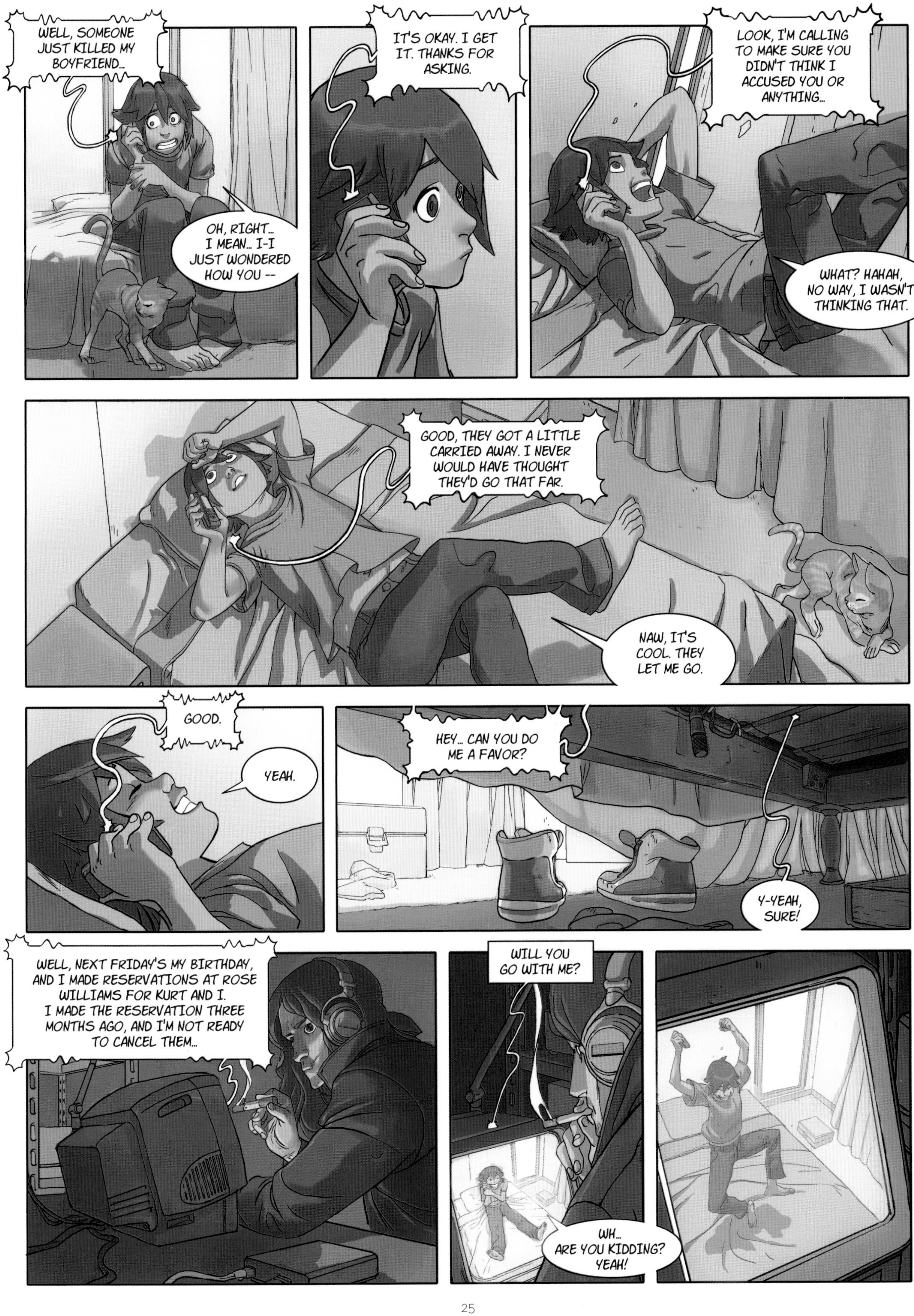
WELL, SOMEONE JUST KILLED MY BOYFRIEND...
OH, RIGHT... I MEAN... I-I JUST WONDERED HOW YOU --
IT'S OKAY. I GET IT. THANKS FOR ASKING.
LOOK, I'M CALLING TO MAKE SURE YOU DIDN'T THINK I ACCUSED YOU OR ANYTHING...
WHAT? HAHAH, NO WAY, I WASN'T THINKING THAT.
GOOD, THEY GOT A LITTLE CARRIED AWAY. I NEVER WOULD HAVE THOUGHT THEY'D GO THAT FAR.
NAW, IT'S COOL. THEY LET ME GO.
GOOD.
YEAH.
HEY... CAN YOU DO ME A FAVOR?
Y-YEAH, SURE!
WELL, NEXT FRIDAY'S MY BIRTHDAY, AND I MADE RESERVATIONS AT ROSE WILLIAMS FOR KURT AND I. I MADE THE RESERVATION THREE MONTHS AGO, AND I'M NOT READY TO CANCEL THEM...
WILL YOU GO WITH ME?
WH... ARE YOU KIDDING? YEAH!

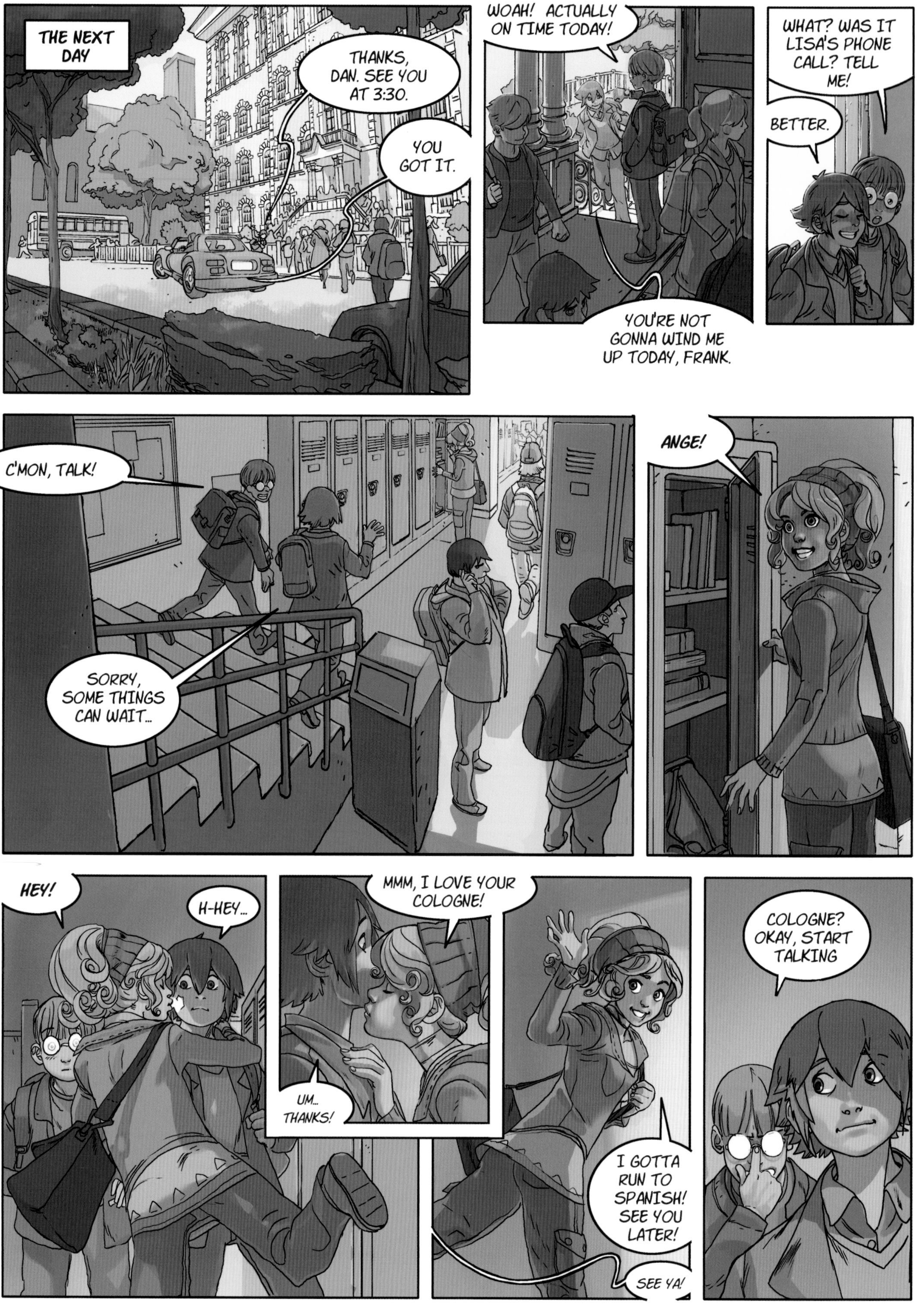
THE NEXT DAY
THANKS, DAN. SEE YOU AT 3:30.
YOU GOT IT.
WOAH! ACTUALLY ON TIME TODAY!
YOU'RE NOT GONNA WIND ME UP TODAY, FRANK.
WHAT? WAS IT LISA'S PHONE CALL? TELL ME!
BETTER.
C'MON, TALK!
SORRY, SOME THINGS CAN WAIT...
ANGE!
HEY!
H-HEY...
MMM, I LOVE YOUR COLOGNE!
UM... THANKS!
I GOTTA RUN TO SPANISH! SEE YOU LATER!
SEE YA!
COLOGNE? OKAY, START TALKING

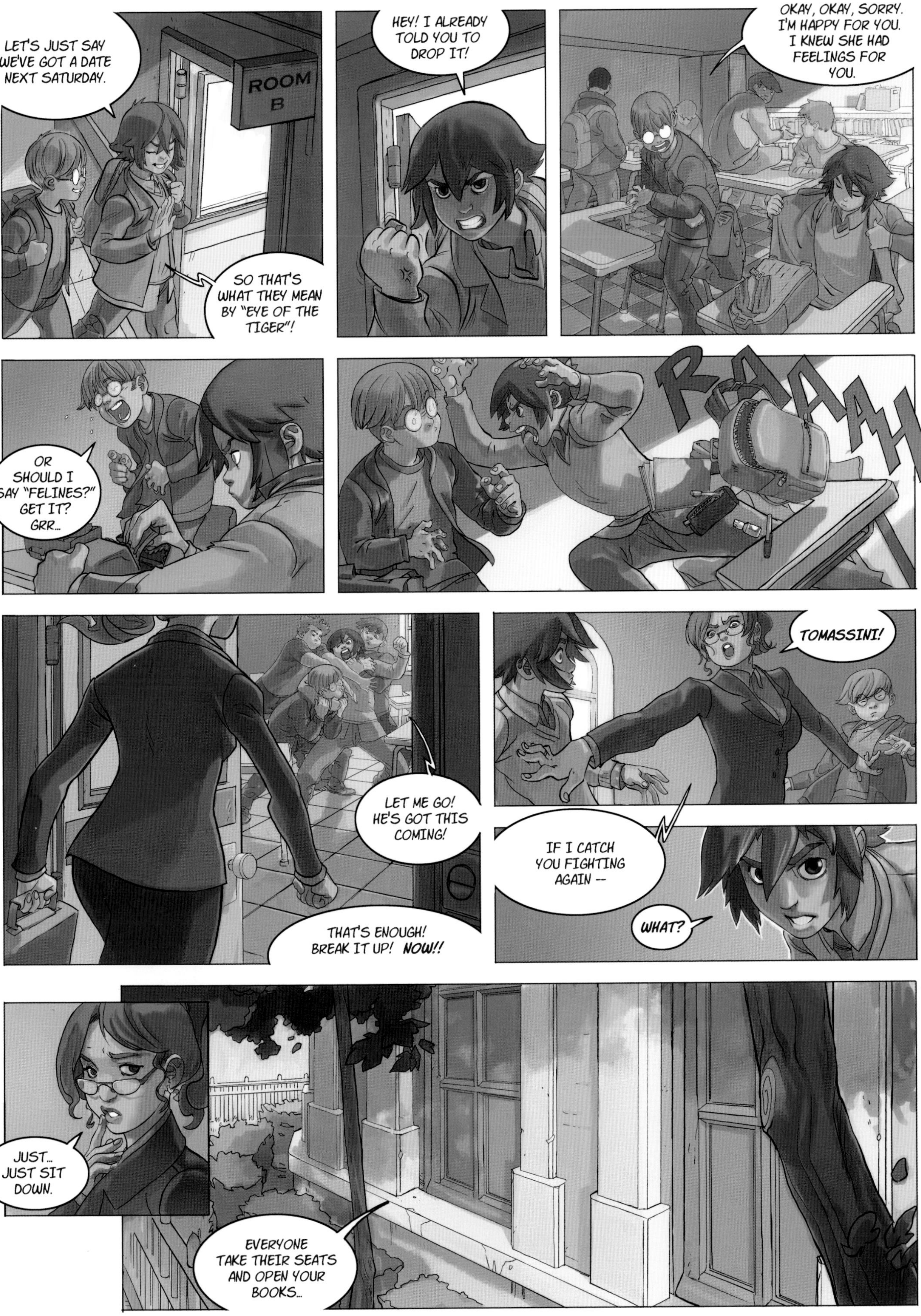
LET'S JUST SAY WE'VE GOT A DATE NEXT SATURDAY.
ROOM B
SO THAT'S WHAT THEY MEAN BY "EYE OF THE TIGER"!
HEY! I ALREADY TOLD YOU TO DROP IT!
OKAY, OKAY, SORRY. I'M HAPPY FOR YOU. I KNEW SHE HAD FEELINGS FOR YOU.
OR SHOULD I SAY "FELINES?" GET IT? GRR...
RAAAH
LET ME GO! HE'S GOT THIS COMING!
THAT'S ENOUGH! BREAK IT UP! NOW!!
TOMASSINI!
IF I CATCH YOU FIGHTING AGAIN --
WHAT?
JUST... JUST SIT DOWN.
EVERYONE TAKE THEIR SEATS AND OPEN YOUR BOOKS...

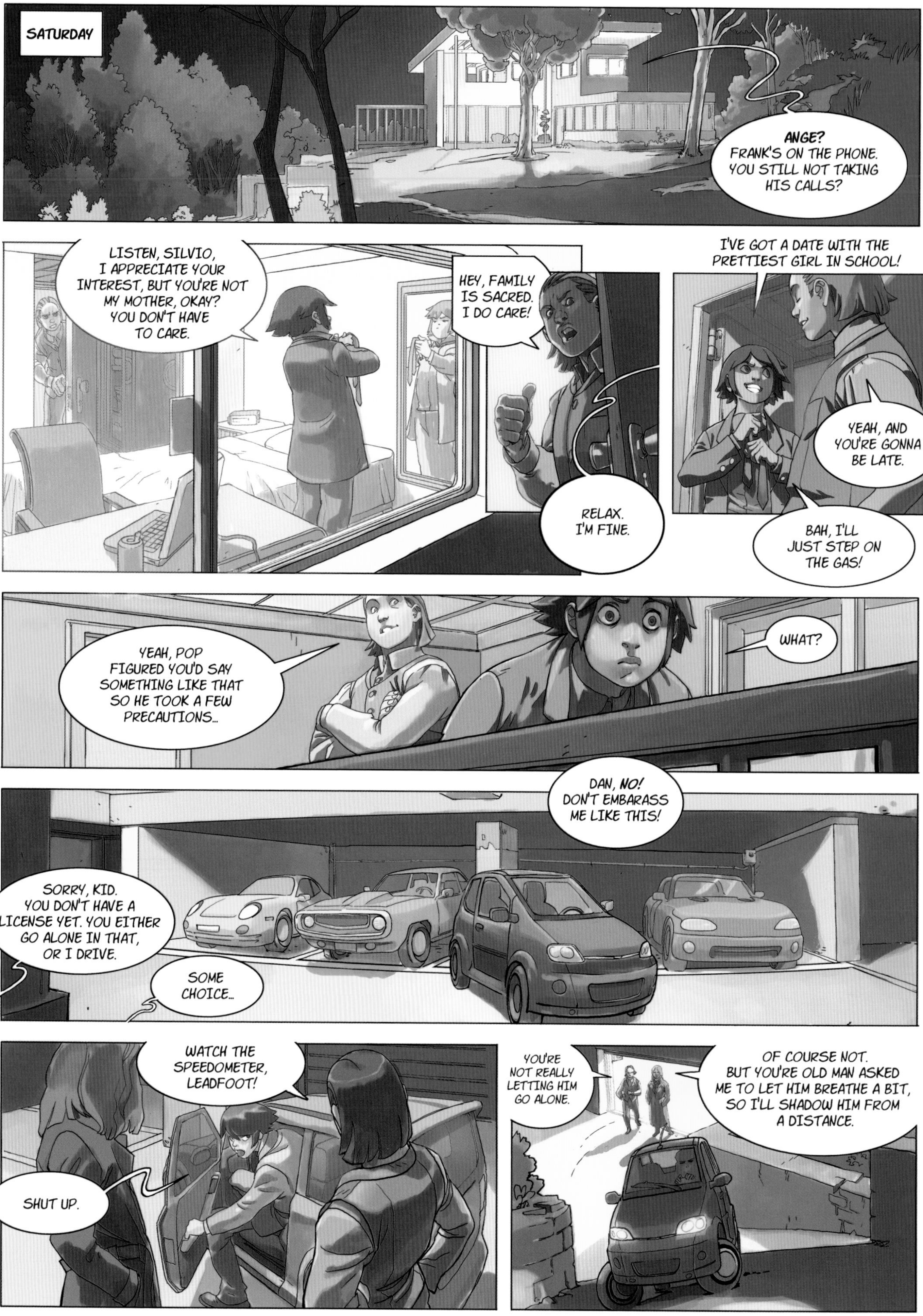
SATURDAY
ANGE? FRANK'S ON THE PHONE. YOU STILL NOT TAKING HIS CALLS?
LISTEN, SILVIO, I APPRECIATE YOUR INTEREST, BUT YOU'RE NOT MY MOTHER, OKAY? YOU DON'T HAVE TO CARE.
HEY, FAMILY IS SACRED. I DO CARE!
RELAX. I'M FINE.
I'VE GOT A DATE WITH THE PRETTIEST GIRL IN SCHOOL!
YEAH, AND YOU'RE GONNA BE LATE.
BAH, I'LL JUST STEP ON THE GAS!
YEAH, POP FIGURED YOU'D SAY SOMETHING LIKE THAT SO HE TOOK A FEW PRECAUTIONS...
WHAT?
DAN, NO! DON'T EMBARASS ME LIKE THIS!
SORRY, KID. YOU DON'T HAVE A LICENSE YET. YOU EITHER GO ALONE IN THAT, OR I DRIVE.
SOME CHOICE...
WATCH THE SPEEDOMETER, LEADFOOT!
SHUT UP.
YOU'RE NOT REALLY LETTING HIM GO ALONE.
OF COURSE NOT. BUT YOU'RE OLD MAN ASKED ME TO LET HIM BREATHE A BIT, SO I'LL SHADOW HIM FROM A DISTANCE.

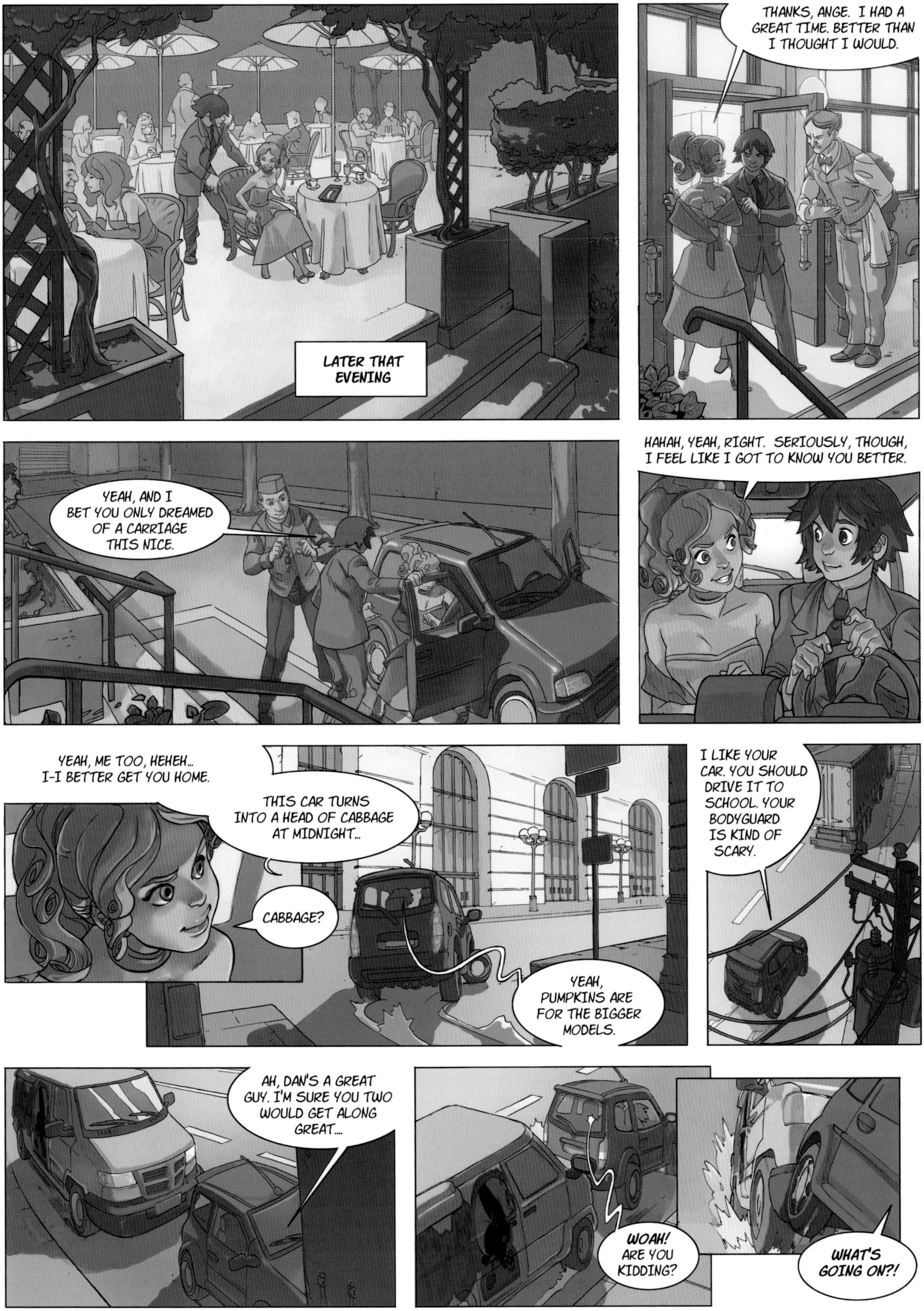
LATER THAT EVENING
THANKS, ANGE. I HAD A GREAT TIME. BETTER THAN I THOUGHT I WOULD.
YEAH, AND I BET YOU ONLY DREAMED OF A CARRIAGE THIS NICE.
HAHAH, YEAH, RIGHT. SERIOUSLY, THOUGH, I FEEL LIKE I GOT TO KNOW YOU BETTER.
YEAH, ME TOO, HEHEH... I-I BETTER GET YOU HOME.
THIS CAR TURNS INTO A HEAD OF CABBAGE AT MIDNIGHT...
CABBAGE?
YEAH, PUMPKINS ARE FOR THE BIGGER MODELS.
I LIKE YOUR CAR. YOU SHOULD DRIVE IT TO SCHOOL. YOUR BODYGUARD IS KIND OF SCARY.
AH, DAN'S A GREAT GUY. I'M SURE YOU TWO WOULD GET ALONG GREAT....
WOAH! ARE YOU KIDDING?
WHAT'S GOING ON?!

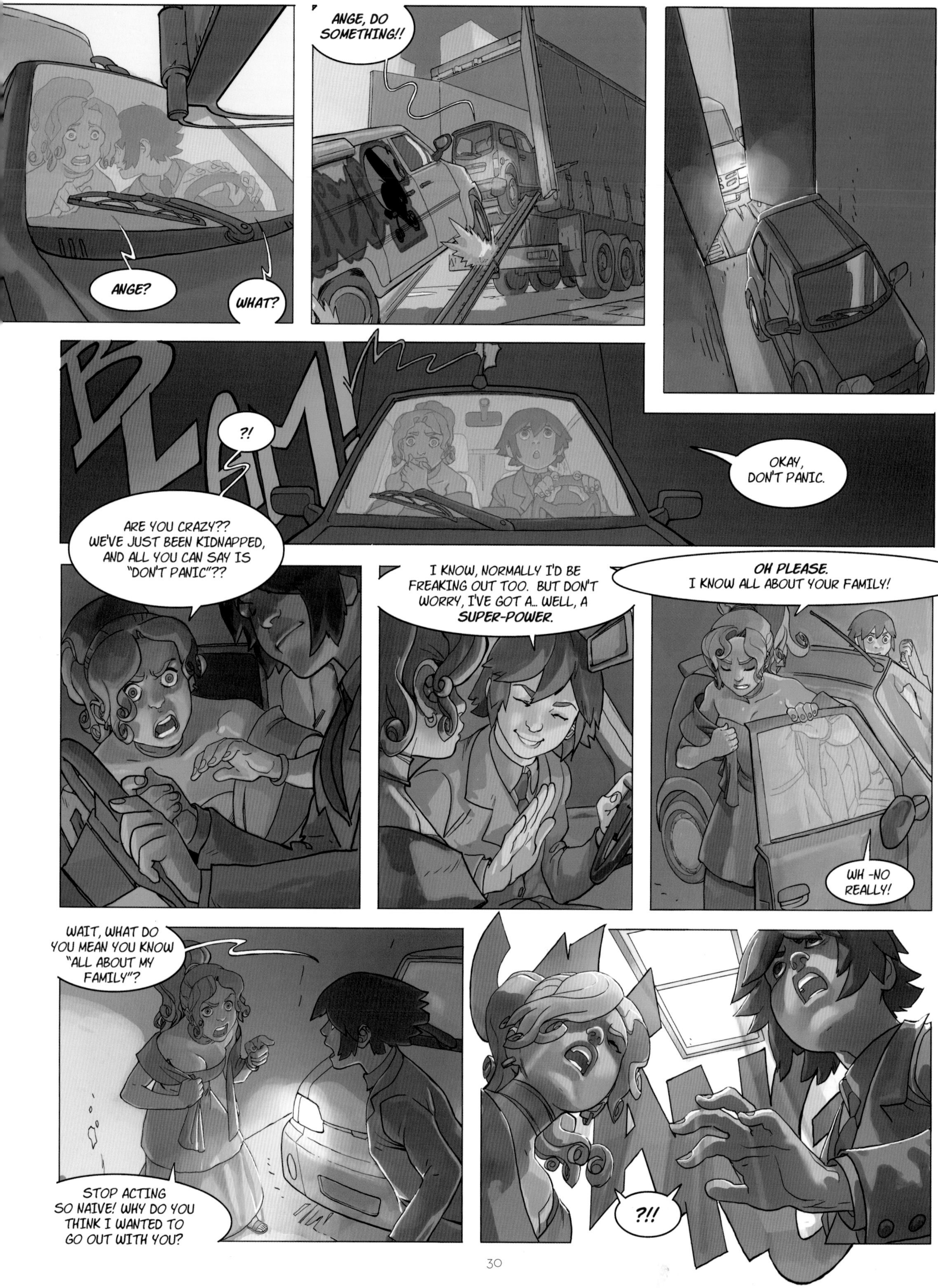
ANGE?
WHAT?
ANGE, DO SOMETHING!!
BLAM
?!
OKAY, DON'T PANIC.
ARE YOU CRAZY?? WE'VE JUST BEEN KIDNAPPED, AND ALL YOU CAN SAY IS "DON'T PANIC"??
I KNOW, NORMALLY I'D BE FREAKING OUT TOO. BUT DON'T WORRY, I'VE GOT A... WELL, A SUPER-POWER.
OH PLEASE. I KNOW ALL ABOUT YOUR FAMILY!
WH -NO REALLY!
WAIT, WHAT DO YOU MEAN YOU KNOW "ALL ABOUT MY FAMILY"?
STOP ACTING SO NAIVE! WHY DO YOU THINK I WANTED TO GO OUT WITH YOU?
?!!

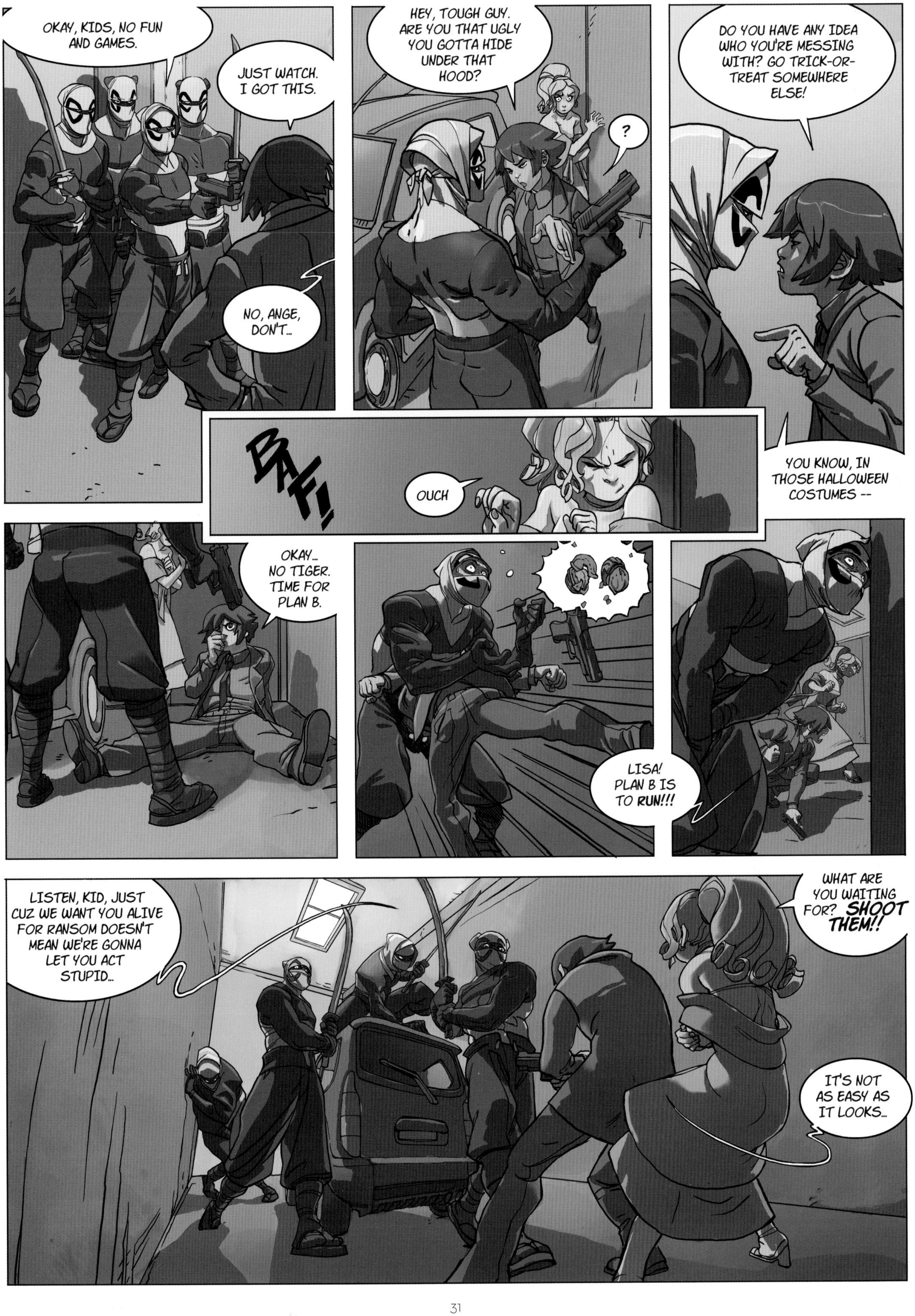
OKAY, KIDS, NO FUN AND GAMES.
JUST WATCH. I GOT THIS.
NO, ANGE, DON'T...
HEY, TOUGH GUY. ARE YOU THAT UGLY YOU GOTTA HIDE UNDER THAT HOOD?
?
DO YOU HAVE ANY IDEA WHO YOU'RE MESSING WITH? GO TRICK-OR-TREAT SOMEWHERE ELSE!
YOU KNOW, IN THOSE HALLOWEEN COSTUMES --
BAF!
OUCH
OKAY... NO TIGER. TIME FOR PLAN B.
LISA! PLAN B IS TO RUN!!!
LISTEN, KID, JUST CUZ WE WANT YOU ALIVE FOR RANSOM DOESN'T MEAN WE'RE GONNA LET YOU ACT STUPID...
WHAT ARE YOU WAITING FOR? SHOOT THEM!!
IT'S NOT AS EASY AS IT LOOKS...

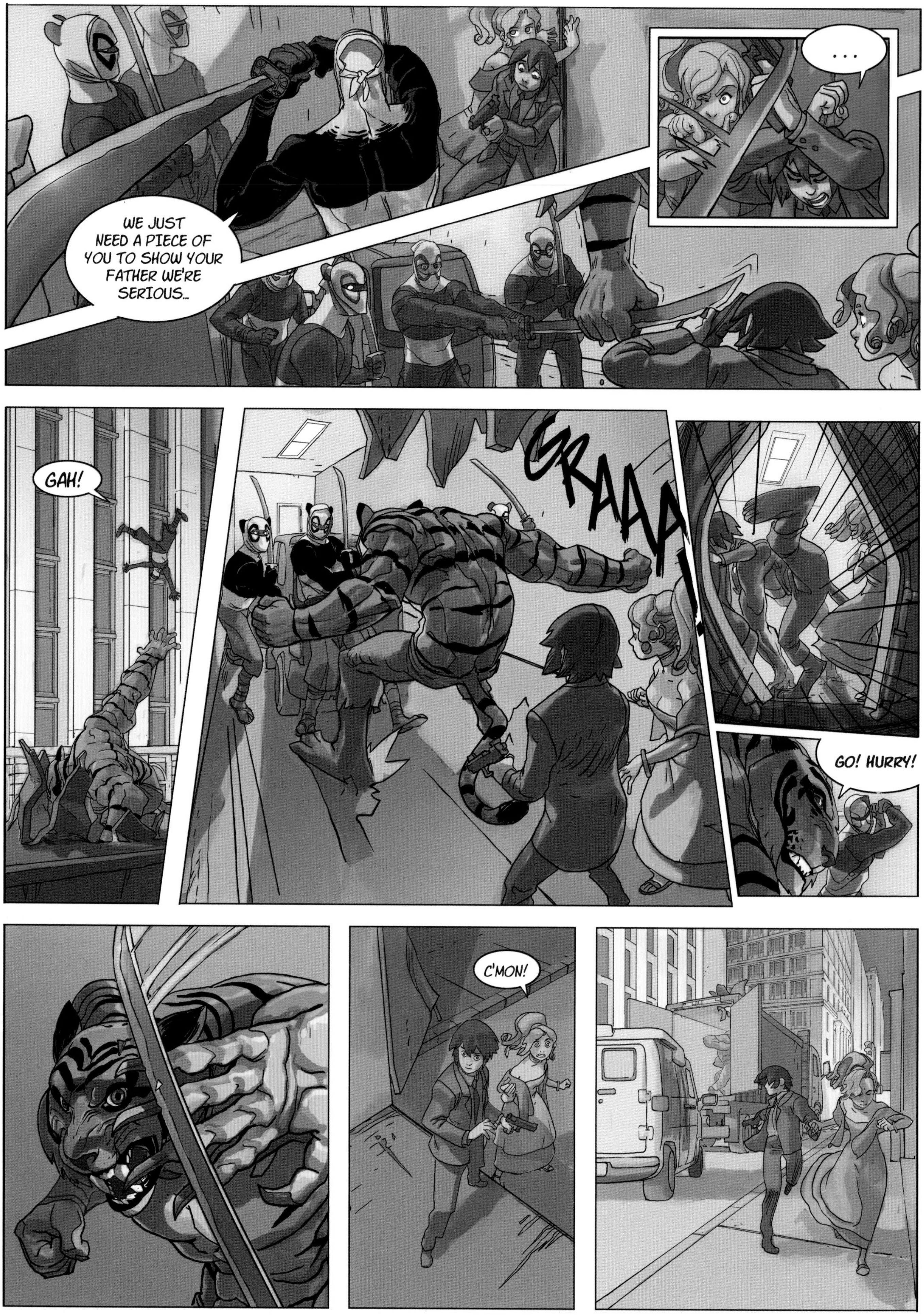
WE JUST NEED A PIECE OF YOU TO SHOW YOUR FATHER WE'RE SERIOUS...
...
GAH!
GRAAAA
GO! HURRY!
C'MON!

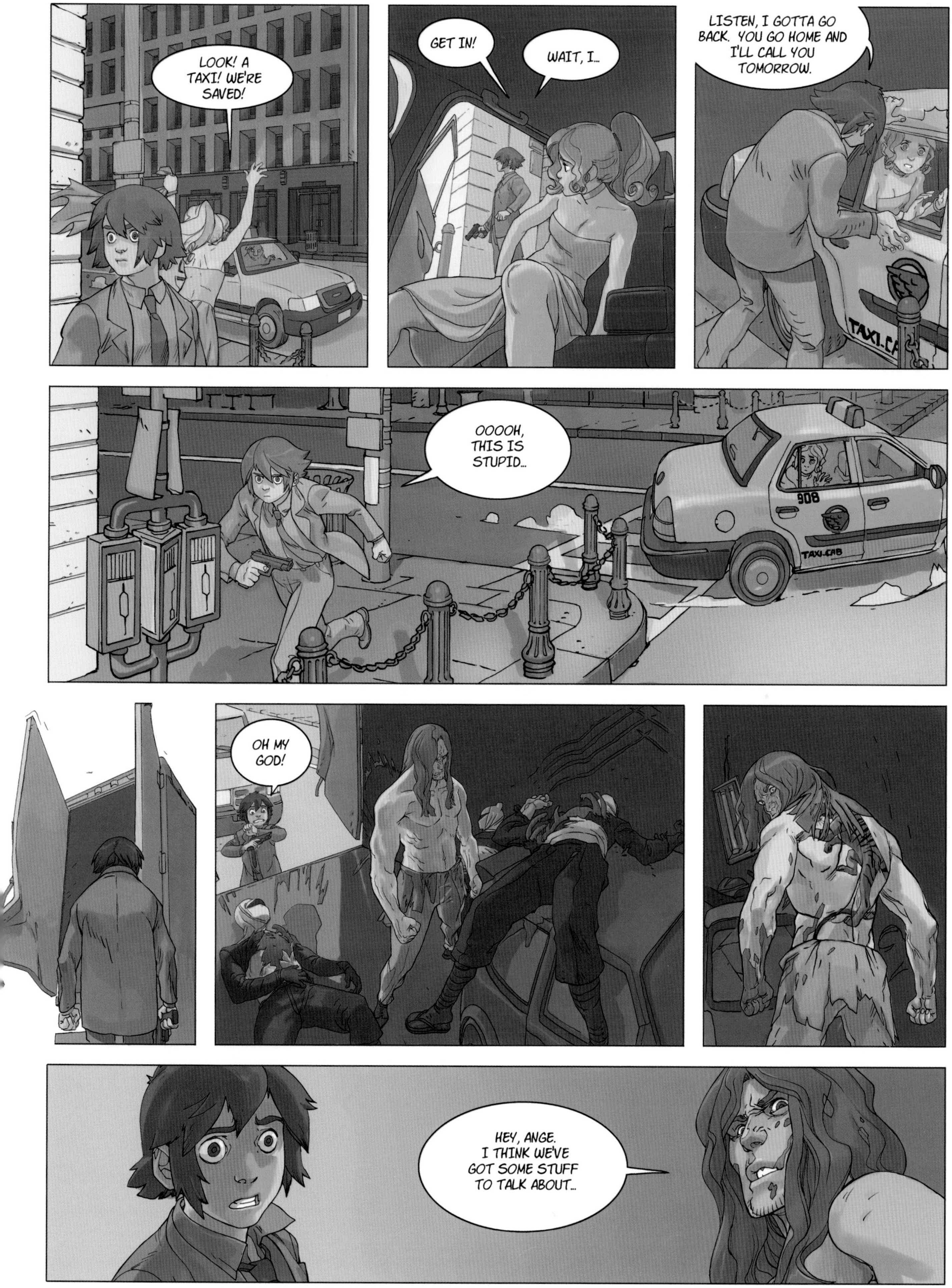
LOOK! A TAXI! WE'RE SAVED!
GET IN!
WAIT, I...
LISTEN, I GOTTA GO BACK. YOU GO HOME AND I'LL CALL YOU TOMORROW.
TAXI.CAB
OOOOH, THIS IS STUPID...
908
TAXI.CAB
OH MY GOD!
HEY, ANGE. I THINK WE'VE GOT SOME STUFF TO TALK ABOUT...

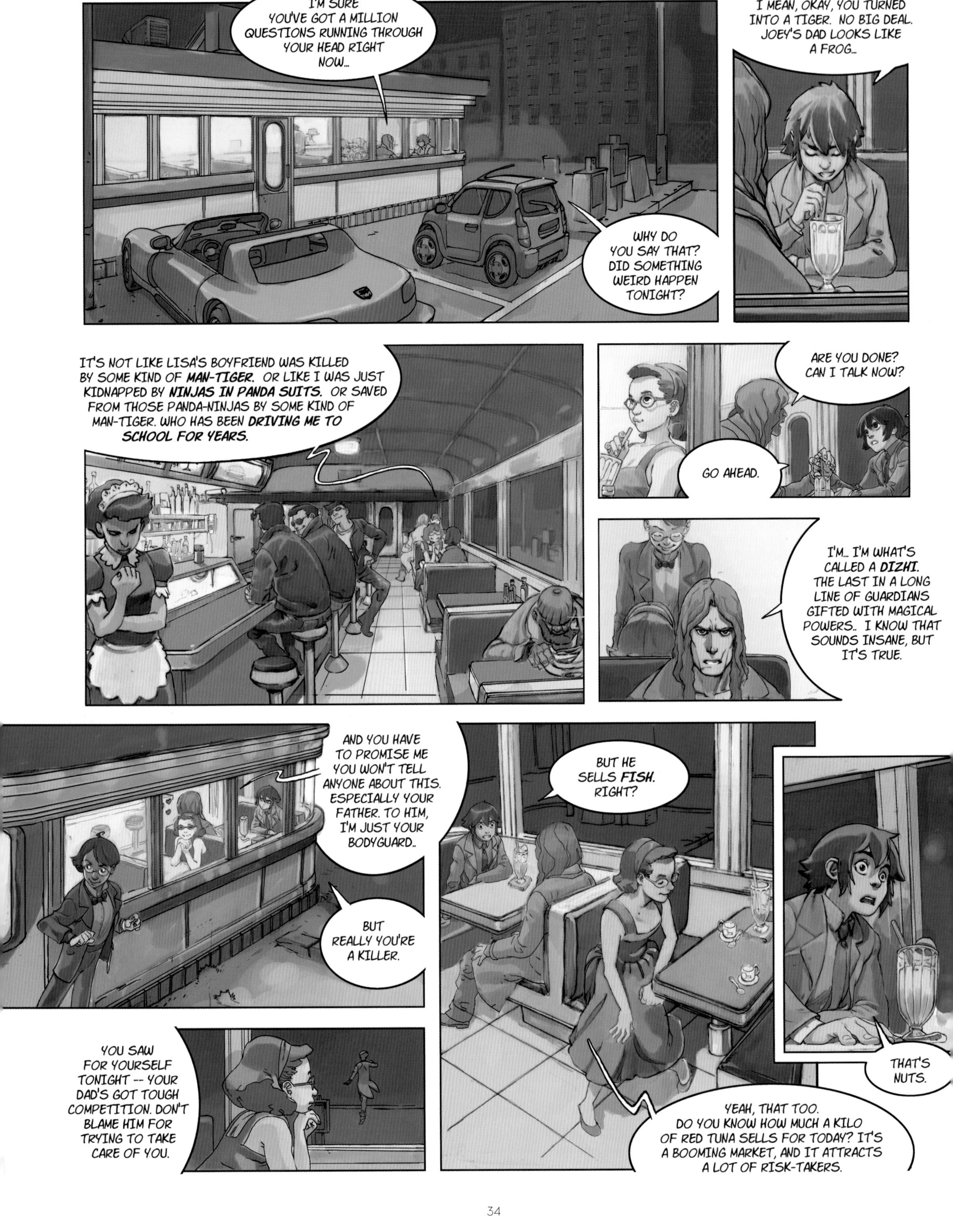
I'M SURE YOU'VE GOT A MILLION QUESTIONS RUNNING THROUGH YOUR HEAD RIGHT NOW...
WHY DO YOU SAY THAT? DID SOMETHING WEIRD HAPPEN TONIGHT?
I MEAN, OKAY, YOU TURNED INTO A TIGER. NO BIG DEAL. JOEY'S DAD LOOKS LIKE A FROG...
IT'S NOT LIKE LISA'S BOYFRIEND WAS KILLED BY SOME KIND OF MAN-TIGER. OR LIKE I WAS JUST KIDNAPPED BY NINJAS IN PANDA SUITS. OR SAVED FROM THOSE PANDA-NINJAS BY SOME KIND OF MAN-TIGER. WHO HAS BEEN DRIVING ME TO SCHOOL FOR YEARS.
ARE YOU DONE? CAN I TALK NOW?
GO AHEAD.
I'M... I'M WHAT'S CALLED A DIZHI. THE LAST IN A LONG LINE OF GUARDIANS GIFTED WITH MAGICAL POWERS.. I KNOW THAT SOUNDS INSANE, BUT IT'S TRUE.
AND YOU HAVE TO PROMISE ME YOU WON'T TELL ANYONE ABOUT THIS. ESPECIALLY YOUR FATHER. TO HIM, I'M JUST YOUR BODYGUARD..
BUT REALLY YOU'RE A KILLER.
BUT HE SELLS FISH. RIGHT?
THAT'S NUTS.
YOU SAW FOR YOURSELF TONIGHT -- YOUR DAD'S GOT TOUGH COMPETITION. DON'T BLAME HIM FOR TRYING TO TAKE CARE OF YOU.
YEAH, THAT TOO. DO YOU KNOW HOW MUCH A KILO OF RED TUNA SELLS FOR TODAY? IT'S A BOOMING MARKET, AND IT ATTRACTS A LOT OF RISK-TAKERS.

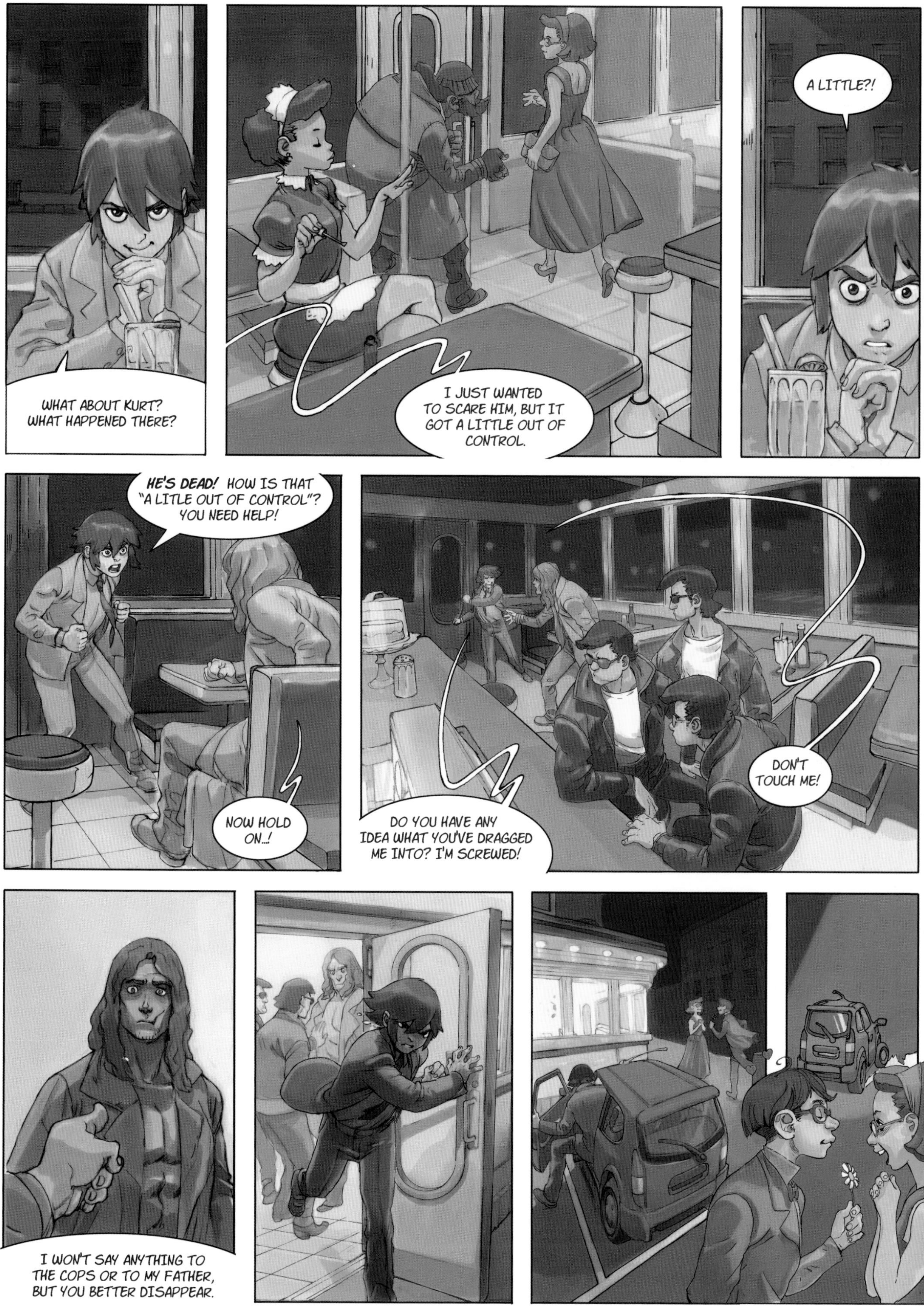
WHAT ABOUT KURT? WHAT HAPPENED THERE?
I JUST WANTED TO SCARE HIM, BUT IT GOT A LITTLE OUT OF CONTROL.
A LITTLE?!
HE'S DEAD! HOW IS THAT "A LITLE OUT OF CONTROL"? YOU NEED HELP!
NOW HOLD ON...!
DO YOU HAVE ANY IDEA WHAT YOU'VE DRAGGED ME INTO? I'M SCREWED!
DON'T TOUCH ME!
I WON'T SAY ANYTHING TO THE COPS OR TO MY FATHER, BUT YOU BETTER DISAPPEAR.

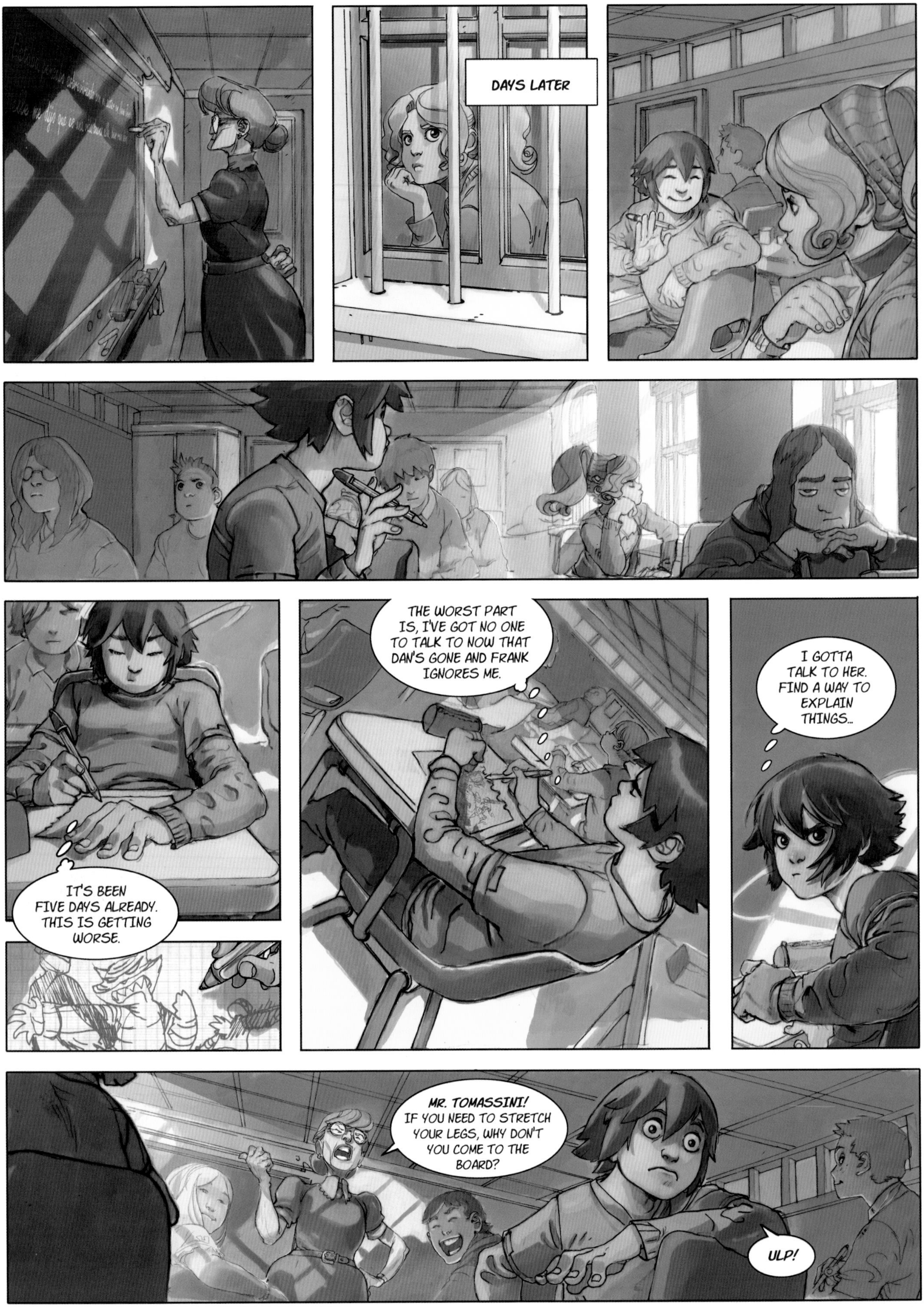
DAYS LATER
IT'S BEEN FIVE DAYS ALREADY. THIS IS GETTING WORSE.
THE WORST PART IS, I'VE GOT NO ONE TO TALK TO NOW THAT DAN'S GONE AND FRANK IGNORES ME.
I GOTTA TALK TO HER. FIND A WAY TO EXPLAIN THINGS...
MR. TOMASSINI! IF YOU NEED TO STRETCH YOUR LEGS, WHY DON'T YOU COME TO THE BOARD?
ULP!

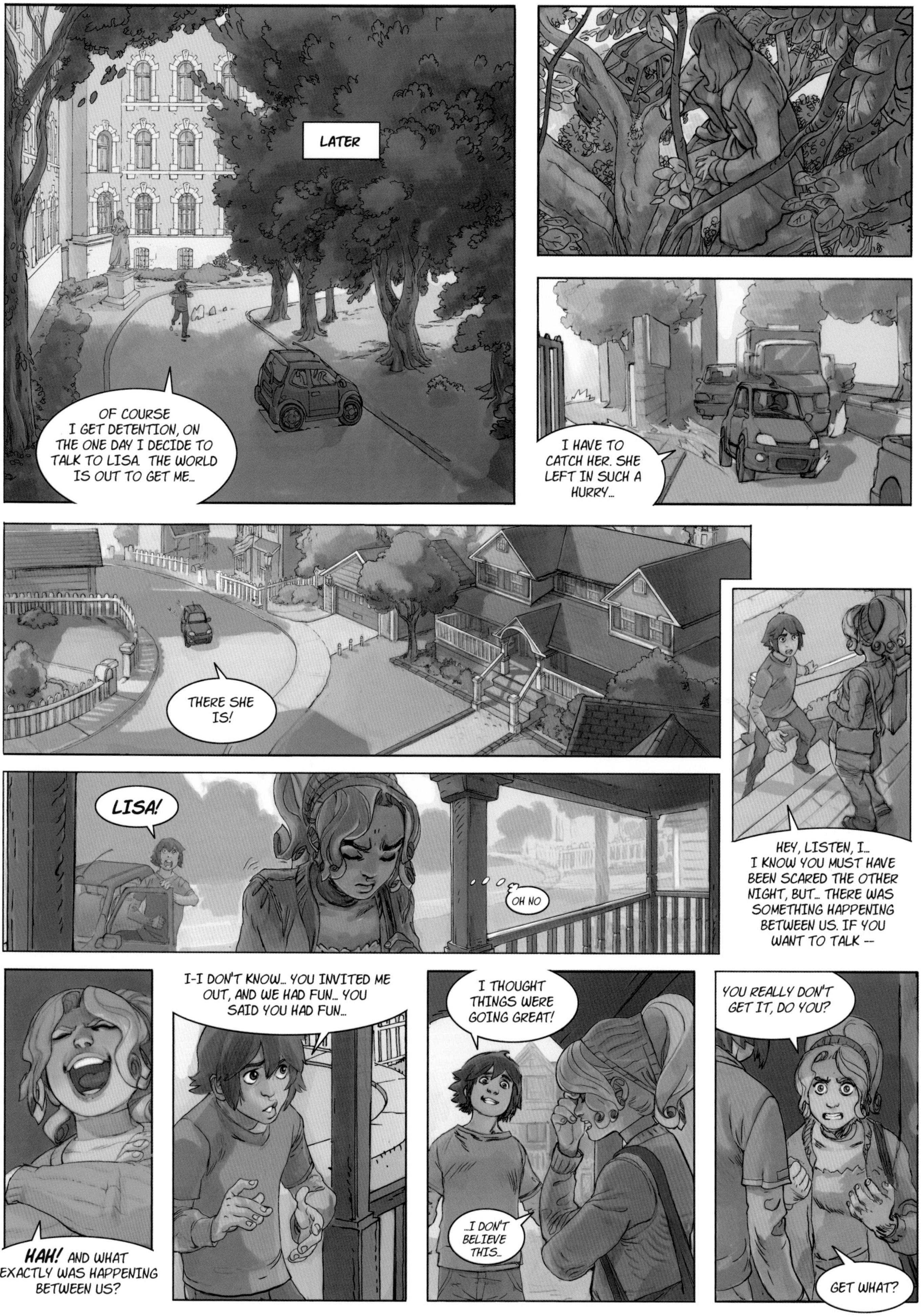
LATER
OF COURSE I GET DETENTION, ON THE ONE DAY I DECIDE TO TALK TO LISA. THE WORLD IS OUT TO GET ME...
I HAVE TO CATCH HER. SHE LEFT IN SUCH A HURRY...
THERE SHE IS!
LISA!
OH NO
HEY, LISTEN, I... I KNOW YOU MUST HAVE BEEN SCARED THE OTHER NIGHT, BUT... THERE WAS SOMETHING HAPPENING BETWEEN US. IF YOU WANT TO TALK --
HAH! AND WHAT EXACTLY WAS HAPPENING BETWEEN US?
I-I DON'T KNOW... YOU INVITED ME OUT, AND WE HAD FUN... YOU SAID YOU HAD FUN...
I THOUGHT THINGS WERE GOING GREAT!
...I DON'T BELIEVE THIS...
YOU REALLY DON'T GET IT, DO YOU?
GET WHAT?

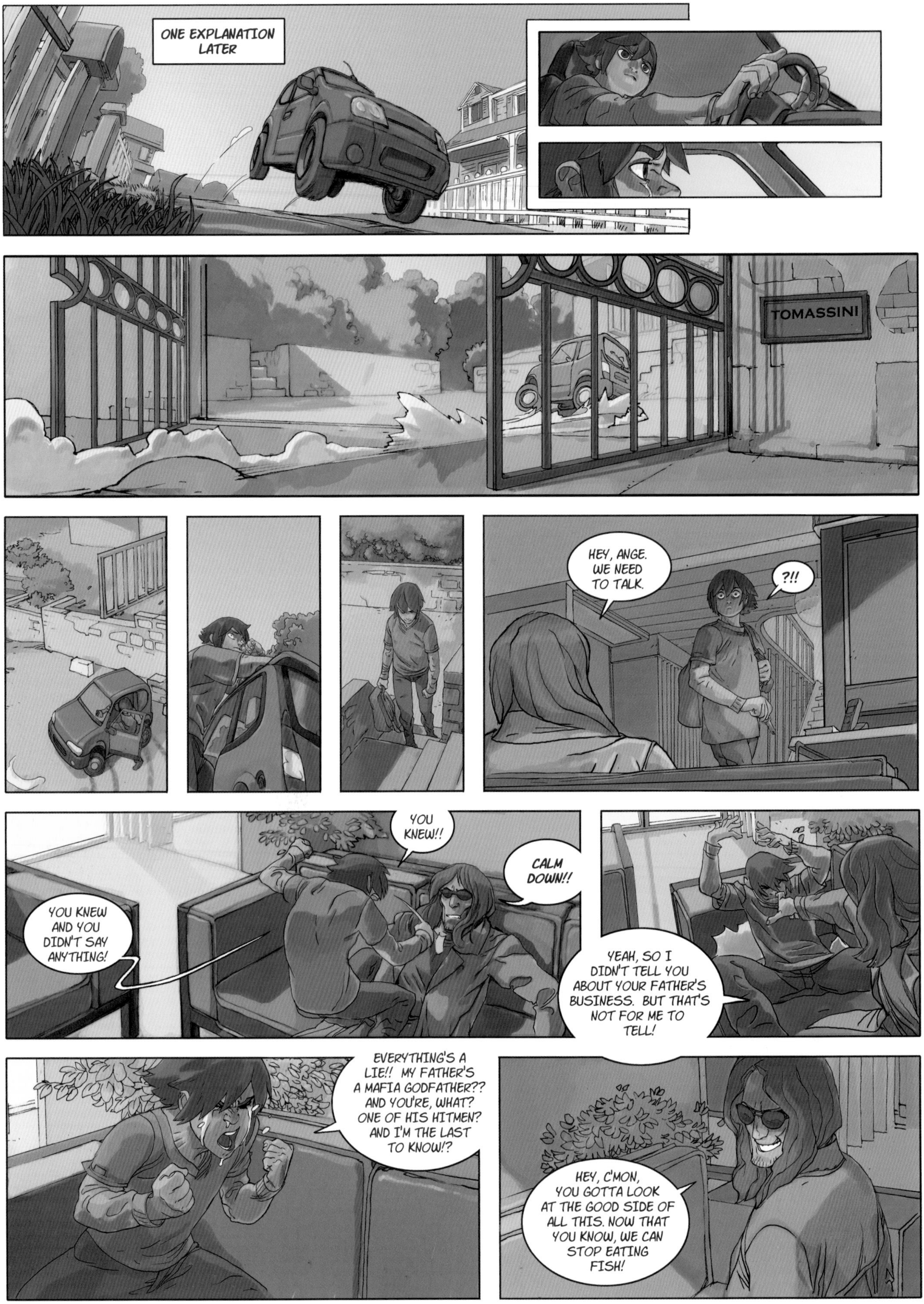
ONE EXPLANATION LATER
TOMASSINI
HEY, ANGE. WE NEED TO TALK.
?!!
YOU KNEW!!
YOU KNEW AND YOU DIDN'T SAY ANYTHING!
CALM DOWN!!
YEAH, SO I DIDN'T TELL YOU ABOUT YOUR FATHER'S BUSINESS. BUT THAT'S NOT FOR ME TO TELL!
EVERYTHING'S A LIE!! MY FATHER'S A MAFIA GODFATHER?? AND YOU'RE, WHAT? ONE OF HIS HITMEN? AND I'M THE LAST TO KNOW!?
HEY, C'MON, YOU GOTTA LOOK AT THE GOOD SIDE OF ALL THIS. NOW THAT YOU KNOW, WE CAN STOP EATING FISH!

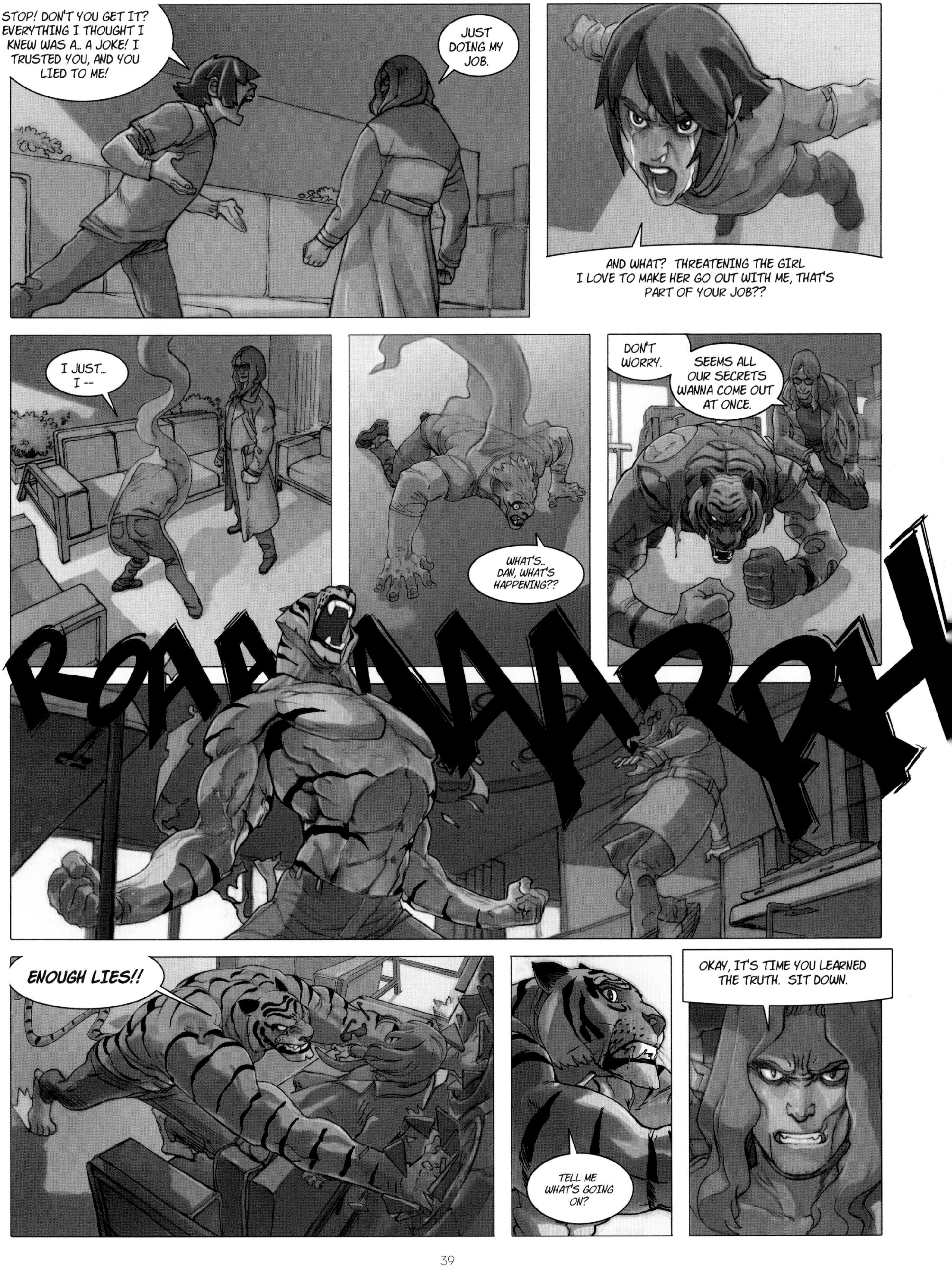
STOP! DON'T YOU GET IT? EVERYTHING I THOUGHT I KNEW WAS A... A JOKE! I TRUSTED YOU, AND YOU LIED TO ME!
JUST DOING MY JOB.
AND WHAT? THREATENING THE GIRL I LOVE TO MAKE HER GO OUT WITH ME, THAT'S PART OF YOUR JOB??
I JUST... I --
WHAT'S... DAN, WHAT'S HAPPENING??
DON'T WORRY.
SEEMS ALL OUR SECRETS WANNA COME OUT AT ONCE.
ROAAAAARRH
ENOUGH LIES!!
TELL ME WHAT'S GOING ON?
OKAY, IT'S TIME YOU LEARNED THE TRUTH. SIT DOWN.

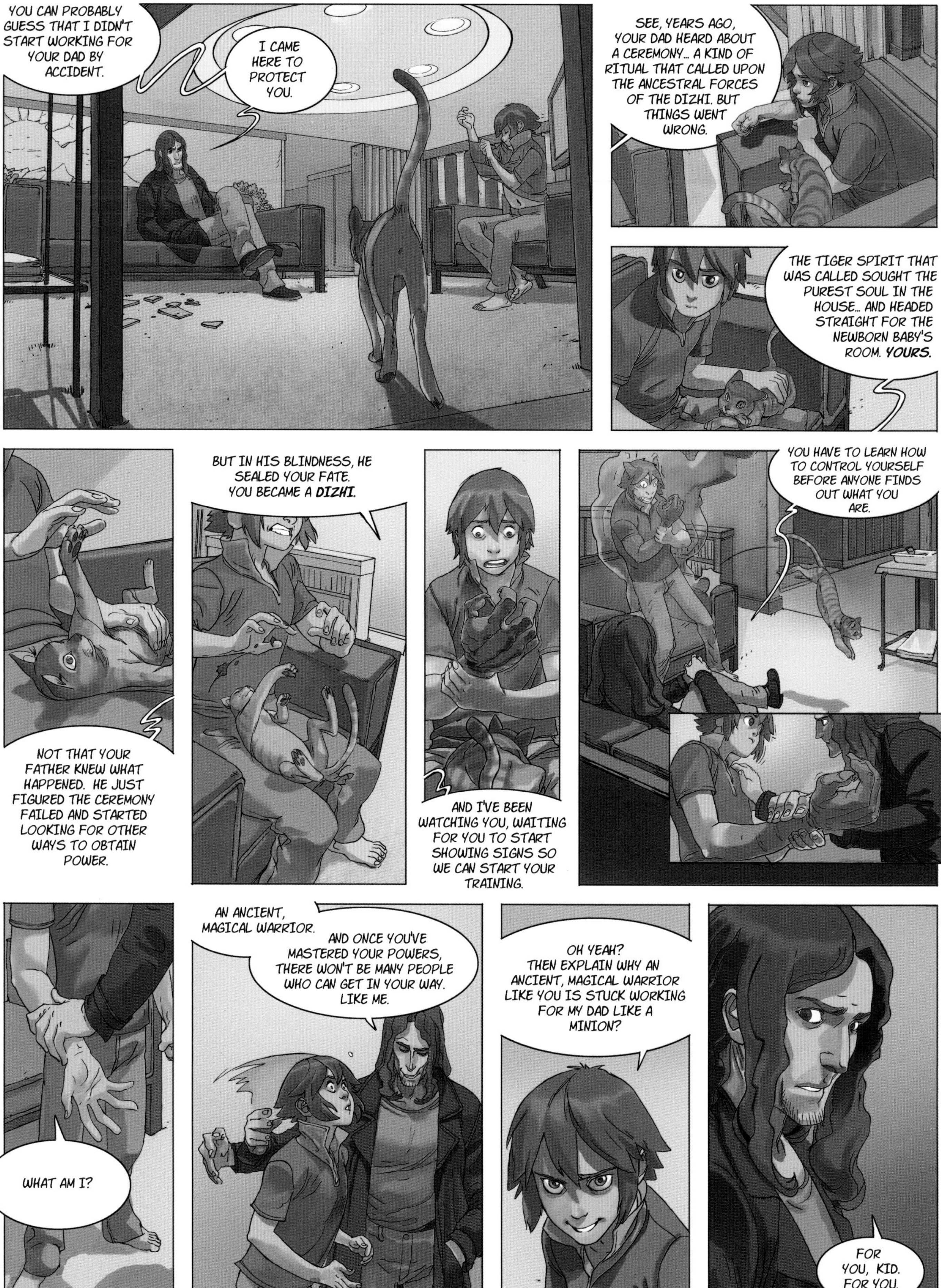

YOU CAN PROBABLY GUESS THAT I DIDN'T START WORKING FOR YOUR DAD BY ACCIDENT.
I CAME HERE TO PROTECT YOU.
SEE, YEARS AGO, YOUR DAD HEARD ABOUT A CEREMONY... A KIND OF RITUAL THAT CALLED UPON THE ANCESTRAL FORCES OF THE DIZHI. BUT THINGS WENT WRONG.
THE TIGER SPIRIT THAT WAS CALLED SOUGHT THE PUREST SOUL IN THE HOUSE... AND HEADED STRAIGHT FOR THE NEWBORN BABY'S ROOM. YOURS.
NOT THAT YOUR FATHER KNEW WHAT HAPPENED. HE JUST FIGURED THE CEREMONY FAILED AND STARTED LOOKING FOR OTHER WAYS TO OBTAIN POWER.
BUT IN HIS BLINDNESS, HE SEALED YOUR FATE. YOU BECAME A DIZHI.
AND I'VE BEEN WATCHING YOU, WAITING FOR YOU TO START SHOWING SIGNS SO WE CAN START YOUR TRAINING.
YOU HAVE TO LEARN HOW TO CONTROL YOURSELF BEFORE ANYONE FINDS OUT WHAT YOU ARE.
WHAT AM I?
AN ANCIENT, MAGICAL WARRIOR.
AND ONCE YOU'VE MASTERED YOUR POWERS, THERE WON'T BE MANY PEOPLE WHO CAN GET IN YOUR WAY. LIKE ME.
OH YEAH? THEN EXPLAIN WHY AN ANCIENT, MAGICAL WARRIOR LIKE YOU IS STUCK WORKING FOR MY DAD LIKE A MINION?
FOR YOU, KID. FOR YOU.

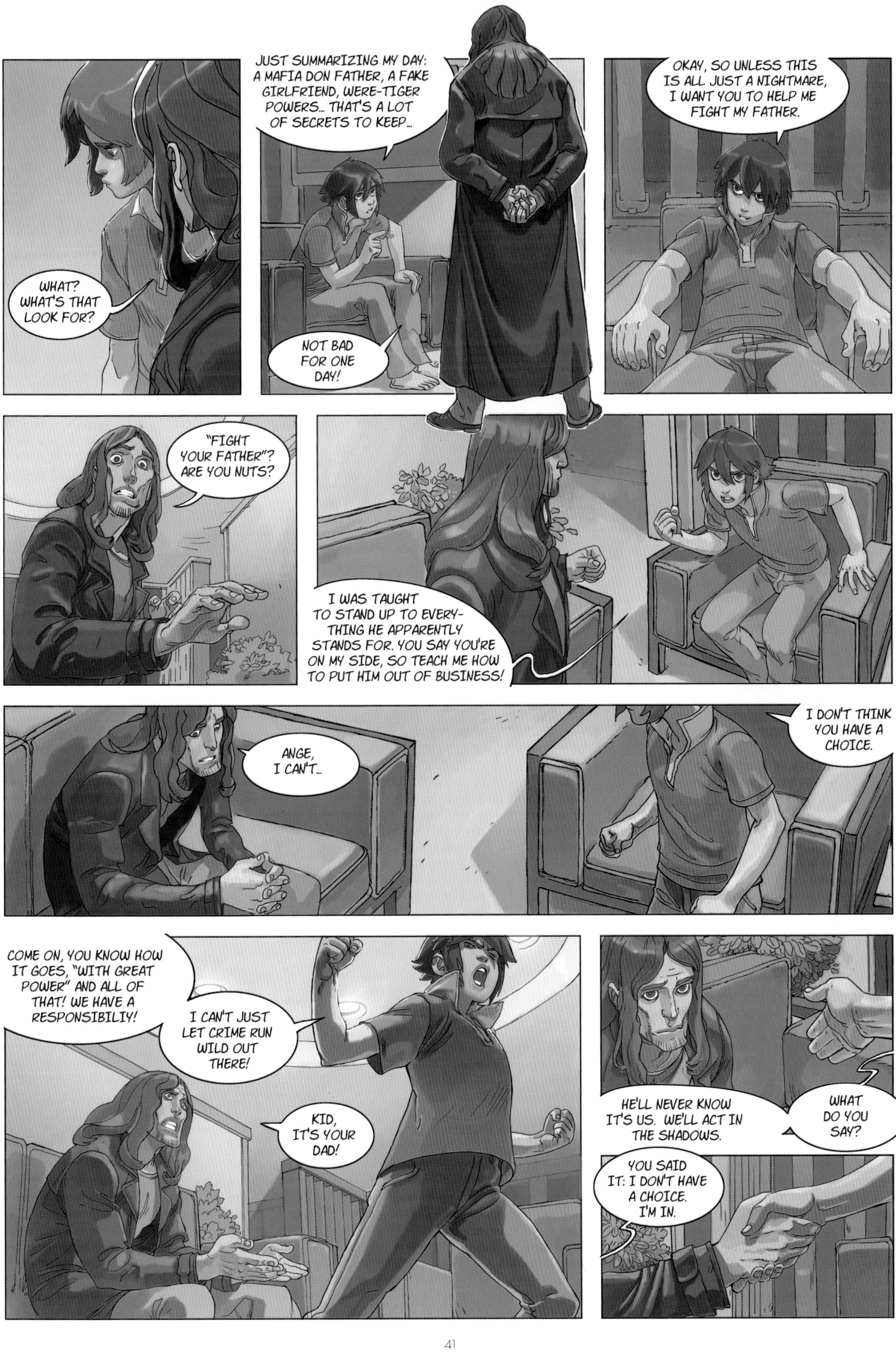
WHAT? WHAT'S THAT LOOK FOR?
JUST SUMMARIZING MY DAY: A MAFIA DON FATHER, A FAKE GIRLFRIEND, WERE-TIGER POWERS... THAT'S A LOT OF SECRETS TO KEEP...
NOT BAD FOR ONE DAY!
OKAY, SO UNLESS THIS IS ALL JUST A NIGHTMARE, I WANT YOU TO HELP ME FIGHT MY FATHER.
"FIGHT YOUR FATHER"? ARE YOU NUTS?
I WAS TAUGHT TO STAND UP TO EVERY-THING HE APPARENTLY STANDS FOR. YOU SAY YOU'RE ON MY SIDE, SO TEACH ME HOW TO PUT HIM OUT OF BUSINESS!
ANGE, I CAN'T...
I DON'T THINK YOU HAVE A CHOICE.
COME ON, YOU KNOW HOW IT GOES, "WITH GREAT POWER" AND ALL OF THAT! WE HAVE A RESPONSIBILIY!
I CAN'T JUST LET CRIME RUN WILD OUT THERE!
KID, IT'S YOUR DAD!
HE'LL NEVER KNOW IT'S US. WE'LL ACT IN THE SHADOWS.
WHAT DO YOU SAY?
YOU SAID IT: I DON'T HAVE A CHOICE. I'M IN.

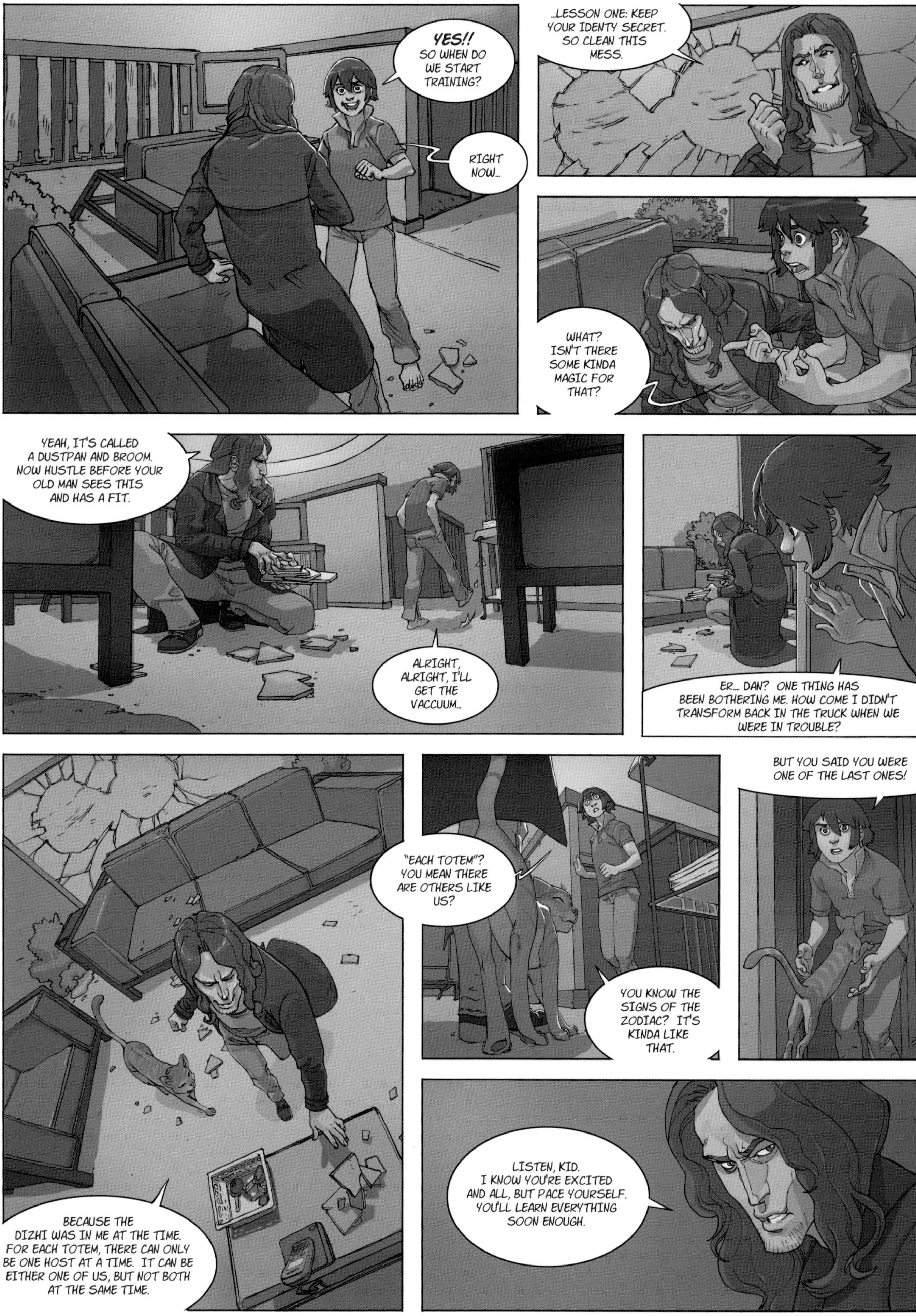
YES!! SO WHEN DO WE START TRAINING?
RIGHT NOW...
...LESSON ONE: KEEP YOUR IDENTY SECRET. SO CLEAN THIS MESS.
WHAT? ISN'T THERE SOME KINDA MAGIC FOR THAT?
YEAH, IT'S CALLED A DUSTPAN AND BROOM. NOW HUSTLE BEFORE YOUR OLD MAN SEES THIS AND HAS A FIT.
ALRIGHT, ALRIGHT, I'LL GET THE VACCUUM...
ER... DAN? ONE THING HAS BEEN BOTHERING ME. HOW COME I DIDN'T TRANSFORM BACK IN THE TRUCK WHEN WE WERE IN TROUBLE?
BECAUSE THE DIZHI WAS IN ME AT THE TIME. FOR EACH TOTEM, THERE CAN ONLY BE ONE HOST AT A TIME. IT CAN BE EITHER ONE OF US, BUT NOT BOTH AT THE SAME TIME.
"EACH TOTEM"? YOU MEAN THERE ARE OTHERS LIKE US?
YOU KNOW THE SIGNS OF THE ZODIAC? IT'S KINDA LIKE THAT.
BUT YOU SAID YOU WERE ONE OF THE LAST ONES!
LISTEN, KID. I KNOW YOU'RE EXCITED AND ALL, BUT PACE YOURSELF. YOU'LL LEARN EVERYTHING SOON ENOUGH.

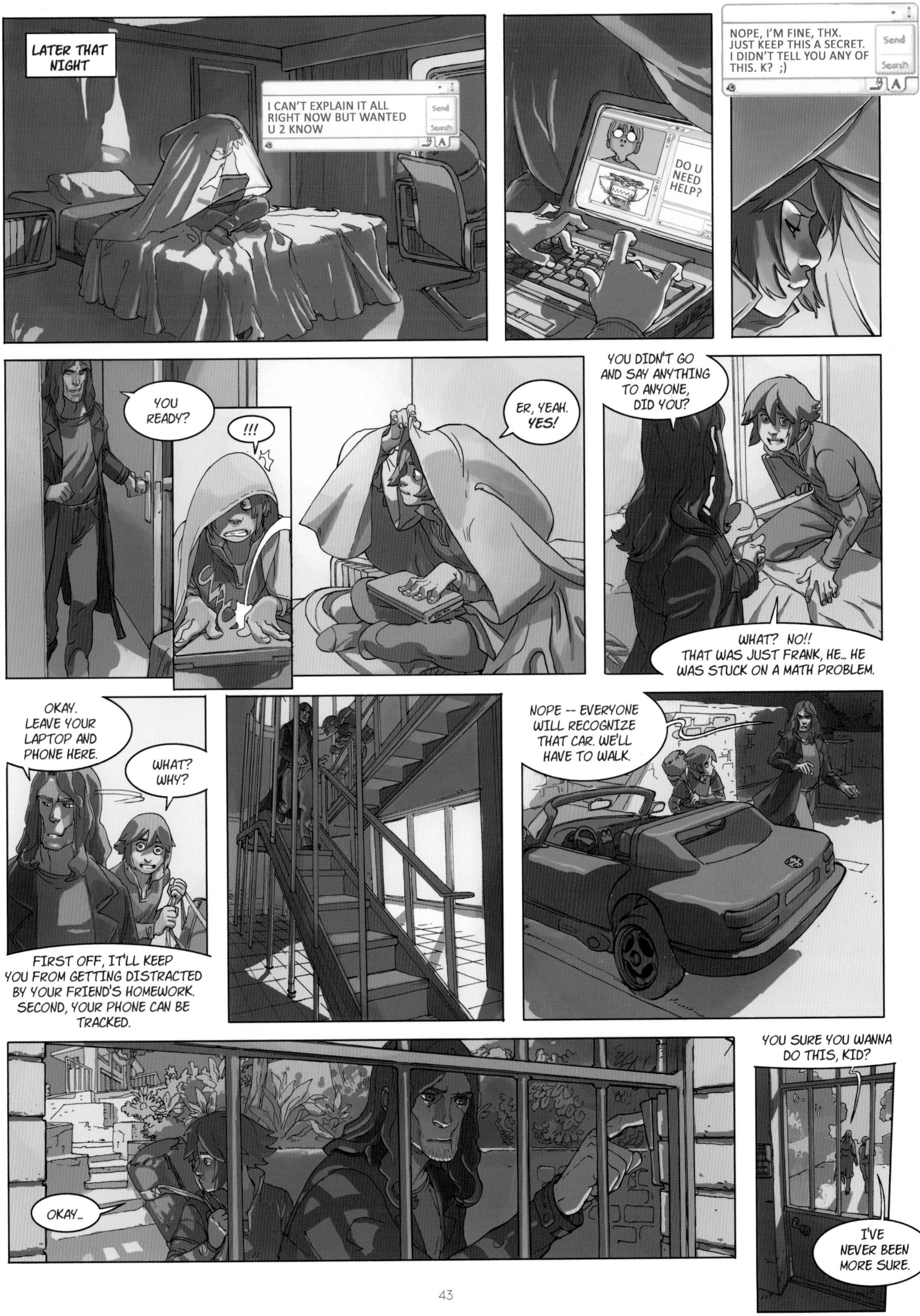

LATER THAT NIGHT
I CAN'T EXPLAIN IT ALL RIGHT NOW BUT WANTED U 2 KNOW
Send
Search
DO U NEED HELP?
NOPE, I'M FINE, THX. JUST KEEP THIS A SECRET. I DIDN'T TELL YOU ANY OF THIS. K? ;)
Send
Search
YOU READY?
!!!
ER, YEAH. YES!
YOU DIDN'T GO AND SAY ANYTHING TO ANYONE, DID YOU?
WHAT? NO!! THAT WAS JUST FRANK, HE... HE WAS STUCK ON A MATH PROBLEM.
OKAY. LEAVE YOUR LAPTOP AND PHONE HERE.
WHAT? WHY?
FIRST OFF, IT'LL KEEP YOU FROM GETTING DISTRACTED BY YOUR FRIEND'S HOMEWORK. SECOND, YOUR PHONE CAN BE TRACKED.
NOPE -- EVERYONE WILL RECOGNIZE THAT CAR. WE'LL HAVE TO WALK.
OKAY...
YOU SURE YOU WANNA DO THIS, KID?
I'VE NEVER BEEN MORE SURE.

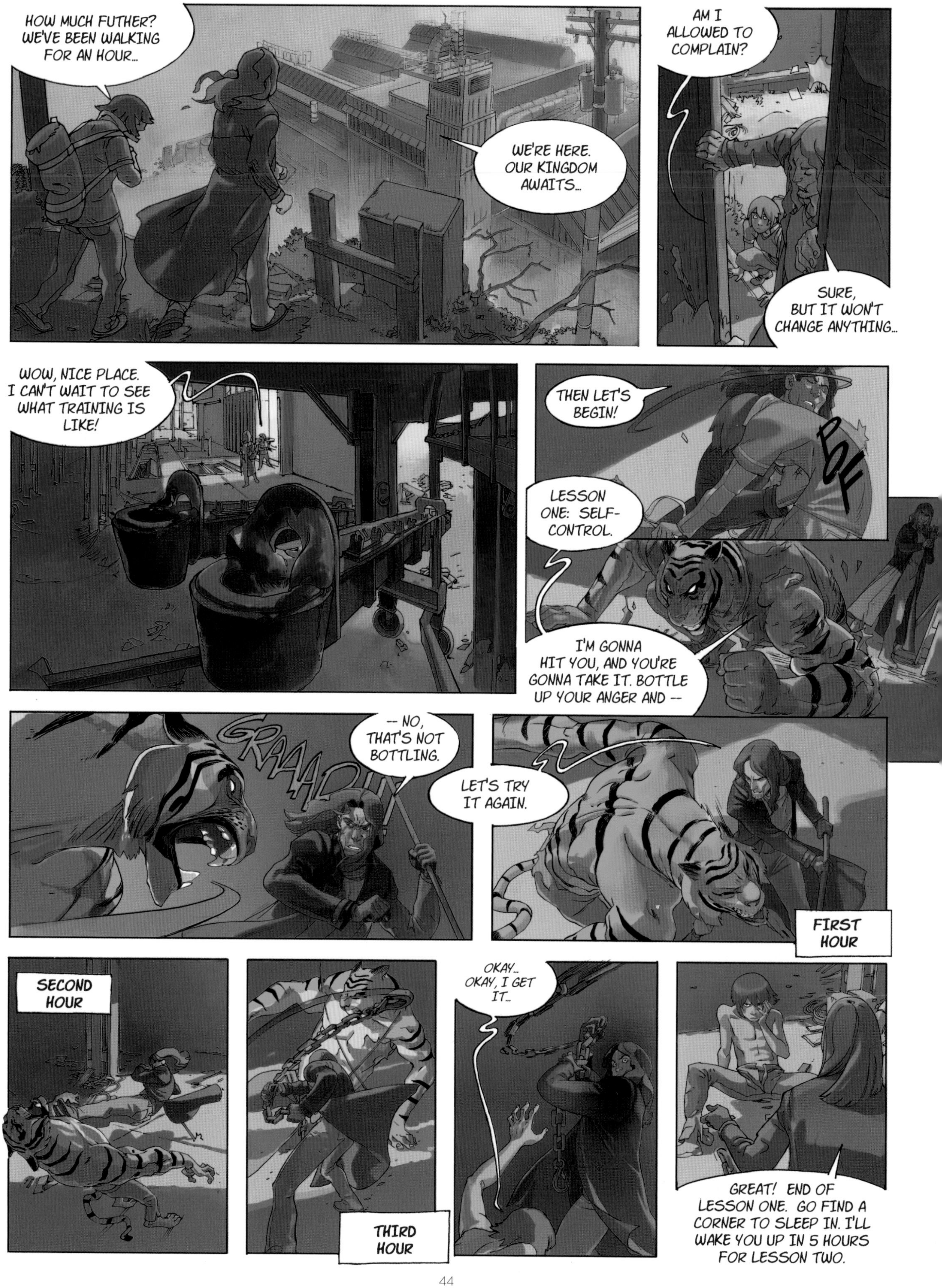
HOW MUCH FUTHER? WE'VE BEEN WALKING FOR AN HOUR...
WE'RE HERE. OUR KINGDOM AWAITS...
AM I ALLOWED TO COMPLAIN?
SURE, BUT IT WON'T CHANGE ANYTHING...
WOW, NICE PLACE. I CAN'T WAIT TO SEE WHAT TRAINING IS LIKE!
THEN LET'S BEGIN!
POF
LESSON ONE: SELF-CONTROL.
I'M GONNA HIT YOU, AND YOU'RE GONNA TAKE IT. BOTTLE UP YOUR ANGER AND --
GRAAAAH!
-- NO, THAT'S NOT BOTTLING.
LET'S TRY IT AGAIN.
FIRST HOUR
SECOND HOUR
THIRD HOUR
OKAY... OKAY, I GET IT...
GREAT! END OF LESSON ONE. GO FIND A CORNER TO SLEEP IN. I'LL WAKE YOU UP IN 5 HOURS FOR LESSON TWO.

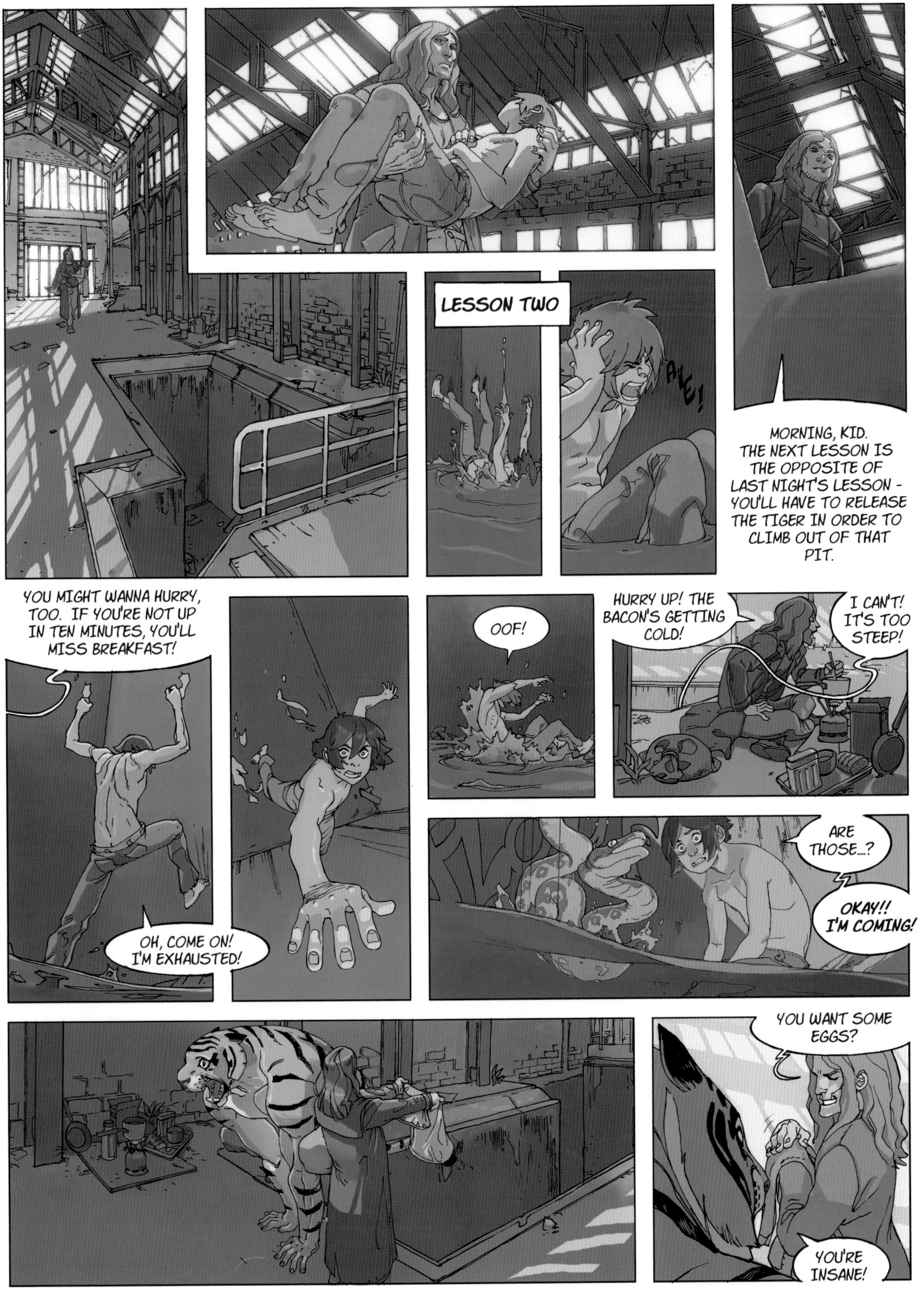
LESSON TWO
AÏE!
MORNING, KID. THE NEXT LESSON IS THE OPPOSITE OF LAST NIGHT'S LESSON - YOU'LL HAVE TO RELEASE THE TIGER IN ORDER TO CLIMB OUT OF THAT PIT.
YOU MIGHT WANNA HURRY, TOO. IF YOU'RE NOT UP IN TEN MINUTES, YOU'LL MISS BREAKFAST!
OH, COME ON! I'M EXHAUSTED!
OOF!
HURRY UP! THE BACON'S GETTING COLD!
I CAN'T! IT'S TOO STEEP!
ARE THOSE...?
OKAY!! I'M COMING!
YOU WANT SOME EGGS?
YOU'RE INSANE!

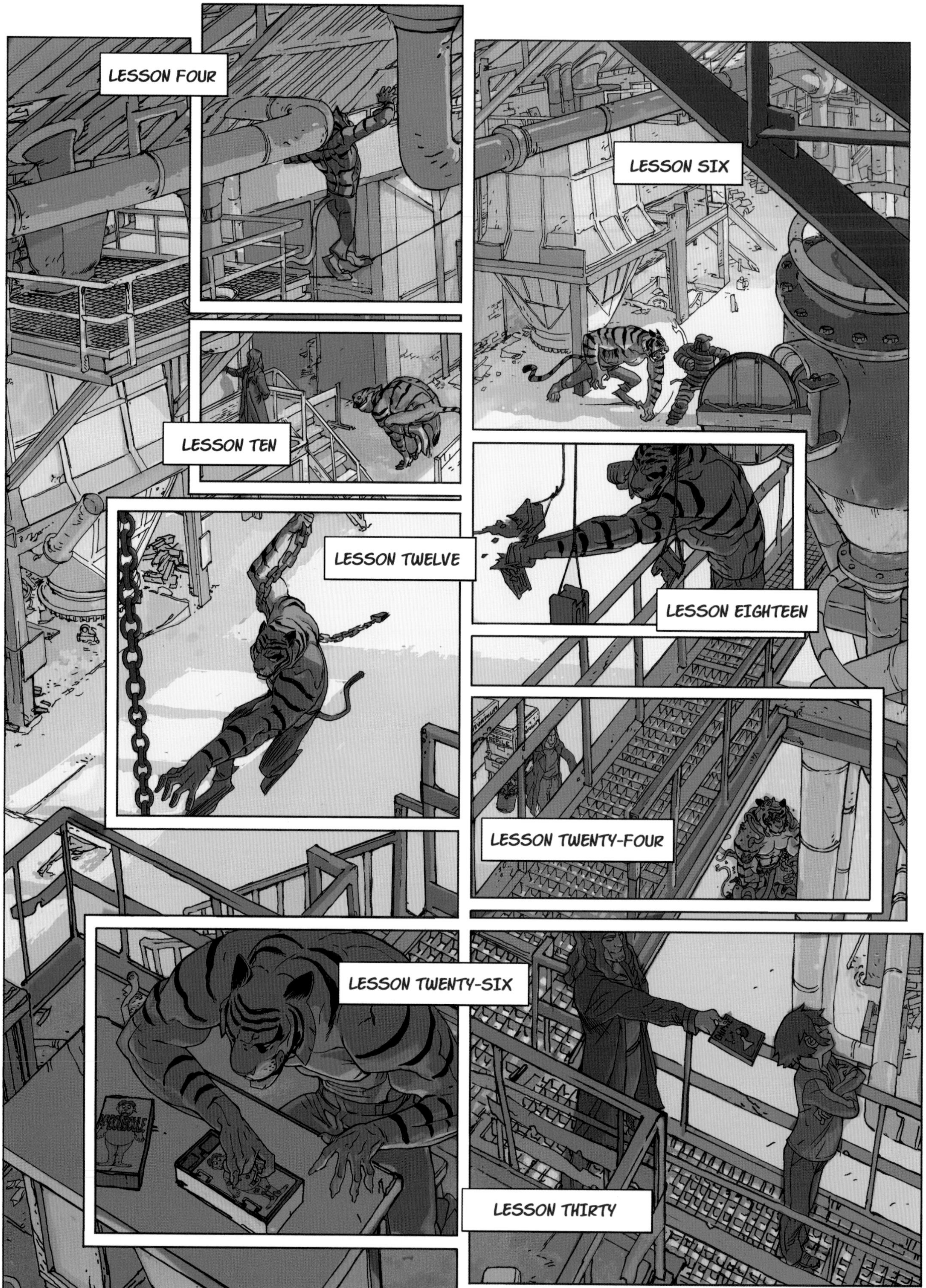
LESSON FOUR
LESSON SIX
LESSON TEN
LESSON TWELVE
LESSON EIGHTEEN
LESSON TWENTY-FOUR
LESSON TWENTY-SIX
LESSON THIRTY

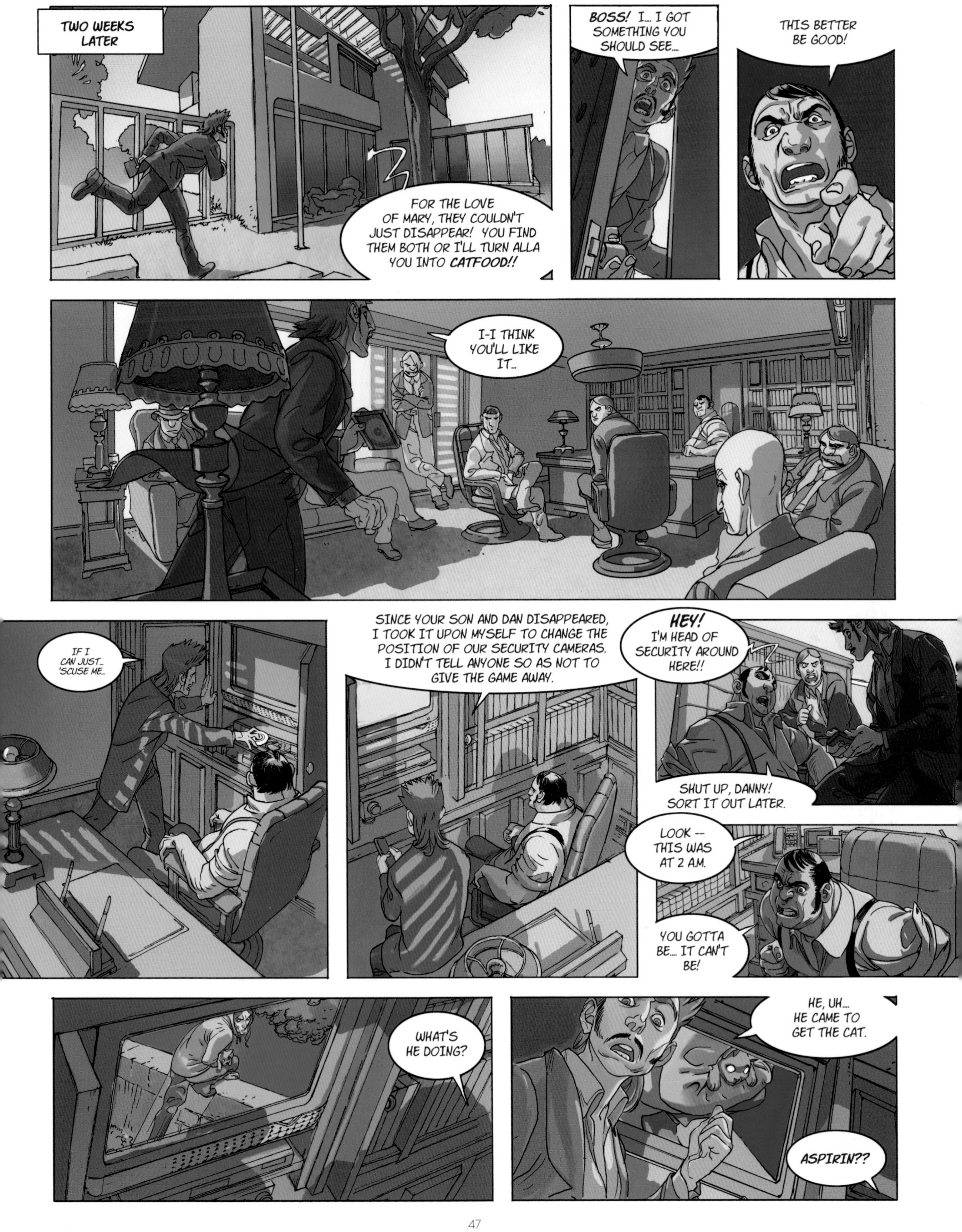

TWO WEEKS LATER
FOR THE LOVE OF MARY, THEY COULDN'T JUST DISAPPEAR! YOU FIND THEM BOTH OR I'LL TURN ALLA YOU INTO CATFOOD!!
BOSS! I... I GOT SOMETHING YOU SHOULD SEE...
THIS BETTER BE GOOD!
I-I THINK YOU'LL LIKE IT...
IF I CAN JUST... 'SCUSE ME...
SINCE YOUR SON AND DAN DISAPPEARED, I TOOK IT UPON MYSELF TO CHANGE THE POSITION OF OUR SECURITY CAMERAS. I DIDN'T TELL ANYONE SO AS NOT TO GIVE THE GAME AWAY.
HEY! I'M HEAD OF SECURITY AROUND HERE!!
SHUT UP, DANNY! SORT IT OUT LATER.
LOOK -- THIS WAS AT 2 A.M.
YOU GOTTA BE... IT CAN'T BE!
WHAT'S HE DOING?
HE, UH... HE CAME TO GET THE CAT.
ASPIRIN??

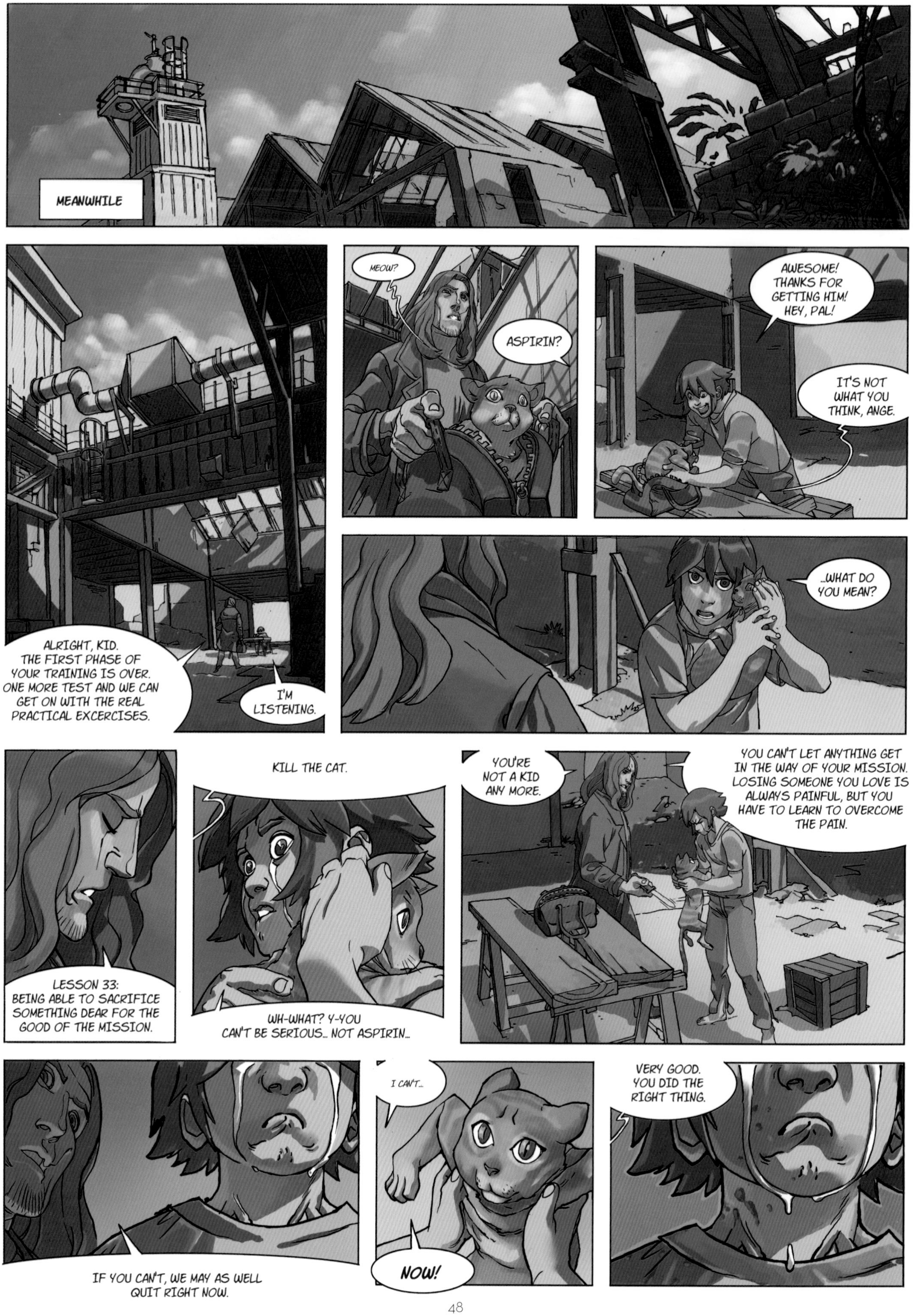
MEANWHILE
ALRIGHT, KID. THE FIRST PHASE OF YOUR TRAINING IS OVER. ONE MORE TEST AND WE CAN GET ON WITH THE REAL PRACTICAL EXCERCISES.
I'M LISTENING.
MEOW?
ASPIRIN?
AWESOME! THANKS FOR GETTING HIM! HEY, PAL!
IT'S NOT WHAT YOU THINK, ANGE.
...WHAT DO YOU MEAN?
LESSON 33: BEING ABLE TO SACRIFICE SOMETHING DEAR FOR THE GOOD OF THE MISSION.
KILL THE CAT.
WH-WHAT? Y-YOU CAN'T BE SERIOUS... NOT ASPIRIN...
YOU'RE NOT A KID ANY MORE.
YOU CAN'T LET ANYTHING GET IN THE WAY OF YOUR MISSION. LOSING SOMEONE YOU LOVE IS ALWAYS PAINFUL, BUT YOU HAVE TO LEARN TO OVERCOME THE PAIN.
IF YOU CAN'T, WE MAY AS WELL QUIT RIGHT NOW.
I CAN'T...
NOW!
VERY GOOD. YOU DID THE RIGHT THING.

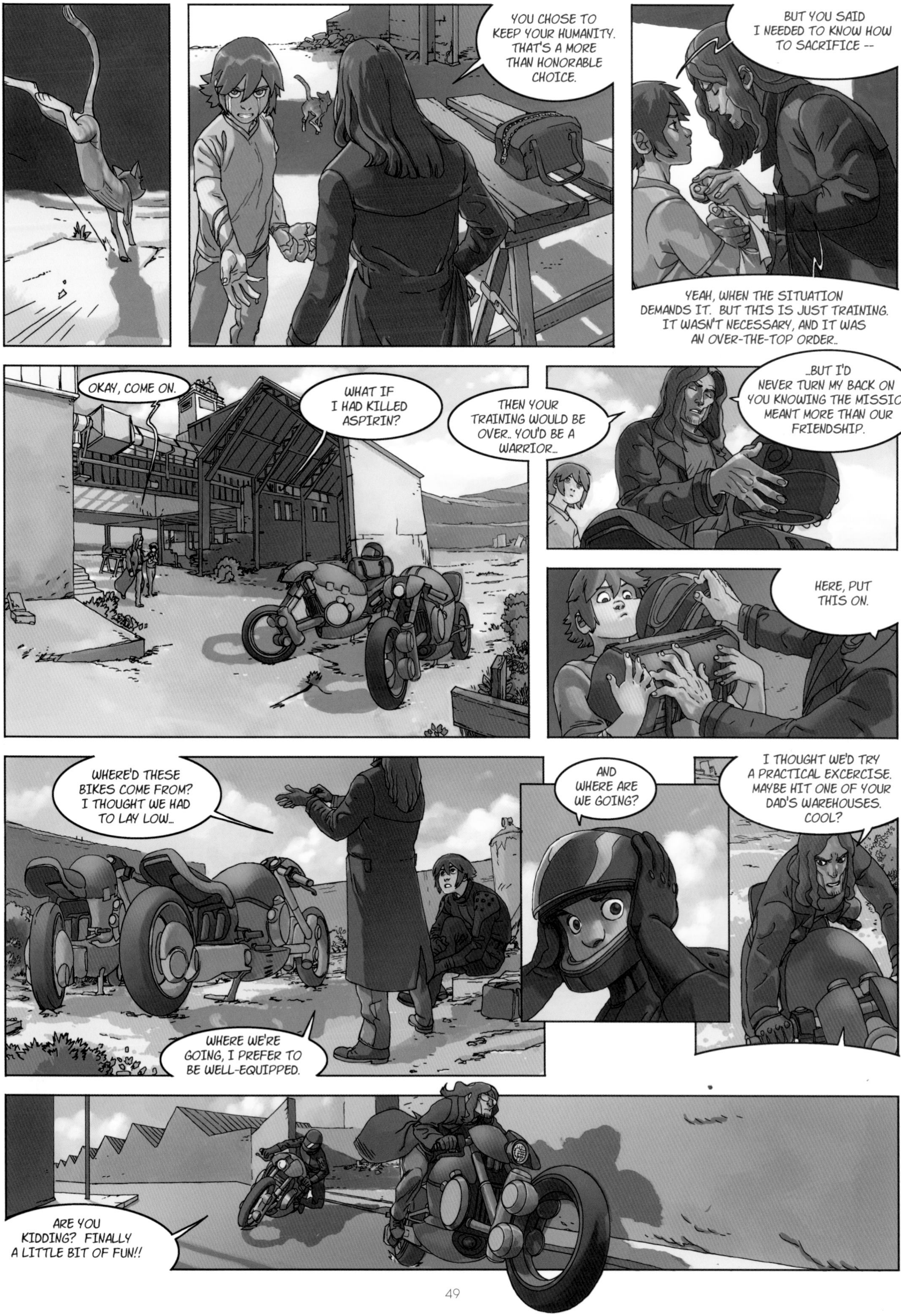
YOU CHOSE TO KEEP YOUR HUMANITY. THAT'S A MORE THAN HONORABLE CHOICE.
BUT YOU SAID I NEEDED TO KNOW HOW TO SACRIFICE --
YEAH, WHEN THE SITUATION DEMANDS IT. BUT THIS IS JUST TRAINING. IT WASN'T NECESSARY, AND IT WAS AN OVER-THE-TOP ORDER..
OKAY, COME ON.
WHAT IF I HAD KILLED ASPIRIN?
THEN YOUR TRAINING WOULD BE OVER.. YOU'D BE A WARRIOR...
...BUT I'D NEVER TURN MY BACK ON YOU KNOWING THE MISSION MEANT MORE THAN OUR FRIENDSHIP.
HERE, PUT THIS ON.
WHERE'D THESE BIKES COME FROM? I THOUGHT WE HAD TO LAY LOW...
WHERE WE'RE GOING, I PREFER TO BE WELL-EQUIPPED.
AND WHERE ARE WE GOING?
I THOUGHT WE'D TRY A PRACTICAL EXCERCISE. MAYBE HIT ONE OF YOUR DAD'S WAREHOUSES. COOL?
ARE YOU KIDDING? FINALLY A LITTLE BIT OF FUN!!

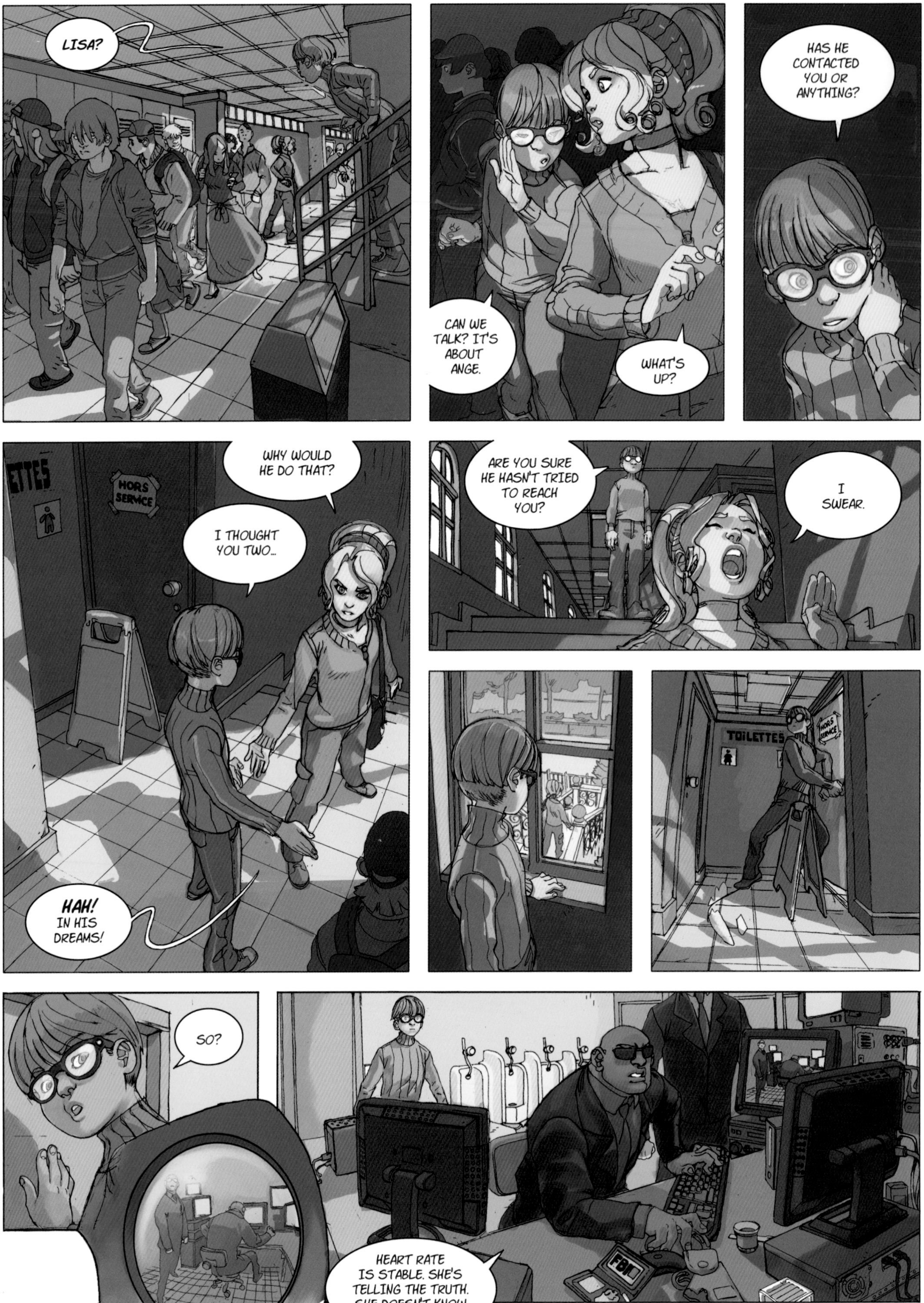
LISA?
CAN WE TALK? IT'S ABOUT ANGE.
WHAT'S UP?
HAS HE CONTACTED YOU OR ANYTHING?
ETTES
HORS SERVICE
WHY WOULD HE DO THAT?
I THOUGHT YOU TWO...
HAH! IN HIS DREAMS!
ARE YOU SURE HE HASN'T TRIED TO REACH YOU?
I SWEAR.
TOILETTES
HORS SERVICE
SO?
HEART RATE IS STABLE. SHE'S TELLING THE TRUTH. SHE DOESN'T KNOW A THING...
FBI

END PART ONE

PART TWO: TABULA RASA

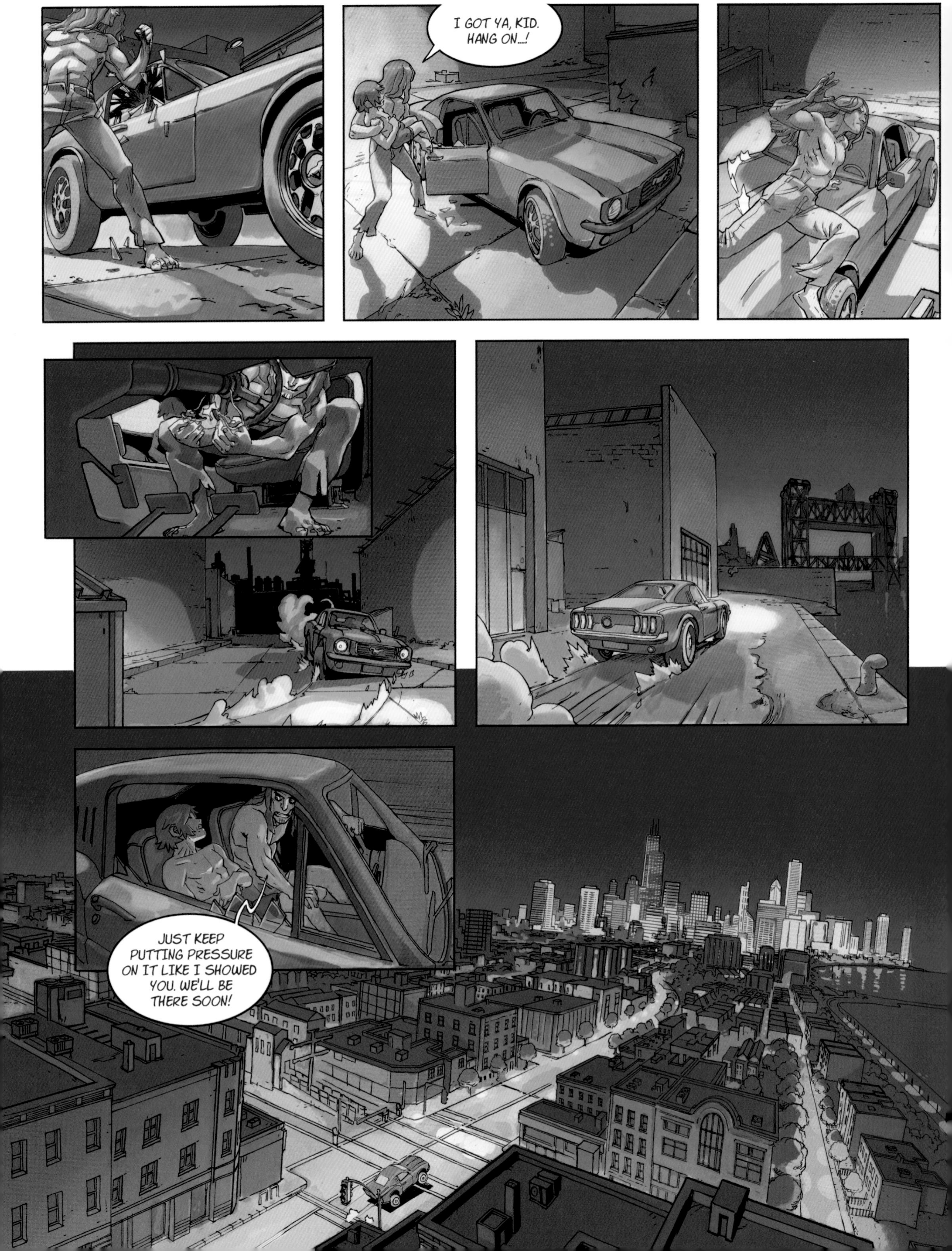
I GOT YA, KID. HANG ON...!
JUST KEEP PUTTING PRESSURE ON IT LIKE I SHOWED YOU. WE'LL BE THERE SOON!

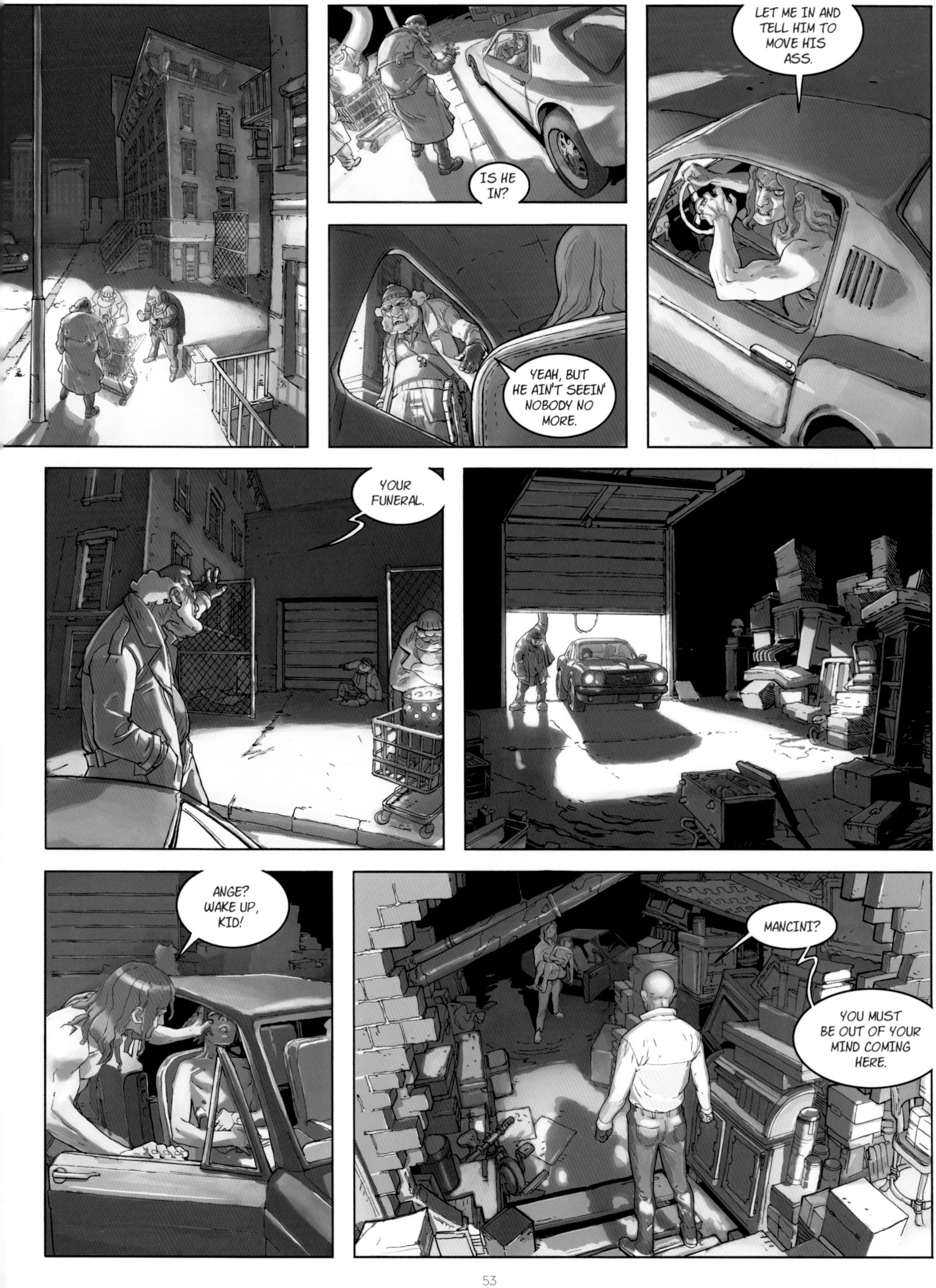
IS HE IN?
LET ME IN AND TELL HIM TO MOVE HIS ASS.
YEAH, BUT HE AIN'T SEEIN' NOBODY NO MORE.
YOUR FUNERAL.
ANGE? WAKE UP, KID!
MANCINI?
YOU MUST BE OUT OF YOUR MIND COMING HERE.

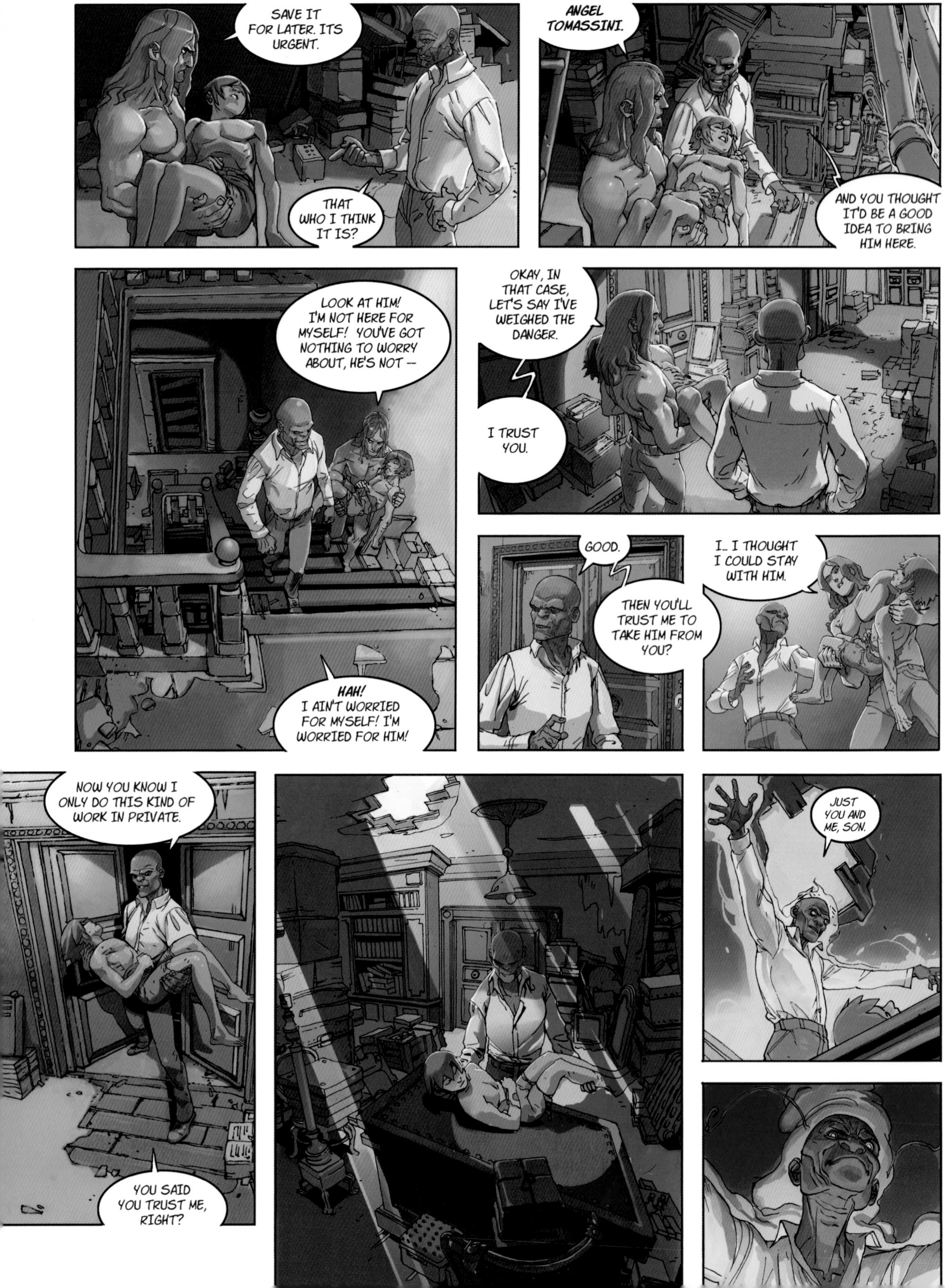
SAVE IT FOR LATER. ITS URGENT.
THAT WHO I THINK IT IS?
ANGEL TOMASSINI.
AND YOU THOUGHT IT'D BE A GOOD IDEA TO BRING HIM HERE.
LOOK AT HIM! I'M NOT HERE FOR MYSELF! YOU'VE GOT NOTHING TO WORRY ABOUT, HE'S NOT --
HAH! I AIN'T WORRIED FOR MYSELF! I'M WORRIED FOR HIM!
OKAY, IN THAT CASE, LET'S SAY I'VE WEIGHED THE DANGER.
I TRUST YOU.
GOOD.
THEN YOU'LL TRUST ME TO TAKE HIM FROM YOU?
I... I THOUGHT I COULD STAY WITH HIM.
NOW YOU KNOW I ONLY DO THIS KIND OF WORK IN PRIVATE.
YOU SAID YOU TRUST ME, RIGHT?
JUST YOU AND ME, SON.

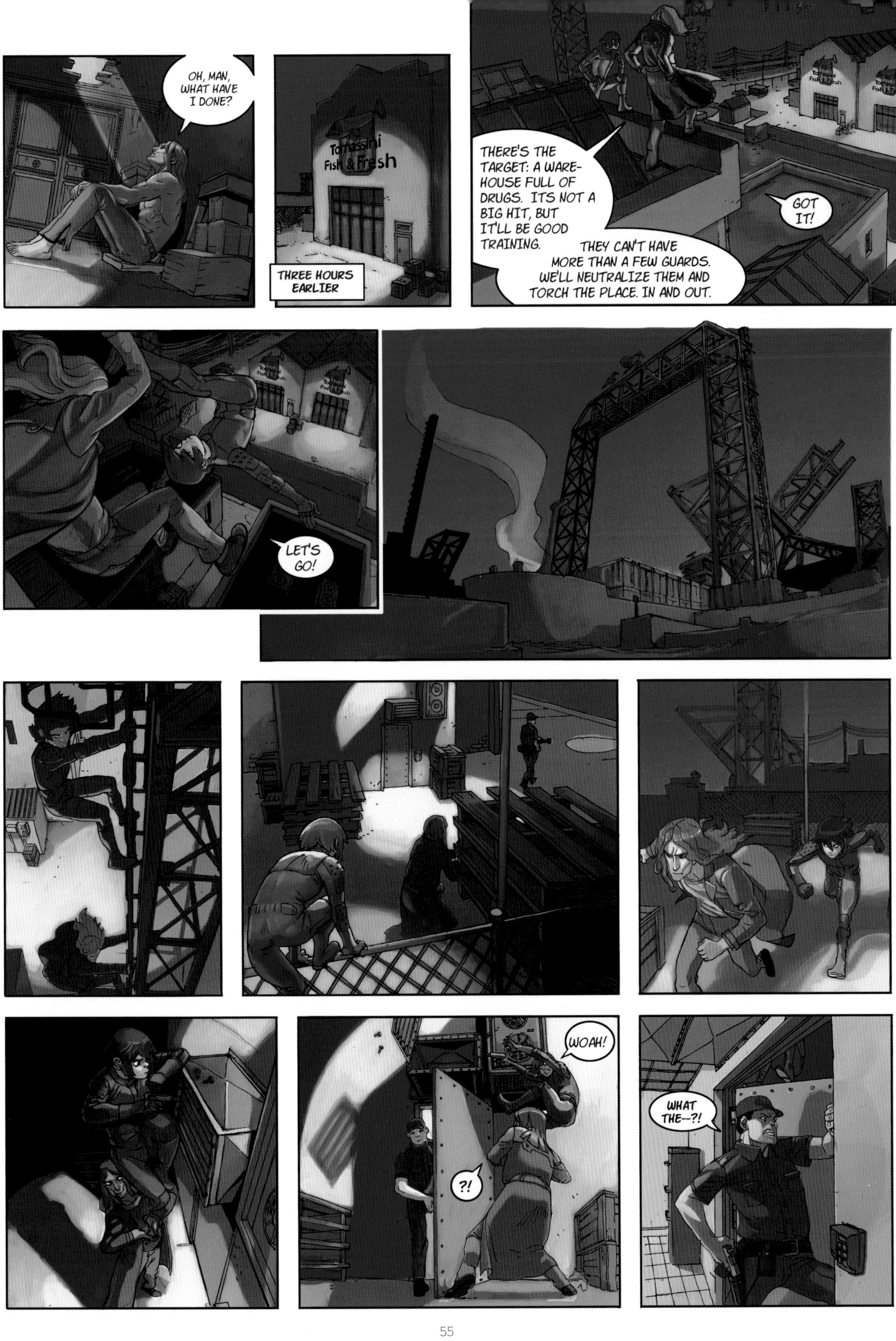
OH, MAN, WHAT HAVE I DONE?
Tomassini Fish & Fresh
THREE HOURS EARLIER
THERE'S THE TARGET: A WARE-HOUSE FULL OF DRUGS. ITS NOT A BIG HIT, BUT IT'LL BE GOOD TRAINING.
THEY CAN'T HAVE MORE THAN A FEW GUARDS. WE'LL NEUTRALIZE THEM AND TORCH THE PLACE. IN AND OUT.
GOT IT!
LET'S GO!
WOAH!
?!
WHAT THE--?!

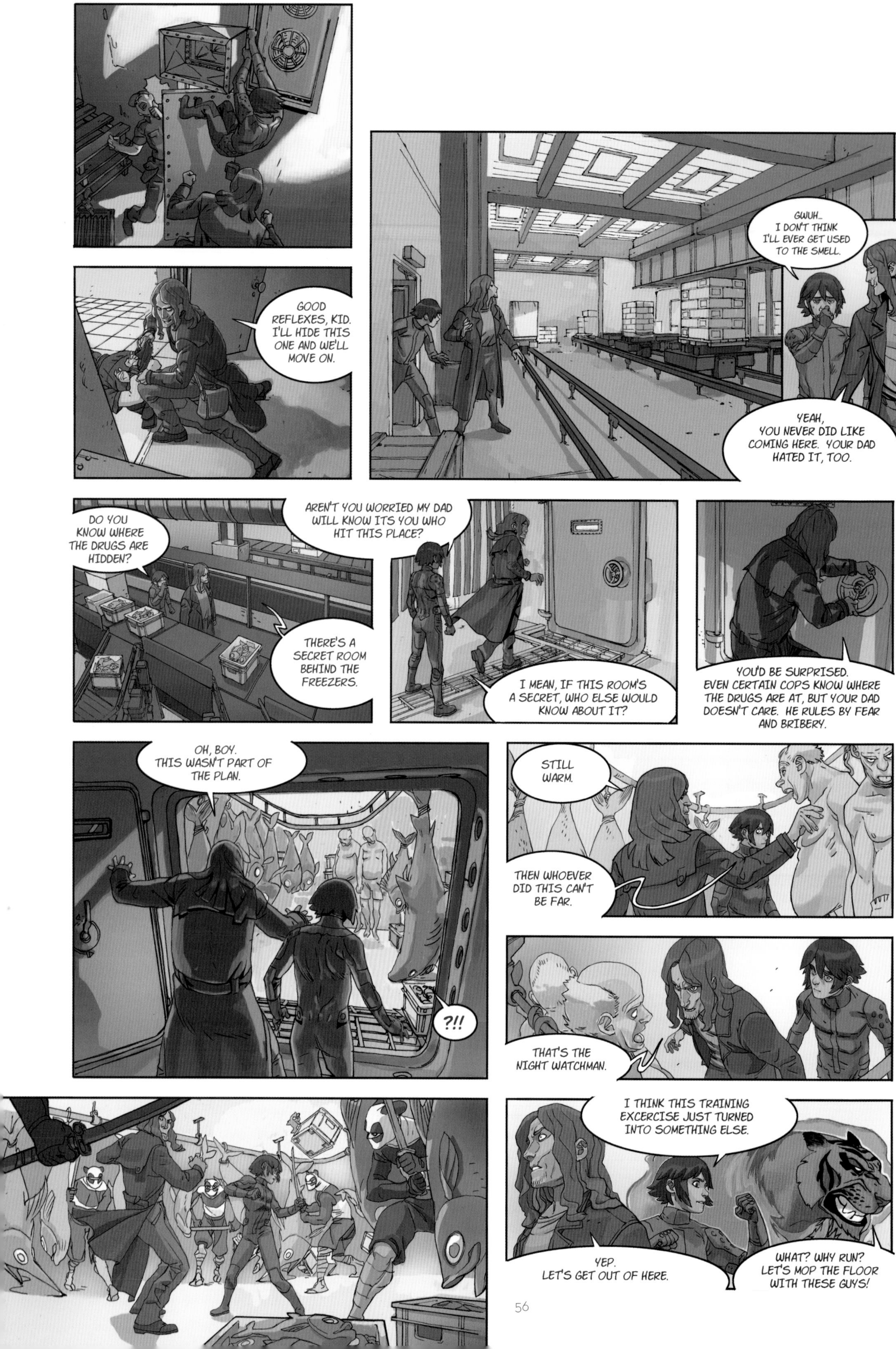
GOOD REFLEXES, KID. I'LL HIDE THIS ONE AND WE'LL MOVE ON.
GWUH... I DON'T THINK I'LL EVER GET USED TO THE SMELL.
YEAH, YOU NEVER DID LIKE COMING HERE. YOUR DAD HATED IT, TOO.
DO YOU KNOW WHERE THE DRUGS ARE HIDDEN?
THERE'S A SECRET ROOM BEHIND THE FREEZERS.
AREN'T YOU WORRIED MY DAD WILL KNOW ITS YOU WHO HIT THIS PLACE?
I MEAN, IF THIS ROOM'S A SECRET, WHO ELSE WOULD KNOW ABOUT IT?
YOU'D BE SURPRISED. EVEN CERTAIN COPS KNOW WHERE THE DRUGS ARE AT, BUT YOUR DAD DOESN'T CARE. HE RULES BY FEAR AND BRIBERY.
OH, BOY. THIS WASN'T PART OF THE PLAN.
?!!
STILL WARM.
THEN WHOEVER DID THIS CAN'T BE FAR.
THAT'S THE NIGHT WATCHMAN.
I THINK THIS TRAINING EXCERCISE JUST TURNED INTO SOMETHING ELSE.
YEP. LET'S GET OUT OF HERE.
WHAT? WHY RUN? LET'S MOP THE FLOOR WITH THESE GUYS!

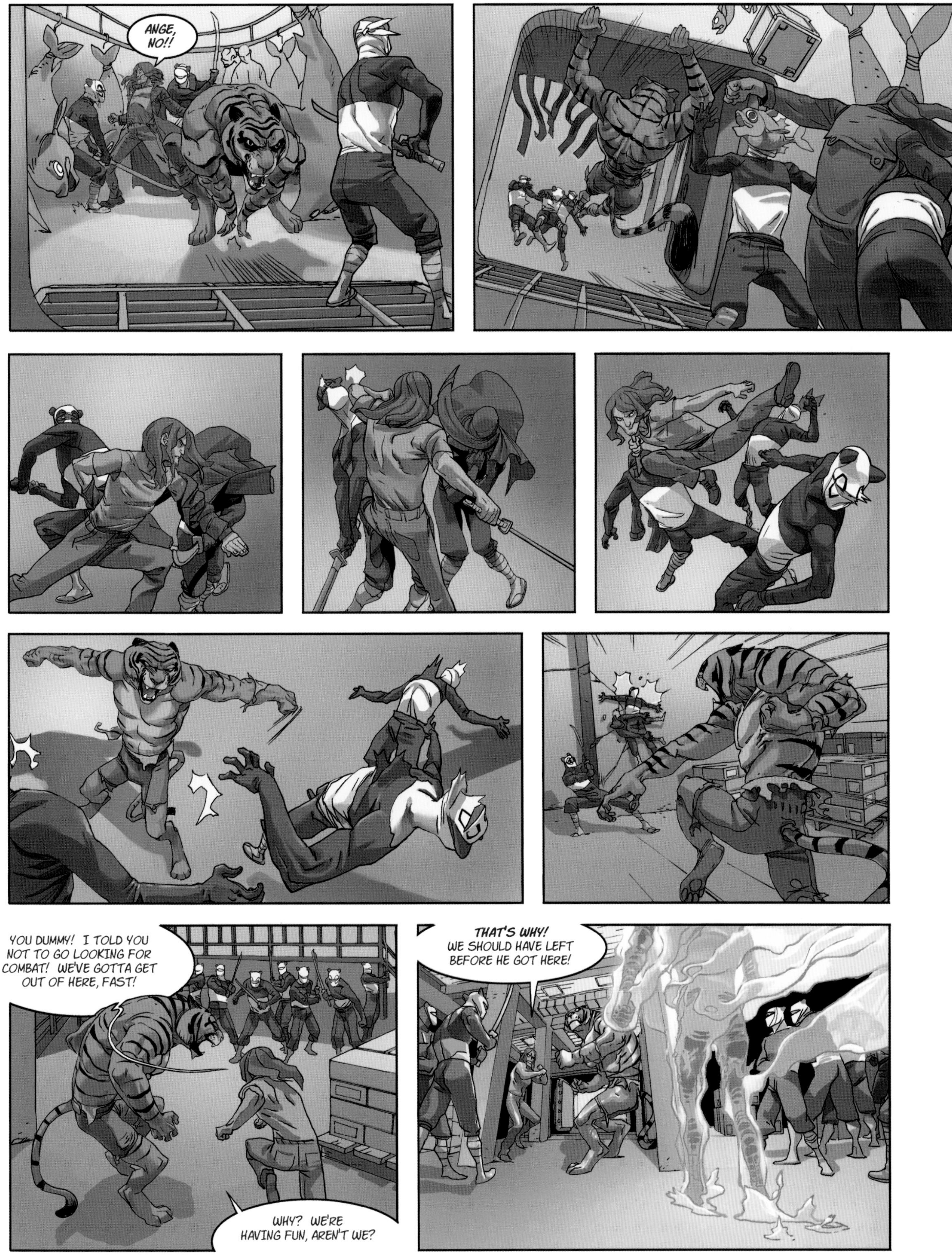
ANGE, NO!!
YOU DUMMY! I TOLD YOU NOT TO GO LOOKING FOR COMBAT! WE'VE GOTTA GET OUT OF HERE, FAST!
WHY? WE'RE HAVING FUN, AREN'T WE?
THAT'S WHY! WE SHOULD HAVE LEFT BEFORE HE GOT HERE!

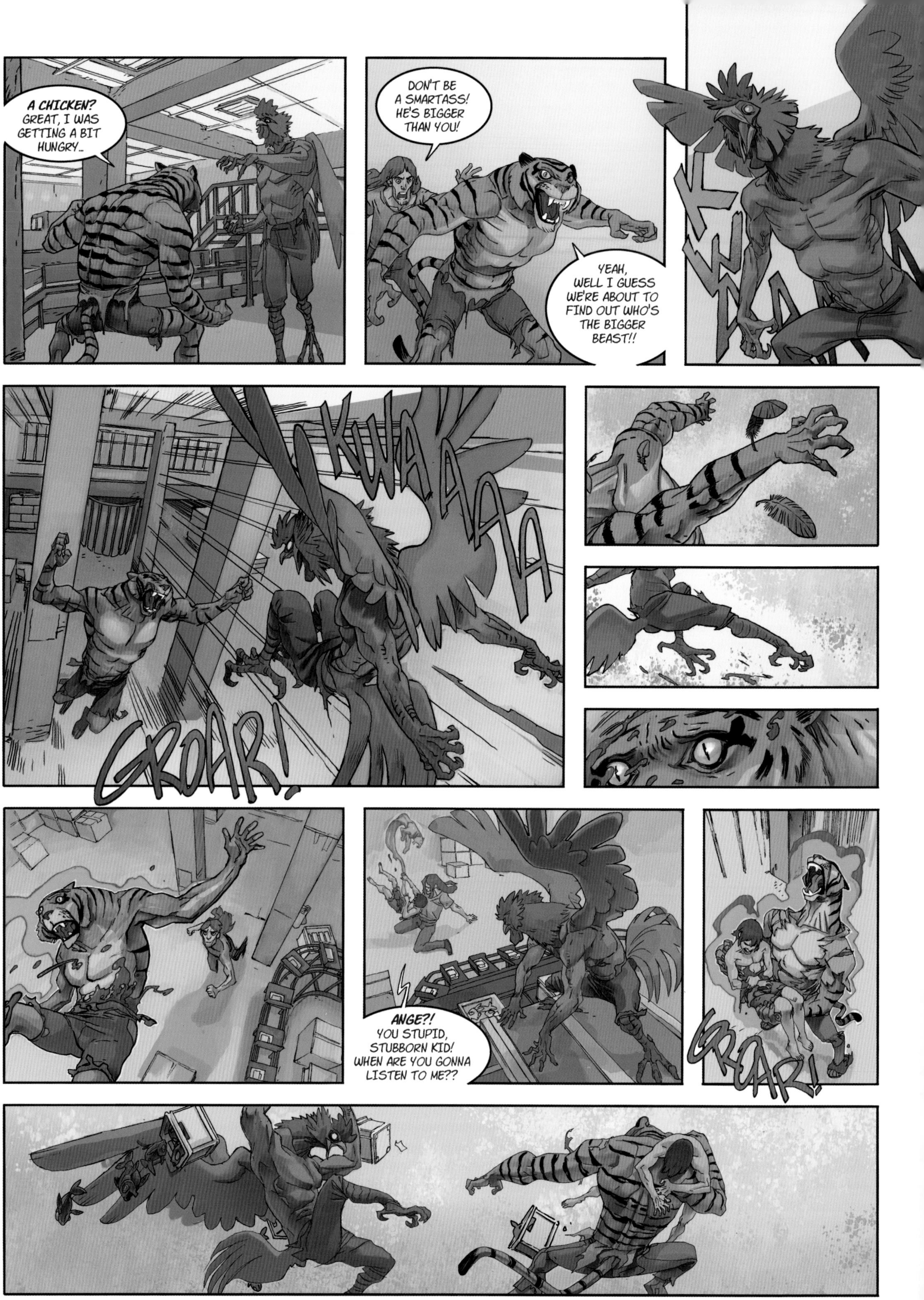

A CHICKEN? GREAT, I WAS GETTING A BIT HUNGRY...
DON'T BE A SMARTASS! HE'S BIGGER THAN YOU!
YEAH, WELL I GUESS WE'RE ABOUT TO FIND OUT WHO'S THE BIGGER BEAST!!
KWAAAAA
GROAR!
ANGE?! YOU STUPID, STUBBORN KID! WHEN ARE YOU GONNA LISTEN TO ME??
GROAR!

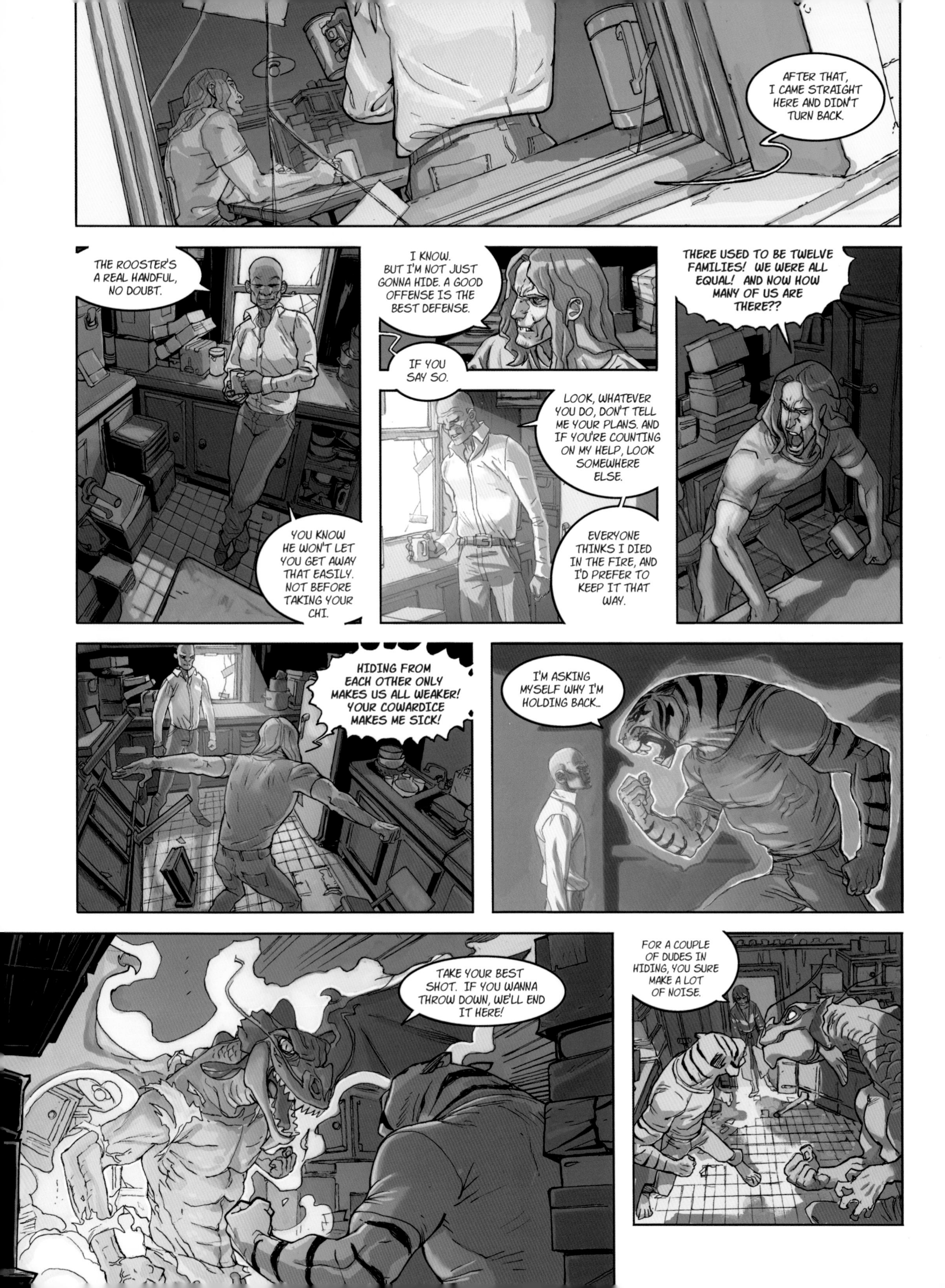
AFTER THAT, I CAME STRAIGHT HERE AND DIDN'T TURN BACK.
THE ROOSTER'S A REAL HANDFUL, NO DOUBT.
YOU KNOW HE WON'T LET YOU GET AWAY THAT EASILY. NOT BEFORE TAKING YOUR CHI.
I KNOW. BUT I'M NOT JUST GONNA HIDE. A GOOD OFFENSE IS THE BEST DEFENSE.
IF YOU SAY SO.
LOOK, WHATEVER YOU DO, DON'T TELL ME YOUR PLANS. AND IF YOU'RE COUNTING ON MY HELP, LOOK SOMEWHERE ELSE.
EVERYONE THINKS I DIED IN THE FIRE, AND I'D PREFER TO KEEP IT THAT WAY.
THERE USED TO BE TWELVE FAMILIES! WE WERE ALL EQUAL! AND NOW HOW MANY OF US ARE THERE??
HIDING FROM EACH OTHER ONLY MAKES US ALL WEAKER! YOUR COWARDICE MAKES ME SICK!
I'M ASKING MYSELF WHY I'M HOLDING BACK...
TAKE YOUR BEST SHOT. IF YOU WANNA THROW DOWN, WE'LL END IT HERE!
FOR A COUPLE OF DUDES IN HIDING, YOU SURE MAKE A LOT OF NOISE.

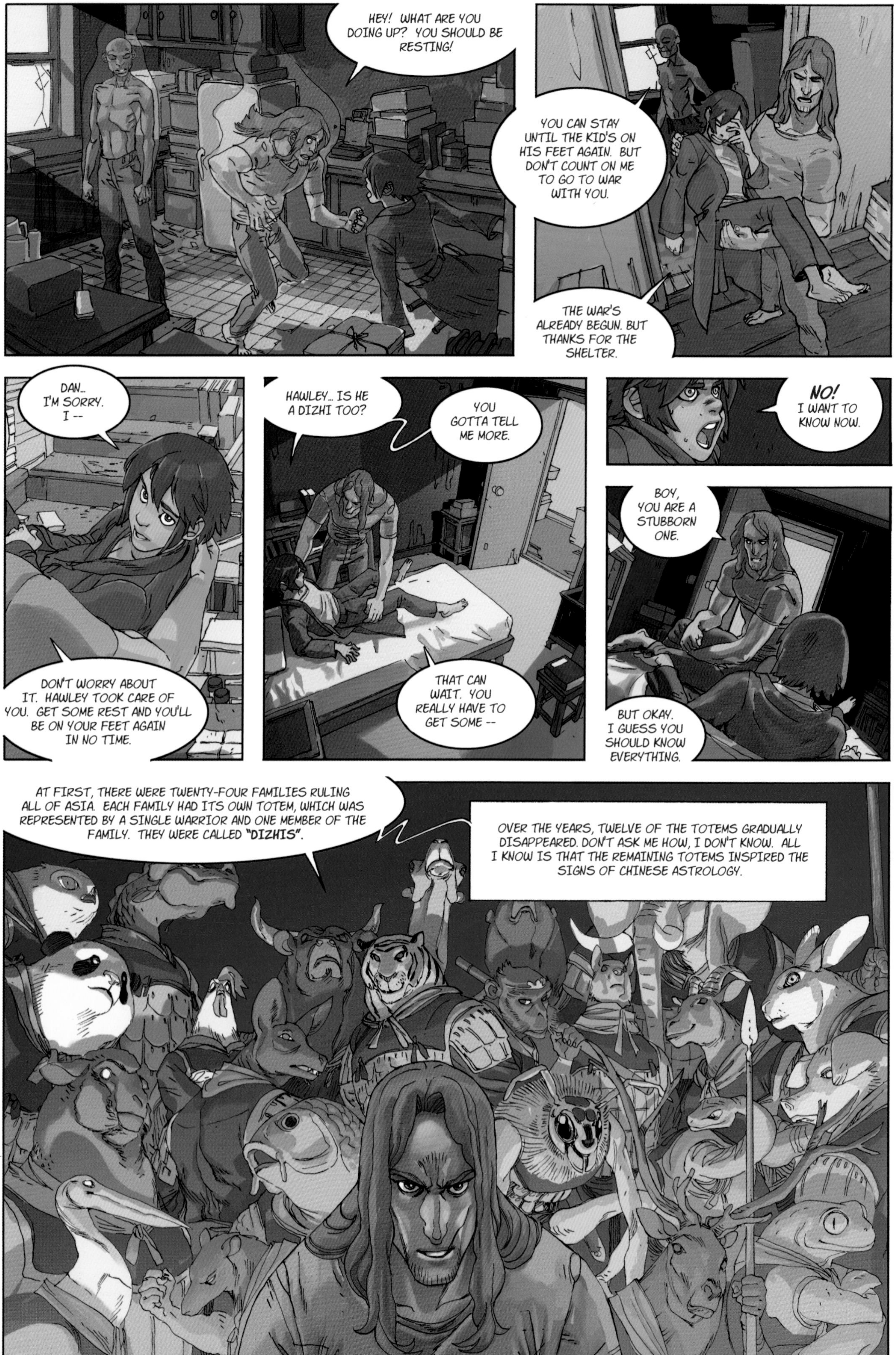

HEY! WHAT ARE YOU DOING UP? YOU SHOULD BE RESTING!
YOU CAN STAY UNTIL THE KID'S ON HIS FEET AGAIN. BUT DON'T COUNT ON ME TO GO TO WAR WITH YOU.
THE WAR'S ALREADY BEGUN. BUT THANKS FOR THE SHELTER.
DAN... I'M SORRY. I --
DON'T WORRY ABOUT IT. HAWLEY TOOK CARE OF YOU. GET SOME REST AND YOU'LL BE ON YOUR FEET AGAIN IN NO TIME.
HAWLEY... IS HE A DIZHI TOO?
YOU GOTTA TELL ME MORE.
THAT CAN WAIT. YOU REALLY HAVE TO GET SOME --
NO! I WANT TO KNOW NOW.
BOY, YOU ARE A STUBBORN ONE.
BUT OKAY. I GUESS YOU SHOULD KNOW EVERYTHING.
AT FIRST, THERE WERE TWENTY-FOUR FAMILIES RULING ALL OF ASIA. EACH FAMILY HAD ITS OWN TOTEM, WHICH WAS REPRESENTED BY A SINGLE WARRIOR AND ONE MEMBER OF THE FAMILY. THEY WERE CALLED **"DIZHIS"**.
OVER THE YEARS, TWELVE OF THE TOTEMS GRADUALLY DISAPPEARED. DON'T ASK ME HOW, I DON'T KNOW. ALL I KNOW IS THAT THE REMAINING TOTEMS INSPIRED THE SIGNS OF CHINESE ASTROLOGY.

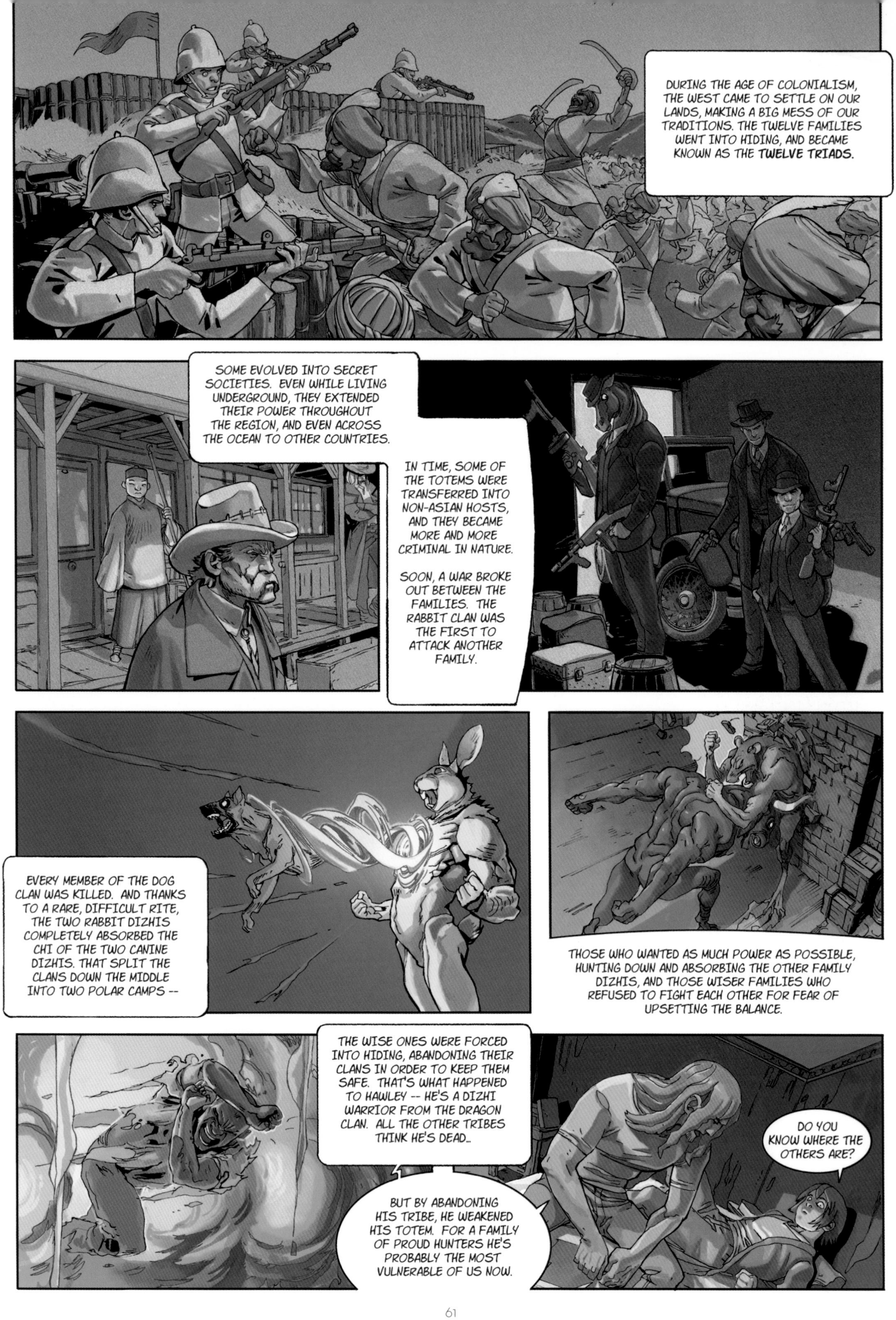
DURING THE AGE OF COLONIALISM, THE WEST CAME TO SETTLE ON OUR LANDS, MAKING A BIG MESS OF OUR TRADITIONS. THE TWELVE FAMILIES WENT INTO HIDING, AND BECAME KNOWN AS THE **TWELVE TRIADS.**
SOME EVOLVED INTO SECRET SOCIETIES. EVEN WHILE LIVING UNDERGROUND, THEY EXTENDED THEIR POWER THROUGHOUT THE REGION, AND EVEN ACROSS THE OCEAN TO OTHER COUNTRIES.
IN TIME, SOME OF THE TOTEMS WERE TRANSFERRED INTO NON-ASIAN HOSTS, AND THEY BECAME MORE AND MORE CRIMINAL IN NATURE.
SOON, A WAR BROKE OUT BETWEEN THE FAMILIES. THE RABBIT CLAN WAS THE FIRST TO ATTACK ANOTHER FAMILY.
EVERY MEMBER OF THE DOG CLAN WAS KILLED. AND THANKS TO A RARE, DIFFICULT RITE, THE TWO RABBIT DIZHIS COMPLETELY ABSORBED THE CHI OF THE TWO CANINE DIZHIS. THAT SPLIT THE CLANS DOWN THE MIDDLE INTO TWO POLAR CAMPS --
THOSE WHO WANTED AS MUCH POWER AS POSSIBLE, HUNTING DOWN AND ABSORBING THE OTHER FAMILY DIZHIS, AND THOSE WISER FAMILIES WHO REFUSED TO FIGHT EACH OTHER FOR FEAR OF UPSETTING THE BALANCE.
THE WISE ONES WERE FORCED INTO HIDING, ABANDONING THEIR CLANS IN ORDER TO KEEP THEM SAFE. THAT'S WHAT HAPPENED TO HAWLEY -- HE'S A DIZHI WARRIOR FROM THE DRAGON CLAN. ALL THE OTHER TRIBES THINK HE'S DEAD...
BUT BY ABANDONING HIS TRIBE, HE WEAKENED HIS TOTEM. FOR A FAMILY OF PROUD HUNTERS HE'S PROBABLY THE MOST VULNERABLE OF US NOW.
DO YOU KNOW WHERE THE OTHERS ARE?

LET ME PUT THIS SIMPLY: IF YOU'RE HERE, YOU KNOW ABOUT "OPERATION: TOTEM".

WE'VE MADE VERY LITTLE HEADWAY IN THE LAST FIVE YEARS, DESPITE TOP-LEVEL SECURITY CLEARANCE AND THE HIGHEST DEGREE OF SECRECY. WE'VE BARELY MANAGED TO IDENTIFY A FEW FLEETING MEMBERS OF TRIAD FAMILIES HARBORING A DIZHI.

AND THAT DOESN'T EVEN INCLUDE THE CLANS WHO REFUSE TO TAKE PART IN THIS MAD RACE FOR ULTIMATE POWER. IF YOU COUNT THEM, WE'RE LOOKING FOR EVEN MORE TOTEMS.

WHAT WE DO KNOW AS OF TODAY IS THAT THERE ARE AT LEAST TWO DIZHIS IN THE AREA.

THE **SOKUMO FAMILY** ARE HARBORING THE TOTEM OF THE ROOSTER. IT IS AN AGGRESSIVE BEAST THAT WE SUSPECT MAY HAVE ABSORBED THE PIG DIZHI.

NEXT IS THE **TOMASSINI FAMILY**, WHO WE BELIEVE MAY HARBOR THE TIGER.

WE'VE HAD A JUNIOR AGENT UNDERCOVER FOR SEVERAL MONTHS NOW MONITORING A MINOR WHO WE BELIEVE FITS THE PROFILE OF A YOUNG DIZHI.

UNFORTUNATELY, THE SUSPECT HAS DISAPPEARED.

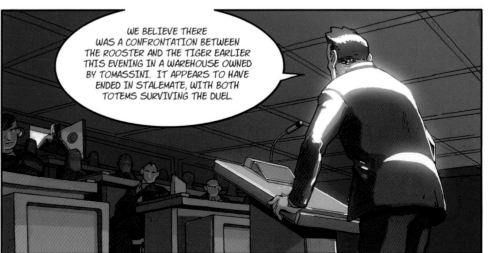

WE BELIEVE THERE WAS A CONFRONTATION BETWEEN THE ROOSTER AND THE TIGER EARLIER THIS EVENING IN A WAREHOUSE OWNED BY TOMASSINI. IT APPEARS TO HAVE ENDED IN STALEMATE, WITH BOTH TOTEMS SURVIVING THE DUEL.

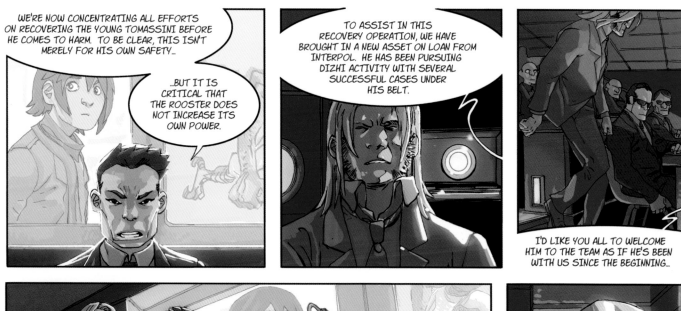

WE'RE NOW CONCENTRATING ALL EFFORTS ON RECOVERING THE YOUNG TOMASSINI BEFORE HE COMES TO HARM. TO BE CLEAR, THIS ISN'T MERELY FOR HIS OWN SAFETY...

...BUT IT IS CRITICAL THAT THE ROOSTER DOES NOT INCREASE ITS OWN POWER.

TO ASSIST IN THIS RECOVERY OPERATION, WE HAVE BROUGHT IN A NEW ASSET ON LOAN FROM INTERPOL. HE HAS BEEN PURSUING DIZHI ACTIVITY WITH SEVERAL SUCCESSFUL CASES UNDER HIS BELT.

I'D LIKE YOU ALL TO WELCOME HIM TO THE TEAM AS IF HE'S BEEN WITH US SINCE THE BEGINNING...

LADIES AND GENTLEMEN, AGENT **OSWALD JONES.**

HELLO.

I'M GONNA SKIP THE USUAL PLEASANTRIES AND ASK YOU TO DO ONE THING FOR ME: **FORGET EVERYTHING YOU THINK YOU'VE LEARNED ABOUT THE DIZHIS.**

FOR ONE THING, THERE'S NO SUCH THING AS A "PACIFIST TOTEM". THEY'RE ALL SOLDIERS AND WARRIORS, CREATED FOR ONE THING AND ONE THING ONLY: **WINNING WARS.** IT DOESN'T MATTER IF THEY'RE KILLING EACH OTHER FOR A WHILE.

OUR MISSION IS TO STOP THEM. TO DESTROY THEM COMPLETELY.

CLEARLY THIS WON'T BE EASY. WE KNOW THAT WHEN YOU KILL ONE OF THEM, THE DIZHI CHI LEAVES ITS BODY AND SEEKS A NEW HOST...

...SO WE NEED TO CAPTURE THEM ALL, ONE BY ONE. AND ONCE WE HAVE THEM ALL, WE EXTERMINATE THEM EN MASSE.

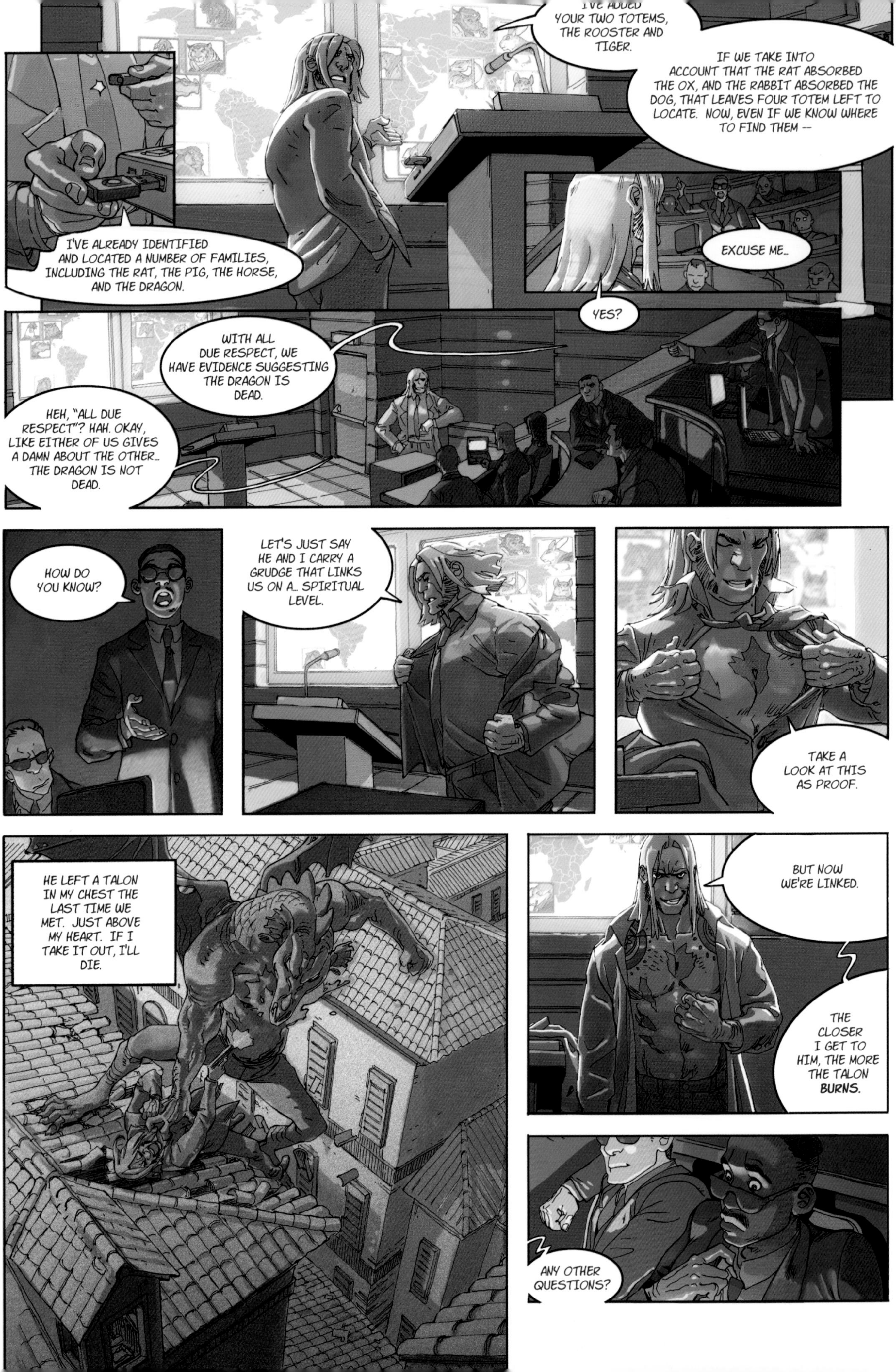
I'VE ADDED YOUR TWO TOTEMS, THE ROOSTER AND TIGER.
IF WE TAKE INTO ACCOUNT THAT THE RAT ABSORBED THE OX, AND THE RABBIT ABSORBED THE DOG, THAT LEAVES FOUR TOTEM LEFT TO LOCATE. NOW, EVEN IF WE KNOW WHERE TO FIND THEM --
I'VE ALREADY IDENTIFIED AND LOCATED A NUMBER OF FAMILIES, INCLUDING THE RAT, THE PIG, THE HORSE, AND THE DRAGON.
EXCUSE ME...
YES?
WITH ALL DUE RESPECT, WE HAVE EVIDENCE SUGGESTING THE DRAGON IS DEAD.
HEH, "ALL DUE RESPECT"? HAH. OKAY, LIKE EITHER OF US GIVES A DAMN ABOUT THE OTHER... THE DRAGON IS NOT DEAD.
HOW DO YOU KNOW?
LET'S JUST SAY HE AND I CARRY A GRUDGE THAT LINKS US ON A... SPIRITUAL LEVEL.
TAKE A LOOK AT THIS AS PROOF.
HE LEFT A TALON IN MY CHEST THE LAST TIME WE MET. JUST ABOVE MY HEART. IF I TAKE IT OUT, I'LL DIE.
BUT NOW WE'RE LINKED.
THE CLOSER I GET TO HIM, THE MORE THE TALON **BURNS.**
ANY OTHER QUESTIONS?

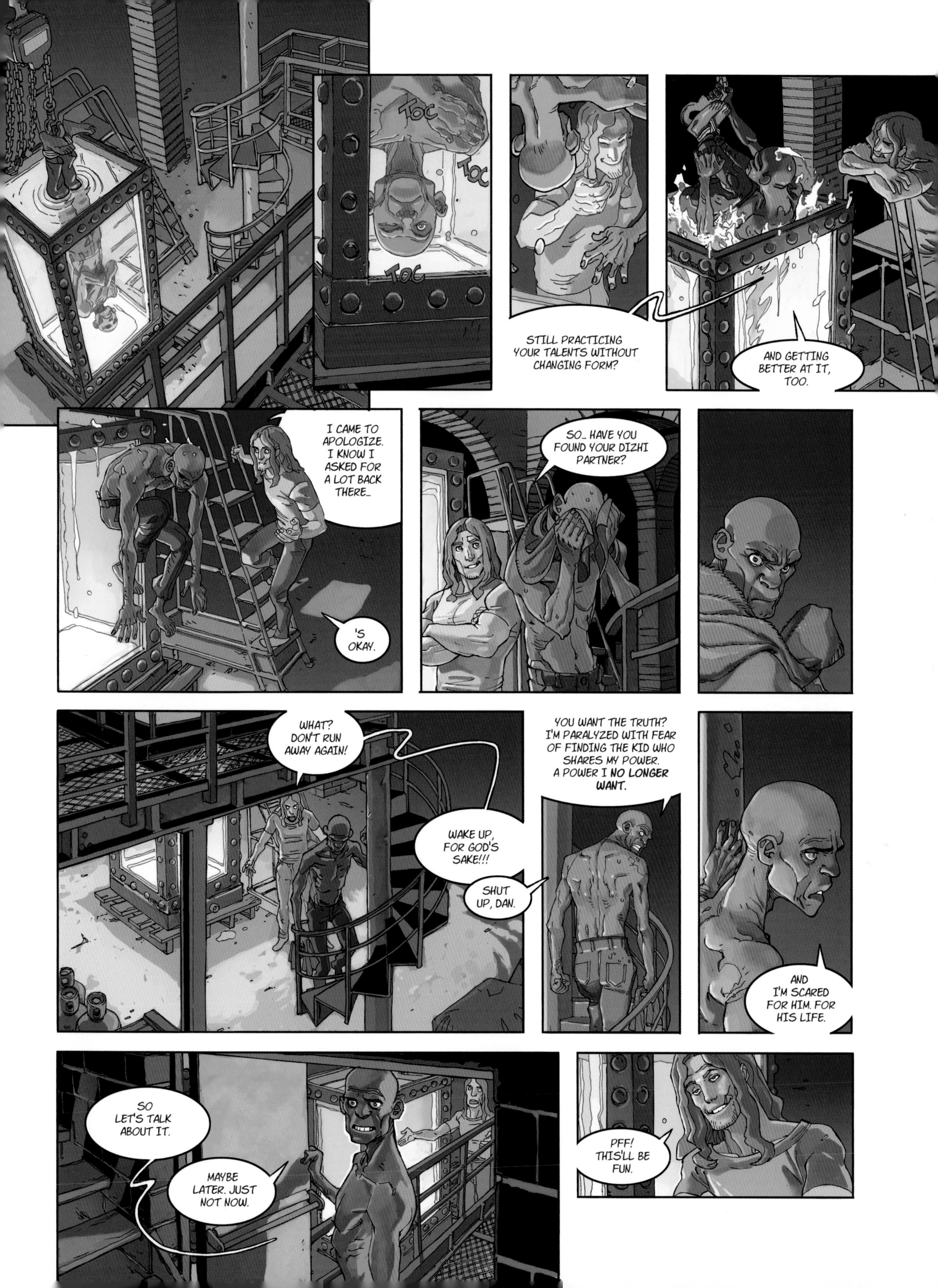
TOC
TOC
TOC
STILL PRACTICING YOUR TALENTS WITHOUT CHANGING FORM?
AND GETTING BETTER AT IT, TOO.
I CAME TO APOLOGIZE. I KNOW I ASKED FOR A LOT BACK THERE...
'S OKAY.
SO... HAVE YOU FOUND YOUR DIZHI PARTNER?
WHAT? DON'T RUN AWAY AGAIN!
WAKE UP, FOR GOD'S SAKE!!!
SHUT UP, DAN.
YOU WANT THE TRUTH? I'M PARALYZED WITH FEAR OF FINDING THE KID WHO SHARES MY POWER. A POWER I NO LONGER WANT.
AND I'M SCARED FOR HIM. FOR HIS LIFE.
SO LET'S TALK ABOUT IT.
MAYBE LATER. JUST NOT NOW.
PFF! THIS'LL BE FUN.

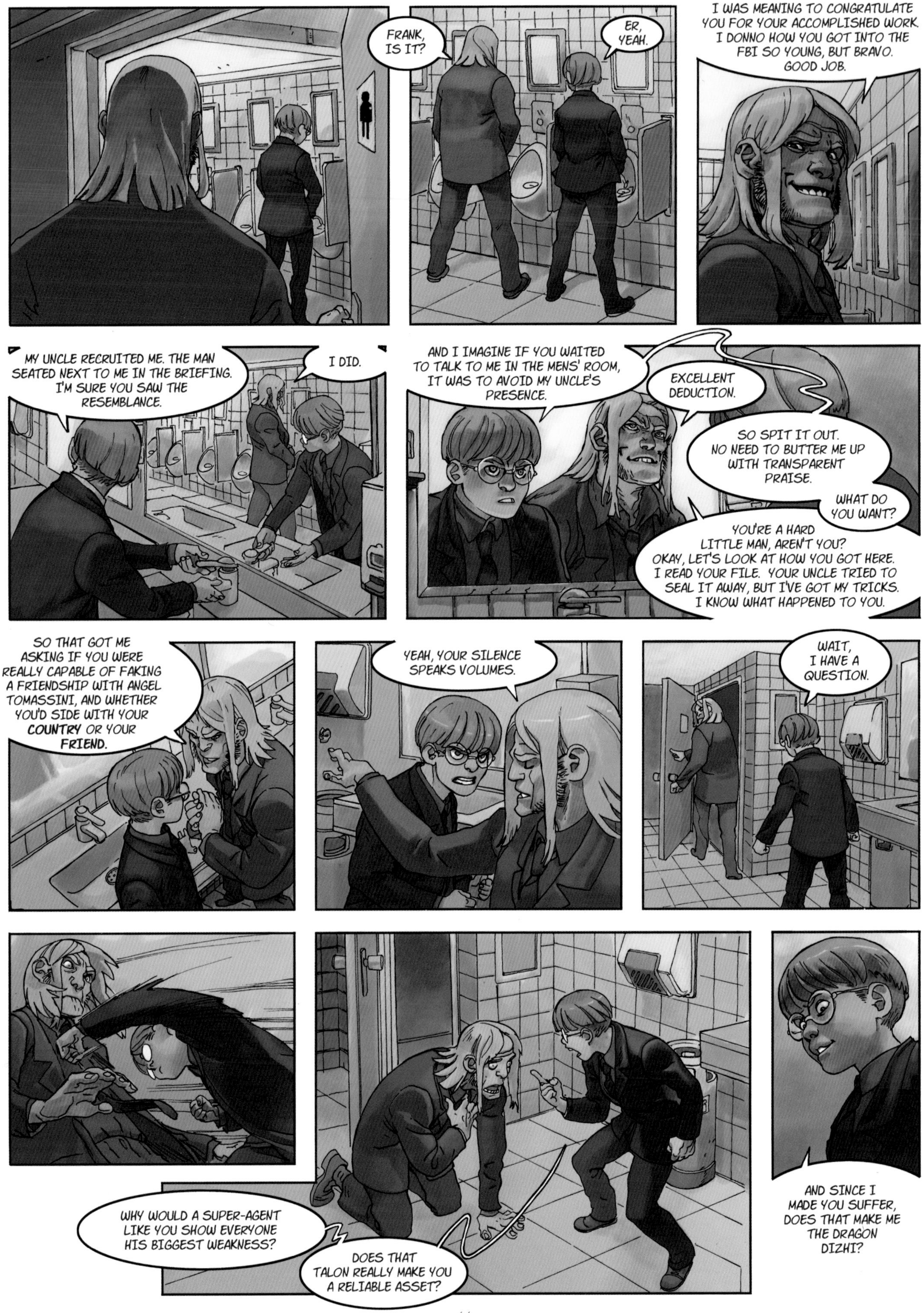
FRANK, IS IT?
ER, YEAH.
I WAS MEANING TO CONGRATULATE YOU FOR YOUR ACCOMPLISHED WORK. I DONNO HOW YOU GOT INTO THE FBI SO YOUNG, BUT BRAVO. GOOD JOB.
MY UNCLE RECRUITED ME. THE MAN SEATED NEXT TO ME IN THE BRIEFING. I'M SURE YOU SAW THE RESEMBLANCE.
I DID.
AND I IMAGINE IF YOU WAITED TO TALK TO ME IN THE MENS' ROOM, IT WAS TO AVOID MY UNCLE'S PRESENCE.
EXCELLENT DEDUCTION.
SO SPIT IT OUT. NO NEED TO BUTTER ME UP WITH TRANSPARENT PRAISE.
WHAT DO YOU WANT?
YOU'RE A HARD LITTLE MAN, AREN'T YOU? OKAY, LET'S LOOK AT HOW YOU GOT HERE. I READ YOUR FILE. YOUR UNCLE TRIED TO SEAL IT AWAY, BUT I'VE GOT MY TRICKS. I KNOW WHAT HAPPENED TO YOU.
SO THAT GOT ME ASKING IF YOU WERE REALLY CAPABLE OF FAKING A FRIENDSHIP WITH ANGEL TOMASSINI, AND WHETHER YOU'D SIDE WITH YOUR **COUNTRY** OR YOUR **FRIEND**.
YEAH, YOUR SILENCE SPEAKS VOLUMES.
WAIT, I HAVE A QUESTION.
WHY WOULD A SUPER-AGENT LIKE YOU SHOW EVERYONE HIS BIGGEST WEAKNESS?
DOES THAT TALON REALLY MAKE YOU A RELIABLE ASSET?
AND SINCE I MADE YOU SUFFER, DOES THAT MAKE ME THE DRAGON DIZHI?

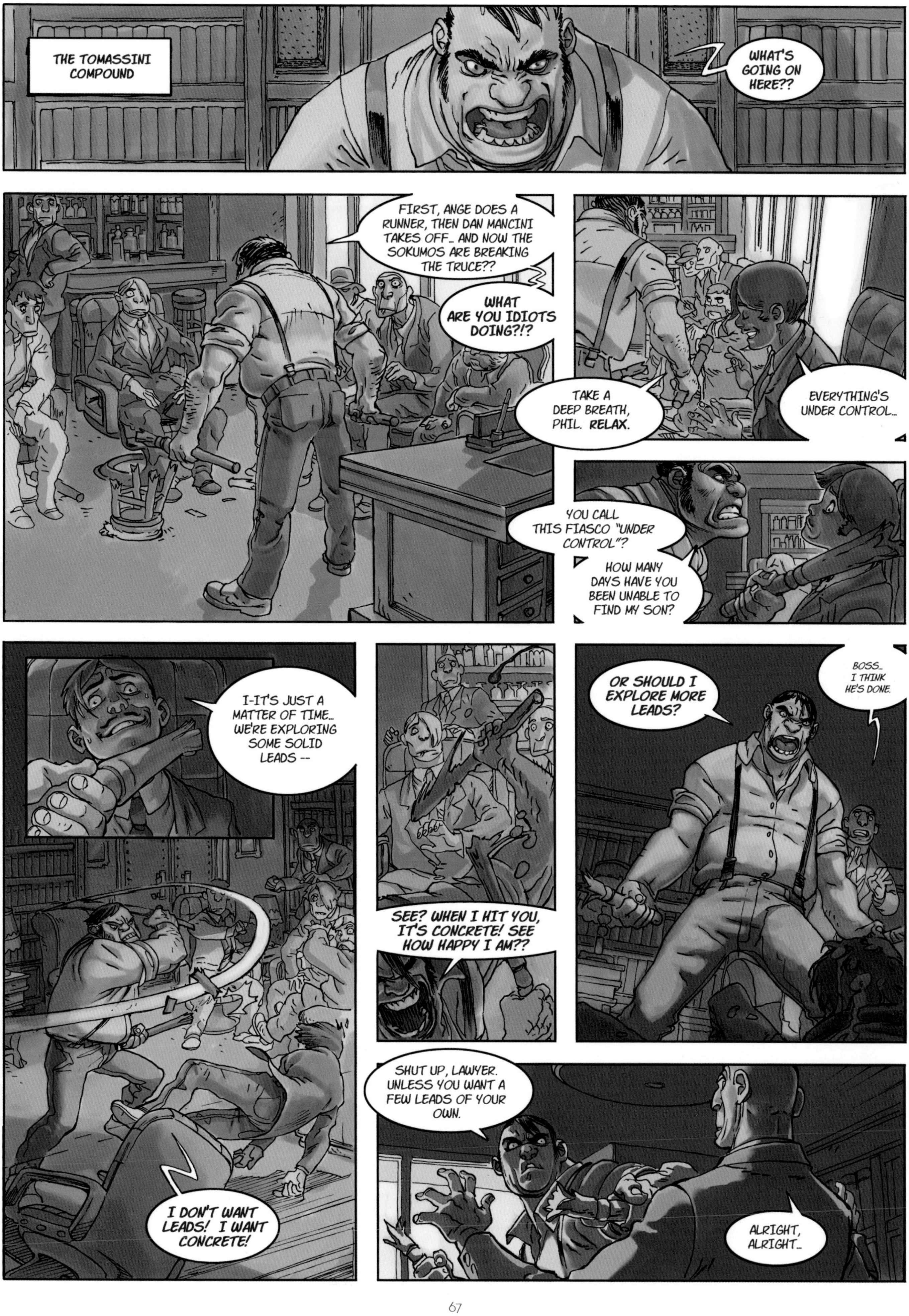
THE TOMASSINI COMPOUND
WHAT'S GOING ON HERE??
FIRST, ANGE DOES A RUNNER, THEN DAN MANCINI TAKES OFF... AND NOW THE SOKUMOS ARE BREAKING THE TRUCE??
WHAT ARE YOU IDIOTS DOING?!?
TAKE A DEEP BREATH, PHIL. RELAX.
EVERYTHING'S UNDER CONTROL...
YOU CALL THIS FIASCO "UNDER CONTROL"?
HOW MANY DAYS HAVE YOU BEEN UNABLE TO FIND MY SON?
I-IT'S JUST A MATTER OF TIME... WE'RE EXPLORING SOME SOLID LEADS --
I DON'T WANT LEADS! I WANT CONCRETE!
SEE? WHEN I HIT YOU, IT'S CONCRETE! SEE HOW HAPPY I AM??
OR SHOULD I EXPLORE MORE LEADS?
BOSS... I THINK HE'S DONE.
SHUT UP, LAWYER. UNLESS YOU WANT A FEW LEADS OF YOUR OWN.
ALRIGHT, ALRIGHT...

SILVIO, GET ME SOME ICE.

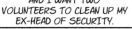

AND I WANT TWO VOLUNTEERS TO CLEAN UP MY EX-HEAD OF SECURITY.

OKAY. LAWYER, YOU'RE GONNA SET UP A MEETING WITH OLD SOKUMO. JERRY, TAKE AS MANY MEN AS YOU NEED AND NAB THE OLD GUY'S LITTLE GIRL, FU-YU OR WHATEVER, THE BALLERINA. SHE'S HIS WEAKNESS....

SILVIO, GET IN HERE. YOU'RE RESPONSIBLE FOR FINDING YOUR BROTHER. TORTURE THAT LITTLE PRICK FRANK IF YOU GOTTA. HE'S GOTTA KNOW SOMETHING.

WHAT?

Y-YOUR ICE.

WHATA YOU ALL STILL DOING HERE?? **MOVE!!!**

WE GOT A WAR TO GET READY FOR!

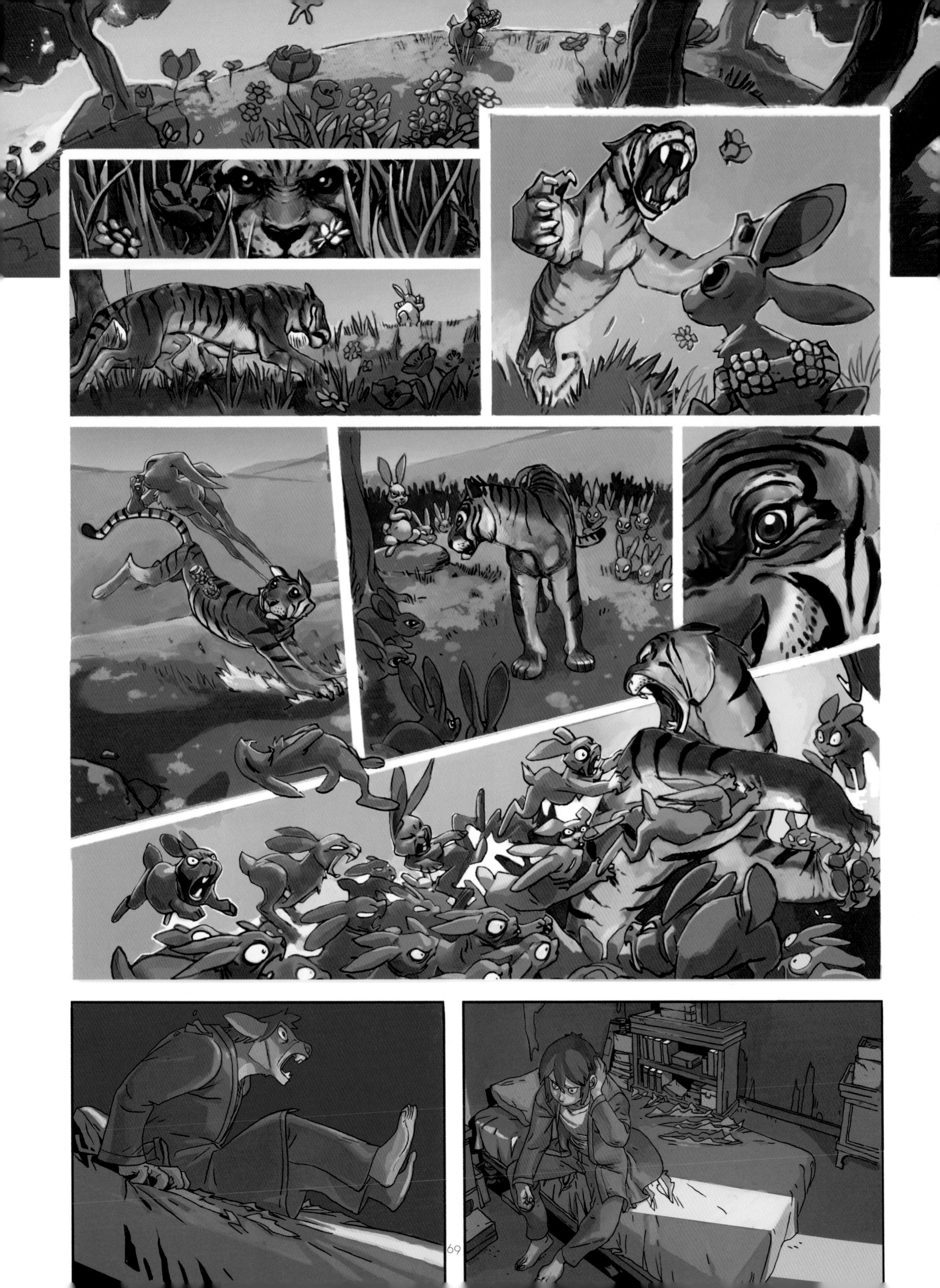

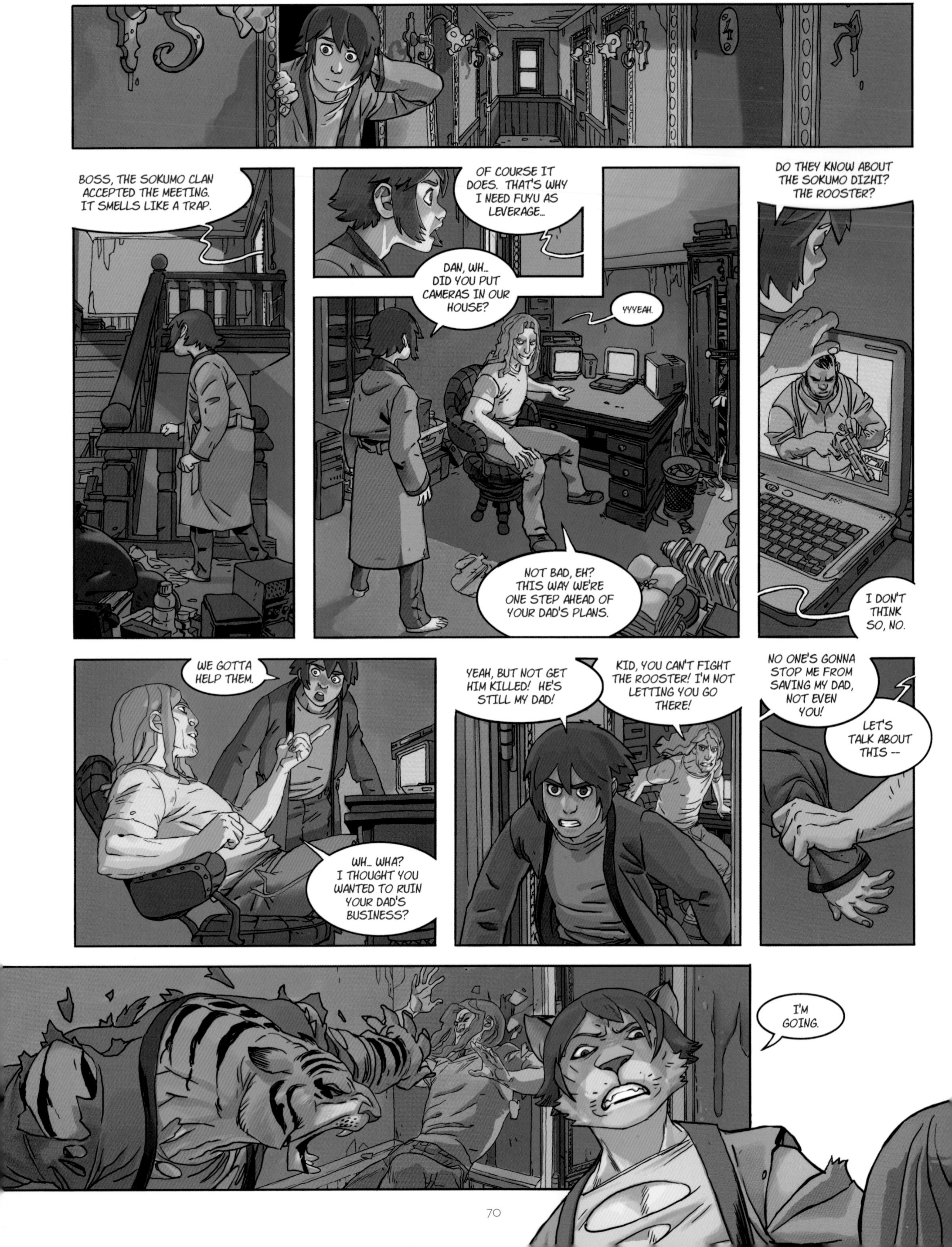
BOSS, THE SOKUMO CLAN ACCEPTED THE MEETING. IT SMELLS LIKE A TRAP.
OF COURSE IT DOES. THAT'S WHY I NEED FUYU AS LEVERAGE...
DAN, WH... DID YOU PUT CAMERAS IN OUR HOUSE?
YYYEAH.
NOT BAD, EH? THIS WAY WE'RE ONE STEP AHEAD OF YOUR DAD'S PLANS.
DO THEY KNOW ABOUT THE SOKUMO DIZHI? THE ROOSTER?
I DON'T THINK SO, NO.
WE GOTTA HELP THEM.
WH... WHA? I THOUGHT YOU WANTED TO RUIN YOUR DAD'S BUSINESS?
YEAH, BUT NOT GET HIM KILLED! HE'S STILL MY DAD!
KID, YOU CAN'T FIGHT THE ROOSTER! I'M NOT LETTING YOU GO THERE!
NO ONE'S GONNA STOP ME FROM SAVING MY DAD, NOT EVEN YOU!
LET'S TALK ABOUT THIS --
I'M GOING.

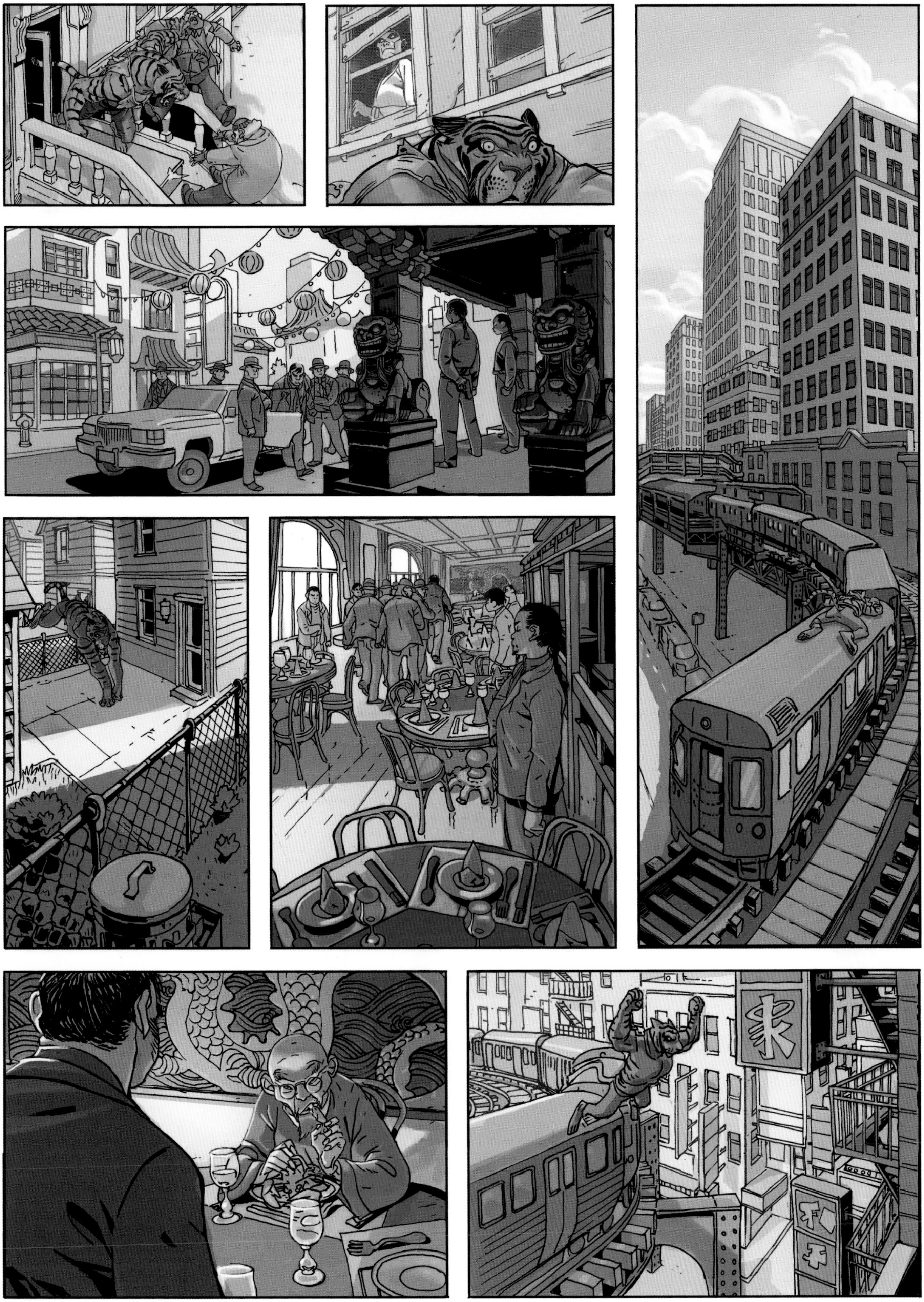

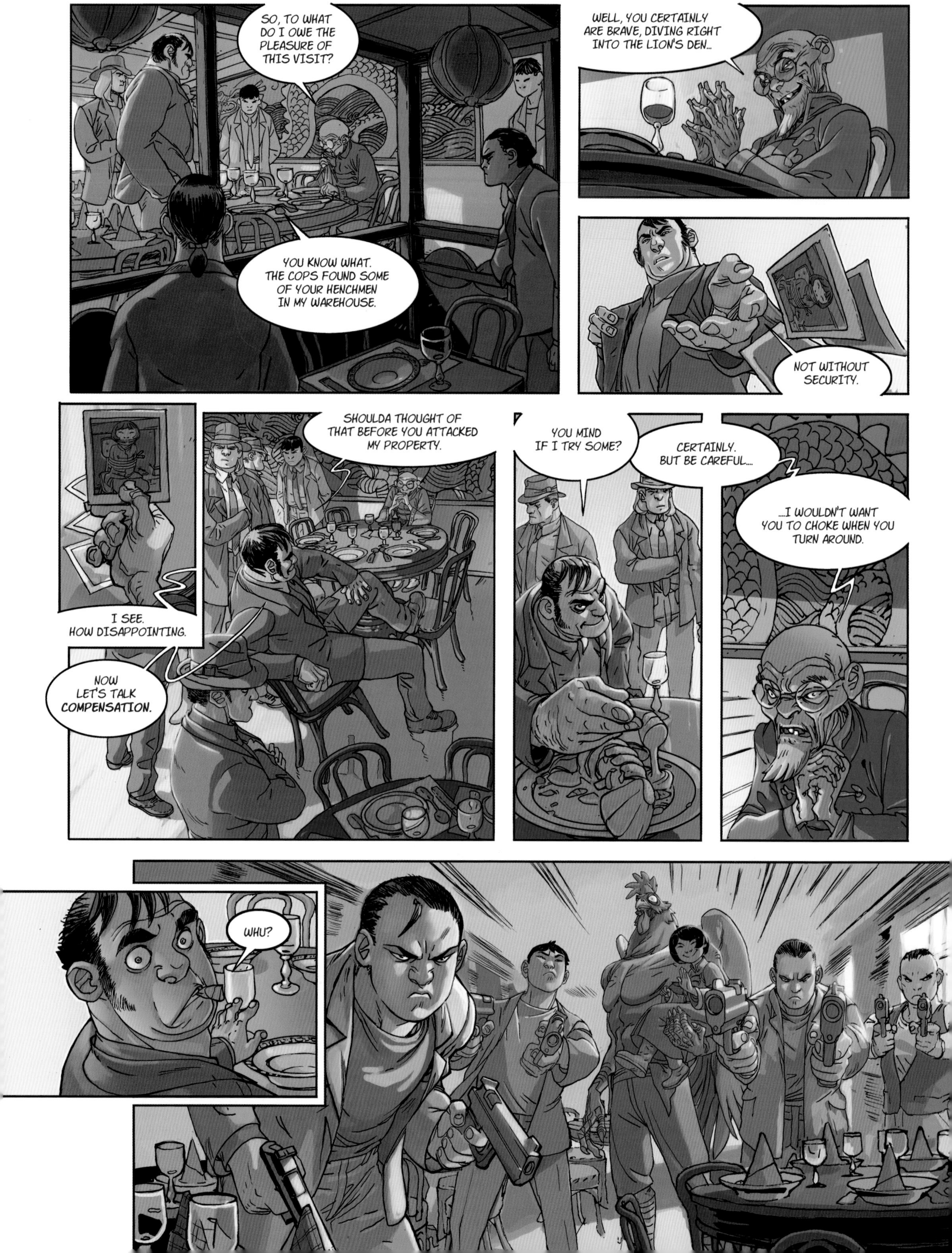
SO, TO WHAT DO I OWE THE PLEASURE OF THIS VISIT?
YOU KNOW WHAT. THE COPS FOUND SOME OF YOUR HENCHMEN IN MY WAREHOUSE.
WELL, YOU CERTAINLY ARE BRAVE, DIVING RIGHT INTO THE LION'S DEN...
NOT WITHOUT SECURITY.
I SEE. HOW DISAPPOINTING.
SHOULDA THOUGHT OF THAT BEFORE YOU ATTACKED MY PROPERTY.
NOW LET'S TALK COMPENSATION.
YOU MIND IF I TRY SOME?
CERTAINLY. BUT BE CAREFUL....
...I WOULDN'T WANT YOU TO CHOKE WHEN YOU TURN AROUND.
WHU?

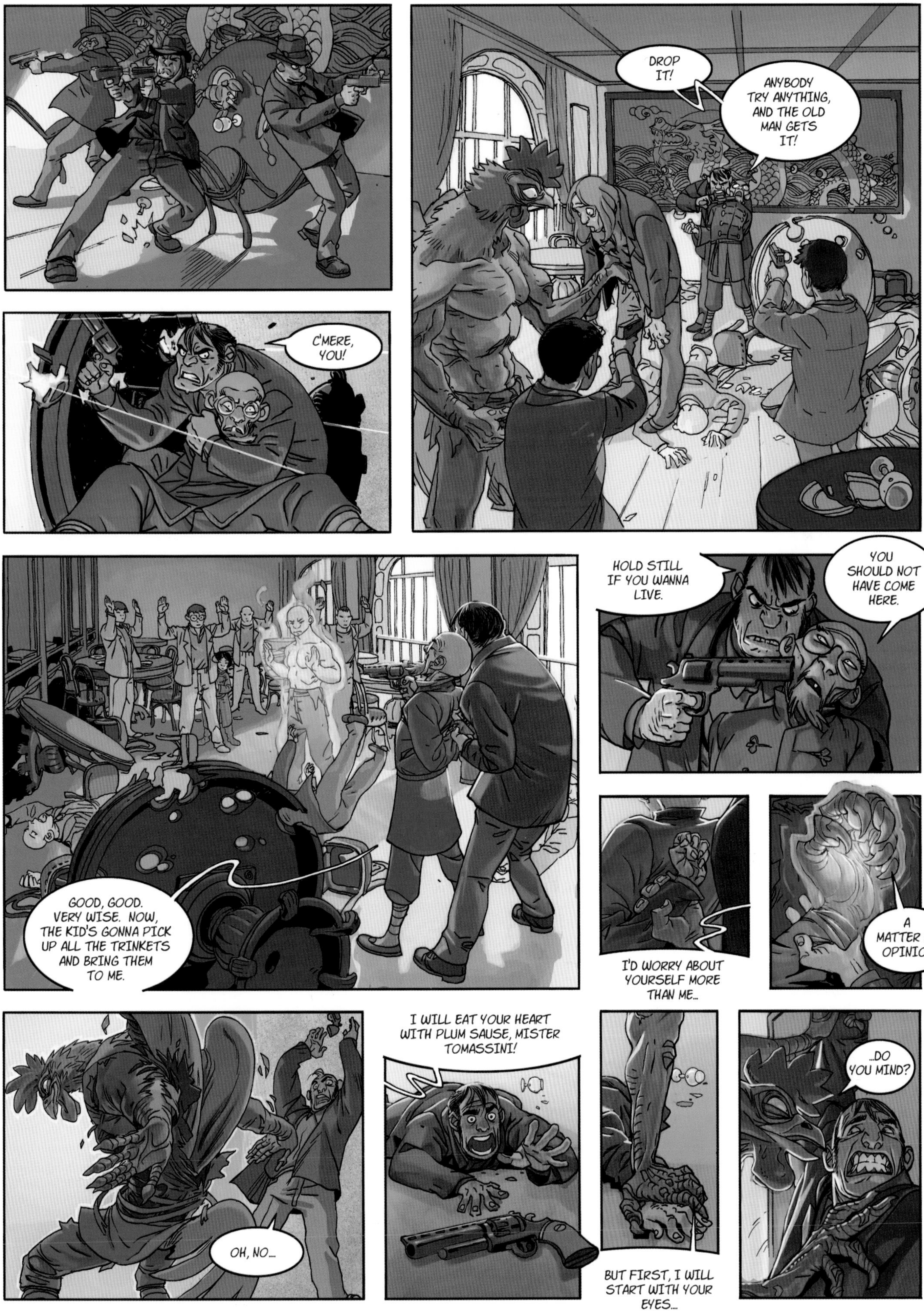
C'MERE, YOU!
DROP IT!
ANYBODY TRY ANYTHING, AND THE OLD MAN GETS IT!
GOOD, GOOD. VERY WISE. NOW, THE KID'S GONNA PICK UP ALL THE TRINKETS AND BRING THEM TO ME.
HOLD STILL IF YOU WANNA LIVE.
YOU SHOULD NOT HAVE COME HERE.
I'D WORRY ABOUT YOURSELF MORE THAN ME...
A MATTER OF OPINION.
OH, NO....
I WILL EAT YOUR HEART WITH PLUM SAUSE, MISTER TOMASSINI!
BUT FIRST, I WILL START WITH YOUR EYES....
...DO YOU MIND?

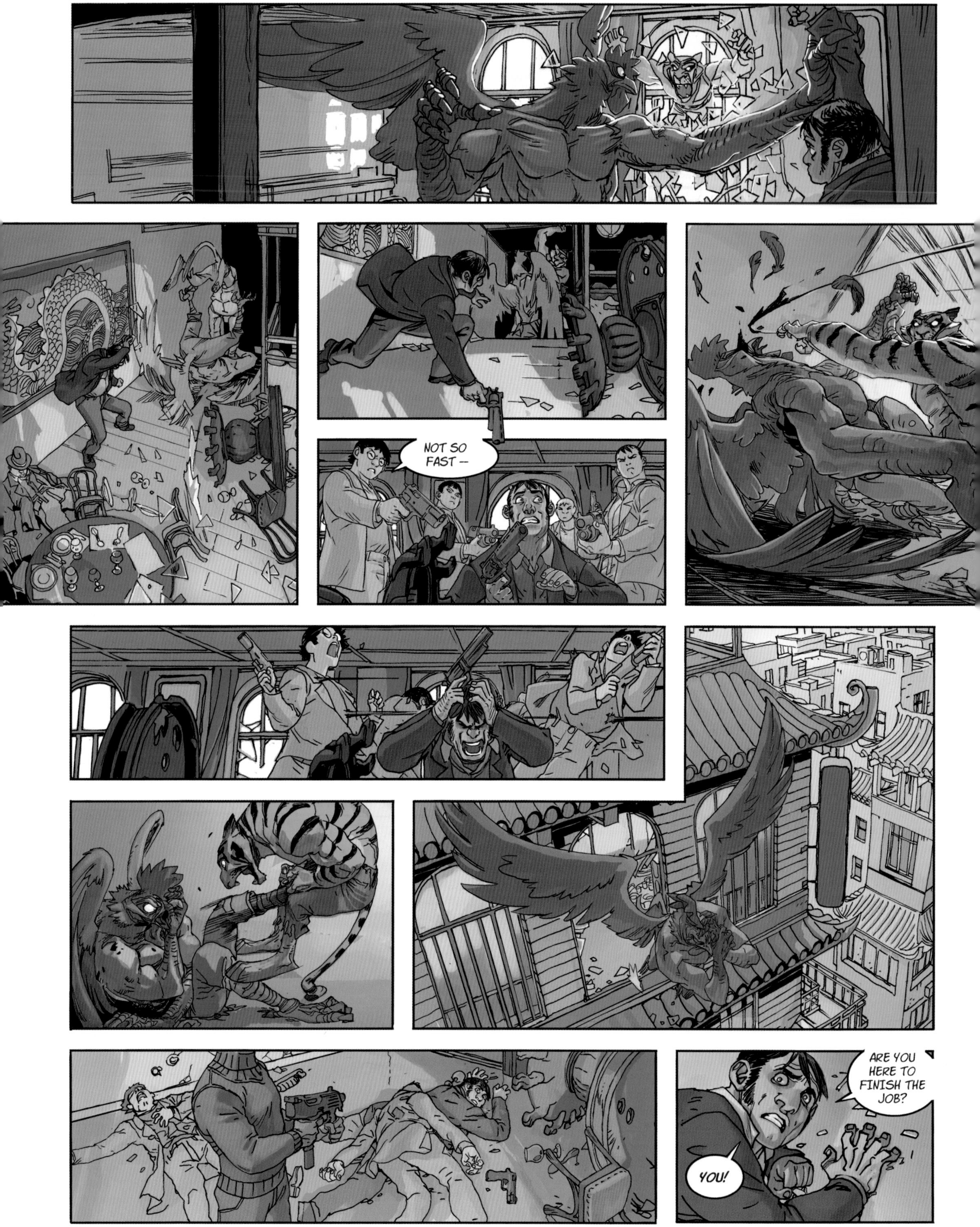
NOT SO FAST --
ARE YOU HERE TO FINISH THE JOB?
YOU!

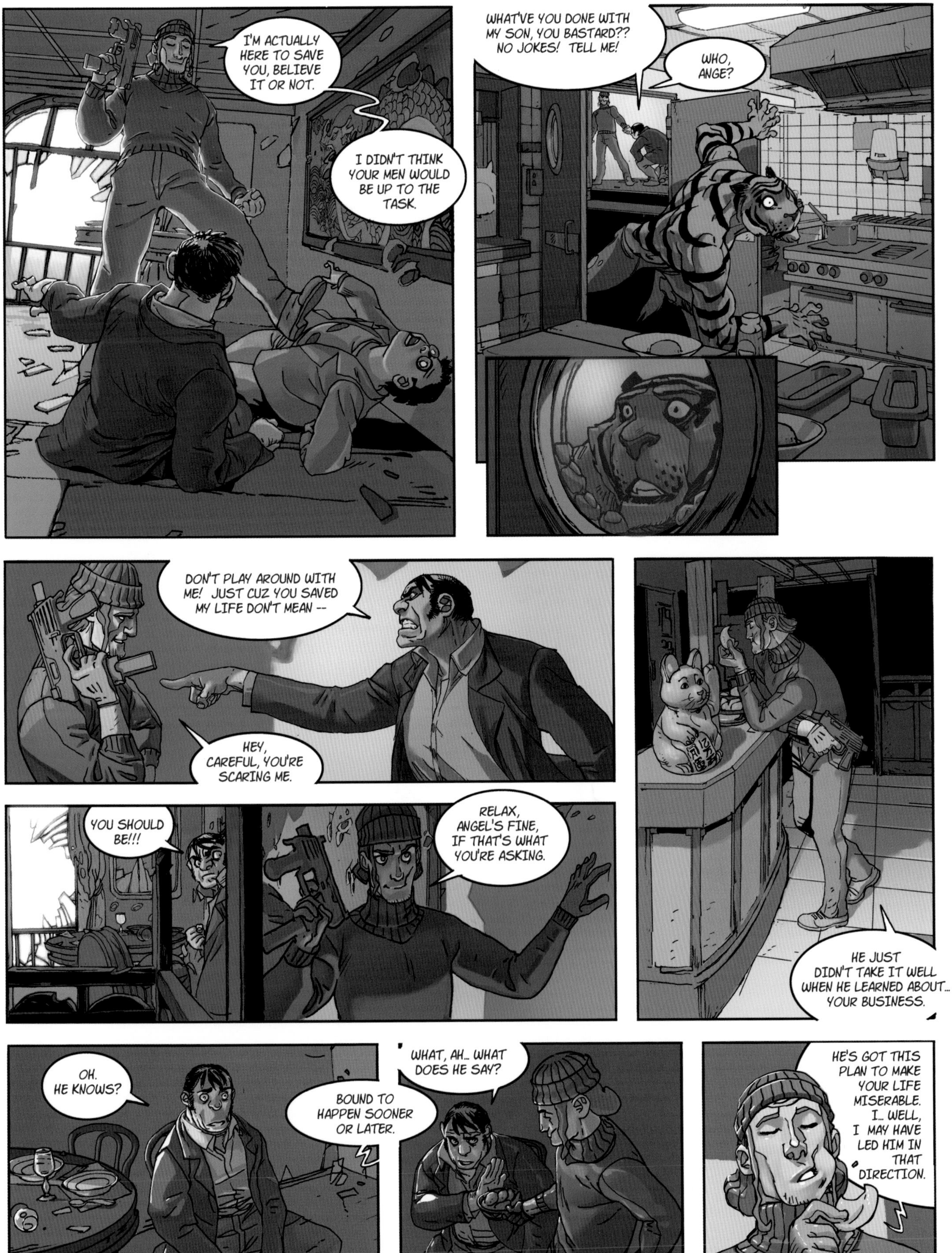
I'M ACTUALLY HERE TO SAVE YOU, BELIEVE IT OR NOT.
I DIDN'T THINK YOUR MEN WOULD BE UP TO THE TASK.
WHAT'VE YOU DONE WITH MY SON, YOU BASTARD?? NO JOKES! TELL ME!
WHO, ANGE?
DON'T PLAY AROUND WITH ME! JUST CUZ YOU SAVED MY LIFE DON'T MEAN --
HEY, CAREFUL, YOU'RE SCARING ME.
YOU SHOULD BE!!!
RELAX, ANGEL'S FINE, IF THAT'S WHAT YOU'RE ASKING.
HE JUST DIDN'T TAKE IT WELL WHEN HE LEARNED ABOUT... YOUR BUSINESS.
OH. HE KNOWS?
BOUND TO HAPPEN SOONER OR LATER.
WHAT, AH... WHAT DOES HE SAY?
HE'S GOT THIS PLAN TO MAKE YOUR LIFE MISERABLE. I... WELL, I MAY HAVE LED HIM IN THAT DIRECTION.

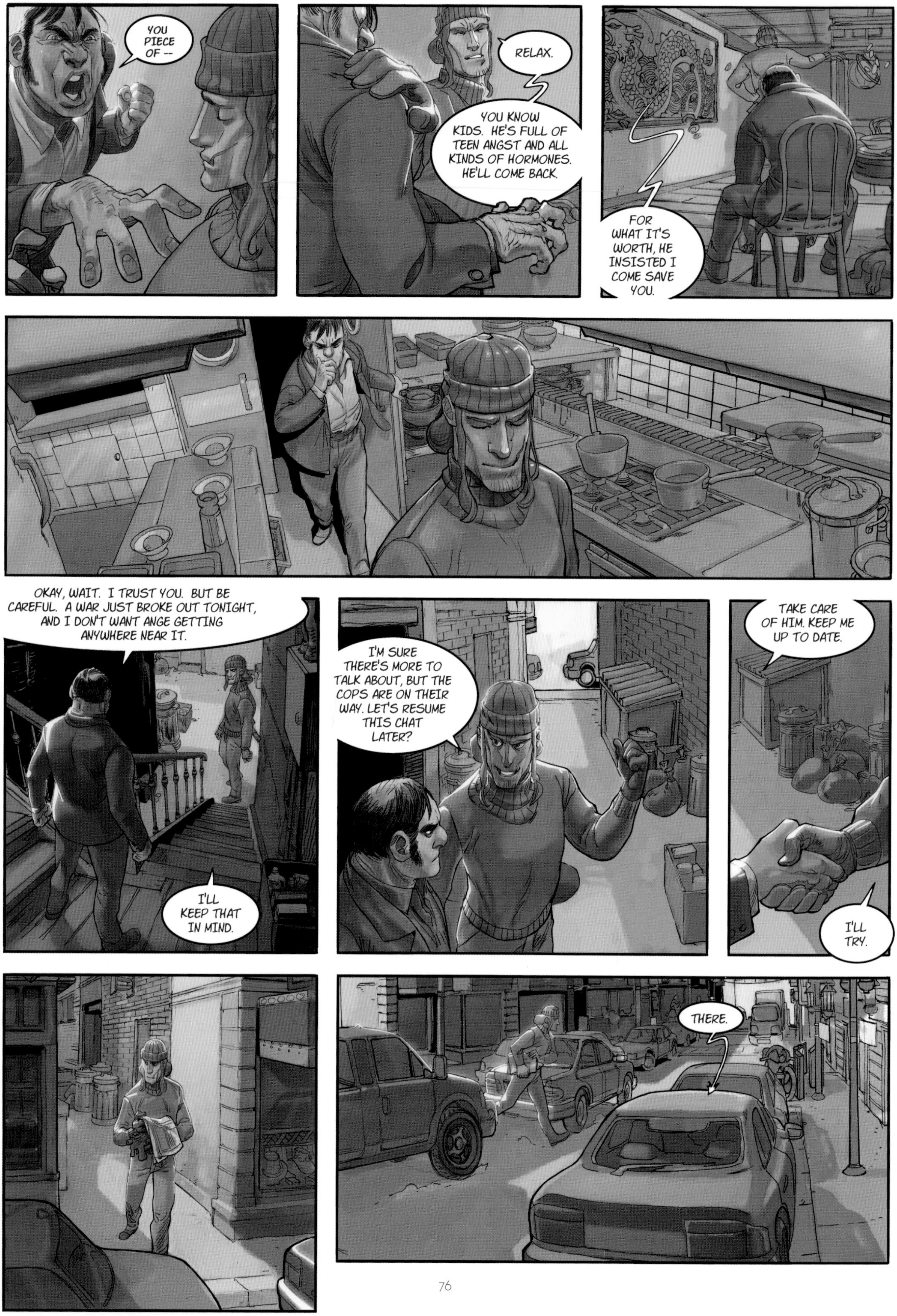

YOU PIECE OF --
RELAX.
YOU KNOW KIDS. HE'S FULL OF TEEN ANGST AND ALL KINDS OF HORMONES. HE'LL COME BACK.
FOR WHAT IT'S WORTH, HE INSISTED I COME SAVE YOU.
OKAY, WAIT. I TRUST YOU. BUT BE CAREFUL. A WAR JUST BROKE OUT TONIGHT, AND I DON'T WANT ANGE GETTING ANYWHERE NEAR IT.
I'LL KEEP THAT IN MIND.
I'M SURE THERE'S MORE TO TALK ABOUT, BUT THE COPS ARE ON THEIR WAY. LET'S RESUME THIS CHAT LATER?
TAKE CARE OF HIM. KEEP ME UP TO DATE.
I'LL TRY.
THERE.

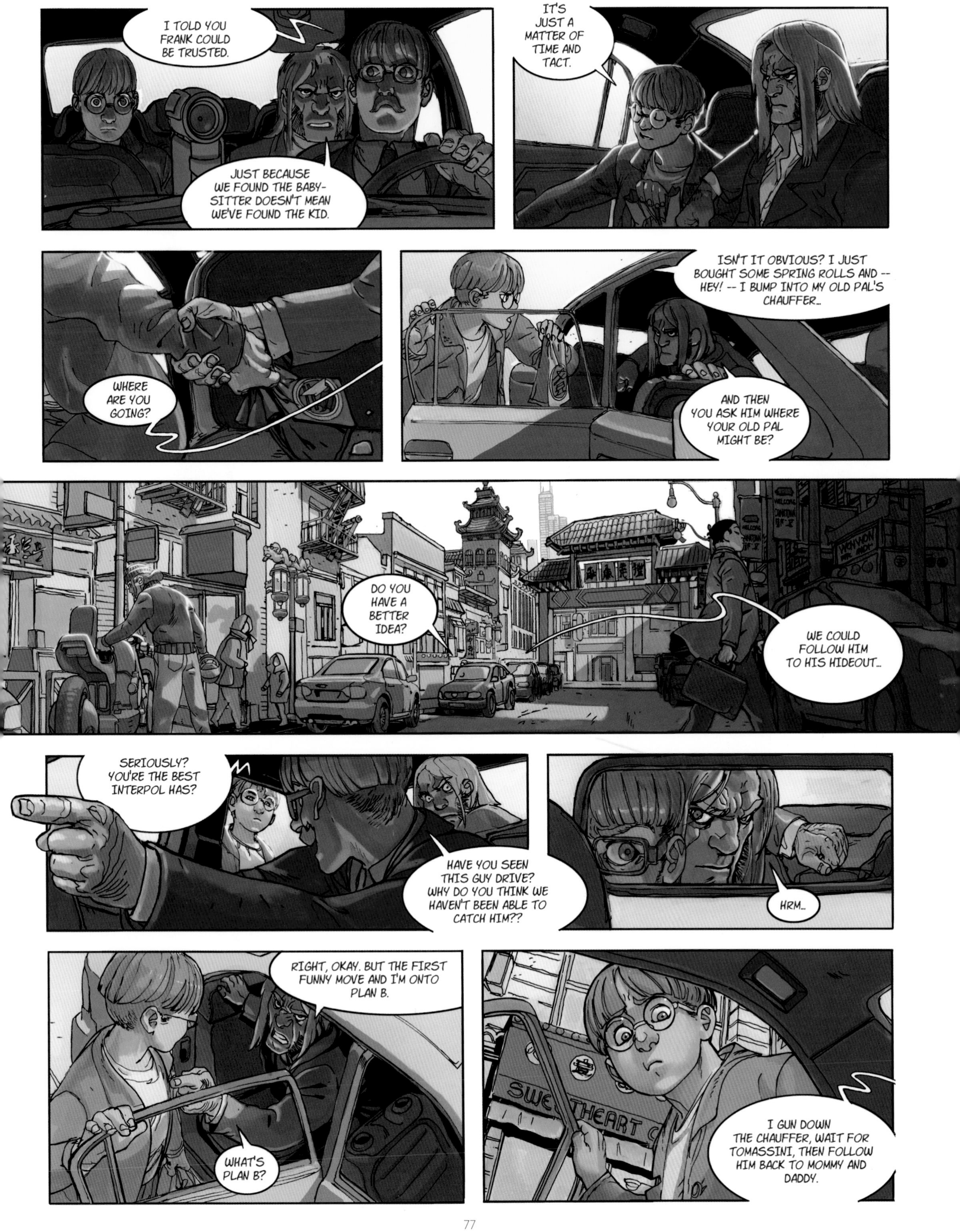

I TOLD YOU FRANK COULD BE TRUSTED.
JUST BECAUSE WE FOUND THE BABY-SITTER DOESN'T MEAN WE'VE FOUND THE KID.
IT'S JUST A MATTER OF TIME AND TACT.
WHERE ARE YOU GOING?
ISN'T IT OBVIOUS? I JUST BOUGHT SOME SPRING ROLLS AND -- HEY! -- I BUMP INTO MY OLD PAL'S CHAUFFER...
AND THEN YOU ASK HIM WHERE YOUR OLD PAL MIGHT BE?
DO YOU HAVE A BETTER IDEA?
WE COULD FOLLOW HIM TO HIS HIDEOUT...
SERIOUSLY? YOU'RE THE BEST INTERPOL HAS?
HAVE YOU SEEN THIS GUY DRIVE? WHY DO YOU THINK WE HAVEN'T BEEN ABLE TO CATCH HIM??
HRM...
RIGHT, OKAY. BUT THE FIRST FUNNY MOVE AND I'M ONTO PLAN B.
WHAT'S PLAN B?
I GUN DOWN THE CHAUFFER, WAIT FOR TOMASSINI, THEN FOLLOW HIM BACK TO MOMMY AND DADDY.

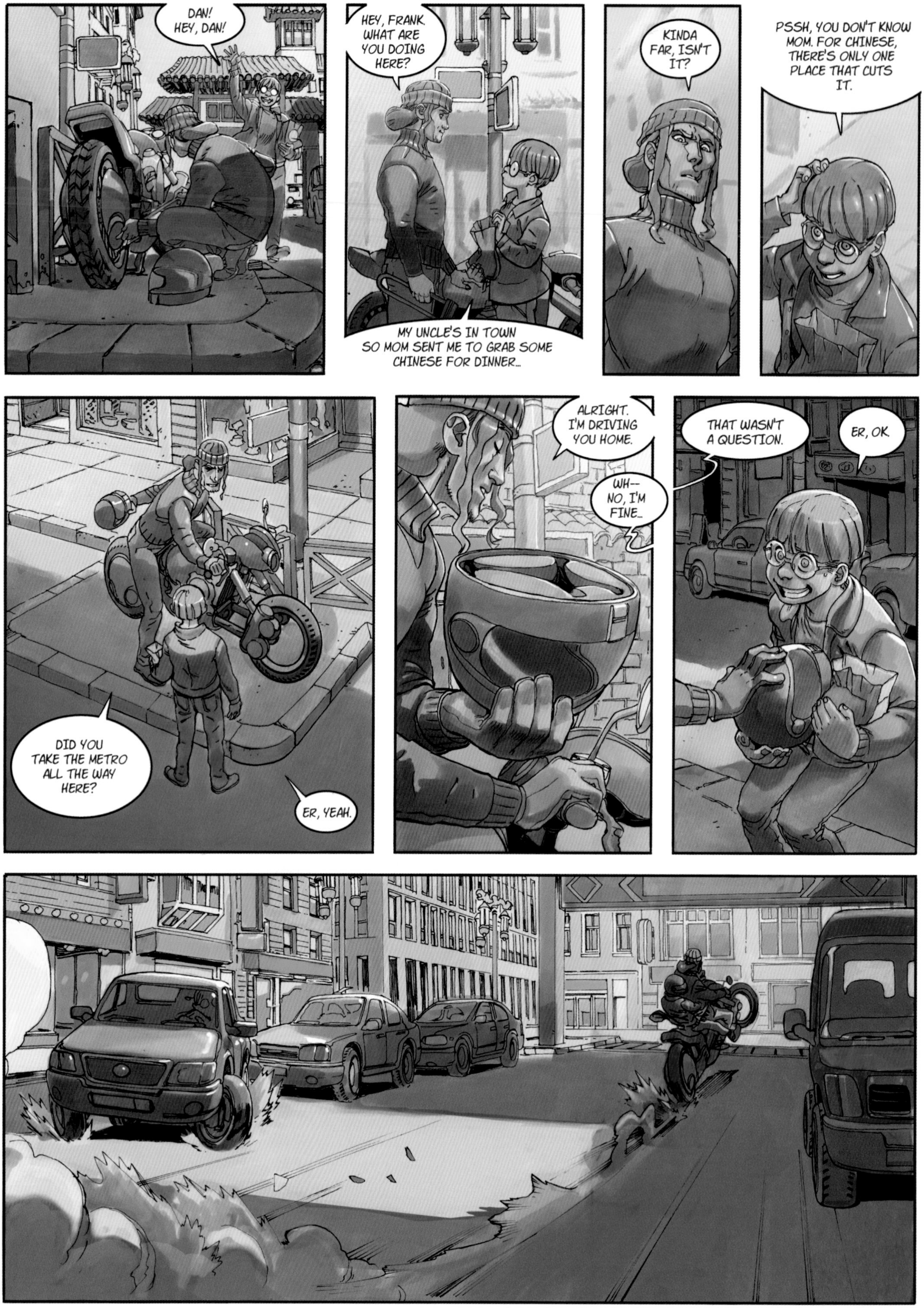
DAN! HEY, DAN!
HEY, FRANK. WHAT ARE YOU DOING HERE?
MY UNCLE'S IN TOWN SO MOM SENT ME TO GRAB SOME CHINESE FOR DINNER...
KINDA FAR, ISN'T IT?
PSSH, YOU DON'T KNOW MOM. FOR CHINESE, THERE'S ONLY ONE PLACE THAT CUTS IT.
DID YOU TAKE THE METRO ALL THE WAY HERE?
ER, YEAH.
ALRIGHT. I'M DRIVING YOU HOME.
WH-- NO, I'M FINE...
THAT WASN'T A QUESTION.
ER, OK.

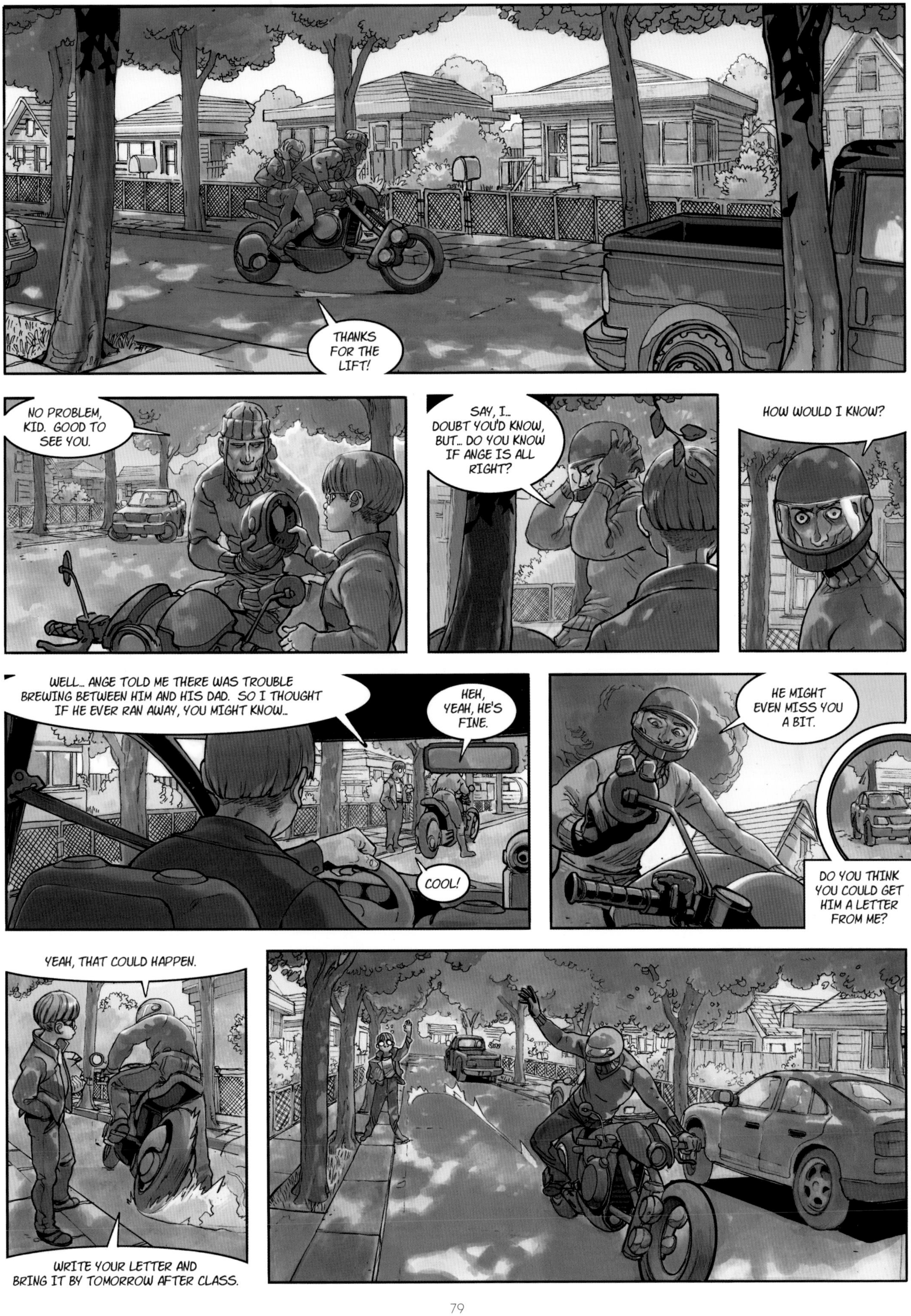
THANKS FOR THE LIFT!
NO PROBLEM, KID. GOOD TO SEE YOU.
SAY, I... DOUBT YOU'D KNOW, BUT... DO YOU KNOW IF ANGE IS ALL RIGHT?
HOW WOULD I KNOW?
WELL... ANGE TOLD ME THERE WAS TROUBLE BREWING BETWEEN HIM AND HIS DAD. SO I THOUGHT IF HE EVER RAN AWAY, YOU MIGHT KNOW...
HEH, YEAH, HE'S FINE.
COOL!
HE MIGHT EVEN MISS YOU A BIT.
DO YOU THINK YOU COULD GET HIM A LETTER FROM ME?
YEAH, THAT COULD HAPPEN.
WRITE YOUR LETTER AND BRING IT BY TOMORROW AFTER CLASS.

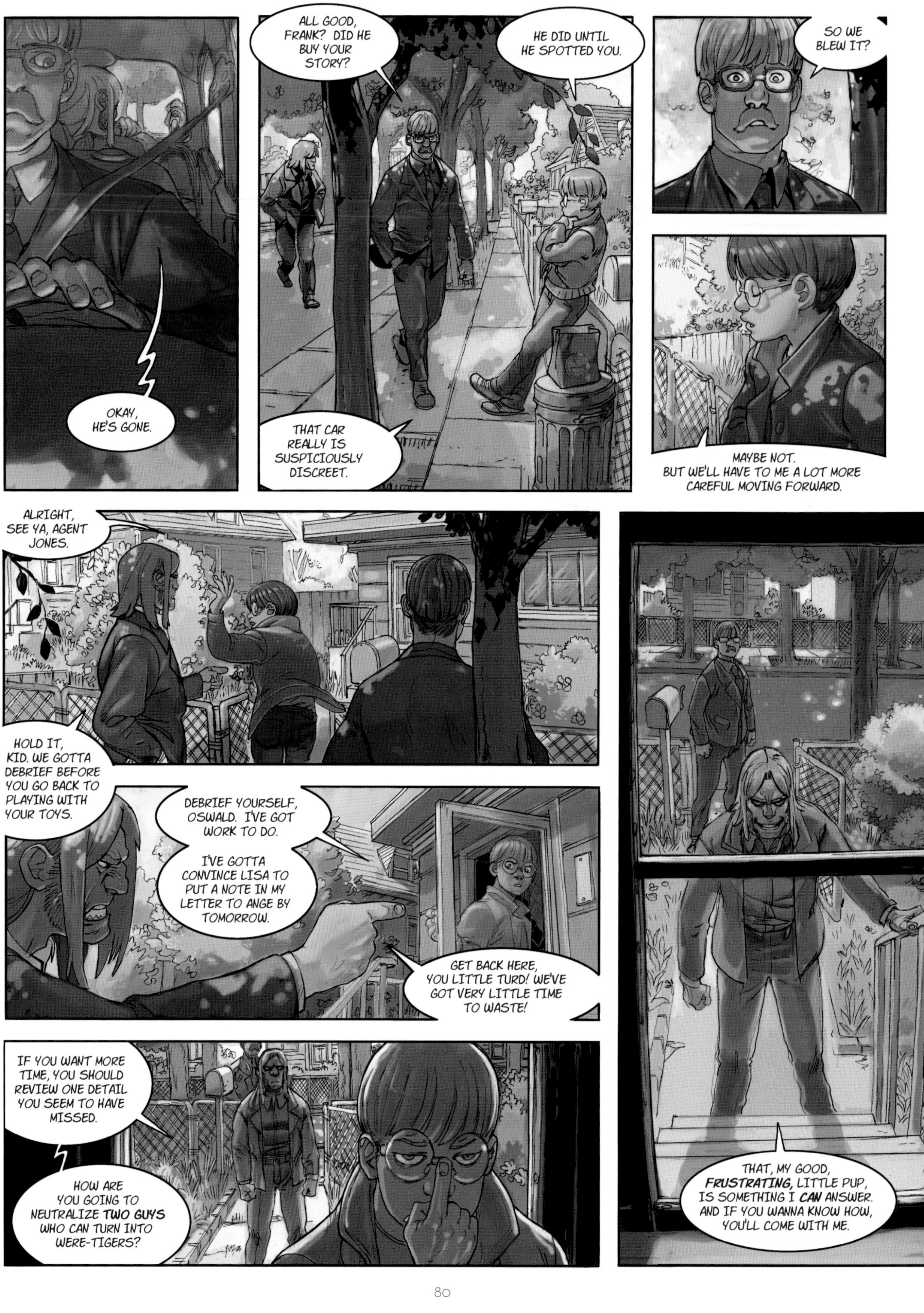
OKAY, HE'S GONE.
ALL GOOD, FRANK? DID HE BUY YOUR STORY?
HE DID UNTIL HE SPOTTED YOU.
THAT CAR REALLY IS SUSPICIOUSLY DISCREET.
SO WE BLEW IT?
MAYBE NOT. BUT WE'LL HAVE TO ME A LOT MORE CAREFUL MOVING FORWARD.
ALRIGHT, SEE YA, AGENT JONES.
HOLD IT, KID. WE GOTTA DEBRIEF BEFORE YOU GO BACK TO PLAYING WITH YOUR TOYS.
DEBRIEF YOURSELF, OSWALD. I'VE GOT WORK TO DO.
I'VE GOTTA CONVINCE LISA TO PUT A NOTE IN MY LETTER TO ANGE BY TOMORROW.
GET BACK HERE, YOU LITTLE TURD! WE'VE GOT VERY LITTLE TIME TO WASTE!
IF YOU WANT MORE TIME, YOU SHOULD REVIEW ONE DETAIL YOU SEEM TO HAVE MISSED.
HOW ARE YOU GOING TO NEUTRALIZE TWO GUYS WHO CAN TURN INTO WERE-TIGERS?
THAT, MY GOOD, FRUSTRATING, LITTLE PUP, IS SOMETHING I CAN ANSWER. AND IF YOU WANNA KNOW HOW, YOU'LL COME WITH ME.

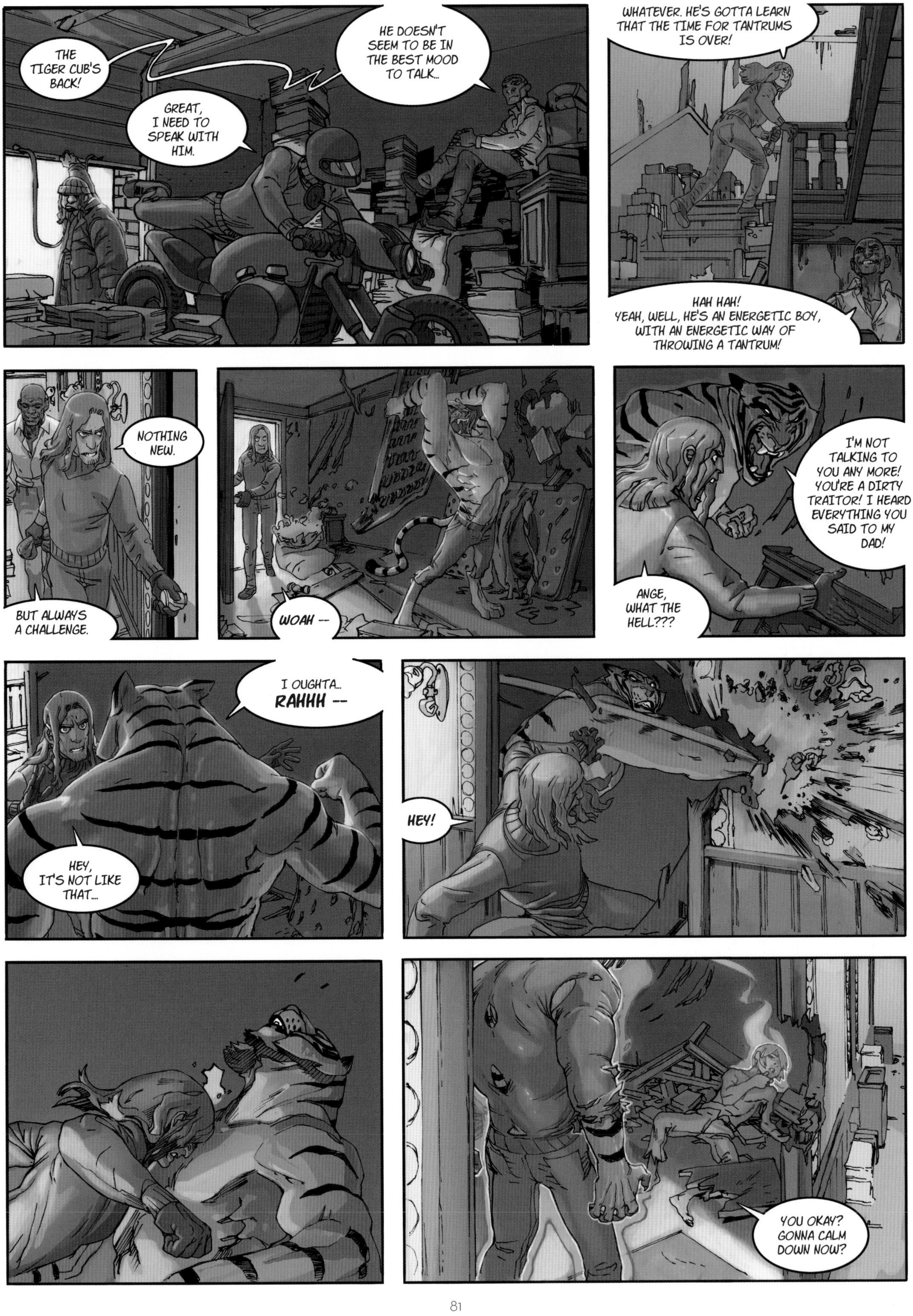
THE TIGER CUB'S BACK!
HE DOESN'T SEEM TO BE IN THE BEST MOOD TO TALK...
GREAT, I NEED TO SPEAK WITH HIM.
WHATEVER. HE'S GOTTA LEARN THAT THE TIME FOR TANTRUMS IS OVER!
HAH HAH! YEAH, WELL, HE'S AN ENERGETIC BOY, WITH AN ENERGETIC WAY OF THROWING A TANTRUM!
NOTHING NEW.
BUT ALWAYS A CHALLENGE.
WOAH --
I'M NOT TALKING TO YOU ANY MORE! YOU'RE A DIRTY TRAITOR! I HEARD EVERYTHING YOU SAID TO MY DAD!
ANGE, WHAT THE HELL???
I OUGHTA... RAHHH --
HEY, IT'S NOT LIKE THAT....
HEY!
YOU OKAY? GONNA CALM DOWN NOW?

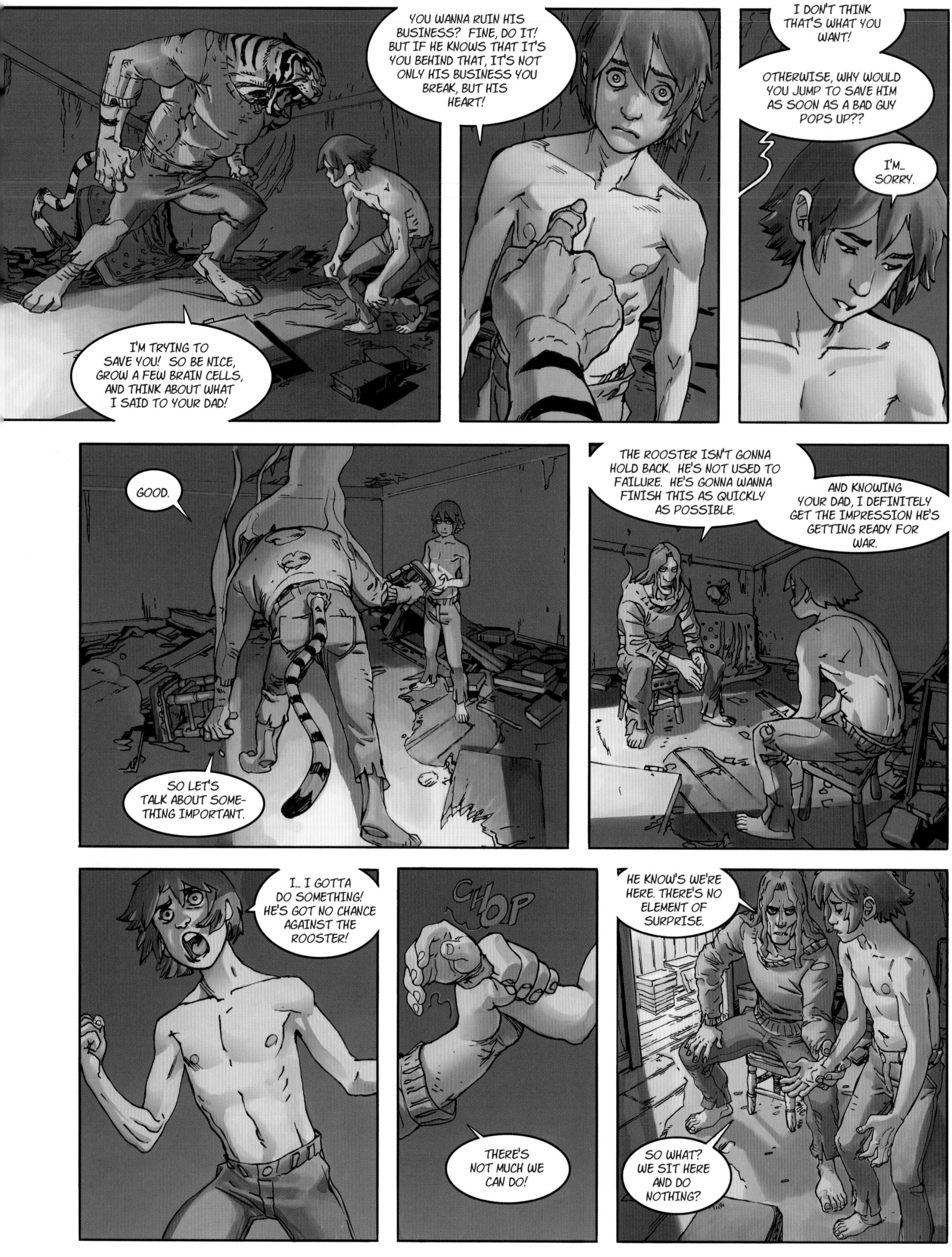
YOU WANNA RUIN HIS BUSINESS? FINE, DO IT! BUT IF HE KNOWS THAT IT'S YOU BEHIND THAT, IT'S NOT ONLY HIS BUSINESS YOU BREAK, BUT HIS HEART!
I'M TRYING TO SAVE YOU! SO BE NICE, GROW A FEW BRAIN CELLS, AND THINK ABOUT WHAT I SAID TO YOUR DAD!
I DON'T THINK THAT'S WHAT YOU WANT!
OTHERWISE, WHY WOULD YOU JUMP TO SAVE HIM AS SOON AS A BAD GUY POPS UP??
I'M... SORRY.
GOOD.
SO LET'S TALK ABOUT SOME-THING IMPORTANT.
THE ROOSTER ISN'T GONNA HOLD BACK. HE'S NOT USED TO FAILURE. HE'S GONNA WANNA FINISH THIS AS QUICKLY AS POSSIBLE.
AND KNOWING YOUR DAD, I DEFINITELY GET THE IMPRESSION HE'S GETTING READY FOR WAR.
I... I GOTTA DO SOMETHING! HE'S GOT NO CHANCE AGAINST THE ROOSTER!
CHOP
THERE'S NOT MUCH WE CAN DO!
HE KNOW'S WE'RE HERE. THERE'S NO ELEMENT OF SURPRISE.
SO WHAT? WE SIT HERE AND DO NOTHING?

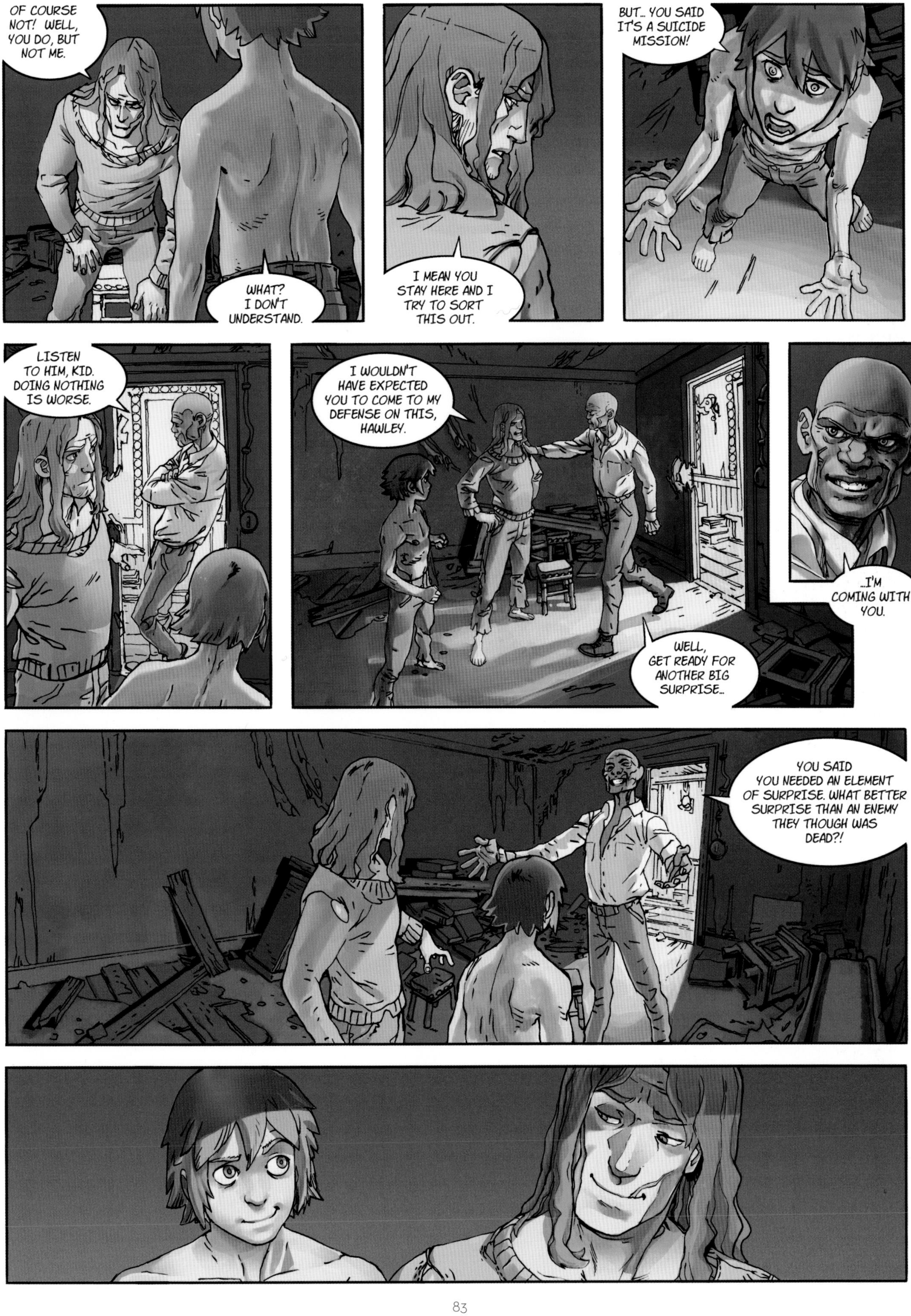
OF COURSE NOT! WELL, YOU DO, BUT NOT ME.
WHAT? I DON'T UNDERSTAND.
I MEAN YOU STAY HERE AND I TRY TO SORT THIS OUT.
BUT... YOU SAID IT'S A SUICIDE MISSION!
LISTEN TO HIM, KID. DOING NOTHING IS WORSE.
I WOULDN'T HAVE EXPECTED YOU TO COME TO MY DEFENSE ON THIS, HAWLEY.
WELL, GET READY FOR ANOTHER BIG SURPRISE...
...I'M COMING WITH YOU.
YOU SAID YOU NEEDED AN ELEMENT OF SURPRISE. WHAT BETTER SURPRISE THAN AN ENEMY THEY THOUGH WAS DEAD?!

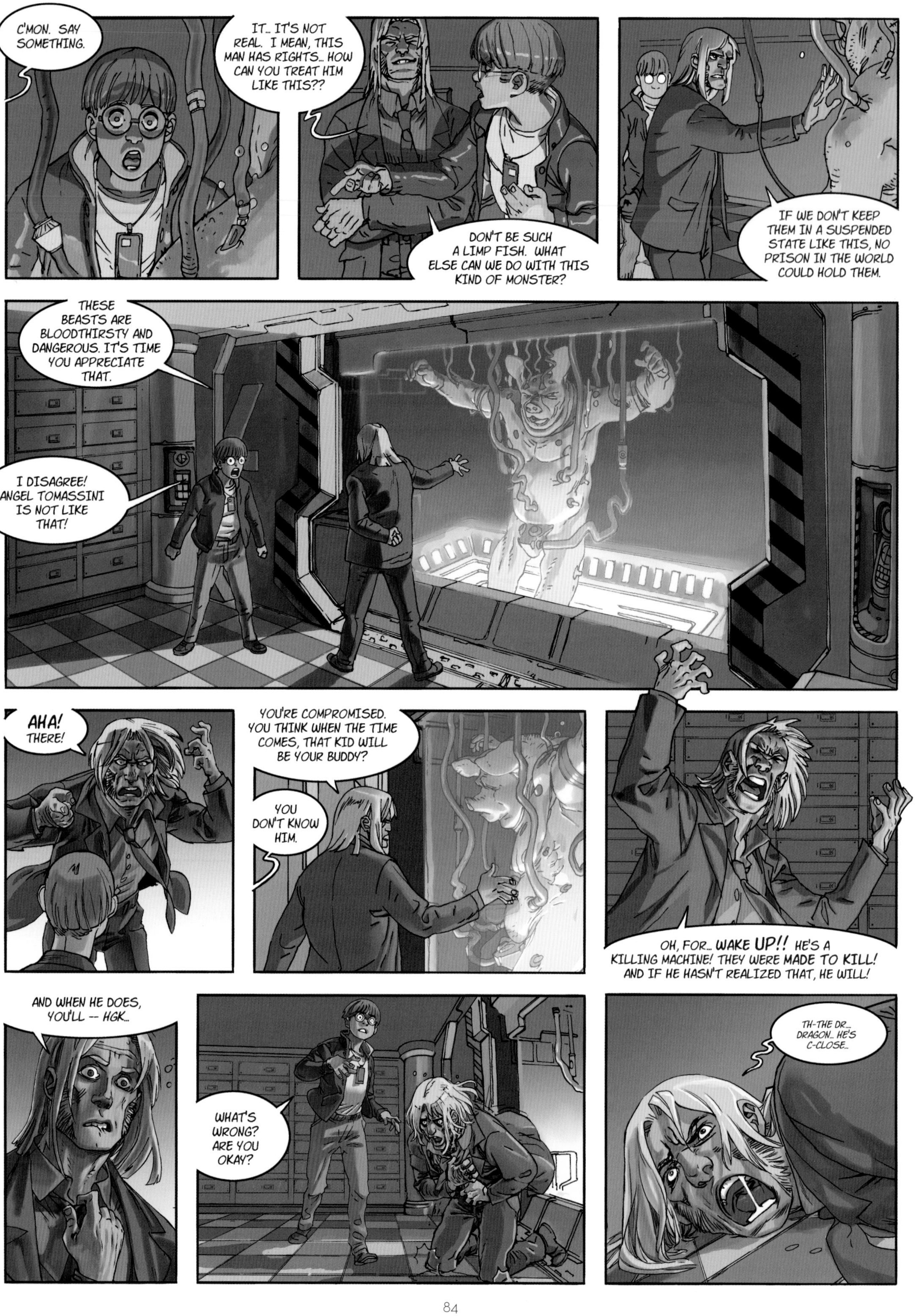
C'MON. SAY SOMETHING.
IT... IT'S NOT REAL. I MEAN, THIS MAN HAS RIGHTS... HOW CAN YOU TREAT HIM LIKE THIS??
DON'T BE SUCH A LIMP FISH. WHAT ELSE CAN WE DO WITH THIS KIND OF MONSTER?
IF WE DON'T KEEP THEM IN A SUSPENDED STATE LIKE THIS, NO PRISON IN THE WORLD COULD HOLD THEM.
THESE BEASTS ARE BLOODTHIRSTY AND DANGEROUS. IT'S TIME YOU APPRECIATE THAT.
I DISAGREE! ANGEL TOMASSINI IS NOT LIKE THAT!
AHA! THERE!
YOU'RE COMPROMISED. YOU THINK WHEN THE TIME COMES, THAT KID WILL BE YOUR BUDDY?
YOU DON'T KNOW HIM.
OH, FOR... WAKE UP!! HE'S A KILLING MACHINE! THEY WERE MADE TO KILL! AND IF HE HASN'T REALIZED THAT, HE WILL!
AND WHEN HE DOES, YOU'LL -- HGK...
WHAT'S WRONG? ARE YOU OKAY?
TH-THE DR... DRAGON... HE'S C-CLOSE...

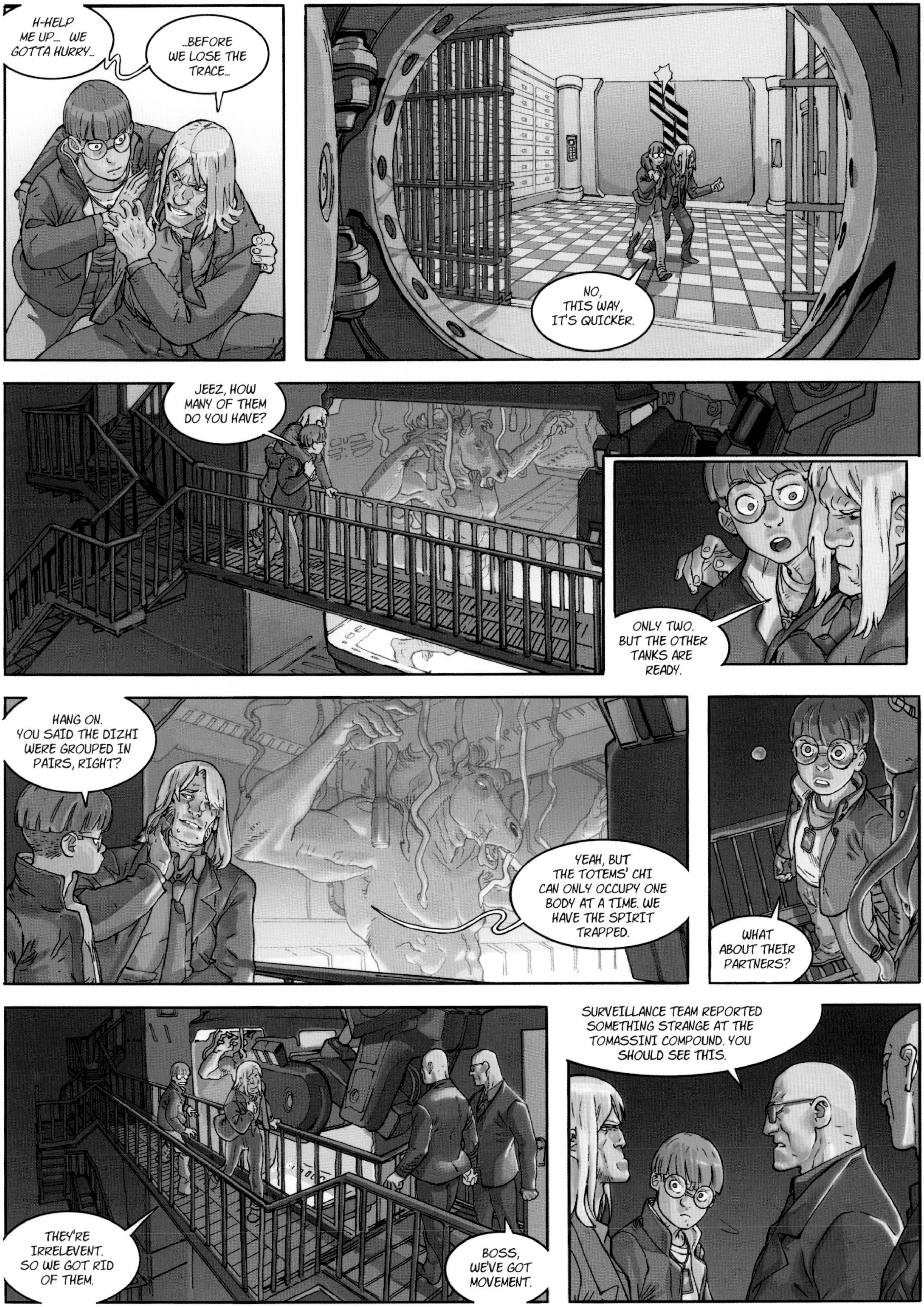
H-HELP ME UP.... WE GOTTA HURRY...
...BEFORE WE LOSE THE TRACE...
NO, THIS WAY, IT'S QUICKER.
JEEZ, HOW MANY OF THEM DO YOU HAVE?
ONLY TWO. BUT THE OTHER TANKS ARE READY.
HANG ON. YOU SAID THE DIZHI WERE GROUPED IN PAIRS, RIGHT?
YEAH, BUT THE TOTEMS' CHI CAN ONLY OCCUPY ONE BODY AT A TIME. WE HAVE THE SPIRIT TRAPPED.
WHAT ABOUT THEIR PARTNERS?
THEY'RE IRRELEVENT. SO WE GOT RID OF THEM.
BOSS, WE'VE GOT MOVEMENT.
SURVEILLANCE TEAM REPORTED SOMETHING STRANGE AT THE TOMASSINI COMPOUND. YOU SHOULD SEE THIS.

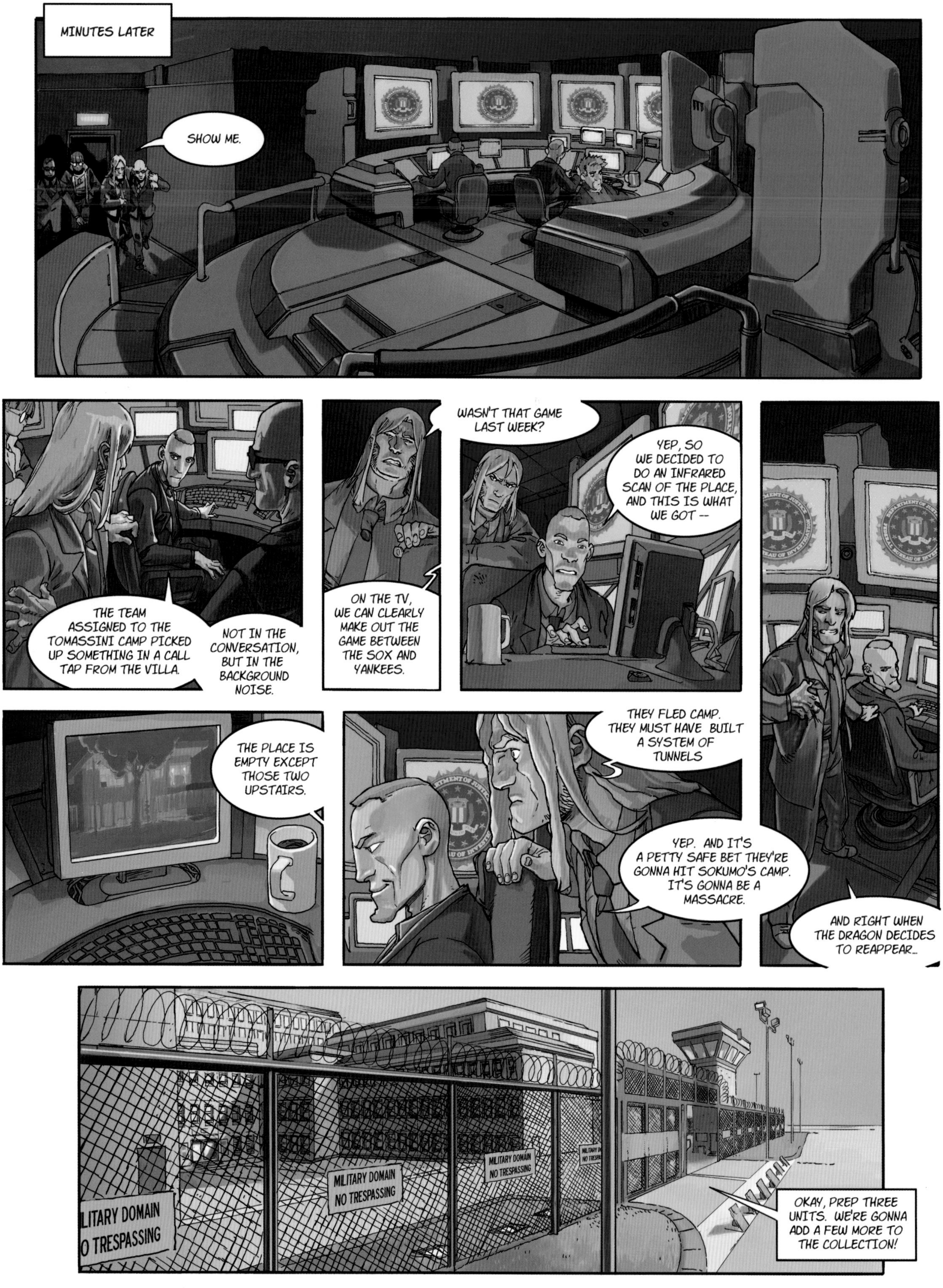
MINUTES LATER
SHOW ME.
THE TEAM ASSIGNED TO THE TOMASSINI CAMP PICKED UP SOMETHING IN A CALL TAP FROM THE VILLA.
NOT IN THE CONVERSATION, BUT IN THE BACKGROUND NOISE.
ON THE TV, WE CAN CLEARLY MAKE OUT THE GAME BETWEEN THE SOX AND YANKEES.
WASN'T THAT GAME LAST WEEK?
YEP, SO WE DECIDED TO DO AN INFRARED SCAN OF THE PLACE, AND THIS IS WHAT WE GOT --
THE PLACE IS EMPTY EXCEPT THOSE TWO UPSTAIRS.
THEY FLED CAMP. THEY MUST HAVE BUILT A SYSTEM OF TUNNELS
YEP. AND IT'S A PETTY SAFE BET THEY'RE GONNA HIT SOKUMO'S CAMP. IT'S GONNA BE A MASSACRE.
AND RIGHT WHEN THE DRAGON DECIDES TO REAPPEAR...
MILITARY DOMAIN NO TRESPASSING
MILITARY DOMAIN NO TRESPASSING
MILITARY DOMAIN NO TRESPASSING
OKAY, PREP THREE UNITS. WE'RE GONNA ADD A FEW MORE TO THE COLLECTION!

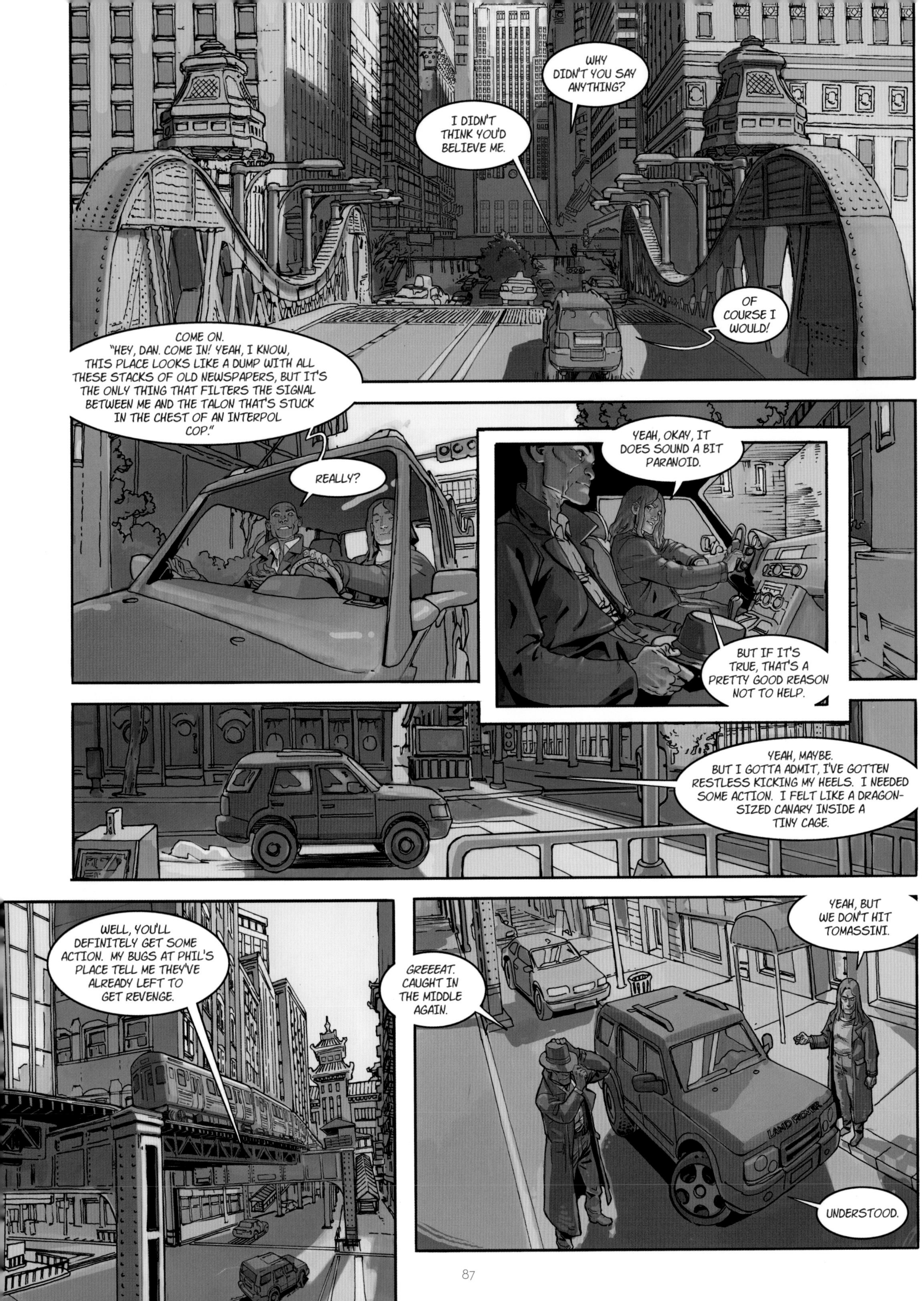
WHY DIDN'T YOU SAY ANYTHING?
I DIDN'T THINK YOU'D BELIEVE ME.
OF COURSE I WOULD!
COME ON. "HEY, DAN. COME IN! YEAH, I KNOW, THIS PLACE LOOKS LIKE A DUMP WITH ALL THESE STACKS OF OLD NEWSPAPERS, BUT IT'S THE ONLY THING THAT FILTERS THE SIGNAL BETWEEN ME AND THE TALON THAT'S STUCK IN THE CHEST OF AN INTERPOL COP."
REALLY?
YEAH, OKAY, IT DOES SOUND A BIT PARANOID.
BUT IF IT'S TRUE, THAT'S A PRETTY GOOD REASON NOT TO HELP.
YEAH, MAYBE. BUT I GOTTA ADMIT, I'VE GOTTEN RESTLESS KICKING MY HEELS. I NEEDED SOME ACTION. I FELT LIKE A DRAGON-SIZED CANARY INSIDE A TINY CAGE.
WELL, YOU'LL DEFINITELY GET SOME ACTION. MY BUGS AT PHIL'S PLACE TELL ME THEY'VE ALREADY LEFT TO GET REVENGE.
GREEEAT. CAUGHT IN THE MIDDLE AGAIN.
YEAH, BUT WE DON'T HIT TOMASSINI.
UNDERSTOOD.

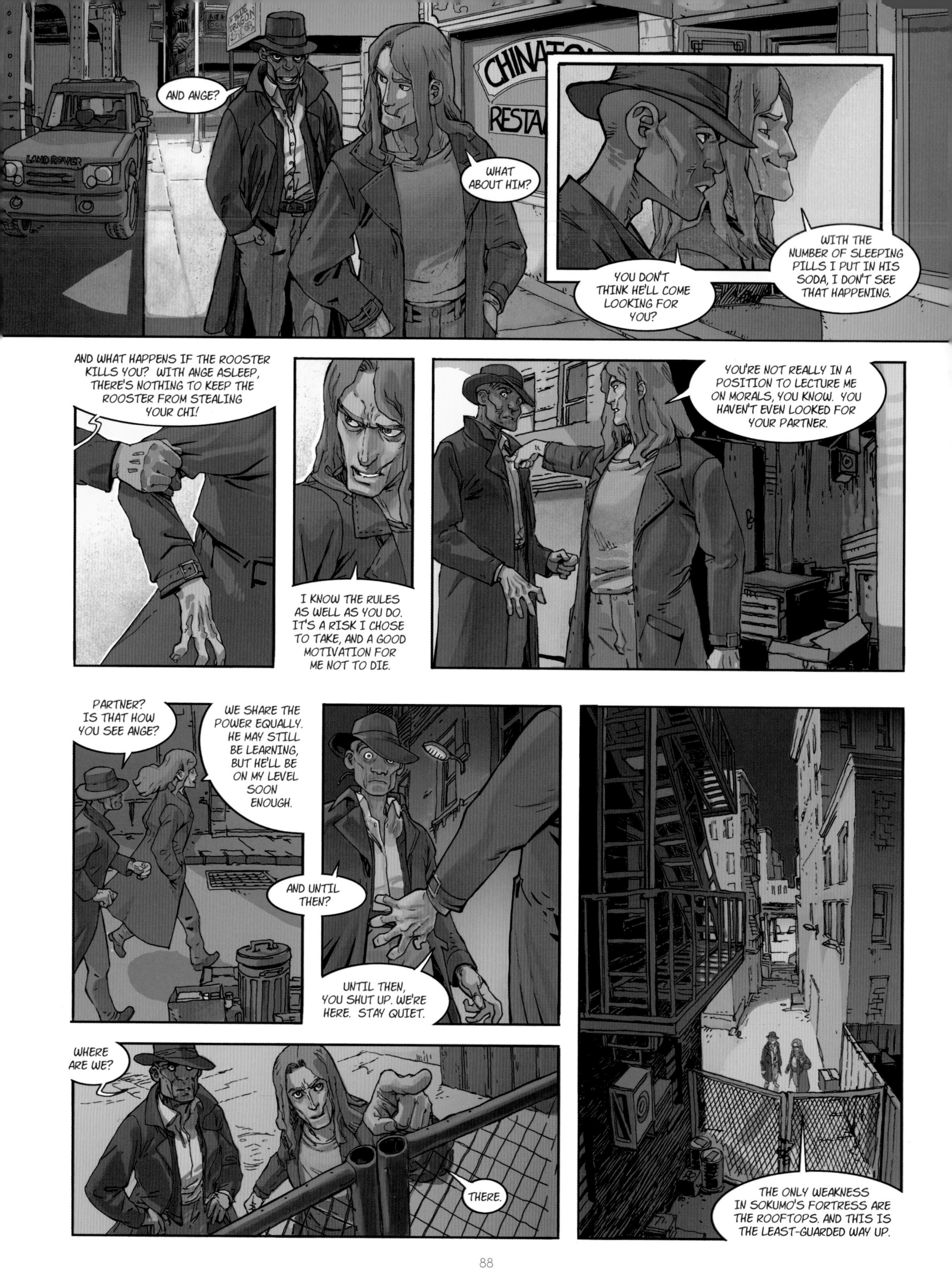

AND ANGE?
WHAT ABOUT HIM?
YOU DON'T THINK HE'LL COME LOOKING FOR YOU?
WITH THE NUMBER OF SLEEPING PILLS I PUT IN HIS SODA, I DON'T SEE THAT HAPPENING.
AND WHAT HAPPENS IF THE ROOSTER KILLS YOU? WITH ANGE ASLEEP, THERE'S NOTHING TO KEEP THE ROOSTER FROM STEALING YOUR CHI!
I KNOW THE RULES AS WELL AS YOU DO. IT'S A RISK I CHOSE TO TAKE, AND A GOOD MOTIVATION FOR ME NOT TO DIE.
YOU'RE NOT REALLY IN A POSITION TO LECTURE ME ON MORALS, YOU KNOW. YOU HAVEN'T EVEN LOOKED FOR YOUR PARTNER.
PARTNER? IS THAT HOW YOU SEE ANGE?
WE SHARE THE POWER EQUALLY. HE MAY STILL BE LEARNING, BUT HE'LL BE ON MY LEVEL SOON ENOUGH.
AND UNTIL THEN?
UNTIL THEN, YOU SHUT UP. WE'RE HERE. STAY QUIET.
WHERE ARE WE?
THERE.
THE ONLY WEAKNESS IN SOKUMO'S FORTRESS ARE THE ROOFTOPS. AND THIS IS THE LEAST-GUARDED WAY UP.

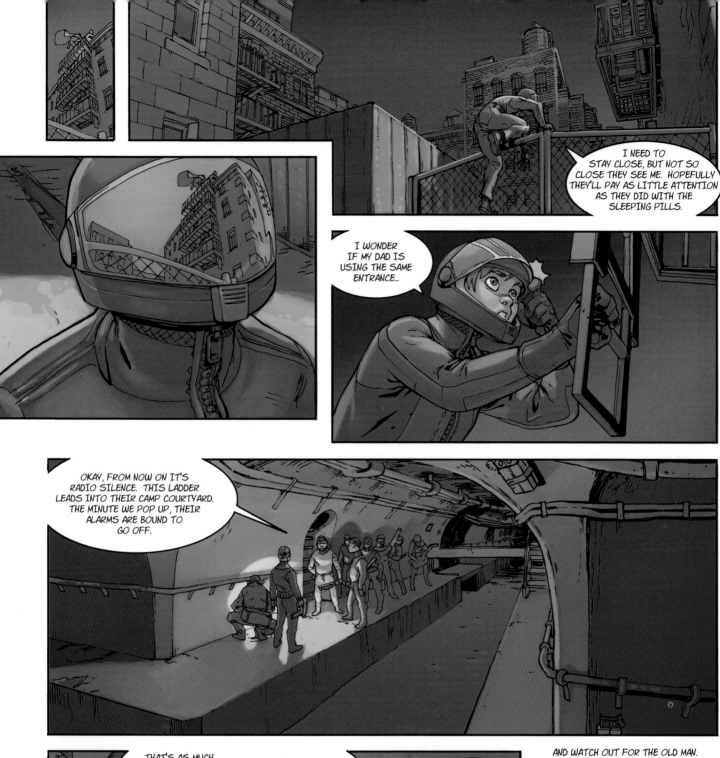

I NEED TO STAY CLOSE, BUT NOT SO CLOSE THEY SEE ME. HOPEFULLY THEY'LL PAY AS LITTLE ATTENTION AS THEY DID WITH THE SLEEPING PILLS.

I WONDER IF MY DAD IS USING THE SAME ENTRANCE...

OKAY, FROM NOW ON IT'S RADIO SILENCE. THIS LADDER LEADS INTO THEIR CAMP COURTYARD. THE MINUTE WE POP UP, THEIR ALARMS ARE BOUND TO GO OFF.

THAT'S AS MUCH SURPRISE AS WE'RE GONNA GET. WE WON'T HAVE A LOT OF TIME BEFORE THEY'RE ON US.

THE GOAL IS TO GET THEM TO CHASE US BACK DOWN HERE. WITH ALL THE C4 CHUCK'S SETTING UP, THEY'LL BE BURIED BEFORE THEY KNOW IT.

AND WATCH OUT FOR THE OLD MAN. IF YOU SEE HIM, YOU SHOOT HIM DEAD ON THE SPOT.

EVEN IF HE'S UNARMED.

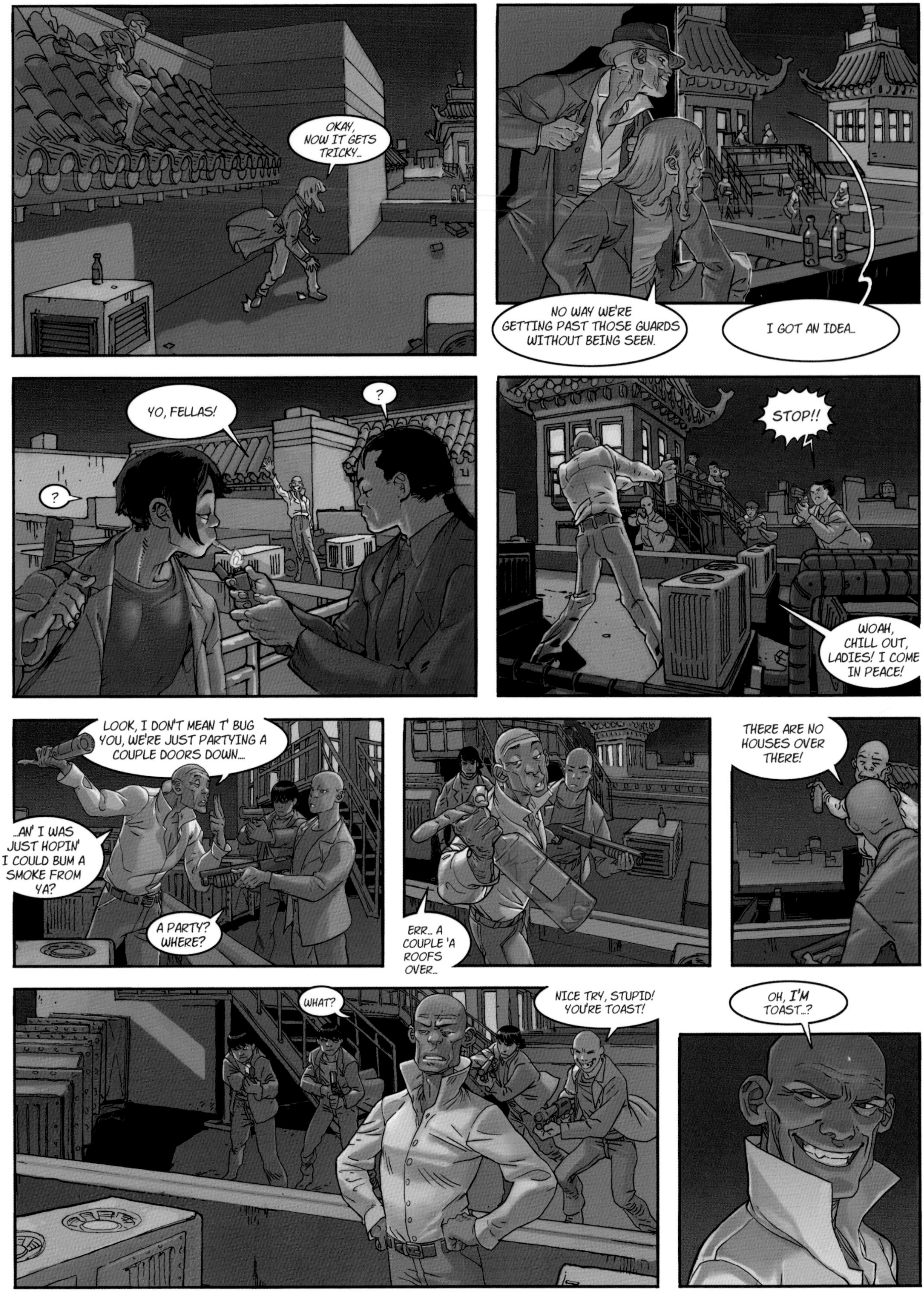
OKAY, NOW IT GETS TRICKY...
NO WAY WE'RE GETTING PAST THOSE GUARDS WITHOUT BEING SEEN.
I GOT AN IDEA...
YO, FELLAS!
?
?
STOP!!
WOAH, CHILL OUT, LADIES! I COME IN PEACE!
LOOK, I DON'T MEAN T' BUG YOU, WE'RE JUST PARTYING A COUPLE DOORS DOWN....
...AN' I WAS JUST HOPIN' I COULD BUM A SMOKE FROM YA?
A PARTY? WHERE?
ERR... A COUPLE 'A ROOFS OVER...
THERE ARE NO HOUSES OVER THERE!
WHAT?
NICE TRY, STUPID! YOU'RE TOAST!
OH, I'M TOAST..?

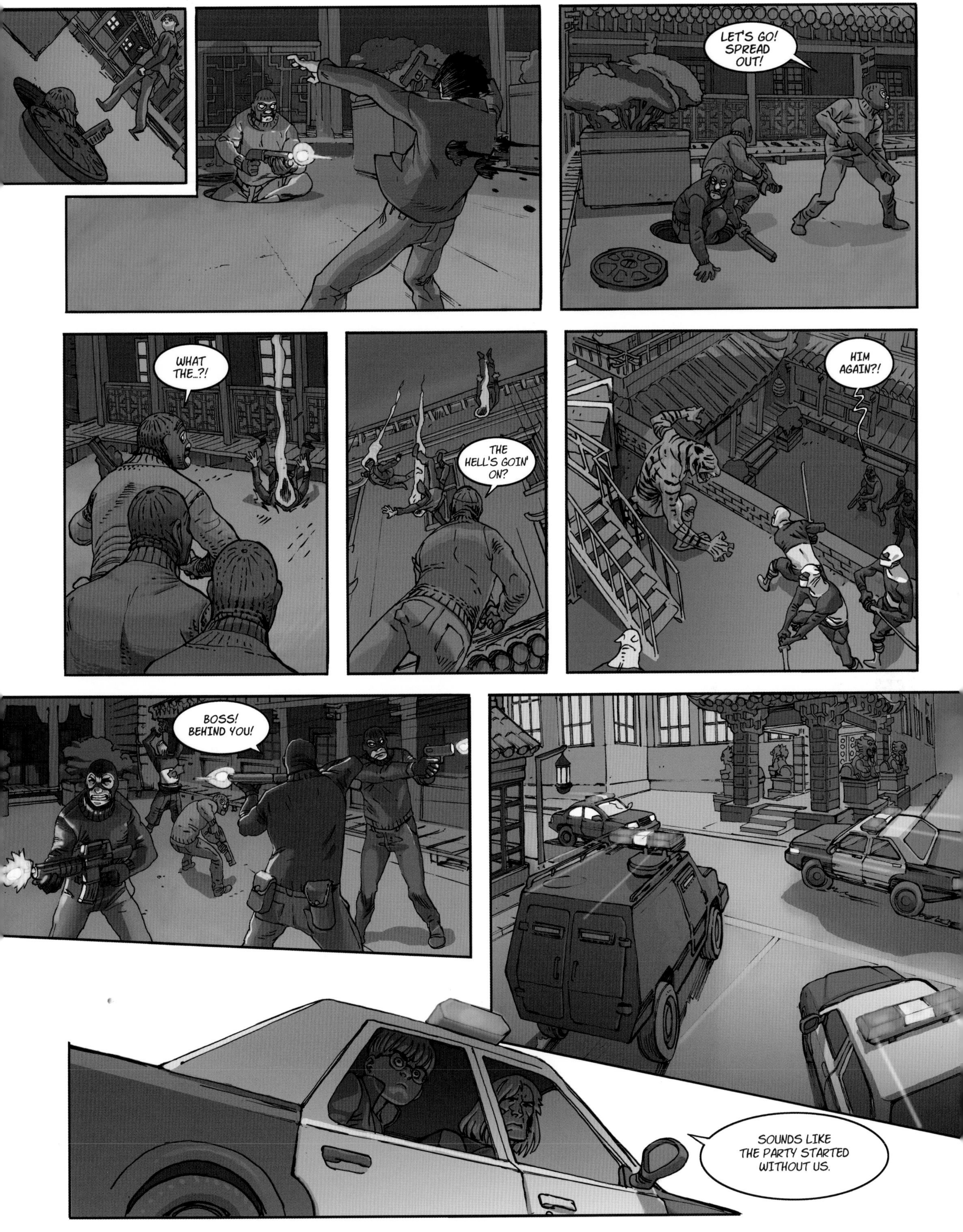
LET'S GO! SPREAD OUT!
WHAT THE...?!
THE HELL'S GOIN' ON?
HIM AGAIN?!
BOSS! BEHIND YOU!
SOUNDS LIKE THE PARTY STARTED WITHOUT US.

STAY HERE, KID!

EVERYONE ELSE, GO!

OH MY GOD...

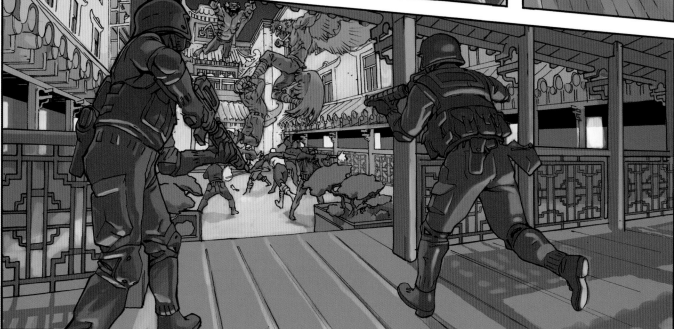

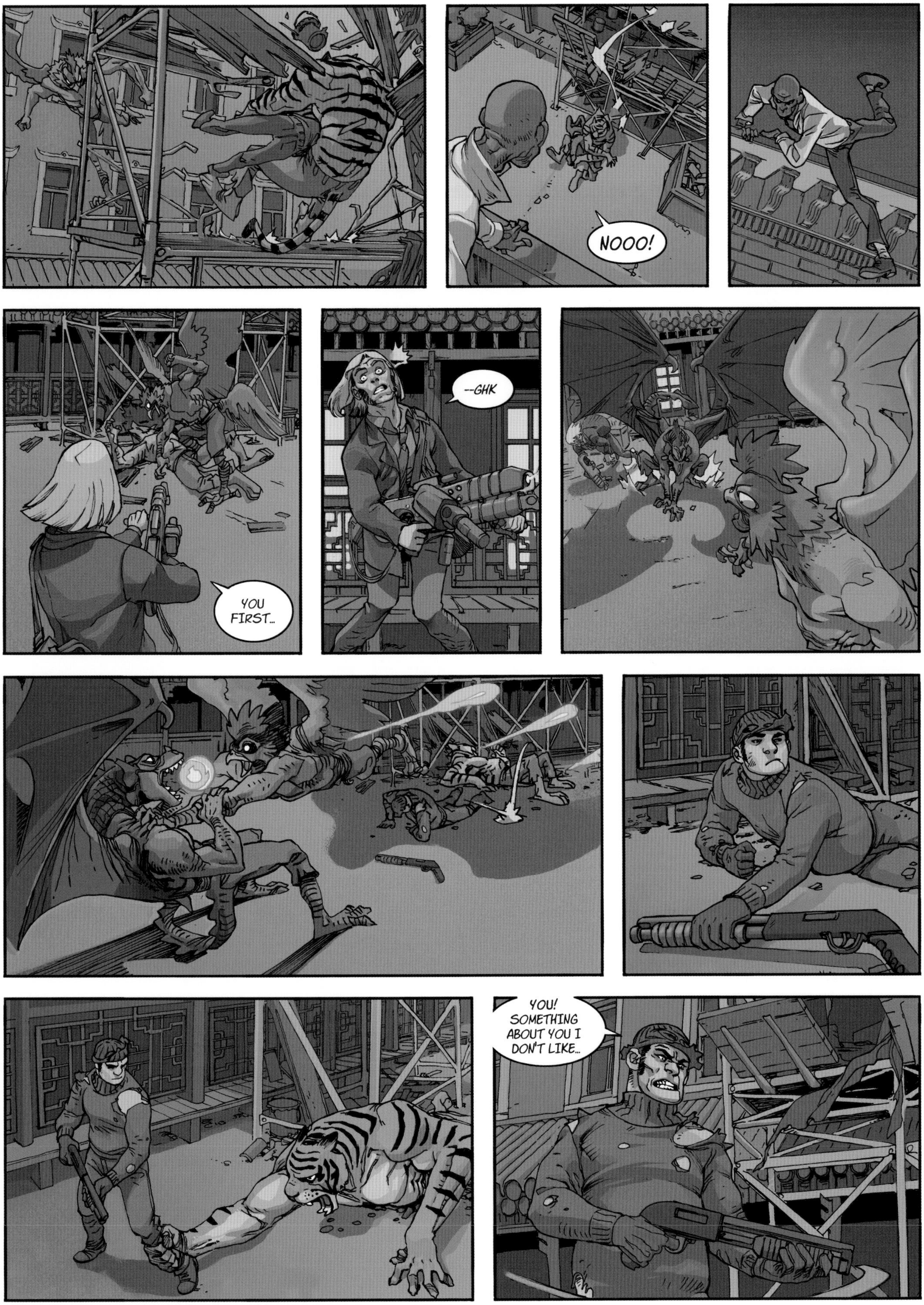
NOOO!
YOU FIRST...
--GHK
YOU! SOMETHING ABOUT YOU I DON'T LIKE...

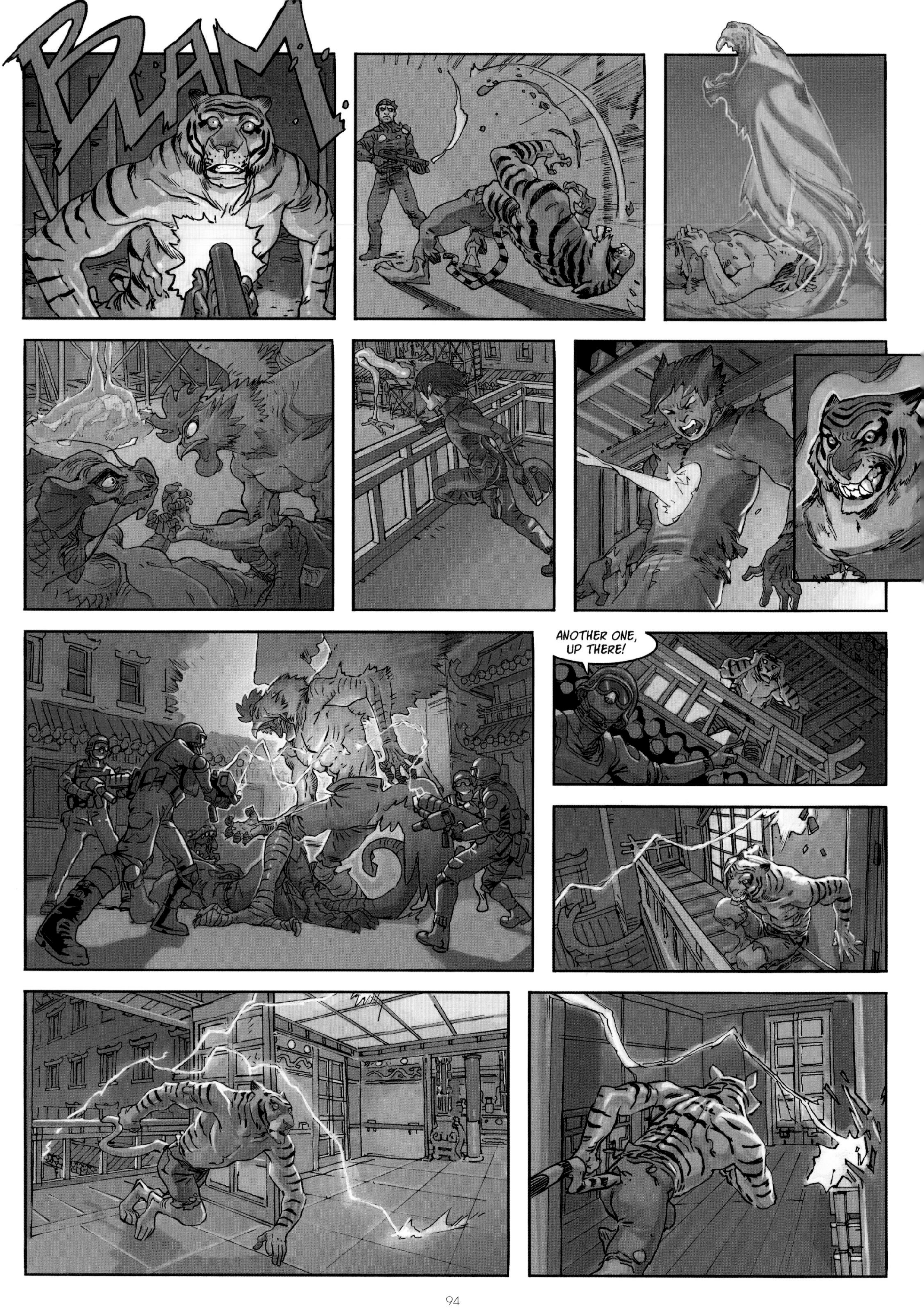
BLAM!
ANOTHER ONE, UP THERE!

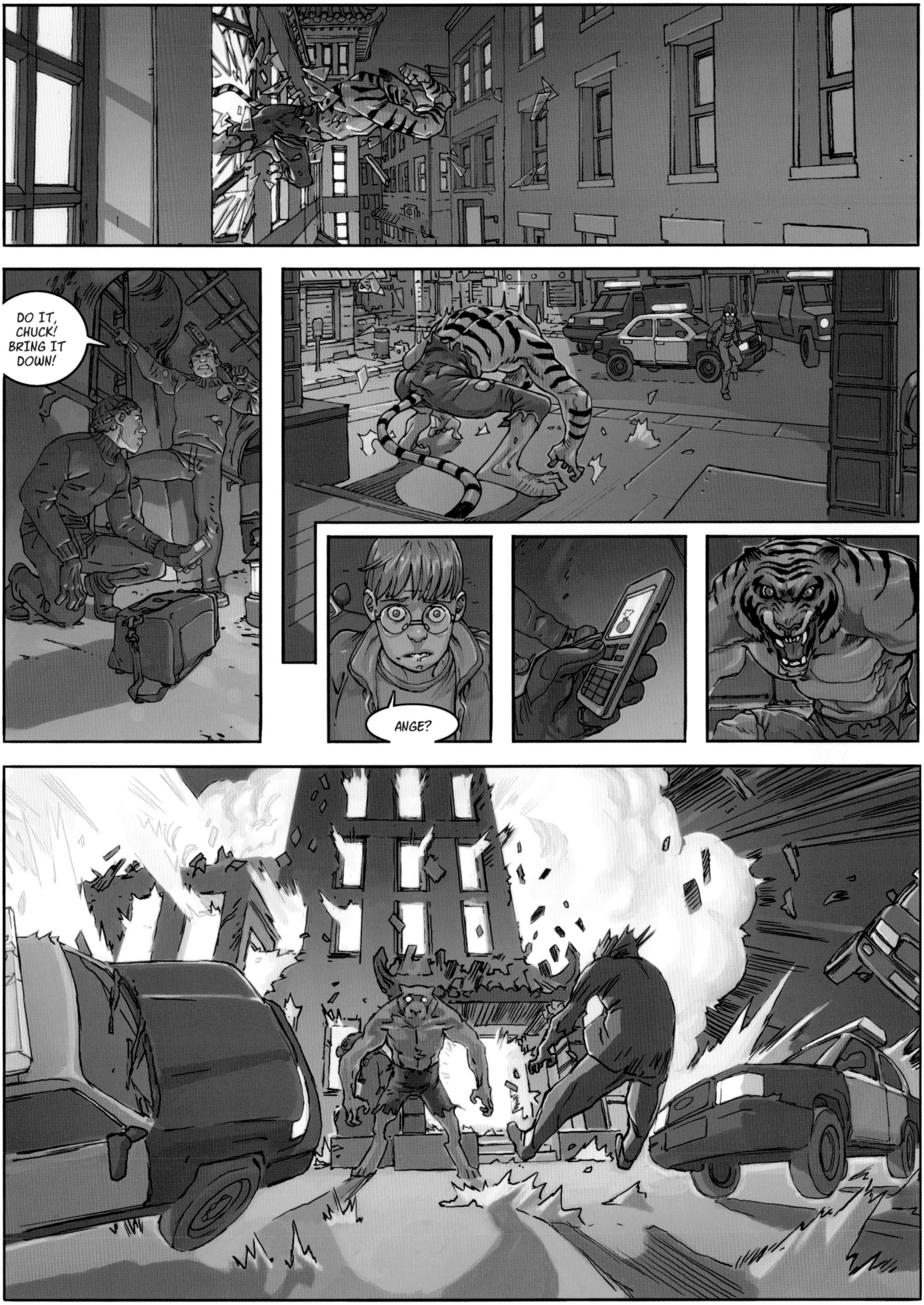
DO IT, CHUCK! BRING IT DOWN!
ANGE?

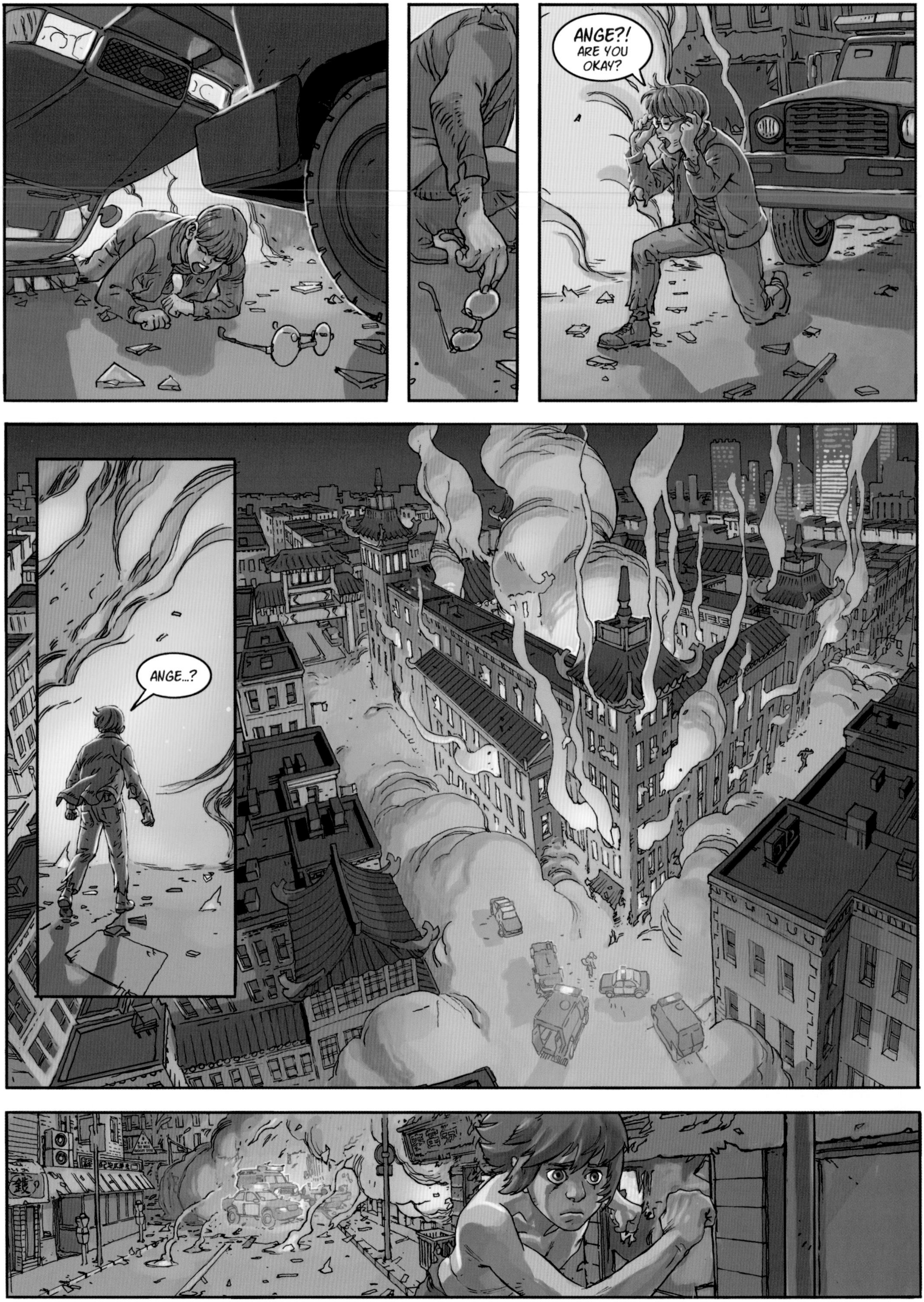
ANGE?! ARE YOU OKAY?
ANGE...?

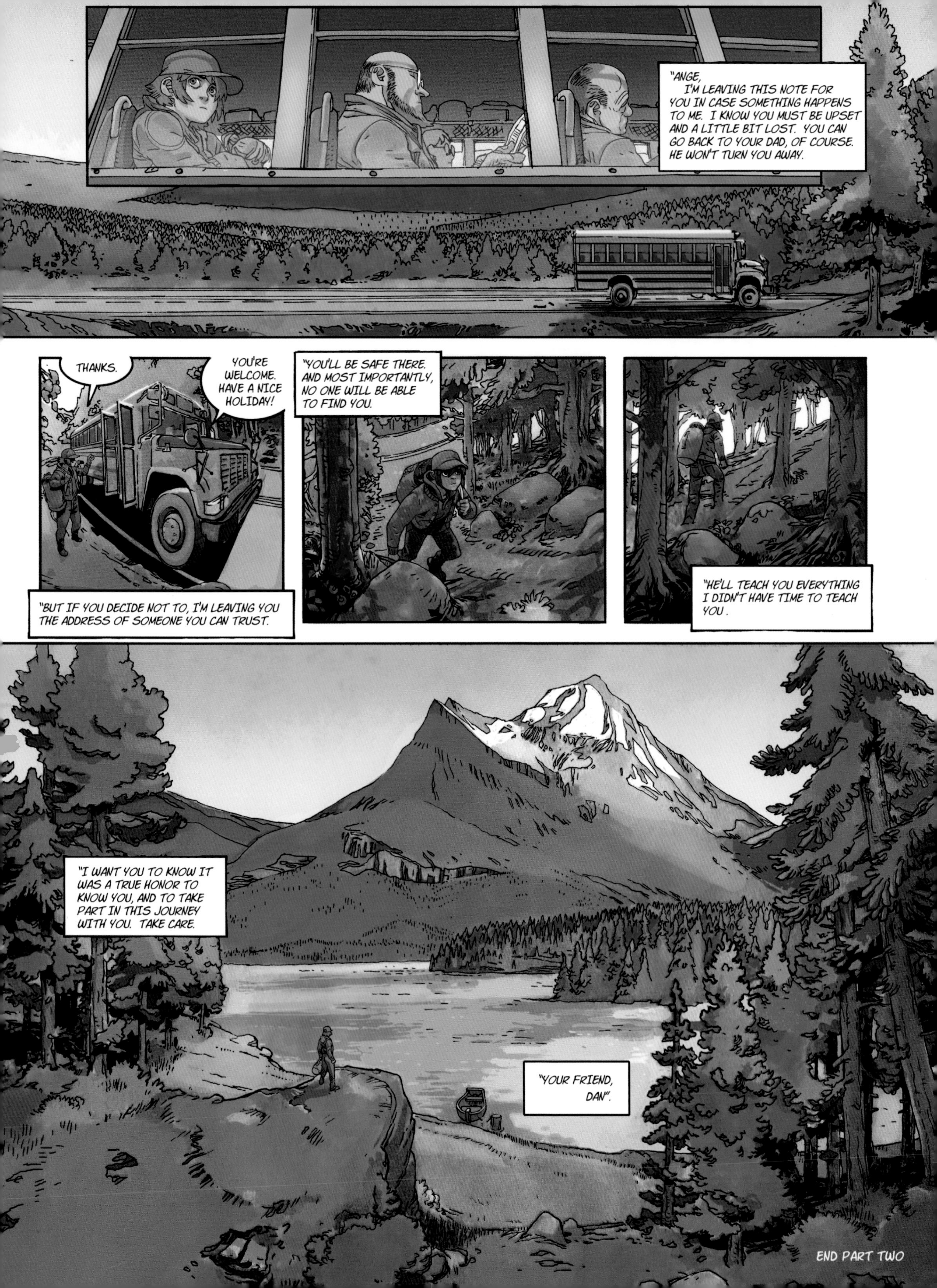
"ANGE,
I'M LEAVING THIS NOTE FOR YOU IN CASE SOMETHING HAPPENS TO ME. I KNOW YOU MUST BE UPSET AND A LITTLE BIT LOST. YOU CAN GO BACK TO YOUR DAD, OF COURSE. HE WON'T TURN YOU AWAY.
THANKS.
YOU'RE WELCOME. HAVE A NICE HOLIDAY!
"BUT IF YOU DECIDE NOT TO, I'M LEAVING YOU THE ADDRESS OF SOMEONE YOU CAN TRUST.
"YOU'LL BE SAFE THERE. AND MOST IMPORTANTLY, NO ONE WILL BE ABLE TO FIND YOU.
"HE'LL TEACH YOU EVERYTHING I DIDN'T HAVE TIME TO TEACH YOU .
"I WANT YOU TO KNOW IT WAS A TRUE HONOR TO KNOW YOU, AND TO TAKE PART IN THIS JOURNEY WITH YOU. TAKE CARE.
"YOUR FRIEND, DAN".
END PART TWO

PART THREE: UNIONS

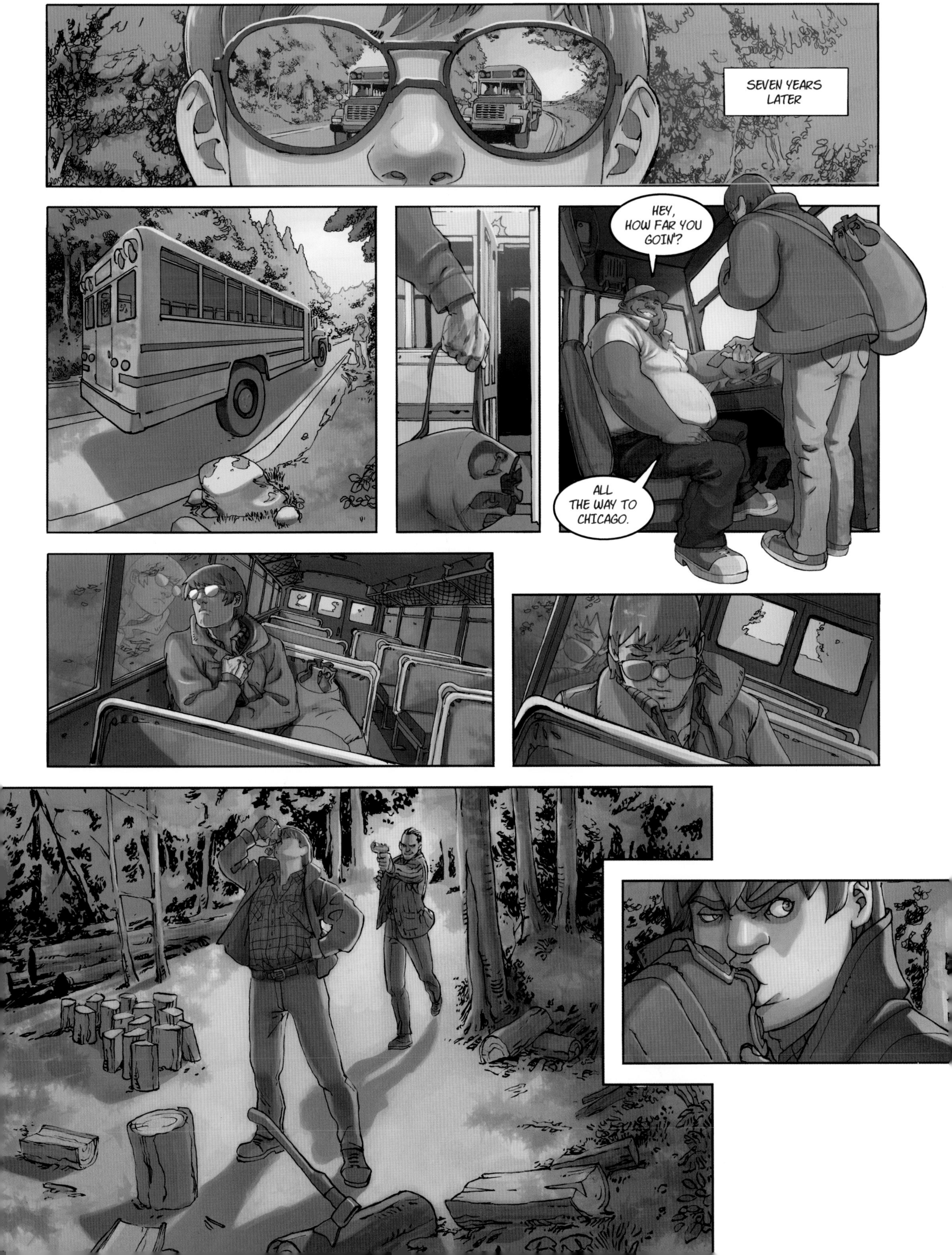
SEVEN YEARS LATER
HEY, HOW FAR YOU GOIN'?
ALL THE WAY TO CHICAGO.

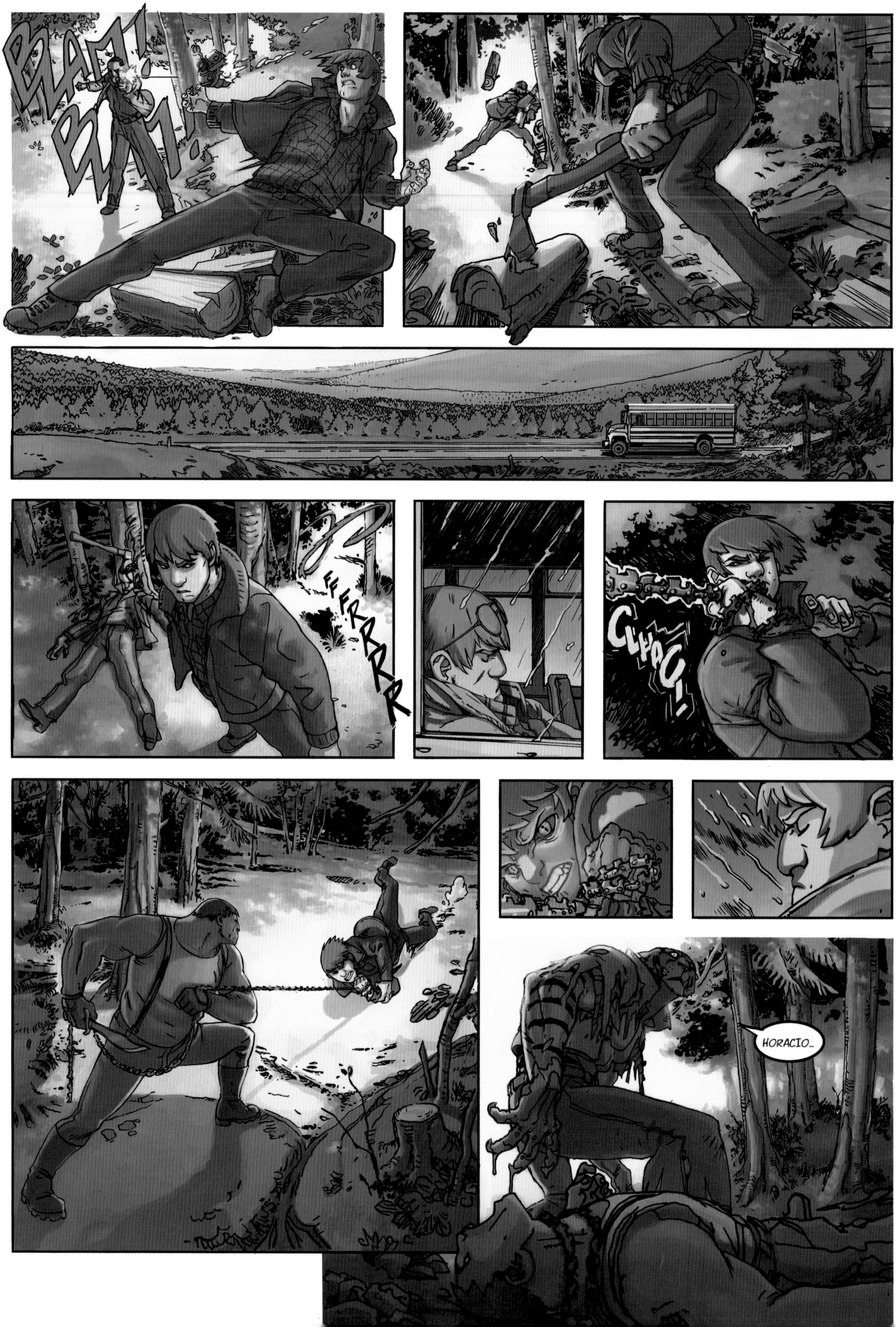
BLAM! BLAM!
FFFRRRRR
CLAAC!
HORACIO...

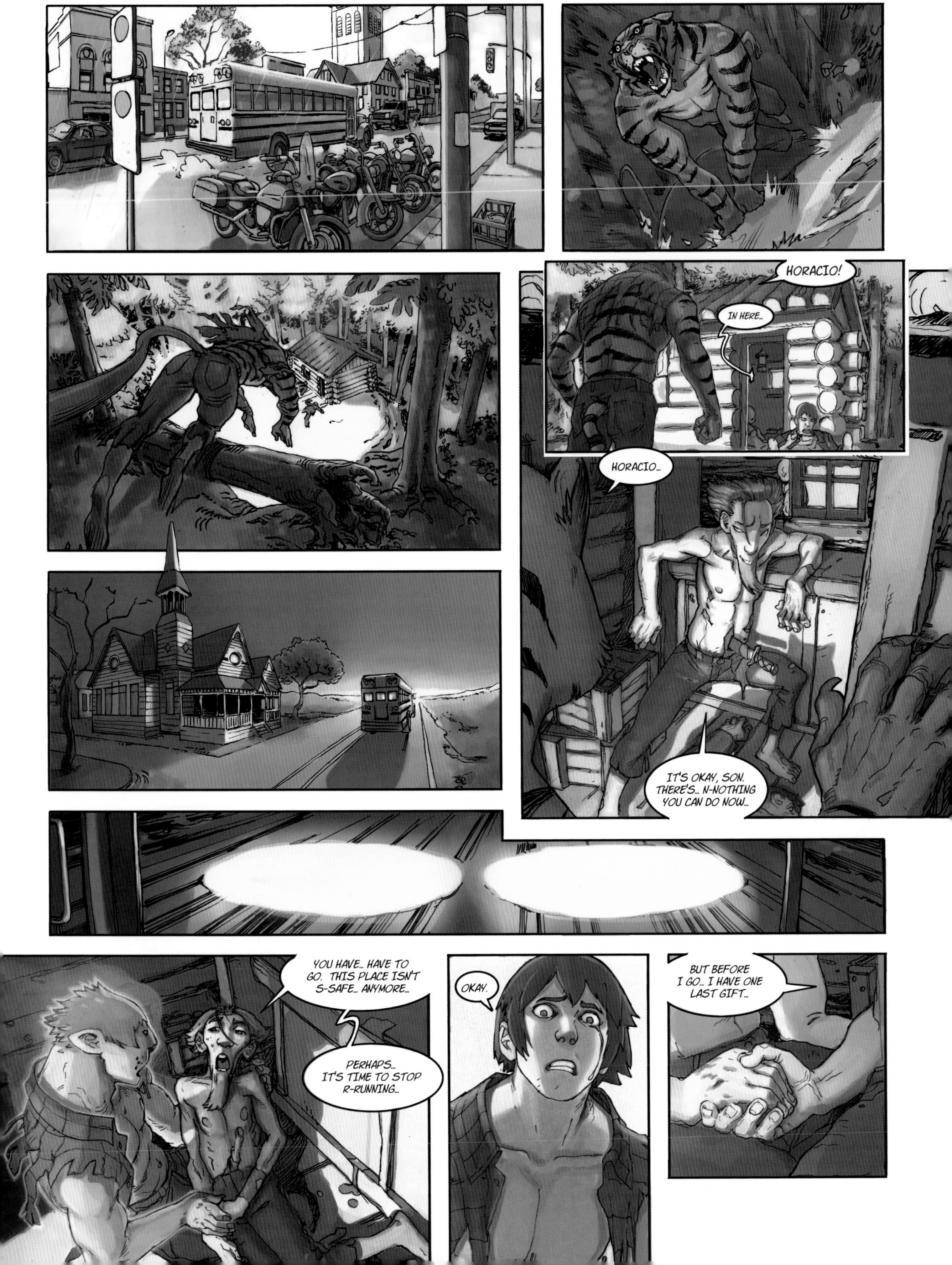
HORACIO!
IN HERE...
HORACIO...
IT'S OKAY, SON. THERE'S... N-NOTHING YOU CAN DO NOW...
YOU HAVE... HAVE TO GO. THIS PLACE ISN'T S-SAFE... ANYMORE...
PERHAPS... IT'S TIME TO STOP R-RUNNING...
OKAY.
BUT BEFORE I GO... I HAVE ONE LAST GIFT...

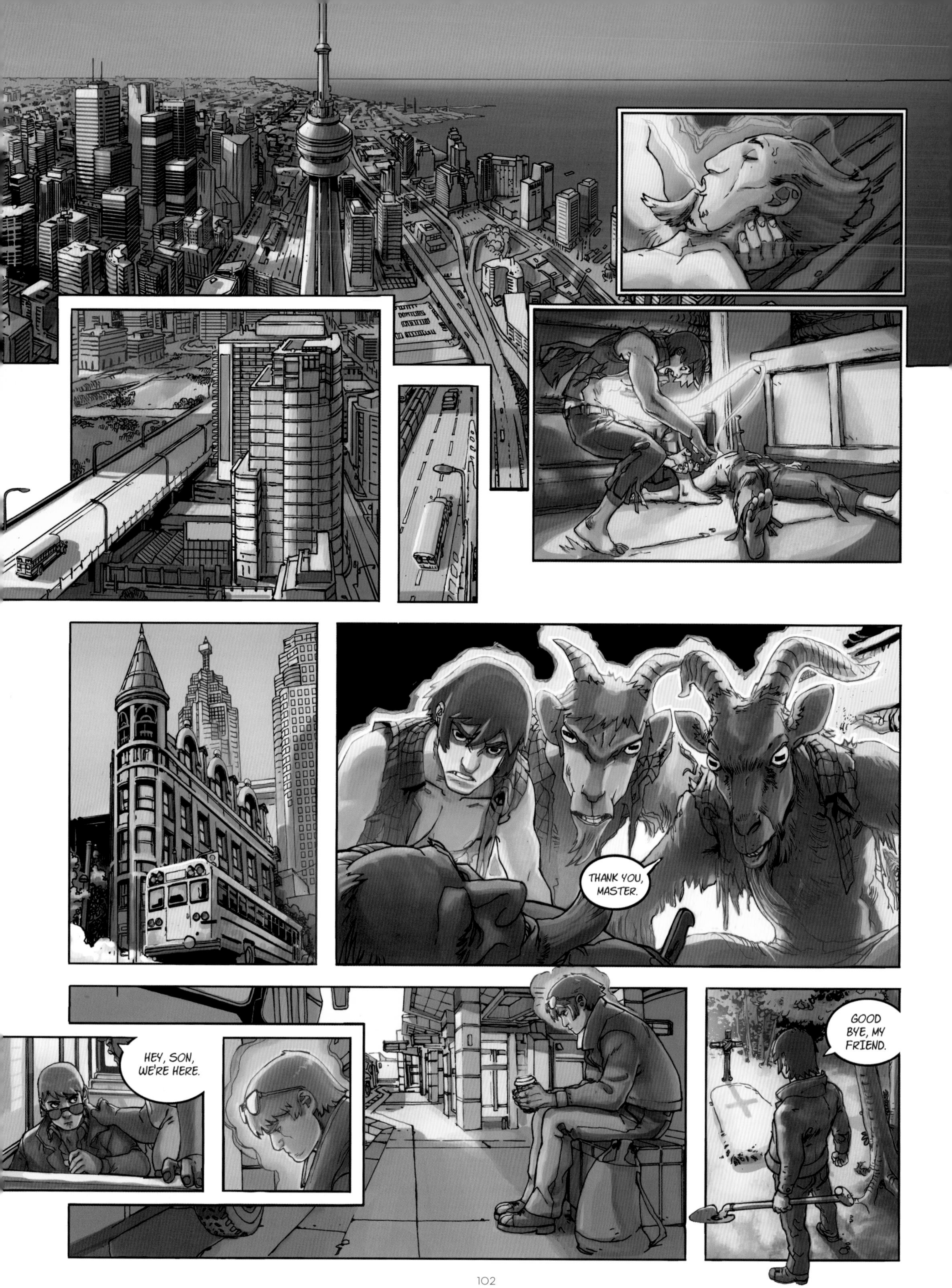
THANK YOU, MASTER.
HEY, SON, WE'RE HERE.
GOOD BYE, MY FRIEND.

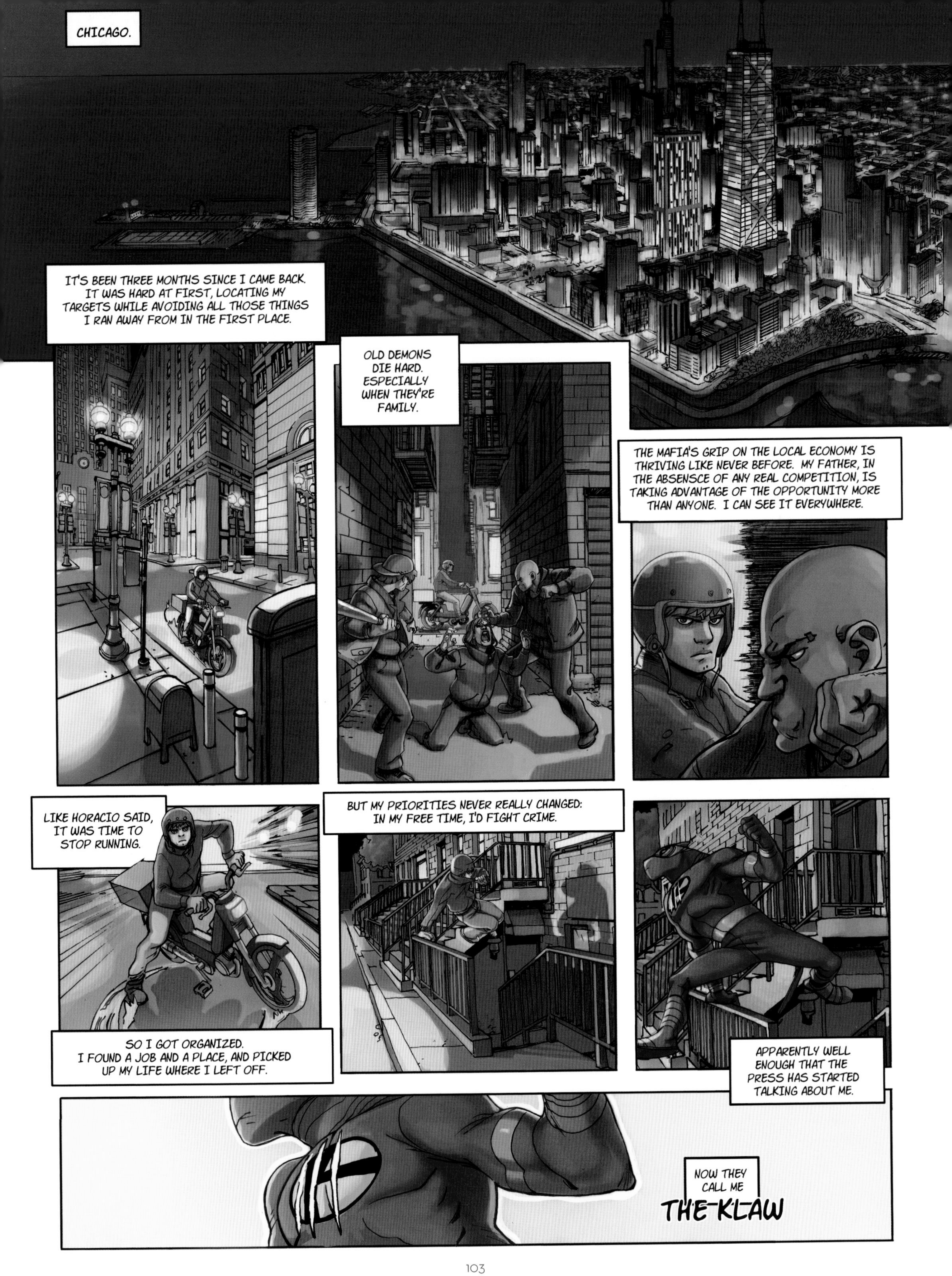
CHICAGO.
IT'S BEEN THREE MONTHS SINCE I CAME BACK. IT WAS HARD AT FIRST, LOCATING MY TARGETS WHILE AVOIDING ALL THOSE THINGS I RAN AWAY FROM IN THE FIRST PLACE.
OLD DEMONS DIE HARD. ESPECIALLY WHEN THEY'RE FAMILY.
THE MAFIA'S GRIP ON THE LOCAL ECONOMY IS THRIVING LIKE NEVER BEFORE. MY FATHER, IN THE ABSENSCE OF ANY REAL COMPETITION, IS TAKING ADVANTAGE OF THE OPPORTUNITY MORE THAN ANYONE. I CAN SEE IT EVERYWHERE.
LIKE HORACIO SAID, IT WAS TIME TO STOP RUNNING.
SO I GOT ORGANIZED. I FOUND A JOB AND A PLACE, AND PICKED UP MY LIFE WHERE I LEFT OFF.
BUT MY PRIORITIES NEVER REALLY CHANGED: IN MY FREE TIME, I'D FIGHT CRIME.
APPARENTLY WELL ENOUGH THAT THE PRESS HAS STARTED TALKING ABOUT ME.
NOW THEY CALL ME
THE KLAW

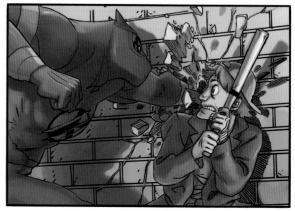

S-STAY BACK, DEMON!!

DEMON?

REAL DEMONS HAVE **HORNS**...

YOU CAN GO.

TH-THANK YOU...

...A-ARE YOU... THE KLAW?

LOOKS LIKE I'VE GOT GOOD PRESS!

YOU DO! KEEP UP THE GOOD WORK! DUTY NEVER SLEEPS!

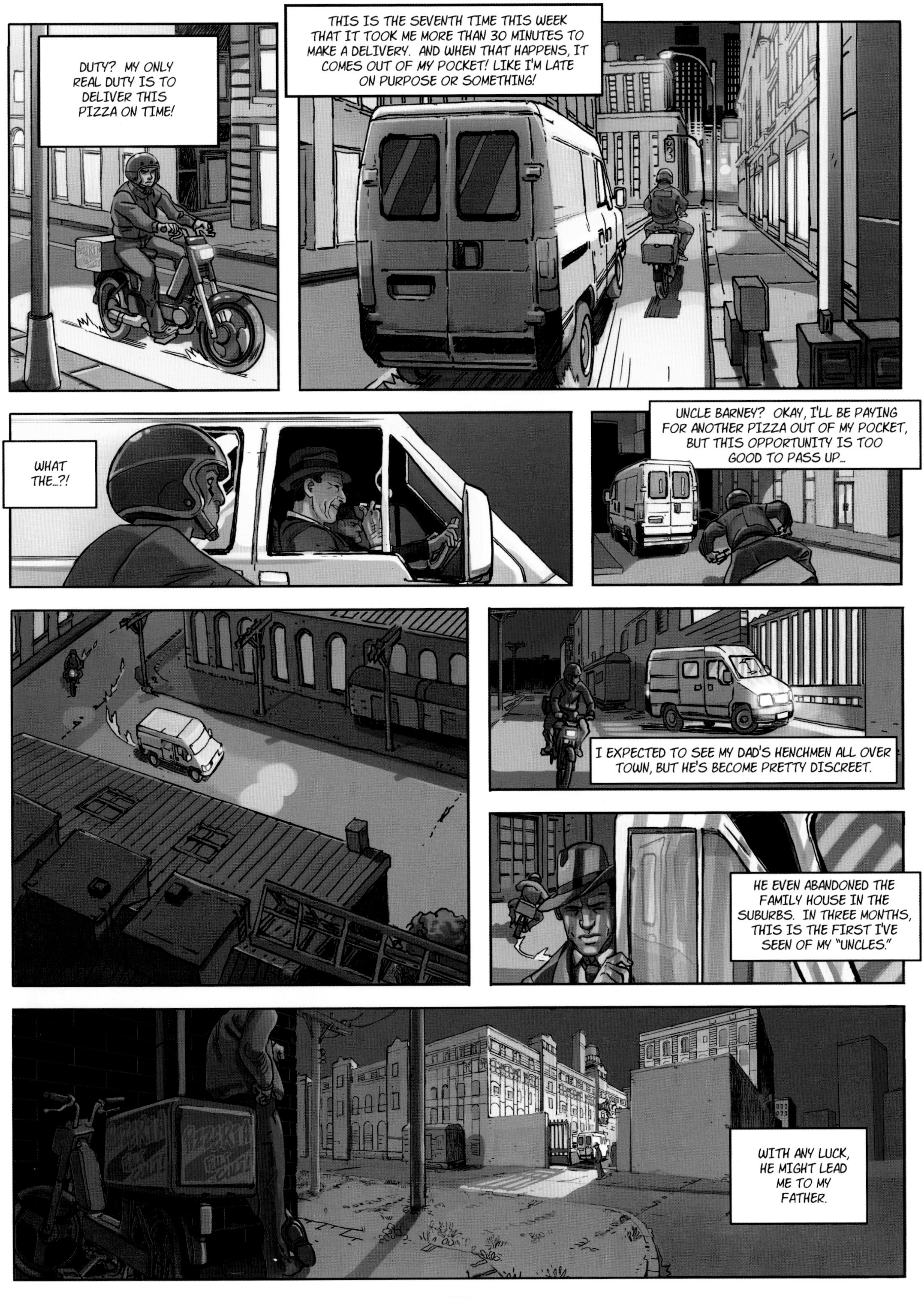
DUTY? MY ONLY REAL DUTY IS TO DELIVER THIS PIZZA ON TIME!
THIS IS THE SEVENTH TIME THIS WEEK THAT IT TOOK ME MORE THAN 30 MINUTES TO MAKE A DELIVERY. AND WHEN THAT HAPPENS, IT COMES OUT OF MY POCKET! LIKE I'M LATE ON PURPOSE OR SOMETHING!
WHAT THE...?!
UNCLE BARNEY? OKAY, I'LL BE PAYING FOR ANOTHER PIZZA OUT OF MY POCKET, BUT THIS OPPORTUNITY IS TOO GOOD TO PASS UP...
I EXPECTED TO SEE MY DAD'S HENCHMEN ALL OVER TOWN, BUT HE'S BECOME PRETTY DISCREET.
HE EVEN ABANDONED THE FAMILY HOUSE IN THE SUBURBS. IN THREE MONTHS, THIS IS THE FIRST I'VE SEEN OF MY "UNCLES."
WITH ANY LUCK, HE MIGHT LEAD ME TO MY FATHER.

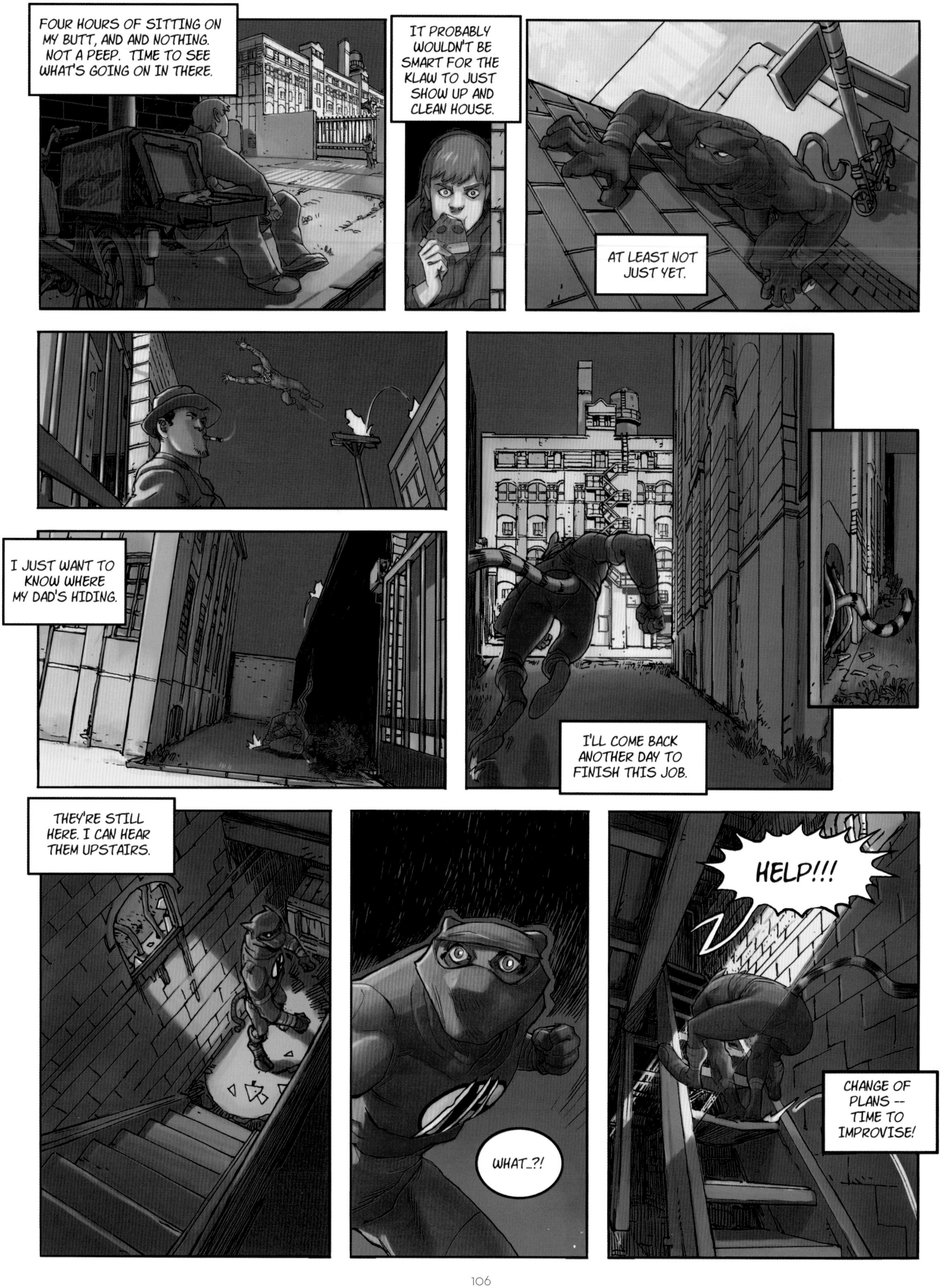
FOUR HOURS OF SITTING ON MY BUTT, AND AND NOTHING. NOT A PEEP. TIME TO SEE WHAT'S GOING ON IN THERE.
IT PROBABLY WOULDN'T BE SMART FOR THE KLAW TO JUST SHOW UP AND CLEAN HOUSE.
AT LEAST NOT JUST YET.
I JUST WANT TO KNOW WHERE MY DAD'S HIDING.
I'LL COME BACK ANOTHER DAY TO FINISH THIS JOB.
THEY'RE STILL HERE. I CAN HEAR THEM UPSTAIRS.
WHAT...?!
HELP!!!
CHANGE OF PLANS -- TIME TO IMPROVISE!

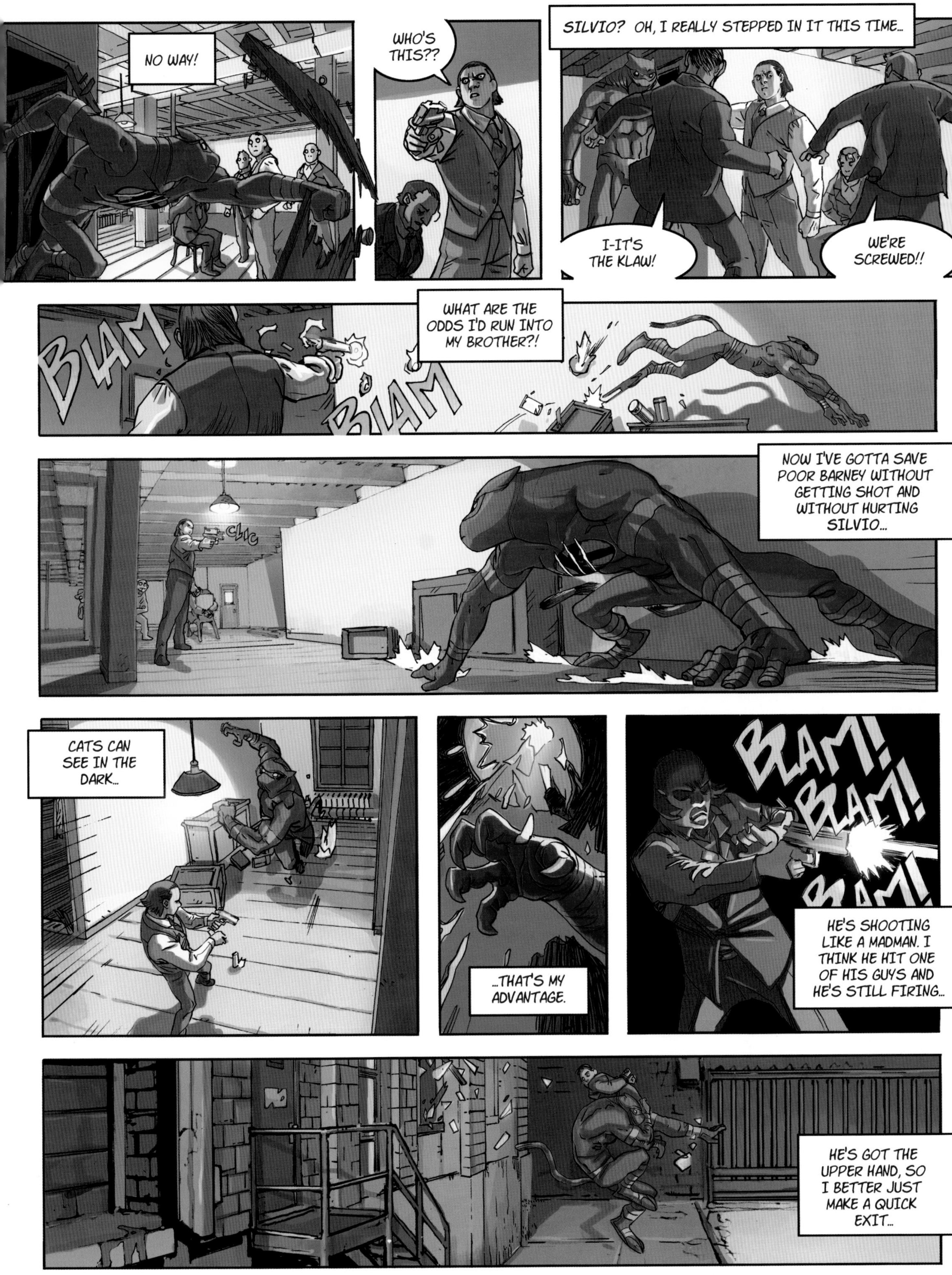
NO WAY!
WHO'S THIS??
SILVIO? OH, I REALLY STEPPED IN IT THIS TIME...
I-IT'S THE KLAW!
WE'RE SCREWED!!
BLAM
WHAT ARE THE ODDS I'D RUN INTO MY BROTHER?!
BLAM
CLIC
NOW I'VE GOTTA SAVE POOR BARNEY WITHOUT GETTING SHOT AND WITHOUT HURTING SILVIO...
CATS CAN SEE IN THE DARK...
...THAT'S MY ADVANTAGE.
BLAM! BLAM!
HE'S SHOOTING LIKE A MADMAN. I THINK HE HIT ONE OF HIS GUYS AND HE'S STILL FIRING...
HE'S GOT THE UPPER HAND, SO I BETTER JUST MAKE A QUICK EXIT...

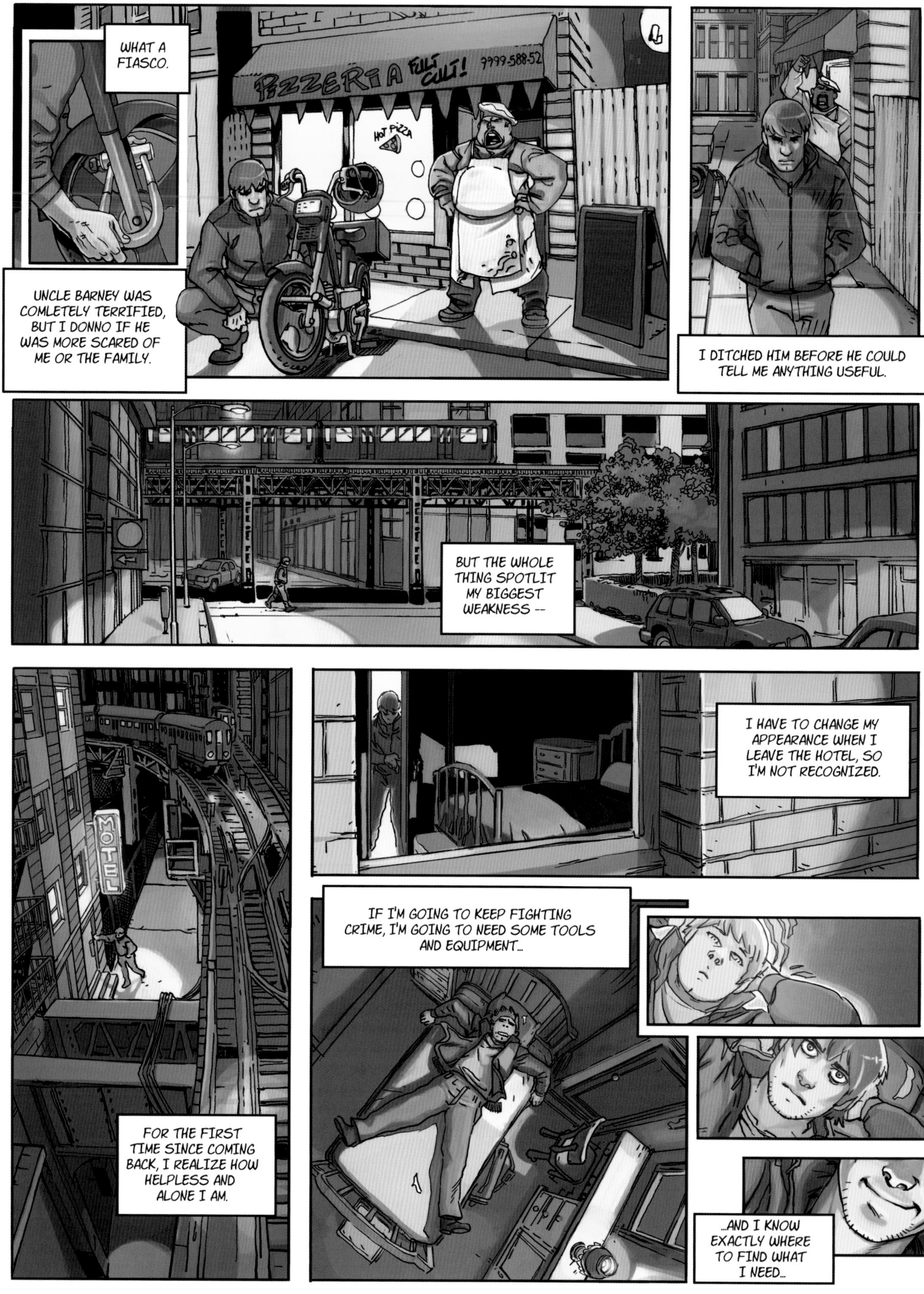

WHAT A FIASCO.
UNCLE BARNEY WAS COMLETELY TERRIFIED, BUT I DONNO IF HE WAS MORE SCARED OF ME OR THE FAMILY.
PIZZERIA FULI CULI! 9999-588-52
HOT PIZZA
I DITCHED HIM BEFORE HE COULD TELL ME ANYTHING USEFUL.
BUT THE WHOLE THING SPOTLIT MY BIGGEST WEAKNESS --
MOTEL
FOR THE FIRST TIME SINCE COMING BACK, I REALIZE HOW HELPLESS AND ALONE I AM.
I HAVE TO CHANGE MY APPEARANCE WHEN I LEAVE THE HOTEL, SO I'M NOT RECOGNIZED.
IF I'M GOING TO KEEP FIGHTING CRIME, I'M GOING TO NEED SOME TOOLS AND EQUIPMENT...
...AND I KNOW EXACTLY WHERE TO FIND WHAT I NEED...

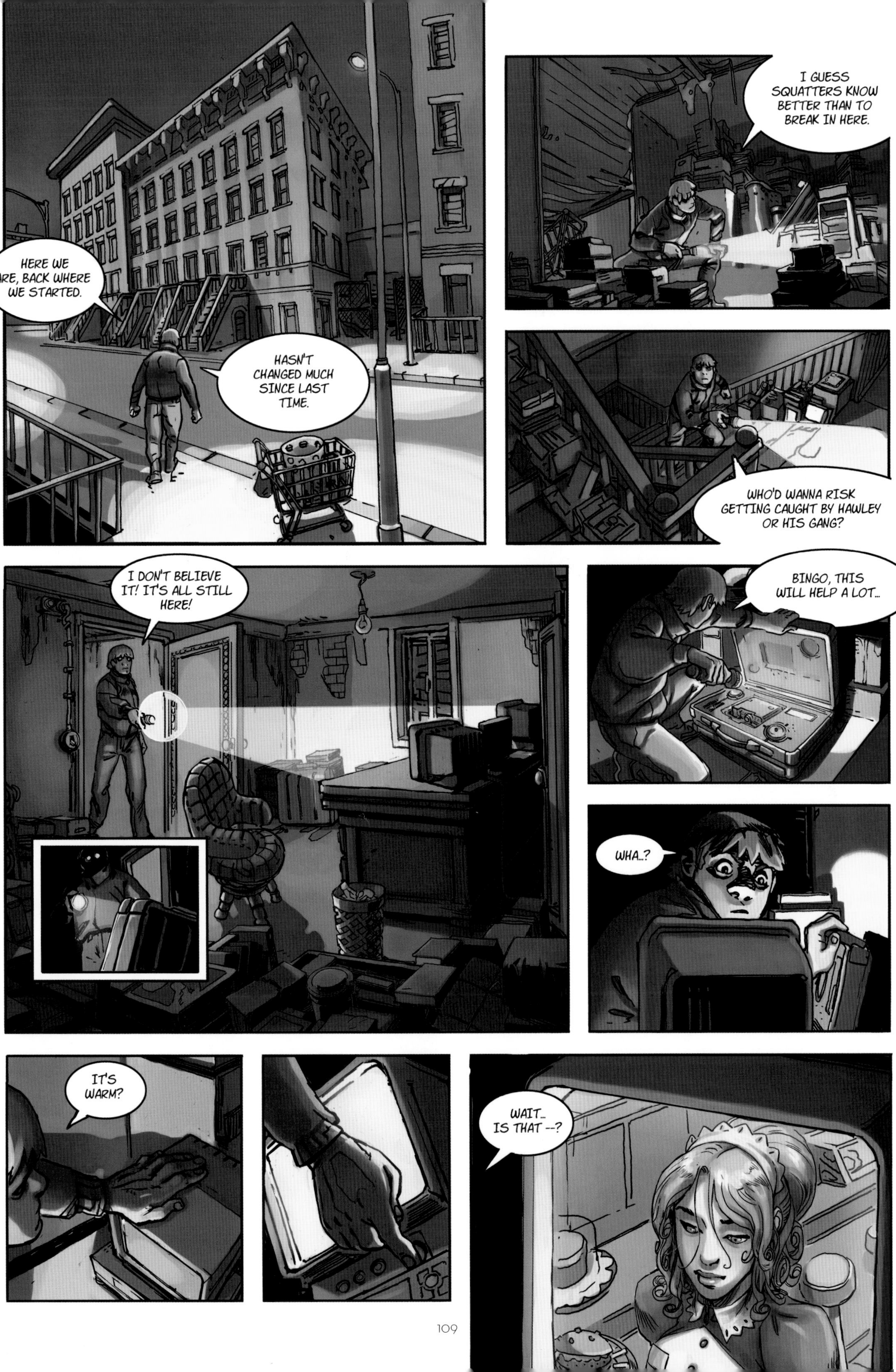
HERE WE ARE, BACK WHERE WE STARTED.
HASN'T CHANGED MUCH SINCE LAST TIME.
I GUESS SQUATTERS KNOW BETTER THAN TO BREAK IN HERE.
WHO'D WANNA RISK GETTING CAUGHT BY HAWLEY OR HIS GANG?
I DON'T BELIEVE IT! IT'S ALL STILL HERE!
BINGO, THIS WILL HELP A LOT...
WHA...?
IT'S WARM?
WAIT... IS THAT --?

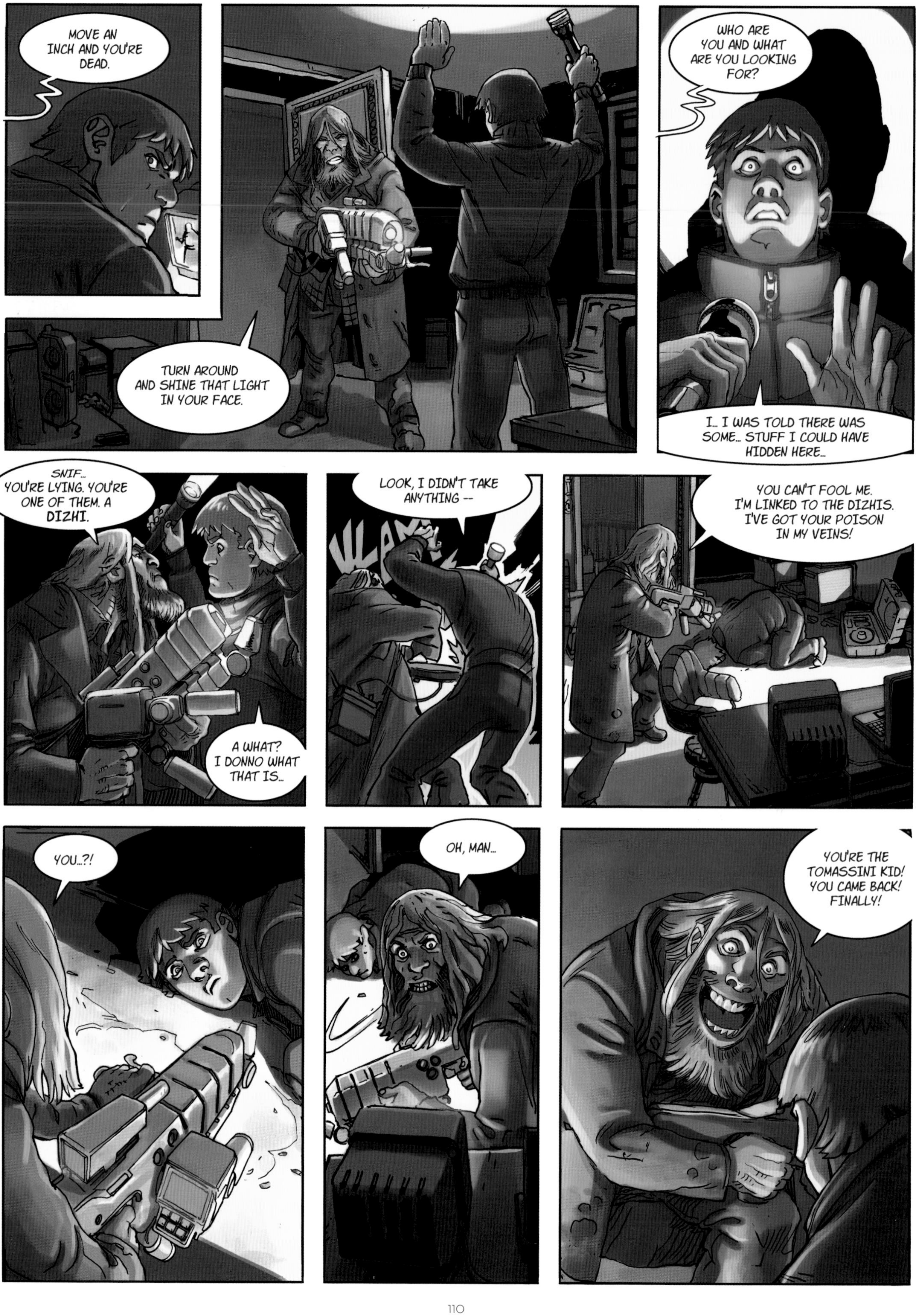
MOVE AN INCH AND YOU'RE DEAD.
TURN AROUND AND SHINE THAT LIGHT IN YOUR FACE.
WHO ARE YOU AND WHAT ARE YOU LOOKING FOR?
I... I WAS TOLD THERE WAS SOME... STUFF I COULD HAVE HIDDEN HERE...
SNIF... YOU'RE LYING. YOU'RE ONE OF THEM. A DIZHI.
A WHAT? I DONNO WHAT THAT IS...
LOOK, I DIDN'T TAKE ANYTHING --
YOU CAN'T FOOL ME. I'M LINKED TO THE DIZHIS. I'VE GOT YOUR POISON IN MY VEINS!
YOU...?!
OH, MAN...
YOU'RE THE TOMASSINI KID! YOU CAME BACK! FINALLY!

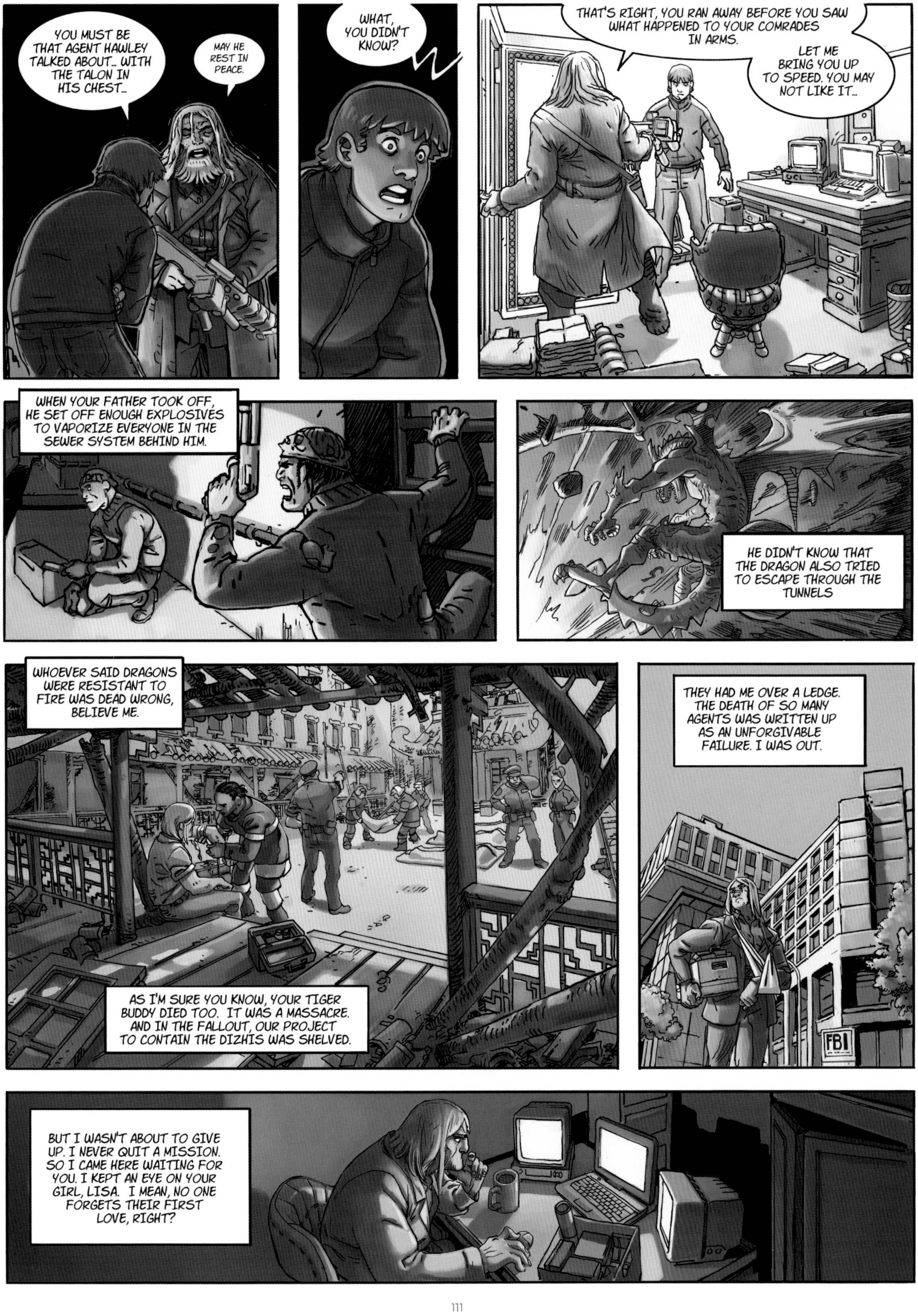

YOU MUST BE THAT AGENT HAWLEY TALKED ABOUT... WITH THE TALON IN HIS CHEST...
MAY HE REST IN PEACE.
WHAT, YOU DIDN'T KNOW?
THAT'S RIGHT, YOU RAN AWAY BEFORE YOU SAW WHAT HAPPENED TO YOUR COMRADES IN ARMS.
LET ME BRING YOU UP TO SPEED. YOU MAY NOT LIKE IT...
WHEN YOUR FATHER TOOK OFF, HE SET OFF ENOUGH EXPLOSIVES TO VAPORIZE EVERYONE IN THE SEWER SYSTEM BEHIND HIM.
HE DIDN'T KNOW THAT THE DRAGON ALSO TRIED TO ESCAPE THROUGH THE TUNNELS
WHOEVER SAID DRAGONS WERE RESISTANT TO FIRE WAS DEAD WRONG, BELIEVE ME.
AS I'M SURE YOU KNOW, YOUR TIGER BUDDY DIED TOO. IT WAS A MASSACRE. AND IN THE FALLOUT, OUR PROJECT TO CONTAIN THE DIZHIS WAS SHELVED.
THEY HAD ME OVER A LEDGE. THE DEATH OF SO MANY AGENTS WAS WRITTEN UP AS AN UNFORGIVABLE FAILURE. I WAS OUT.
FBI
BUT I WASN'T ABOUT TO GIVE UP. I NEVER QUIT A MISSION. SO I CAME HERE WAITING FOR YOU. I KEPT AN EYE ON YOUR GIRL, LISA. I MEAN, NO ONE FORGETS THEIR FIRST LOVE, RIGHT?

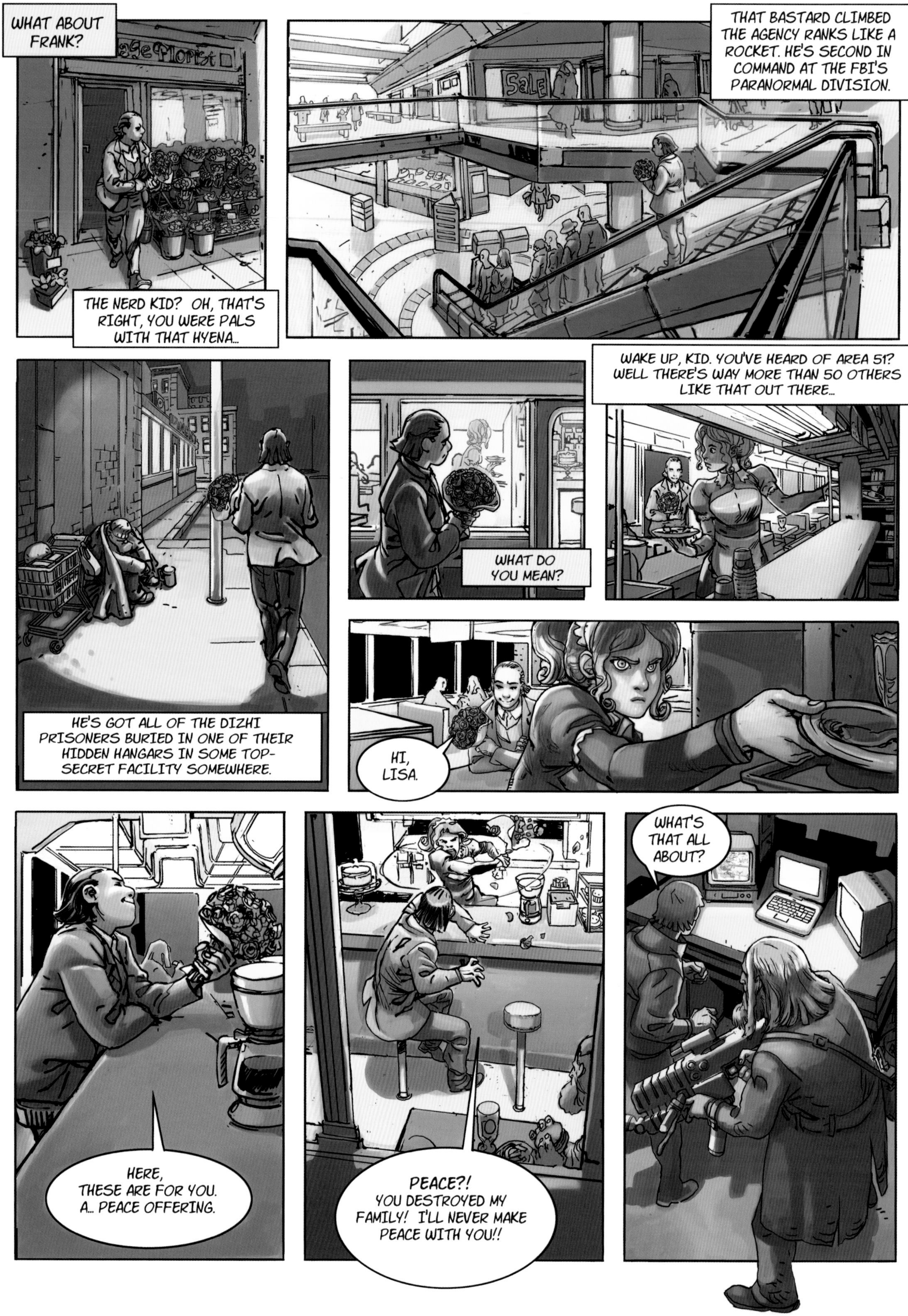
WHAT ABOUT FRANK?
THE NERD KID? OH, THAT'S RIGHT, YOU WERE PALS WITH THAT HYENA...
THAT BASTARD CLIMBED THE AGENCY RANKS LIKE A ROCKET. HE'S SECOND IN COMMAND AT THE FBI'S PARANORMAL DIVISION.
HE'S GOT ALL OF THE DIZHI PRISONERS BURIED IN ONE OF THEIR HIDDEN HANGARS IN SOME TOP-SECRET FACILITY SOMEWHERE.
WHAT DO YOU MEAN?
WAKE UP, KID. YOU'VE HEARD OF AREA 51? WELL THERE'S WAY MORE THAN 50 OTHERS LIKE THAT OUT THERE...
HI, LISA.
HERE, THESE ARE FOR YOU. A... PEACE OFFERING.
PEACE?! YOU DESTROYED MY FAMILY! I'LL NEVER MAKE PEACE WITH YOU!!
WHAT'S THAT ALL ABOUT?

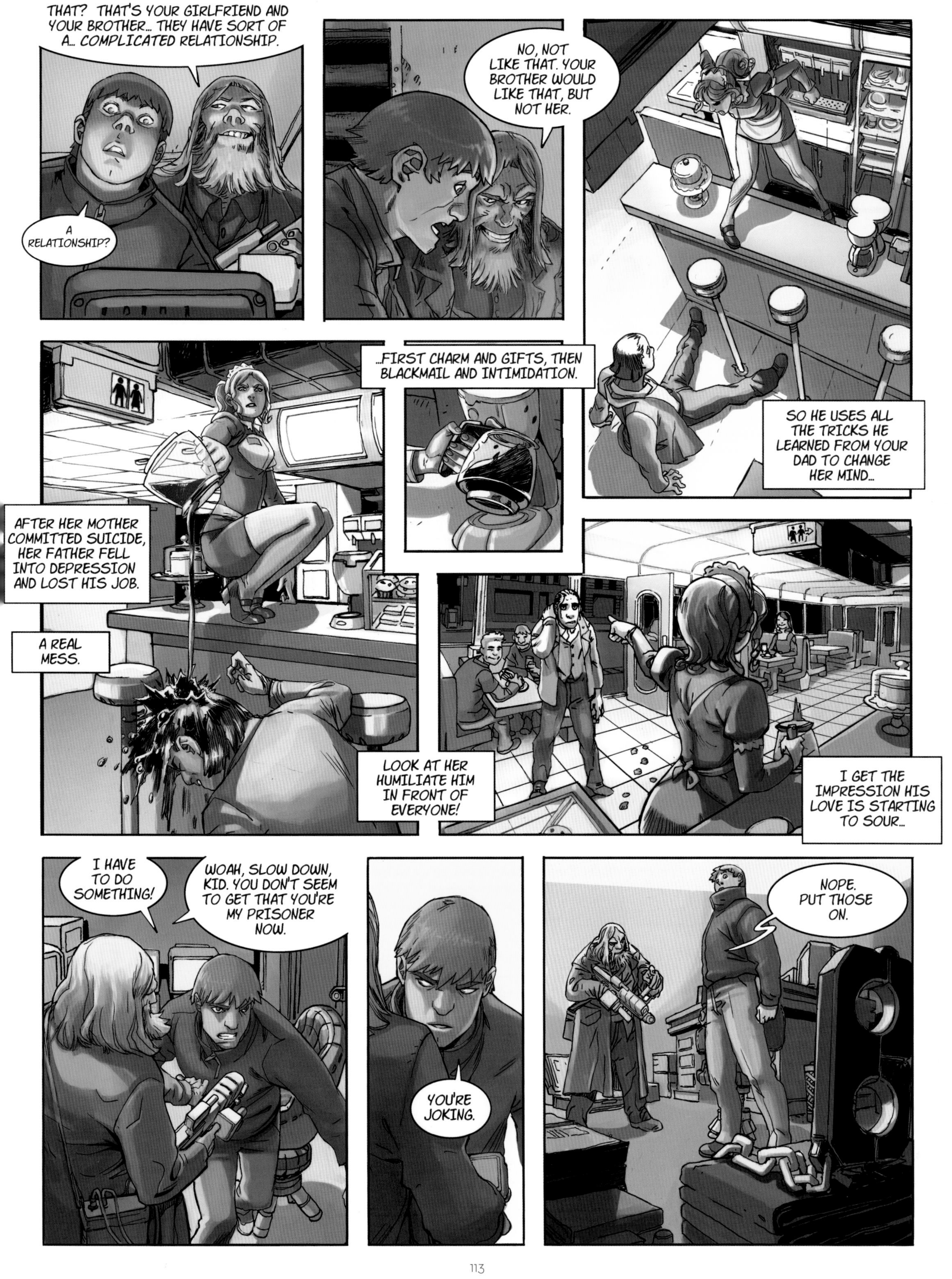
THAT? THAT'S YOUR GIRLFRIEND AND YOUR BROTHER... THEY HAVE SORT OF A... COMPLICATED RELATIONSHIP.
A RELATIONSHIP?
NO, NOT LIKE THAT. YOUR BROTHER WOULD LIKE THAT, BUT NOT HER.
SO HE USES ALL THE TRICKS HE LEARNED FROM YOUR DAD TO CHANGE HER MIND...
...FIRST CHARM AND GIFTS, THEN BLACKMAIL AND INTIMIDATION.
AFTER HER MOTHER COMMITTED SUICIDE, HER FATHER FELL INTO DEPRESSION AND LOST HIS JOB.
A REAL MESS.
LOOK AT HER HUMILIATE HIM IN FRONT OF EVERYONE!
I GET THE IMPRESSION HIS LOVE IS STARTING TO SOUR...
I HAVE TO DO SOMETHING!
WOAH, SLOW DOWN, KID. YOU DON'T SEEM TO GET THAT YOU'RE MY PRISONER NOW.
YOU'RE JOKING.
NOPE. PUT THOSE ON.

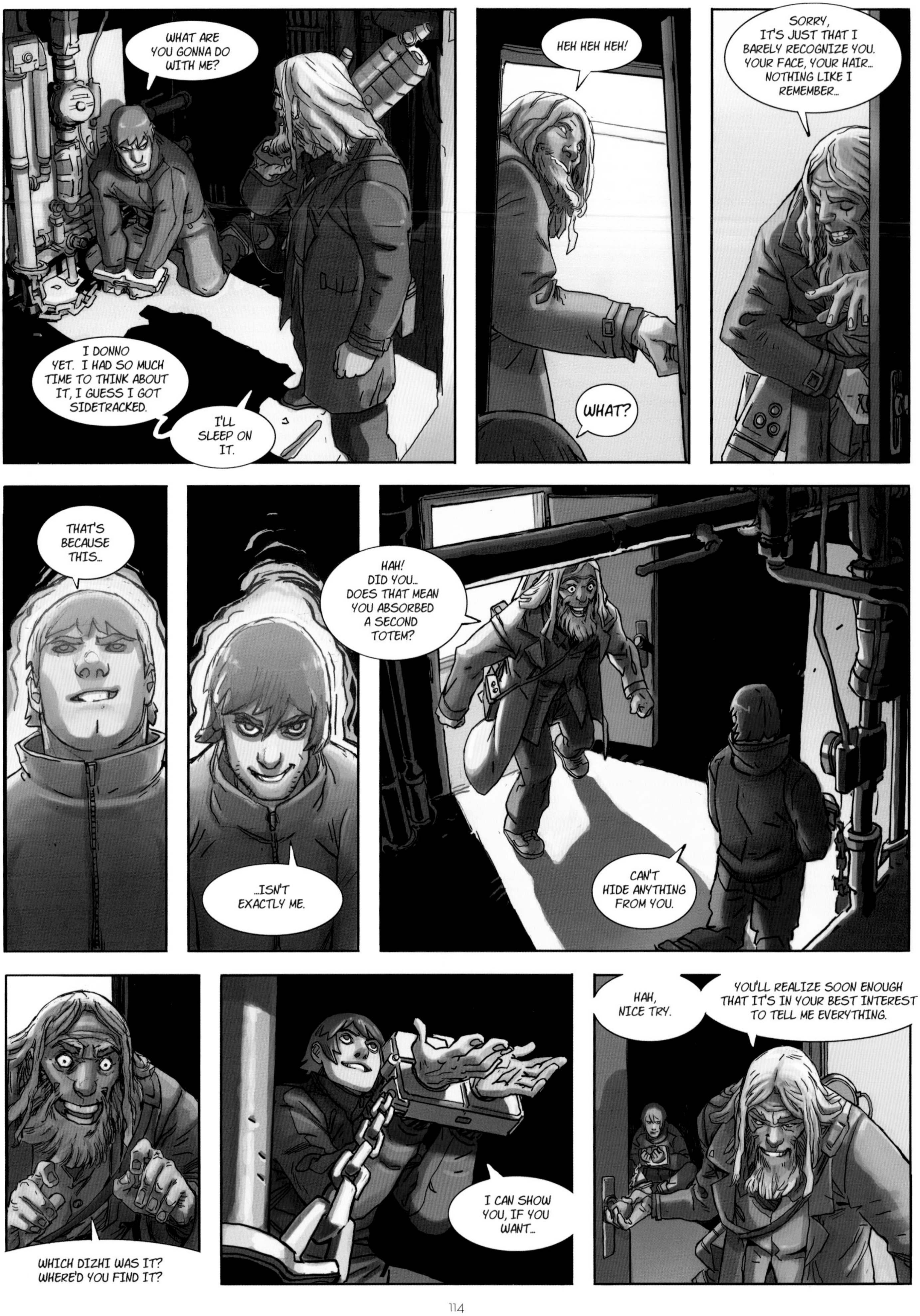
WHAT ARE YOU GONNA DO WITH ME?
I DONNO YET. I HAD SO MUCH TIME TO THINK ABOUT IT, I GUESS I GOT SIDETRACKED.
I'LL SLEEP ON IT.
HEH HEH HEH!
WHAT?
SORRY, IT'S JUST THAT I BARELY RECOGNIZE YOU. YOUR FACE, YOUR HAIR... NOTHING LIKE I REMEMBER...
THAT'S BECAUSE THIS...
...ISN'T EXACTLY ME.
HAH! DID YOU... DOES THAT MEAN YOU ABSORBED A SECOND TOTEM?
CAN'T HIDE ANYTHING FROM YOU.
WHICH DIZHI WAS IT? WHERE'D YOU FIND IT?
I CAN SHOW YOU, IF YOU WANT...
HAH, NICE TRY.
YOU'LL REALIZE SOON ENOUGH THAT IT'S IN YOUR BEST INTEREST TO TELL ME EVERYTHING.

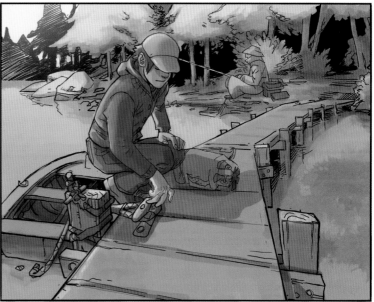

HEY, THERE...

I'M LOOKING FOR HORACIO ENICO...

MISTER?

THERE'S NO ONE BY THAT NAME ON THIS ISLAND.

THIS ISLAND'S PRIVATE PROPERTY.

I... BUT THIS IS THE ADDRESS I WAS GIVEN.

YOU GOT THE WRONG PLACE. GO HOME. YOU'RE NOT WELCOME HERE.

WAIT! I'VE COME A LONG WAY JUST TO GET HERE. IT'LL TAKE HOURS TO GET BACK TO TOWN. IT'LL BE DARK BY THEN.

CAN YOU PUT ME UP FOR THE NIGHT? I'LL LEAVE FIRST THING IN THE MORNING...

YOU SHOULDA THOUGHT OF THAT EARLIER. SORRY.

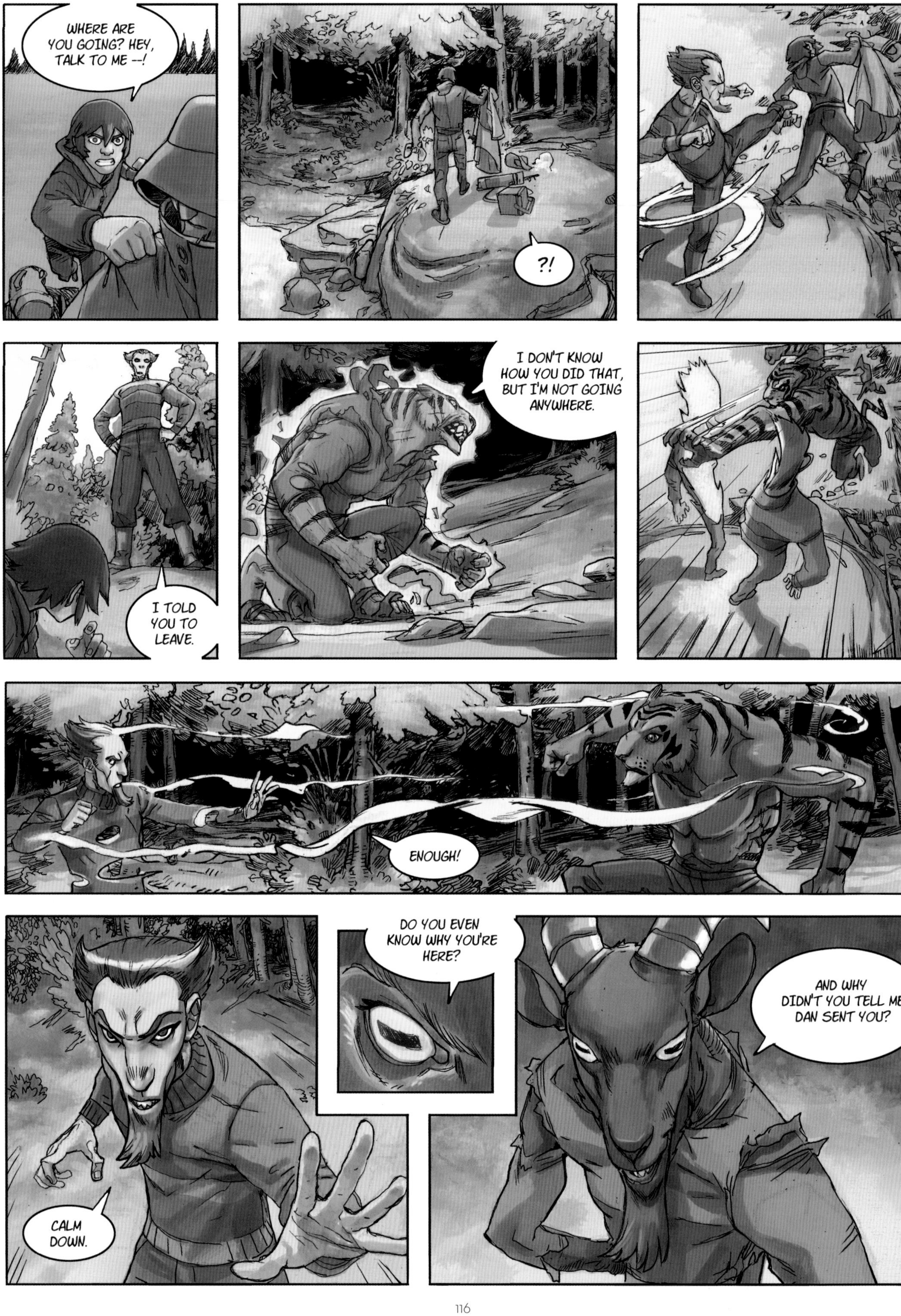
WHERE ARE YOU GOING? HEY, TALK TO ME --!
?!
I TOLD YOU TO LEAVE.
I DON'T KNOW HOW YOU DID THAT, BUT I'M NOT GOING ANYWHERE.
ENOUGH!
CALM DOWN.
DO YOU EVEN KNOW WHY YOU'RE HERE?
AND WHY DIDN'T YOU TELL ME DAN SENT YOU?

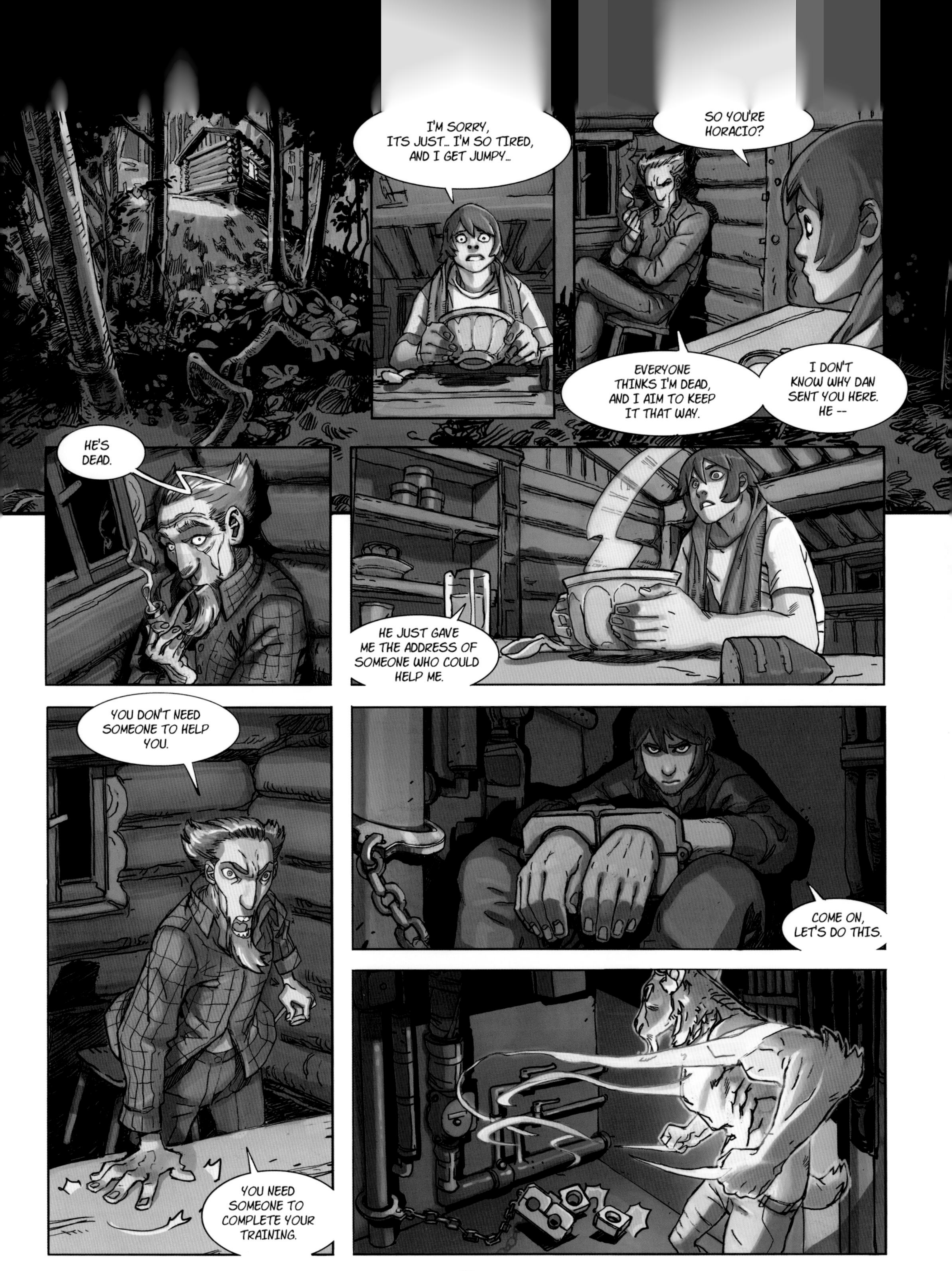

I'M SORRY,
ITS JUST... I'M SO TIRED,
AND I GET JUMPY...
SO YOU'RE
HORACIO?
EVERYONE
THINKS I'M DEAD,
AND I AIM TO KEEP
IT THAT WAY.
I DON'T
KNOW WHY DAN
SENT YOU HERE.
HE --
HE'S
DEAD.
HE JUST GAVE
ME THE ADDRESS OF
SOMEONE WHO COULD
HELP ME.
YOU DON'T NEED
SOMEONE TO HELP
YOU.
YOU NEED
SOMEONE TO
COMPLETE YOUR
TRAINING.
COME ON,
LET'S DO THIS.

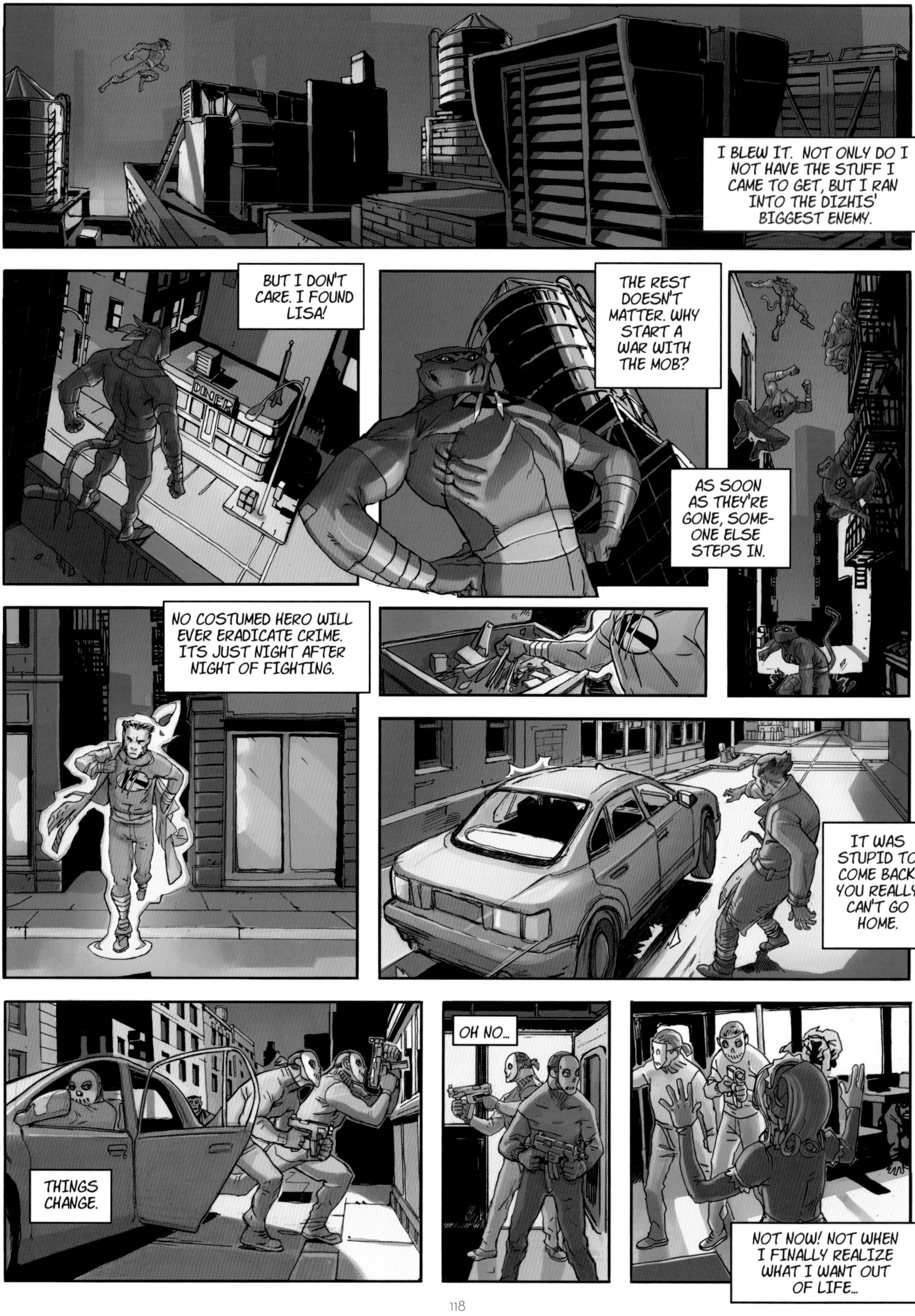
I BLEW IT. NOT ONLY DO I NOT HAVE THE STUFF I CAME TO GET, BUT I RAN INTO THE DIZHIS' BIGGEST ENEMY.
BUT I DON'T CARE. I FOUND LISA!
DINER
THE REST DOESN'T MATTER. WHY START A WAR WITH THE MOB?
AS SOON AS THEY'RE GONE, SOME-ONE ELSE STEPS IN.
NO COSTUMED HERO WILL EVER ERADICATE CRIME. ITS JUST NIGHT AFTER NIGHT OF FIGHTING.
IT WAS STUPID TO COME BACK. YOU REALLY CAN'T GO HOME.
THINGS CHANGE.
OH NO...
NOT NOW! NOT WHEN I FINALLY REALIZE WHAT I WANT OUT OF LIFE...

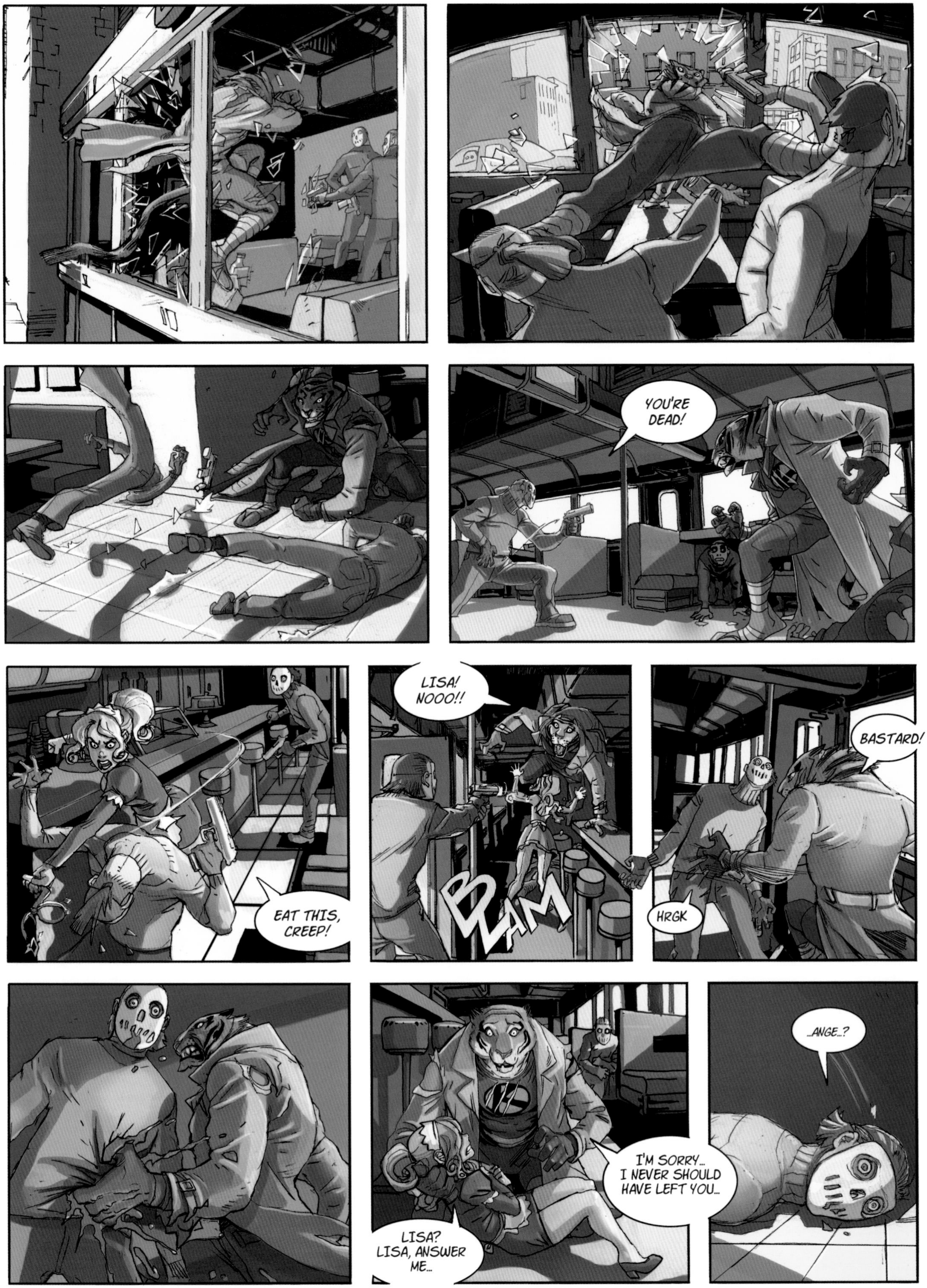
YOU'RE DEAD!
EAT THIS, CREEP!
LISA! NOOO!!
BLAM
BASTARD!
HRGK
I'M SORRY... I NEVER SHOULD HAVE LEFT YOU...
LISA? LISA, ANSWER ME...
...ANGE...?

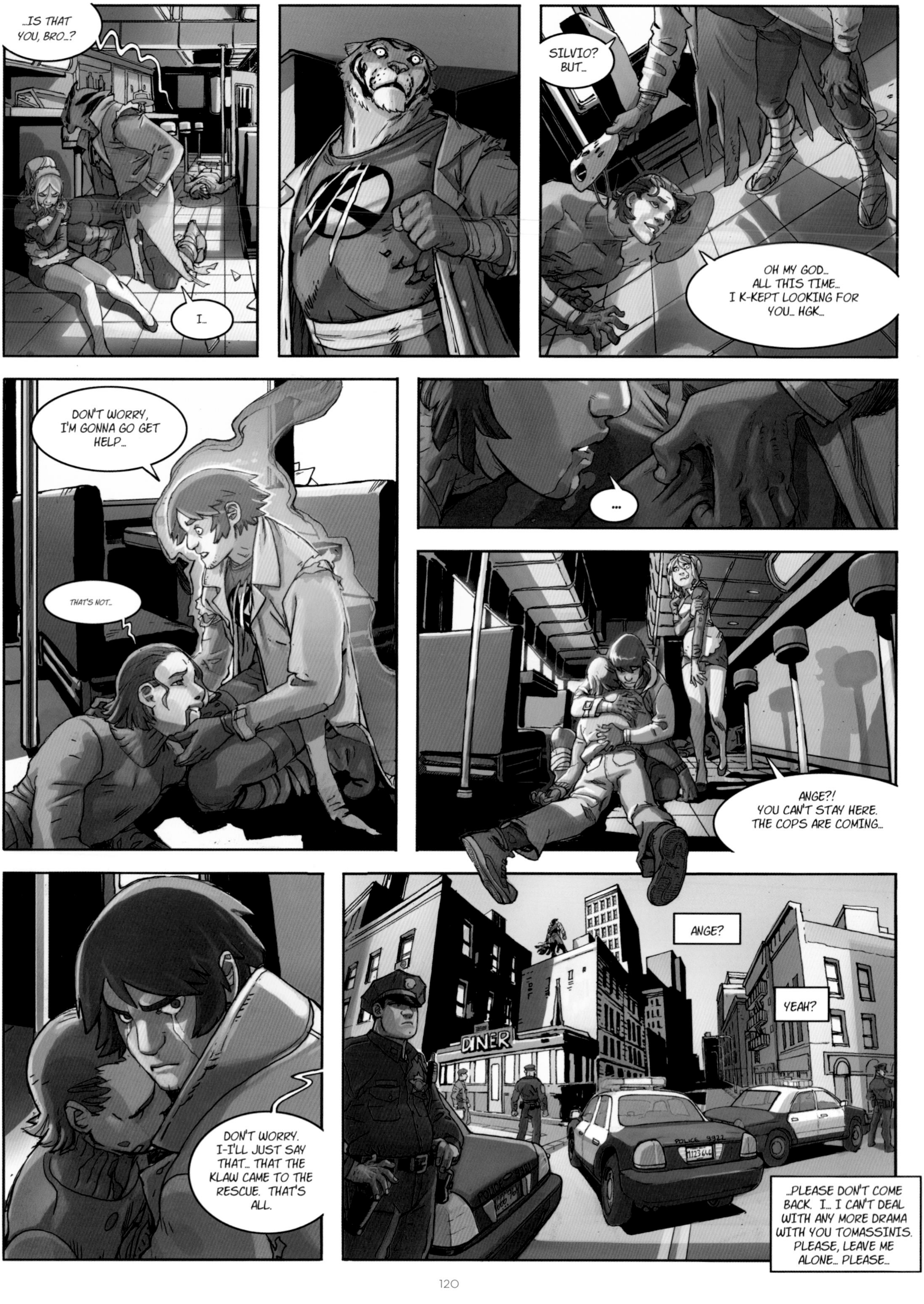
...IS THAT YOU, BRO...?
I...
SILVIO? BUT...
OH MY GOD... ALL THIS TIME... I K-KEPT LOOKING FOR YOU... HGK...
DON'T WORRY, I'M GONNA GO GET HELP...
THAT'S NOT...
...
ANGE?! YOU CAN'T STAY HERE. THE COPS ARE COMING...
DON'T WORRY. I-I'LL JUST SAY THAT... THAT THE KLAW CAME TO THE RESCUE. THAT'S ALL.
ANGE?
YEAH?
DINER
...PLEASE DON'T COME BACK. I... I CAN'T DEAL WITH ANY MORE DRAMA WITH YOU TOMASSINIS. PLEASE, LEAVE ME ALONE... PLEASE...

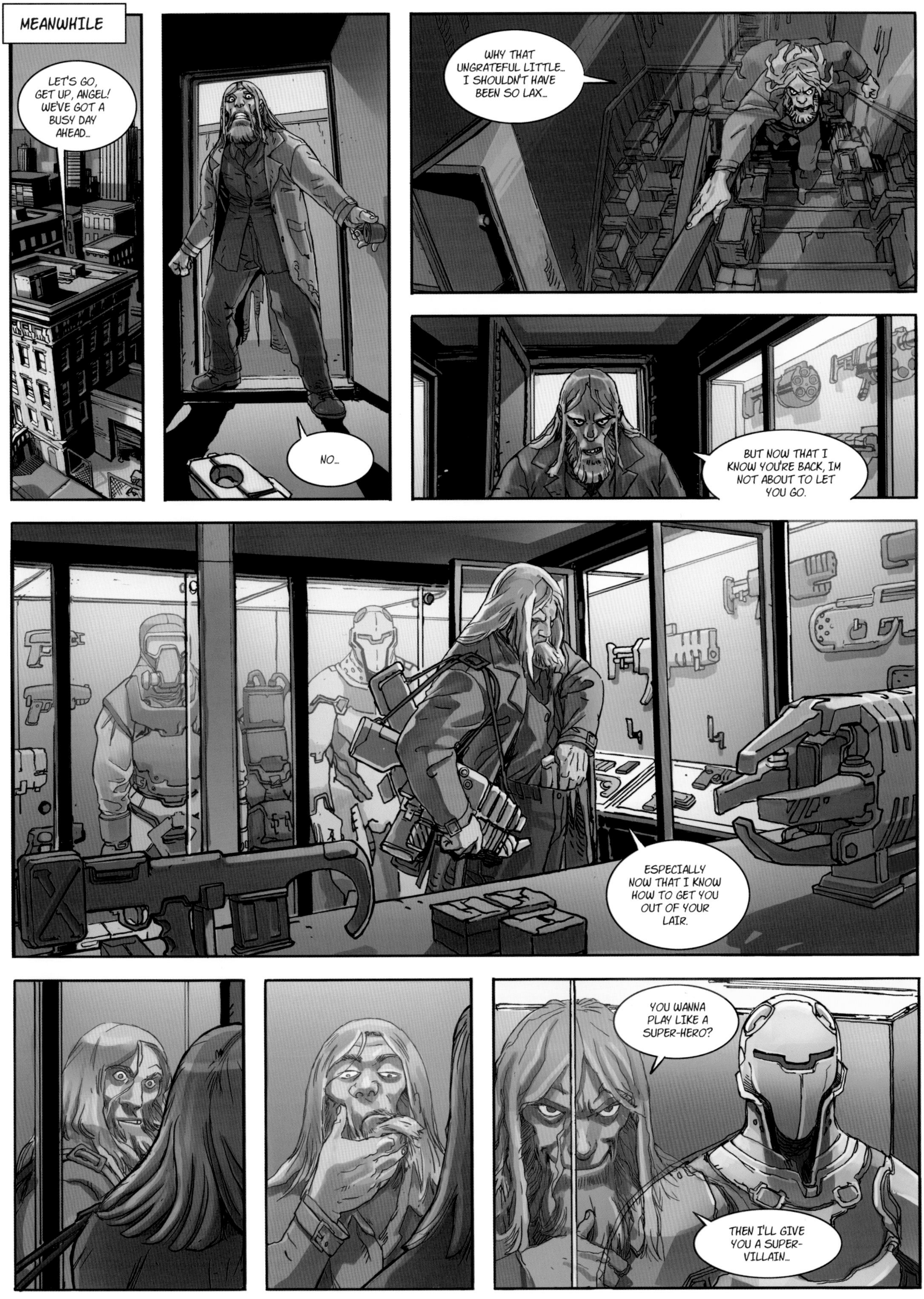
MEANWHILE
LET'S GO, GET UP, ANGEL! WE'VE GOT A BUSY DAY AHEAD...
NO...
WHY THAT UNGRATEFUL LITTLE... I SHOULDN'T HAVE BEEN SO LAX...
BUT NOW THAT I KNOW YOU'RE BACK, IM NOT ABOUT TO LET YOU GO.
ESPECIALLY NOW THAT I KNOW HOW TO GET YOU OUT OF YOUR LAIR.
YOU WANNA PLAY LIKE A SUPER-HERO?
THEN I'LL GIVE YOU A SUPER-VILLAIN...

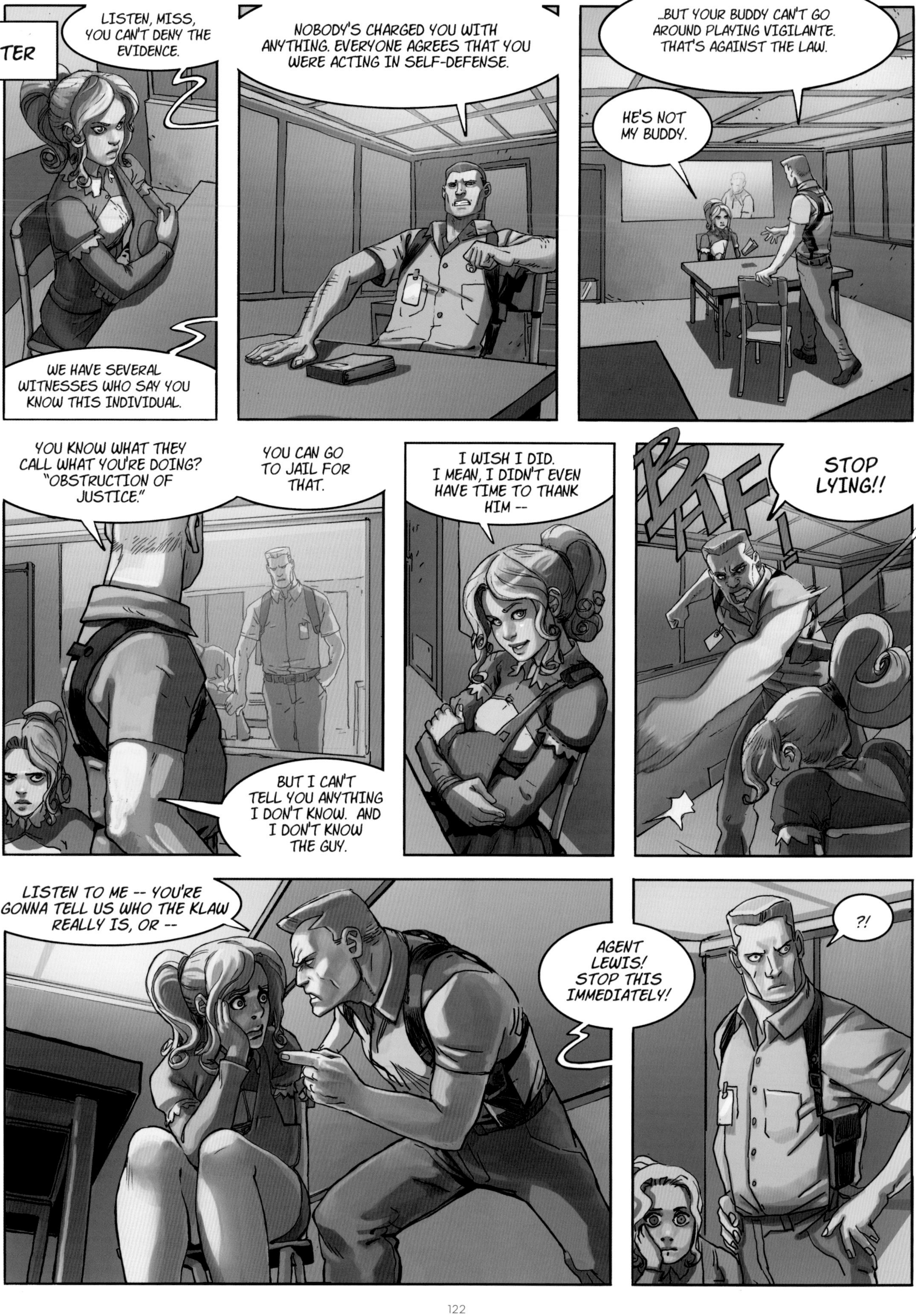
LATER
LISTEN, MISS, YOU CAN'T DENY THE EVIDENCE.
WE HAVE SEVERAL WITNESSES WHO SAY YOU KNOW THIS INDIVIDUAL.
NOBODY'S CHARGED YOU WITH ANYTHING. EVERYONE AGREES THAT YOU WERE ACTING IN SELF-DEFENSE.
...BUT YOUR BUDDY CAN'T GO AROUND PLAYING VIGILANTE. THAT'S AGAINST THE LAW.
HE'S NOT MY BUDDY.
YOU KNOW WHAT THEY CALL WHAT YOU'RE DOING? "OBSTRUCTION OF JUSTICE."
YOU CAN GO TO JAIL FOR THAT.
BUT I CAN'T TELL YOU ANYTHING I DON'T KNOW. AND I DON'T KNOW THE GUY.
I WISH I DID. I MEAN, I DIDN'T EVEN HAVE TIME TO THANK HIM --
BAF!
STOP LYING!!
LISTEN TO ME -- YOU'RE GONNA TELL US WHO THE KLAW REALLY IS, OR --
AGENT LEWIS! STOP THIS IMMEDIATELY!
?!

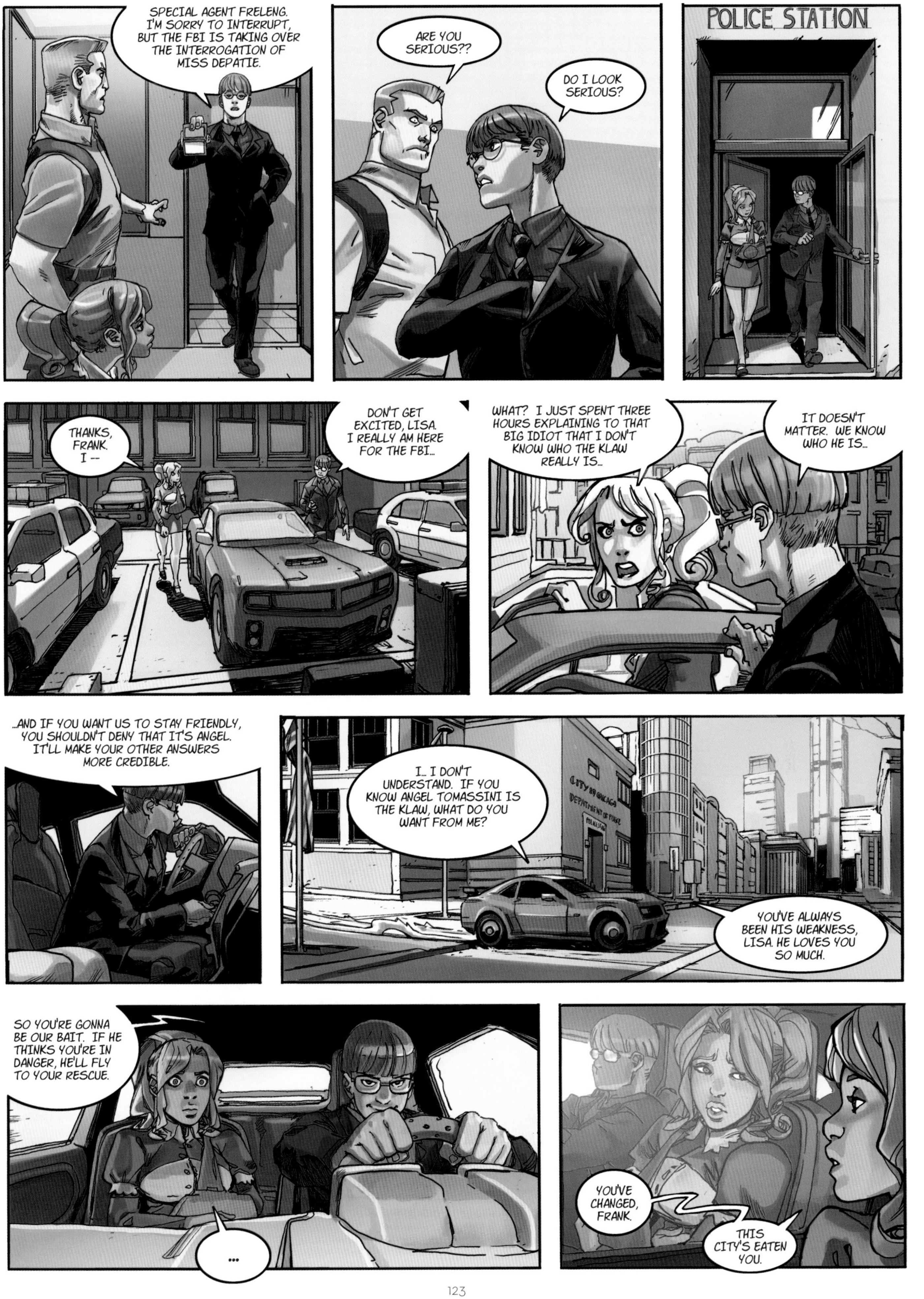

SPECIAL AGENT FRELENG. I'M SORRY TO INTERRUPT, BUT THE FBI IS TAKING OVER THE INTERROGATION OF MISS DEPATIE.
ARE YOU SERIOUS??
DO I LOOK SERIOUS?
POLICE STATION
THANKS, FRANK. I --
DON'T GET EXCITED, LISA. I REALLY AM HERE FOR THE FBI...
WHAT? I JUST SPENT THREE HOURS EXPLAINING TO THAT BIG IDIOT THAT I DON'T KNOW WHO THE KLAW REALLY IS...
IT DOESN'T MATTER. WE KNOW WHO HE IS...
...AND IF YOU WANT US TO STAY FRIENDLY, YOU SHOULDN'T DENY THAT IT'S ANGEL. IT'LL MAKE YOUR OTHER ANSWERS MORE CREDIBLE.
I... I DON'T UNDERSTAND. IF YOU KNOW ANGEL TOMASSINI IS THE KLAW, WHAT DO YOU WANT FROM ME?
YOU'VE ALWAYS BEEN HIS WEAKNESS, LISA. HE LOVES YOU SO MUCH.
SO YOU'RE GONNA BE OUR BAIT. IF HE THINKS YOU'RE IN DANGER, HE'LL FLY TO YOUR RESCUE.
...
YOU'VE CHANGED, FRANK.
THIS CITY'S EATEN YOU.

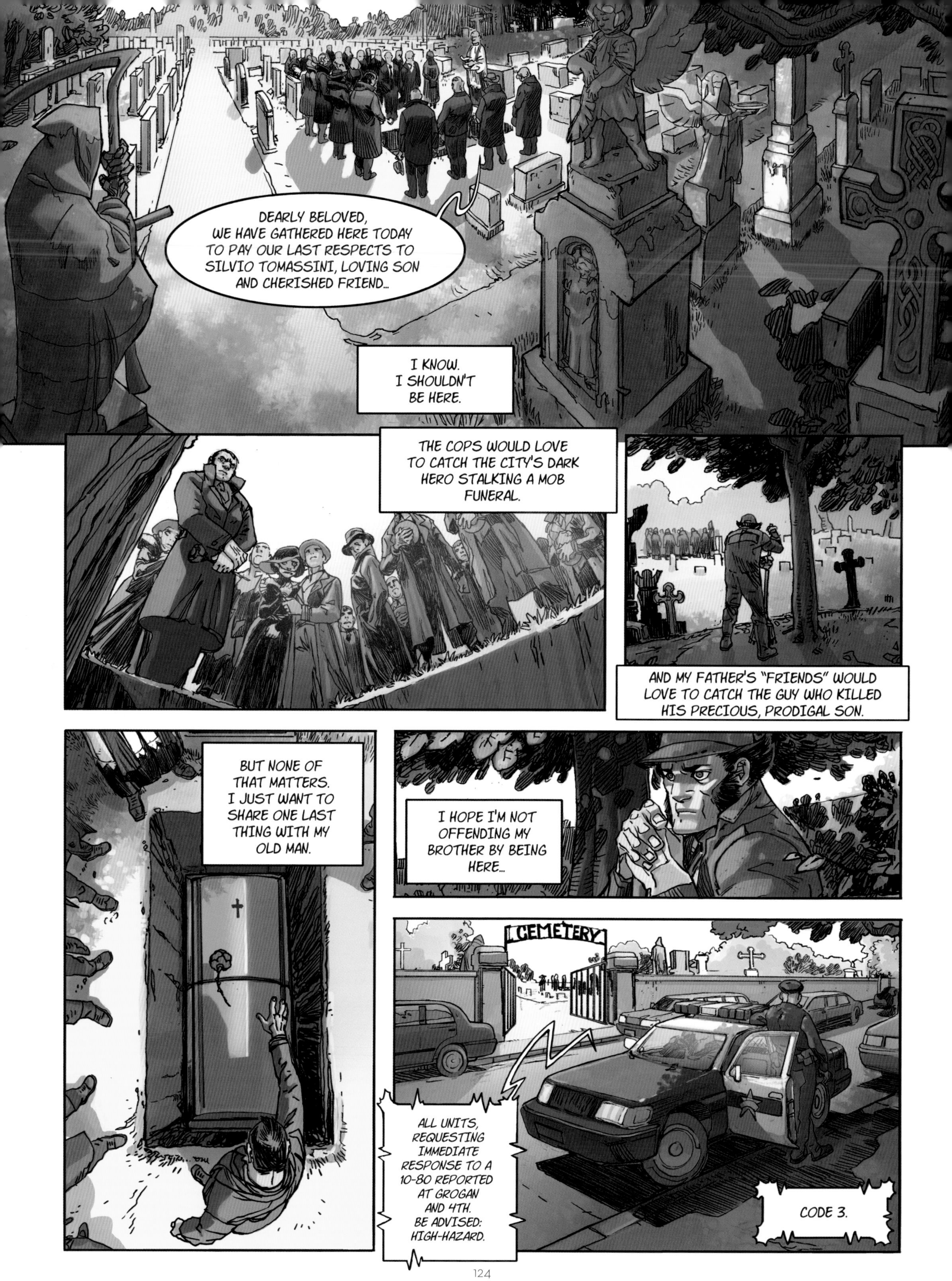
DEARLY BELOVED, WE HAVE GATHERED HERE TODAY TO PAY OUR LAST RESPECTS TO SILVIO TOMASSINI, LOVING SON AND CHERISHED FRIEND...
I KNOW. I SHOULDN'T BE HERE.
THE COPS WOULD LOVE TO CATCH THE CITY'S DARK HERO STALKING A MOB FUNERAL.
AND MY FATHER'S "FRIENDS" WOULD LOVE TO CATCH THE GUY WHO KILLED HIS PRECIOUS, PRODIGAL SON.
BUT NONE OF THAT MATTERS. I JUST WANT TO SHARE ONE LAST THING WITH MY OLD MAN.
I HOPE I'M NOT OFFENDING MY BROTHER BY BEING HERE...
CEMETERY
ALL UNITS, REQUESTING IMMEDIATE RESPONSE TO A 10-80 REPORTED AT GROGAN AND 4TH. BE ADVISED: HIGH-HAZARD.
CODE 3.

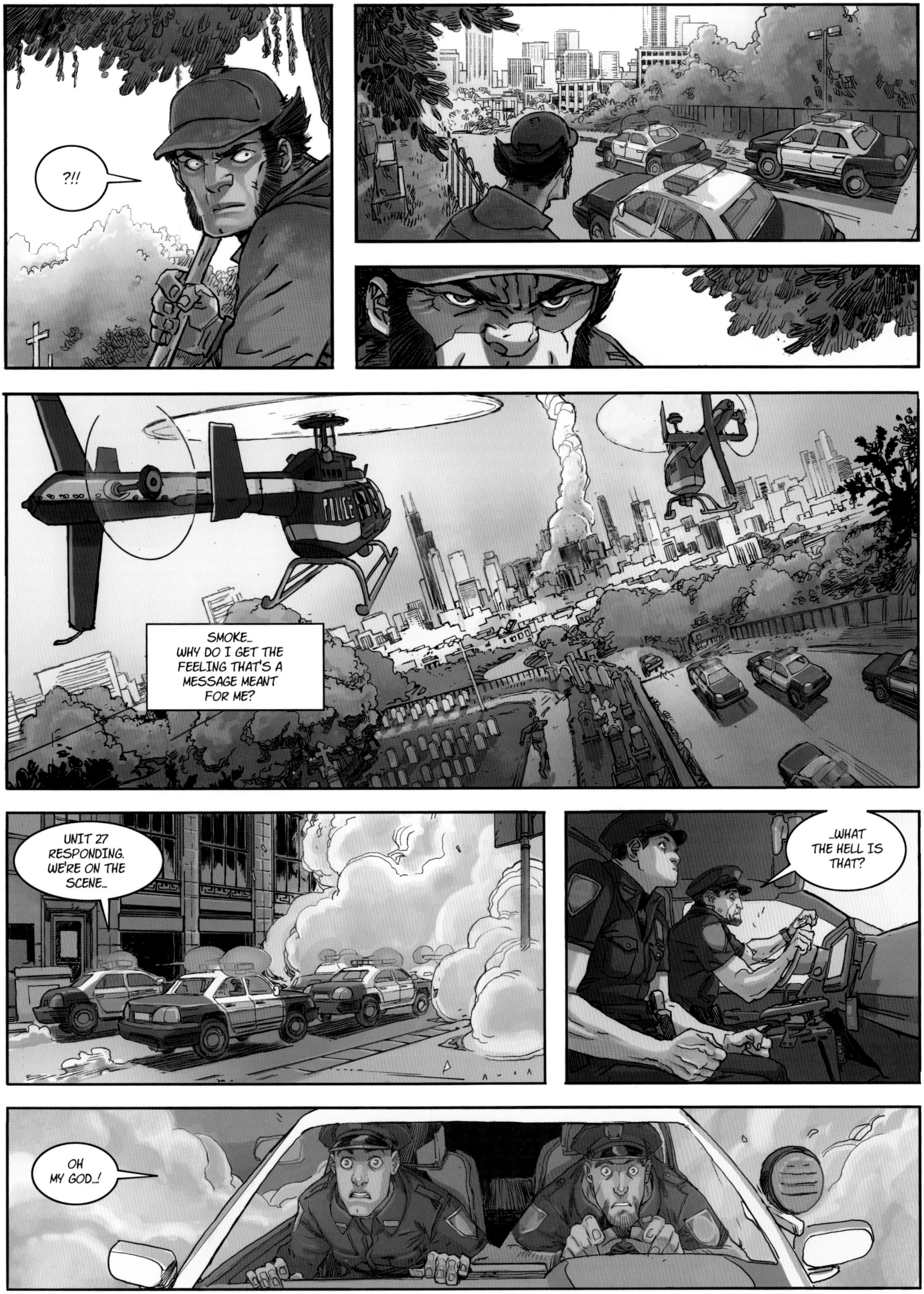
?!!
SMOKE... WHY DO I GET THE FEELING THAT'S A MESSAGE MEANT FOR ME?
POLICE
UNIT 27 RESPONDING. WE'RE ON THE SCENE...
...WHAT THE HELL IS THAT?
OH MY GOD...!

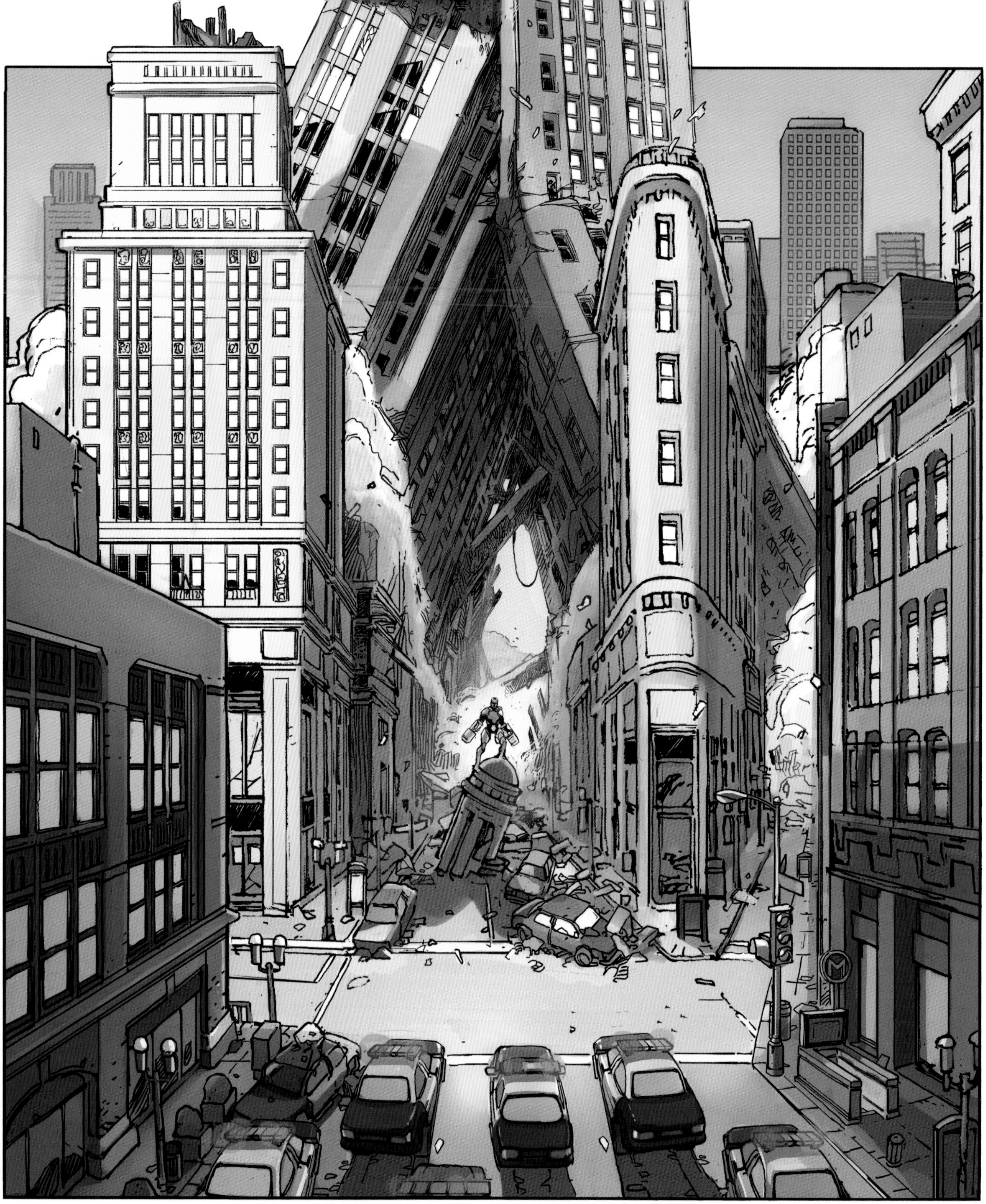

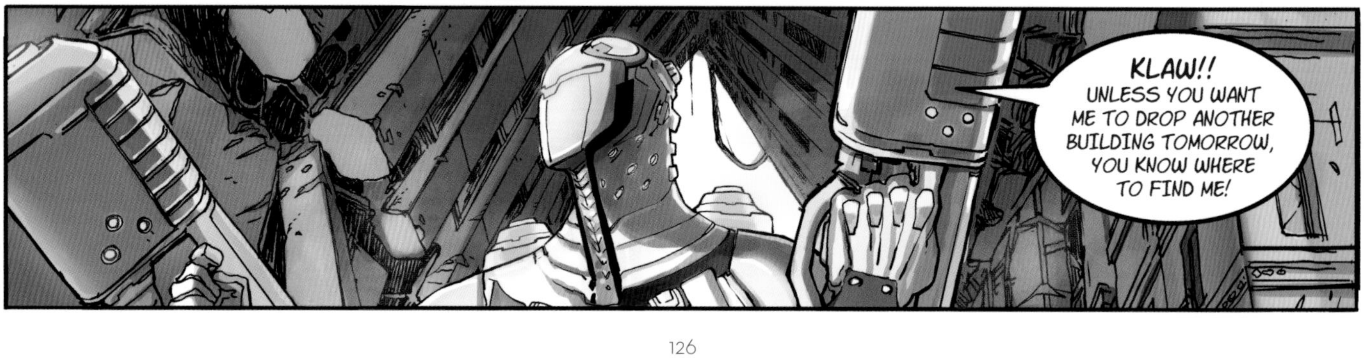
KLAW!! UNLESS YOU WANT ME TO DROP ANOTHER BUILDING TOMORROW, YOU KNOW WHERE TO FIND ME!

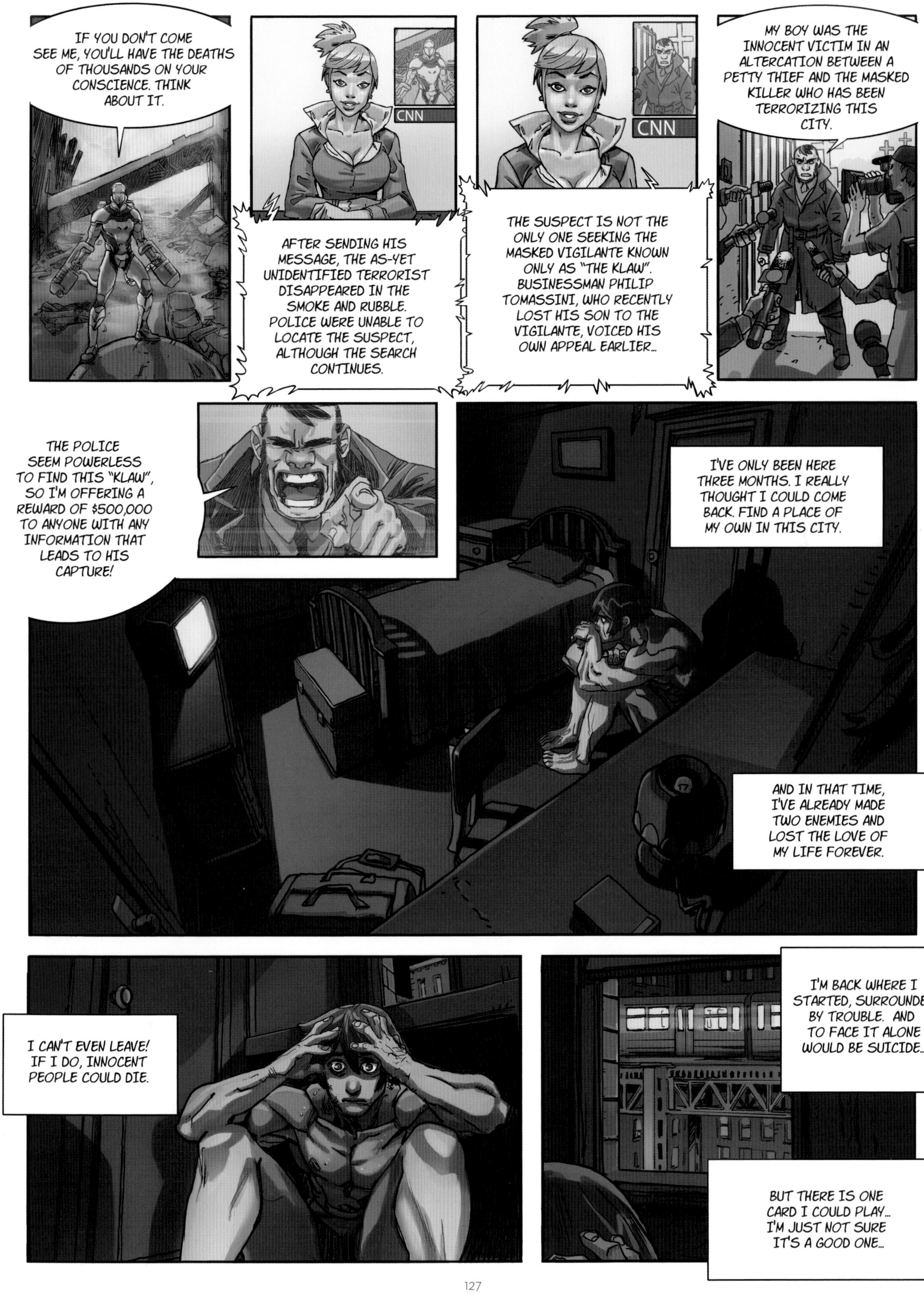

IF YOU DON'T COME SEE ME, YOU'LL HAVE THE DEATHS OF THOUSANDS ON YOUR CONSCIENCE. THINK ABOUT IT.
CNN
AFTER SENDING HIS MESSAGE, THE AS-YET UNIDENTIFIED TERRORIST DISAPPEARED IN THE SMOKE AND RUBBLE. POLICE WERE UNABLE TO LOCATE THE SUSPECT, ALTHOUGH THE SEARCH CONTINUES.
CNN
THE SUSPECT IS NOT THE ONLY ONE SEEKING THE MASKED VIGILANTE KNOWN ONLY AS "THE KLAW". BUSINESSMAN PHILIP TOMASSINI, WHO RECENTLY LOST HIS SON TO THE VIGILANTE, VOICED HIS OWN APPEAL EARLIER...
MY BOY WAS THE INNOCENT VICTIM IN AN ALTERCATION BETWEEN A PETTY THIEF AND THE MASKED KILLER WHO HAS BEEN TERRORIZING THIS CITY.
THE POLICE SEEM POWERLESS TO FIND THIS "KLAW", SO I'M OFFERING A REWARD OF $500,000 TO ANYONE WITH ANY INFORMATION THAT LEADS TO HIS CAPTURE!
I'VE ONLY BEEN HERE THREE MONTHS. I REALLY THOUGHT I COULD COME BACK. FIND A PLACE OF MY OWN IN THIS CITY.
AND IN THAT TIME, I'VE ALREADY MADE TWO ENEMIES AND LOST THE LOVE OF MY LIFE FOREVER.
I CAN'T EVEN LEAVE! IF I DO, INNOCENT PEOPLE COULD DIE.
I'M BACK WHERE I STARTED, SURROUNDED BY TROUBLE. AND TO FACE IT ALONE WOULD BE SUICIDE...
BUT THERE IS ONE CARD I COULD PLAY... I'M JUST NOT SURE IT'S A GOOD ONE...

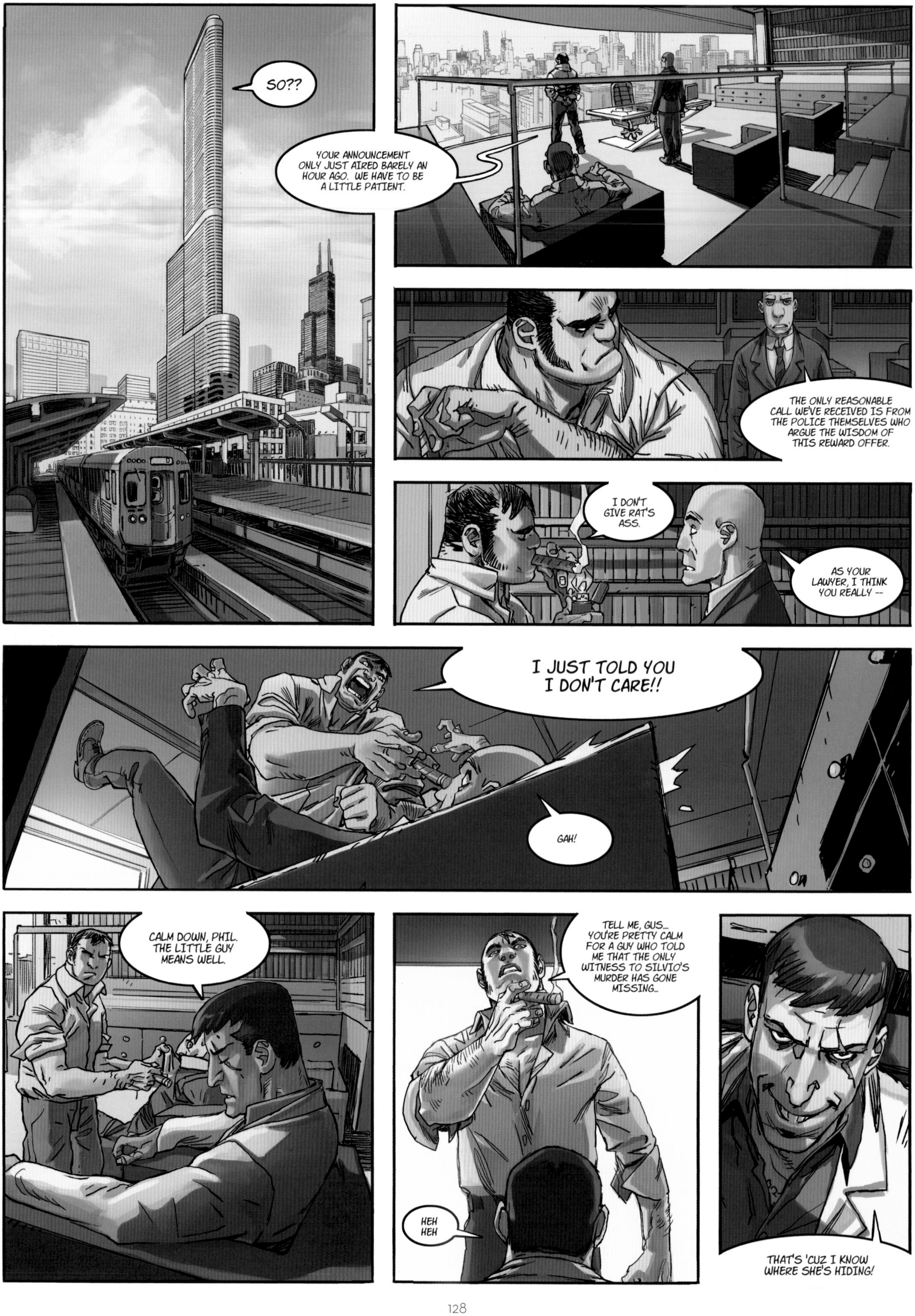
SO??
YOUR ANNOUNCEMENT ONLY JUST AIRED BARELY AN HOUR AGO. WE HAVE TO BE A LITTLE PATIENT.
THE ONLY REASONABLE CALL WE'VE RECEIVED IS FROM THE POLICE THEMSELVES WHO ARGUE THE WISDOM OF THIS REWARD OFFER.
I DON'T GIVE RAT'S ASS.
AS YOUR LAWYER, I THINK YOU REALLY --
I JUST TOLD YOU I DON'T CARE!!
GAH!
CALM DOWN, PHIL. THE LITTLE GUY MEANS WELL.
TELL ME, GUS... YOU'RE PRETTY CALM FOR A GUY WHO TOLD ME THAT THE ONLY WITNESS TO SILVIO'S MURDER HAS GONE MISSING...
HEH HEH
THAT'S 'CUZ I KNOW WHERE SHE'S HIDING!

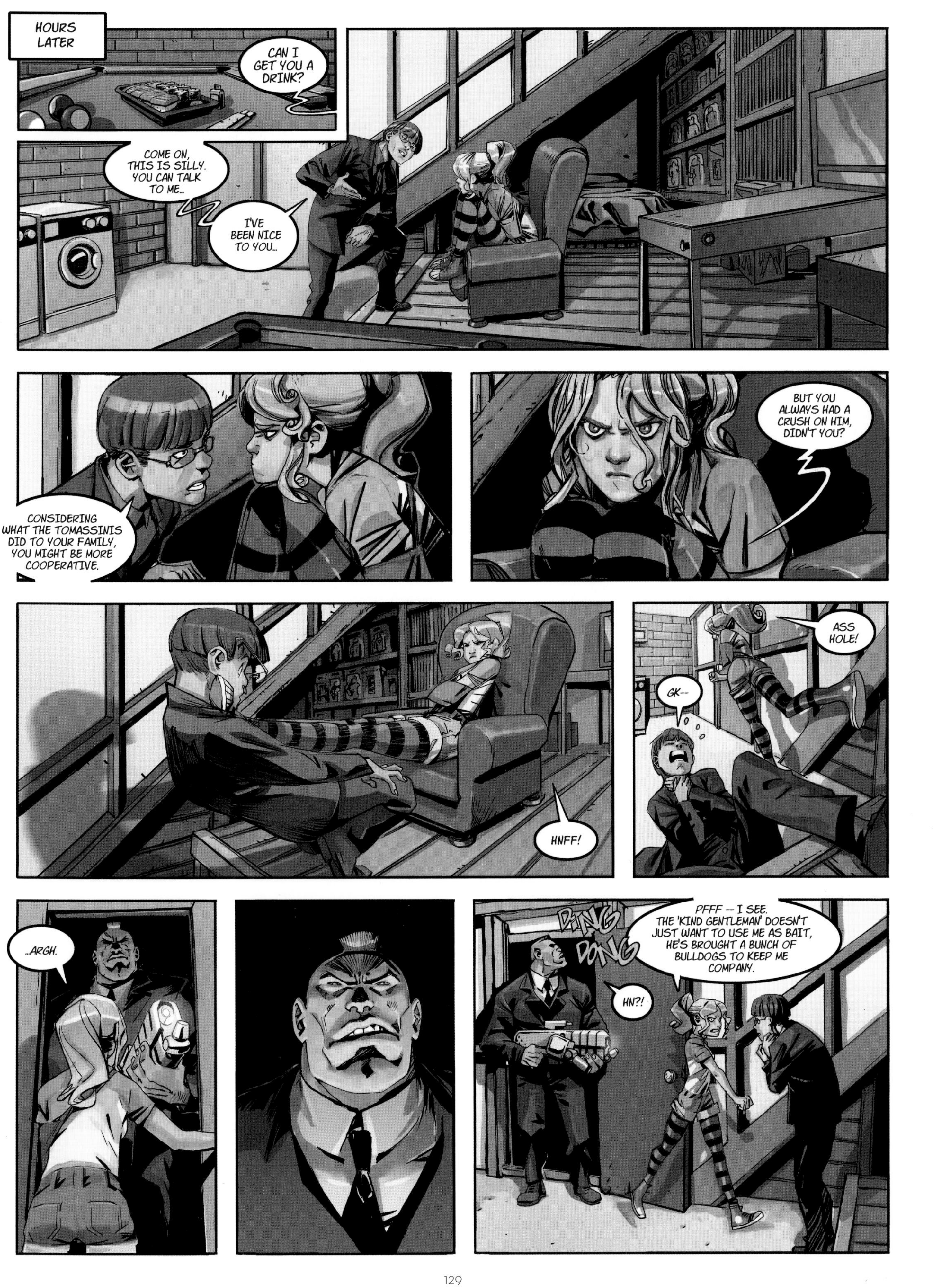
HOURS LATER
CAN I GET YOU A DRINK?
COME ON, THIS IS SILLY. YOU CAN TALK TO ME...
I'VE BEEN NICE TO YOU...
CONSIDERING WHAT THE TOMASSINIS DID TO YOUR FAMILY, YOU MIGHT BE MORE COOPERATIVE.
BUT YOU ALWAYS HAD A CRUSH ON HIM, DIDN'T YOU?
HNFF!
ASS HOLE!
GK--
...ARGH.
DING DONG
PFFF -- I SEE. THE 'KIND GENTLEMAN' DOESN'T JUST WANT TO USE ME AS BAIT, HE'S BROUGHT A BUNCH OF BULLDOGS TO KEEP ME COMPANY.
HN?!

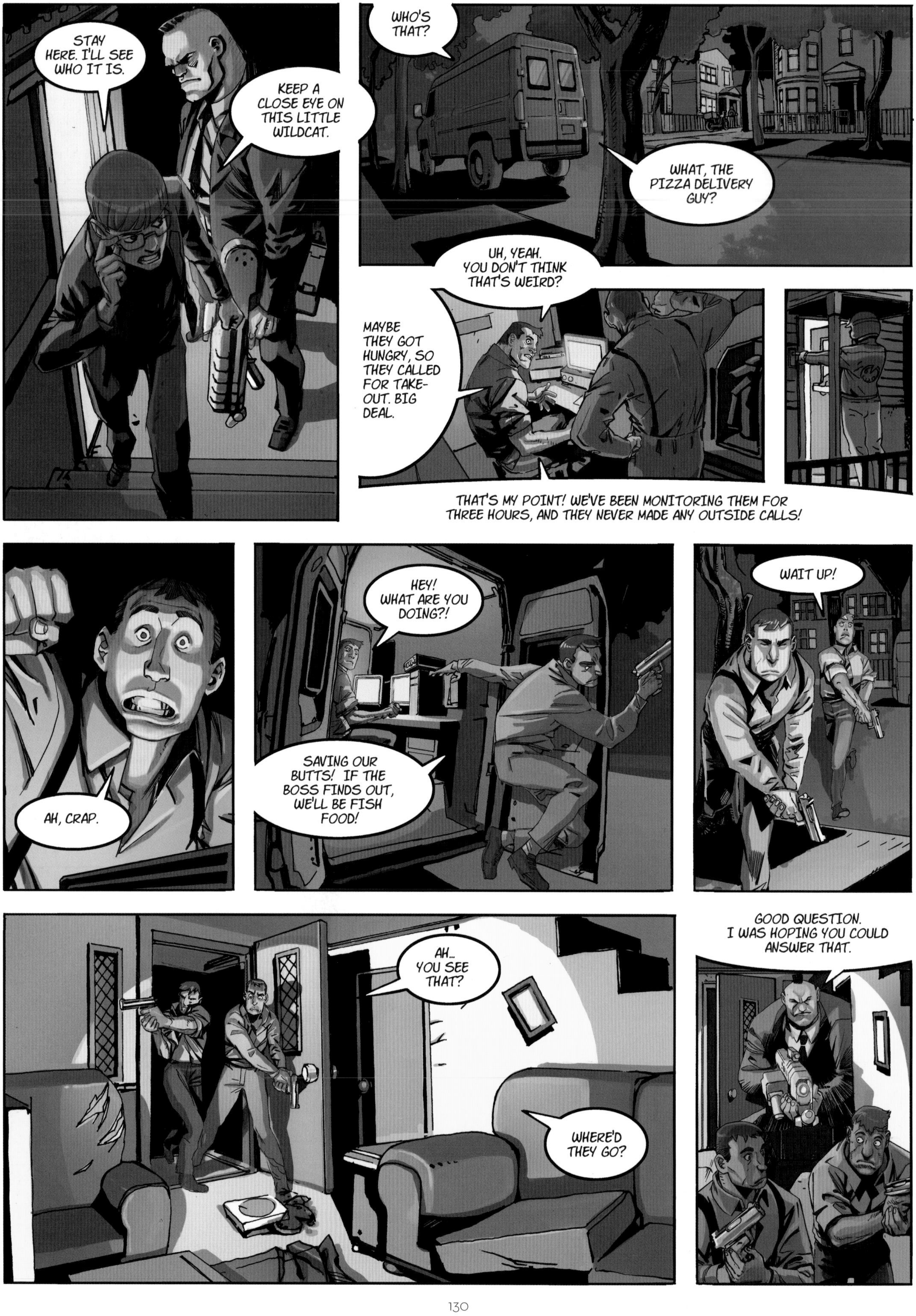
STAY HERE. I'LL SEE WHO IT IS.
KEEP A CLOSE EYE ON THIS LITTLE WILDCAT.
WHO'S THAT?
WHAT, THE PIZZA DELIVERY GUY?
UH, YEAH. YOU DON'T THINK THAT'S WEIRD?
MAYBE THEY GOT HUNGRY, SO THEY CALLED FOR TAKE-OUT. BIG DEAL.
THAT'S MY POINT! WE'VE BEEN MONITORING THEM FOR THREE HOURS, AND THEY NEVER MADE ANY OUTSIDE CALLS!
AH, CRAP.
HEY! WHAT ARE YOU DOING?!
SAVING OUR BUTTS! IF THE BOSS FINDS OUT, WE'LL BE FISH FOOD!
WAIT UP!
AH... YOU SEE THAT?
WHERE'D THEY GO?
GOOD QUESTION. I WAS HOPING YOU COULD ANSWER THAT.

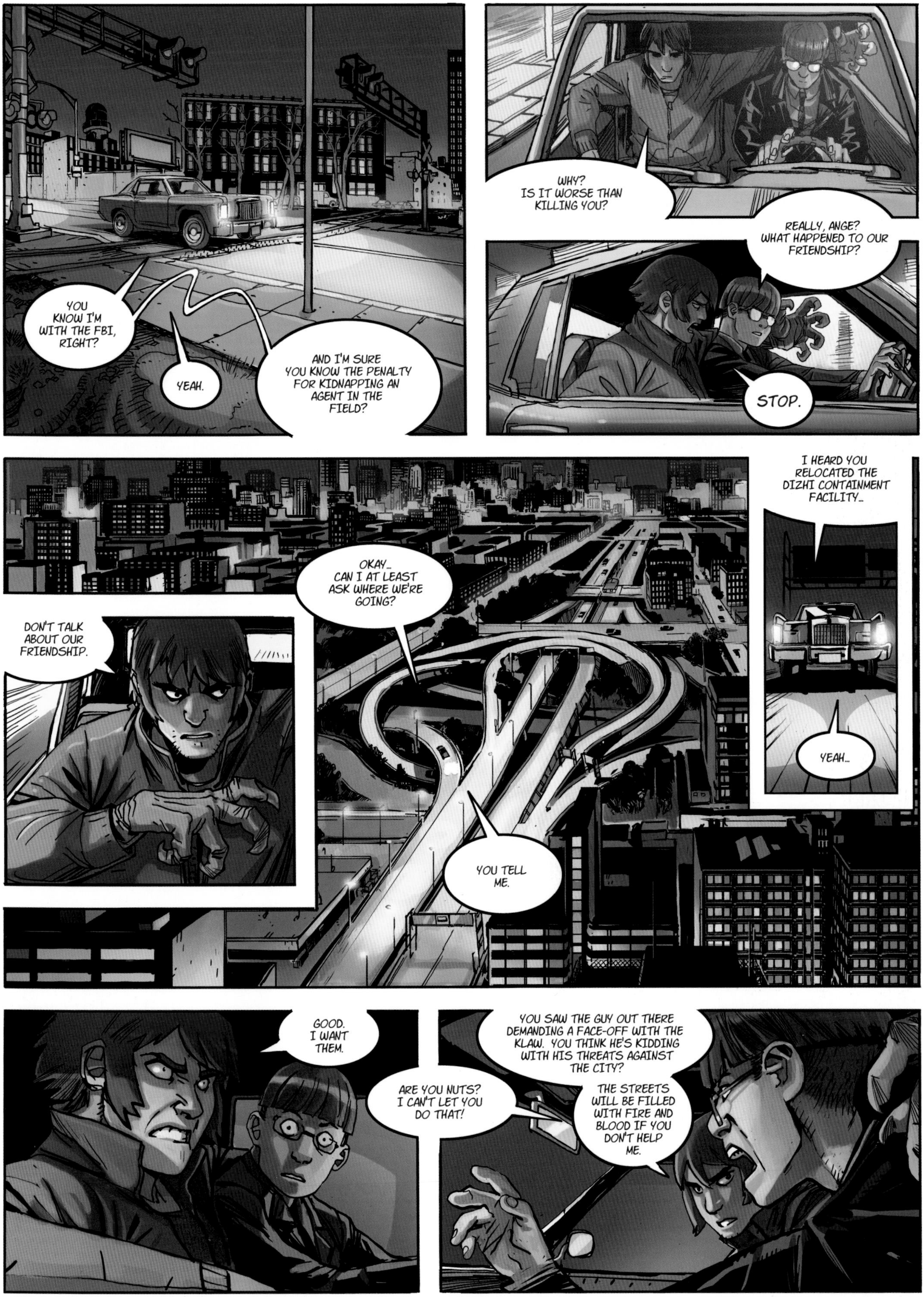

YOU KNOW I'M WITH THE FBI, RIGHT?
YEAH.
AND I'M SURE YOU KNOW THE PENALTY FOR KIDNAPPING AN AGENT IN THE FIELD?
WHY? IS IT WORSE THAN KILLING YOU?
REALLY, ANGE? WHAT HAPPENED TO OUR FRIENDSHIP?
STOP.
DON'T TALK ABOUT OUR FRIENDSHIP.
OKAY... CAN I AT LEAST ASK WHERE WE'RE GOING?
YOU TELL ME.
I HEARD YOU RELOCATED THE DIZHI CONTAINMENT FACILITY...
YEAH...
GOOD. I WANT THEM.
ARE YOU NUTS? I CAN'T LET YOU DO THAT!
YOU SAW THE GUY OUT THERE DEMANDING A FACE-OFF WITH THE KLAW. YOU THINK HE'S KIDDING WITH HIS THREATS AGAINST THE CITY?
THE STREETS WILL BE FILLED WITH FIRE AND BLOOD IF YOU DON'T HELP ME.

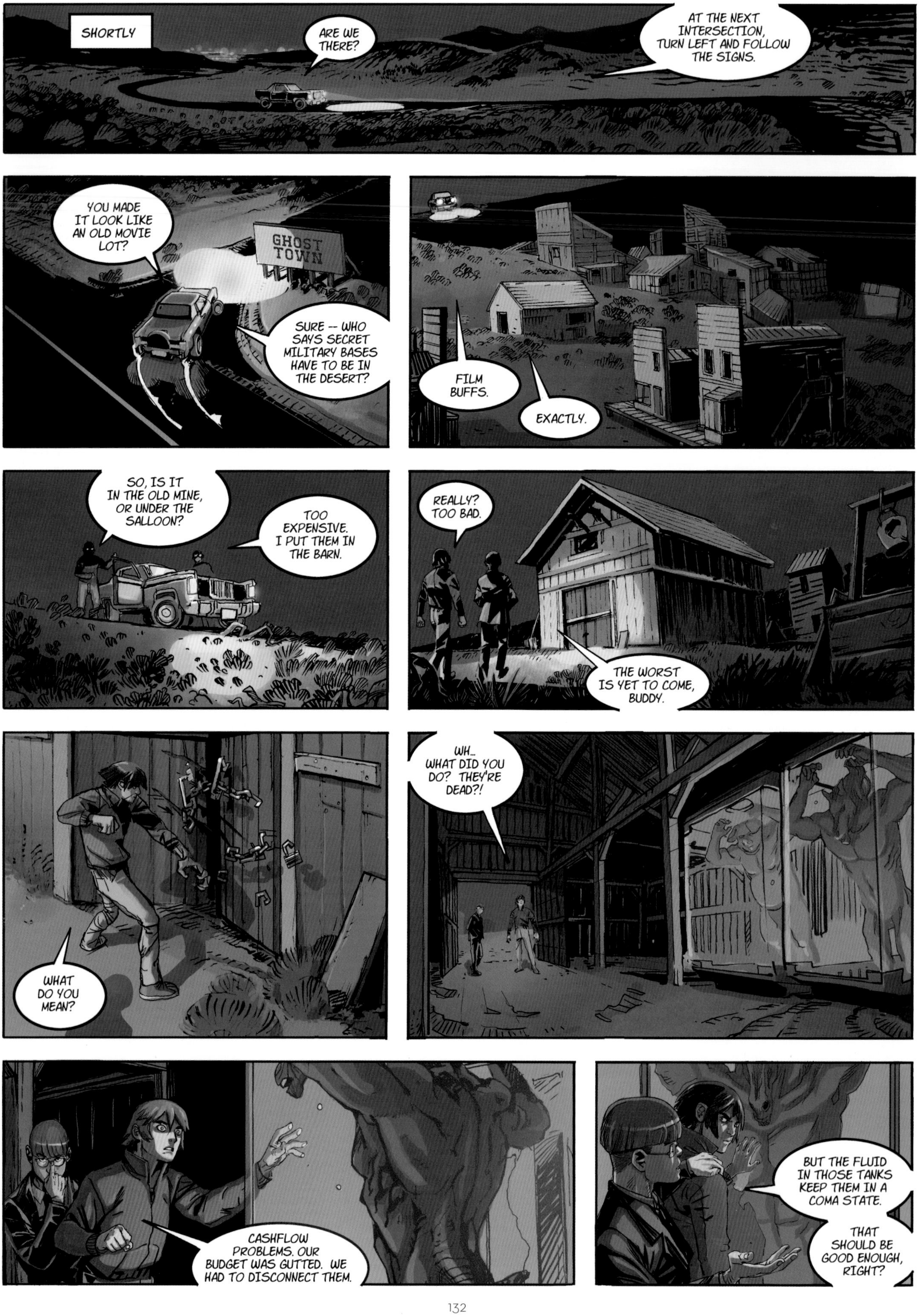
SHORTLY
ARE WE THERE?
AT THE NEXT INTERSECTION, TURN LEFT AND FOLLOW THE SIGNS.
YOU MADE IT LOOK LIKE AN OLD MOVIE LOT?
GHOST TOWN
SURE -- WHO SAYS SECRET MILITARY BASES HAVE TO BE IN THE DESERT?
FILM BUFFS.
EXACTLY.
SO, IS IT IN THE OLD MINE, OR UNDER THE SALOON?
TOO EXPENSIVE. I PUT THEM IN THE BARN.
REALLY? TOO BAD.
THE WORST IS YET TO COME, BUDDY.
WHAT DO YOU MEAN?
WH... WHAT DID YOU DO? THEY'RE DEAD?!
CASHFLOW PROBLEMS. OUR BUDGET WAS GUTTED. WE HAD TO DISCONNECT THEM.
BUT THE FLUID IN THOSE TANKS KEEP THEM IN A COMA STATE.
THAT SHOULD BE GOOD ENOUGH, RIGHT?

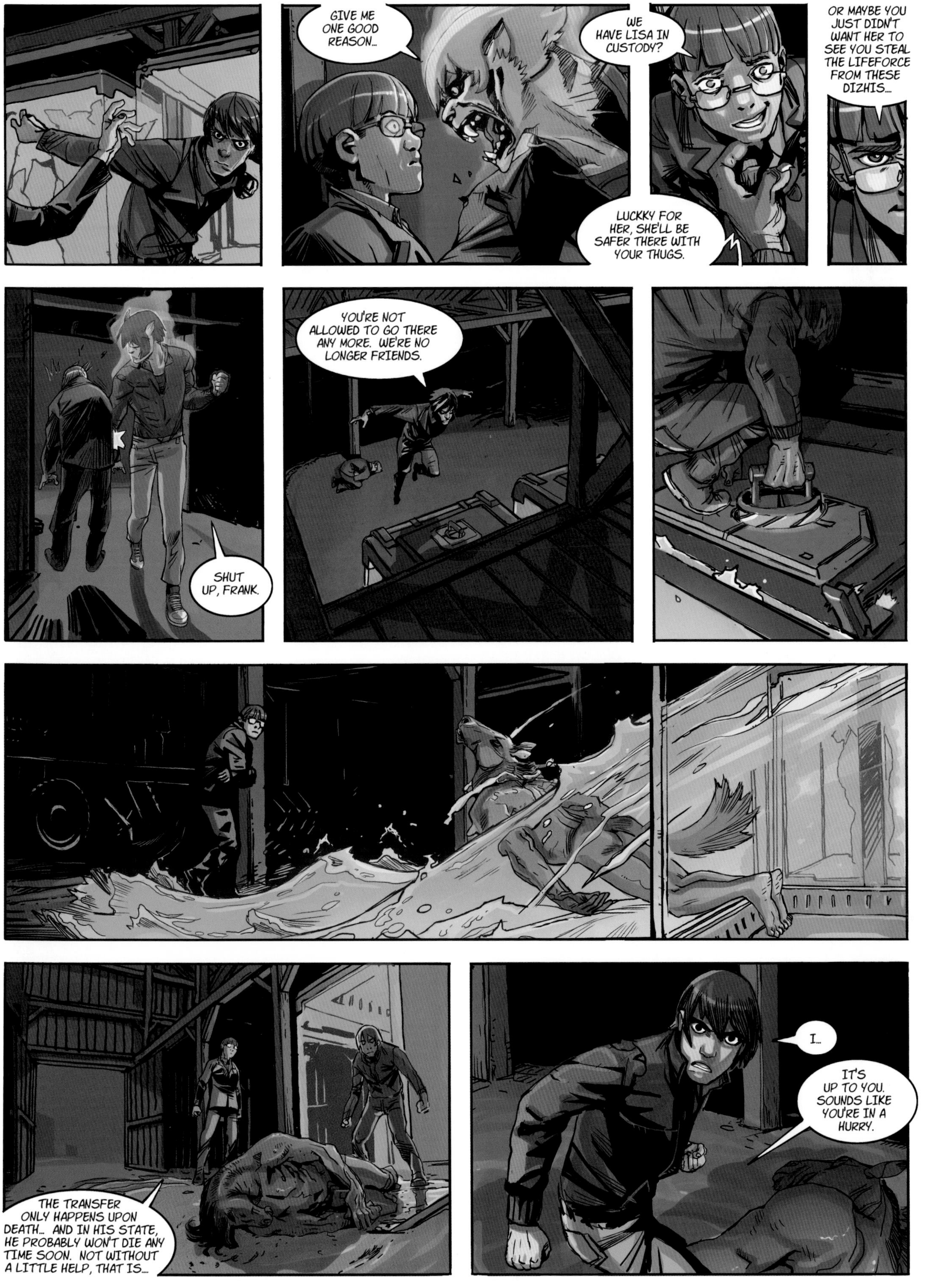
GIVE ME ONE GOOD REASON...
WE HAVE LISA IN CUSTODY?
LUCKKY FOR HER, SHE'LL BE SAFER THERE WITH YOUR THUGS.
OR MAYBE YOU JUST DIDN'T WANT HER TO SEE YOU STEAL THE LIFEFORCE FROM THESE DIZHIS...
SHUT UP, FRANK.
YOU'RE NOT ALLOWED TO GO THERE ANY MORE. WE'RE NO LONGER FRIENDS.
THE TRANSFER ONLY HAPPENS UPON DEATH... AND IN HIS STATE, HE PROBABLY WON'T DIE ANY TIME SOON. NOT WITHOUT A LITTLE HELP, THAT IS...
I...
IT'S UP TO YOU. SOUNDS LIKE YOU'RE IN A HURRY.

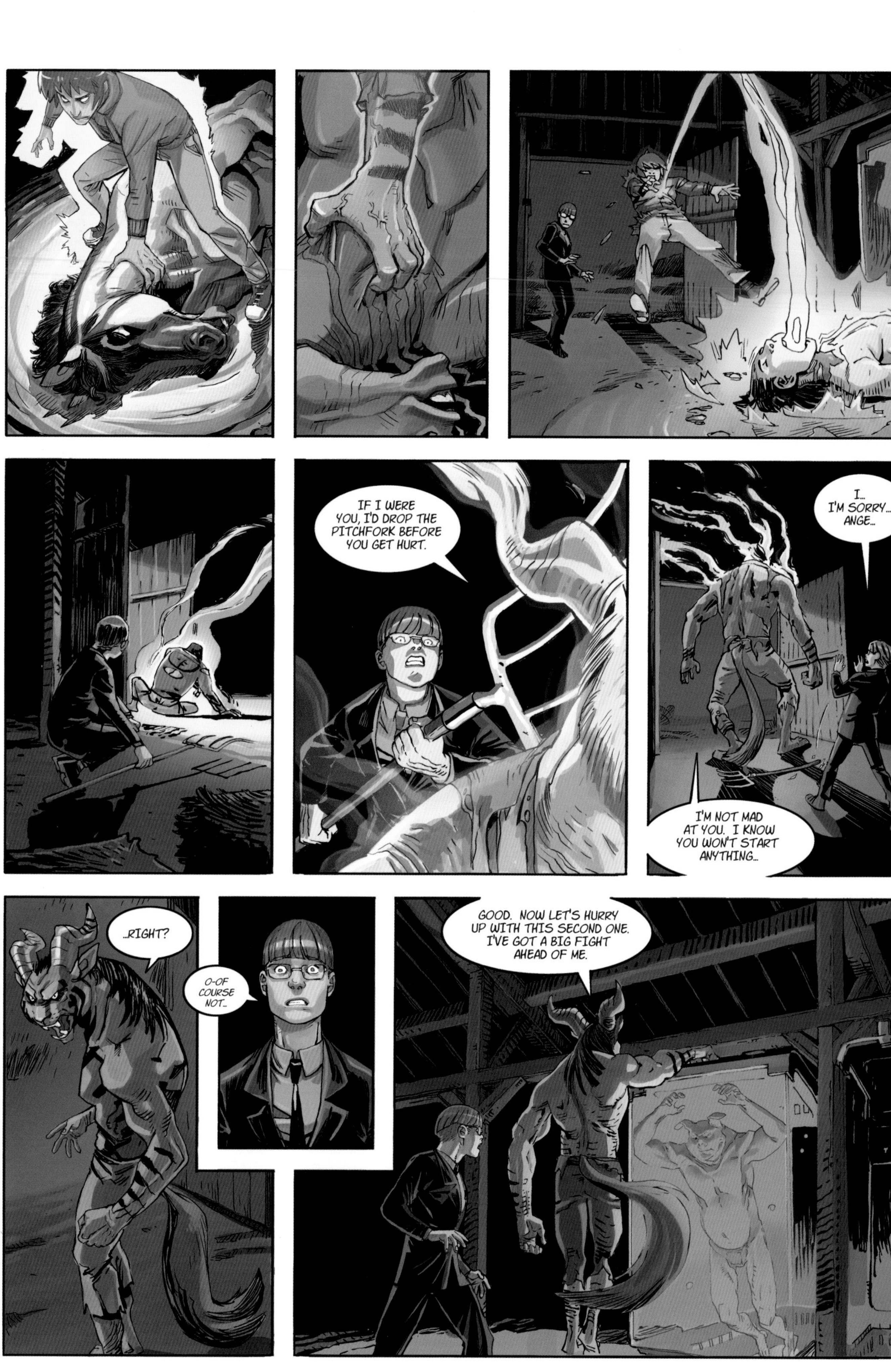

IF I WERE YOU, I'D DROP THE PITCHFORK BEFORE YOU GET HURT.
I... I'M SORRY... ANGE...
I'M NOT MAD AT YOU. I KNOW YOU WON'T START ANYTHING...
...RIGHT?
O-OF COURSE NOT...
GOOD. NOW LET'S HURRY UP WITH THIS SECOND ONE. I'VE GOT A BIG FIGHT AHEAD OF ME.

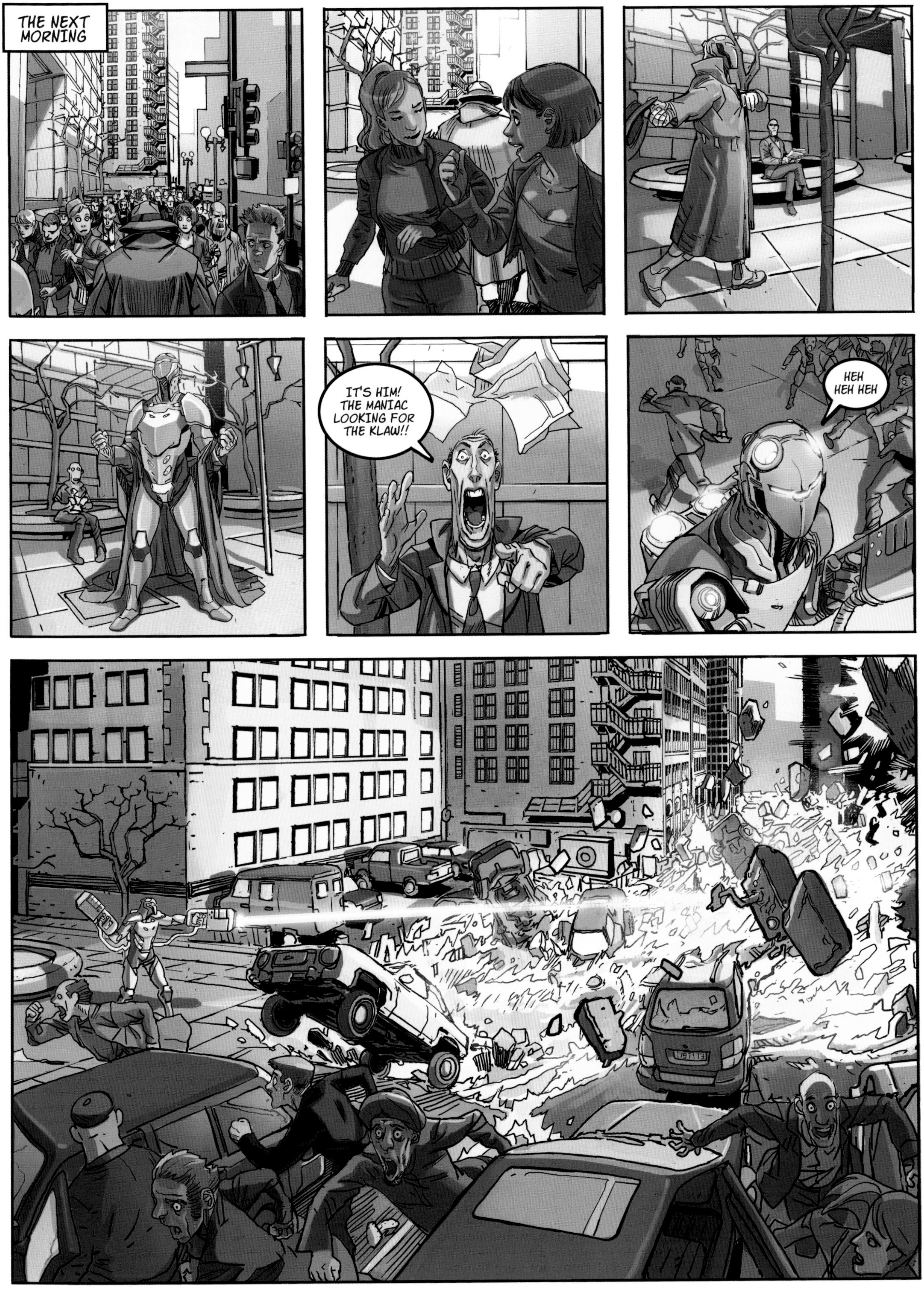
THE NEXT MORNING
IT'S HIM! THE MANIAC LOOKING FOR THE KLAW!!
HEH HEH HEH

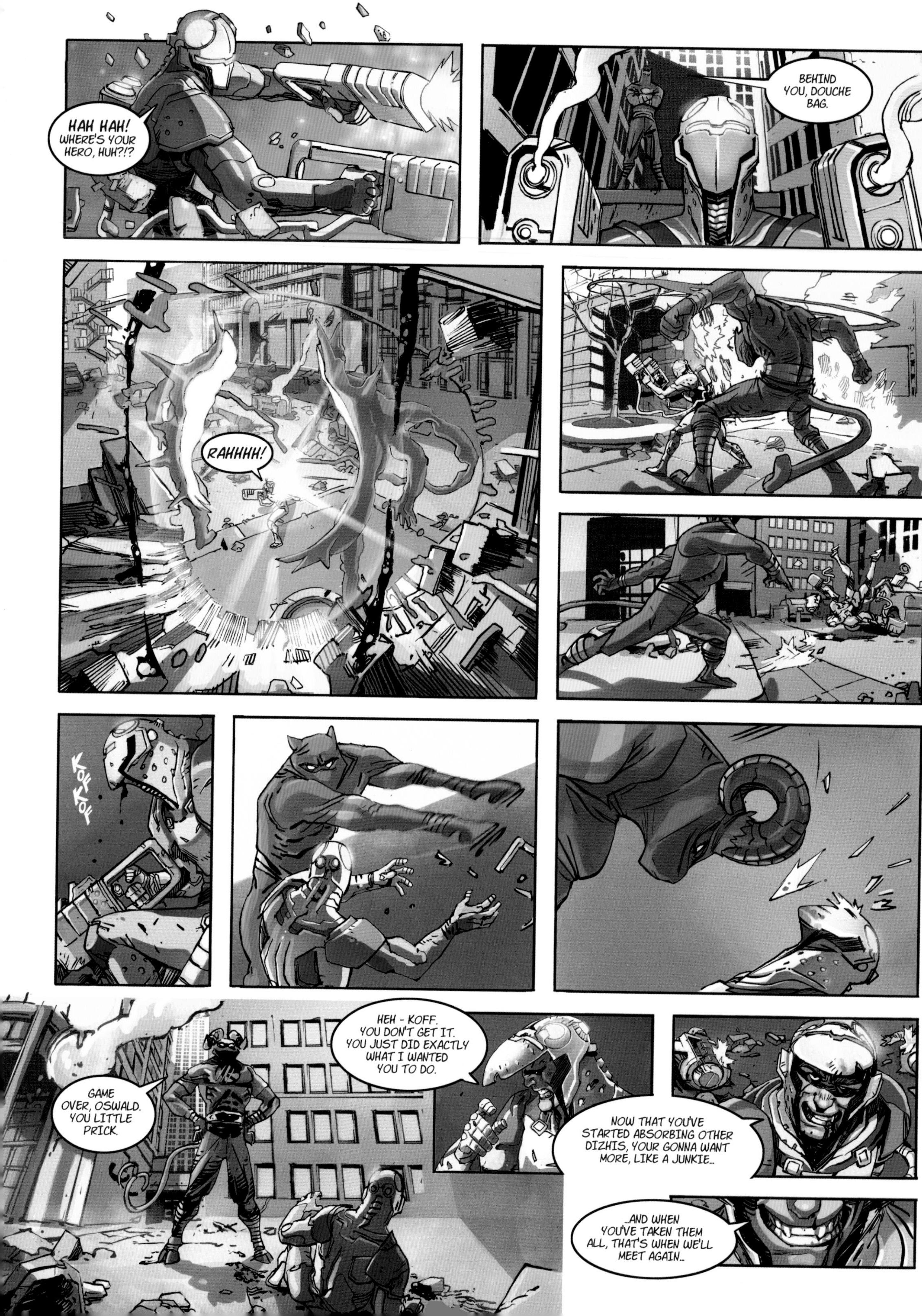
HAH HAH! WHERE'S YOUR HERO, HUH?!?
BEHIND YOU, DOUCHE BAG.
RAHHHH!
KOF KOF
GAME OVER, OSWALD. YOU LITTLE PRICK.
HEH - KOFF. YOU DON'T GET IT. YOU JUST DID EXACTLY WHAT I WANTED YOU TO DO.
NOW THAT YOU'VE STARTED ABSORBING OTHER DIZHIS, YOUR GONNA WANT MORE, LIKE A JUNKIE...
...AND WHEN YOU'VE TAKEN THEM ALL, THAT'S WHEN WE'LL MEET AGAIN...

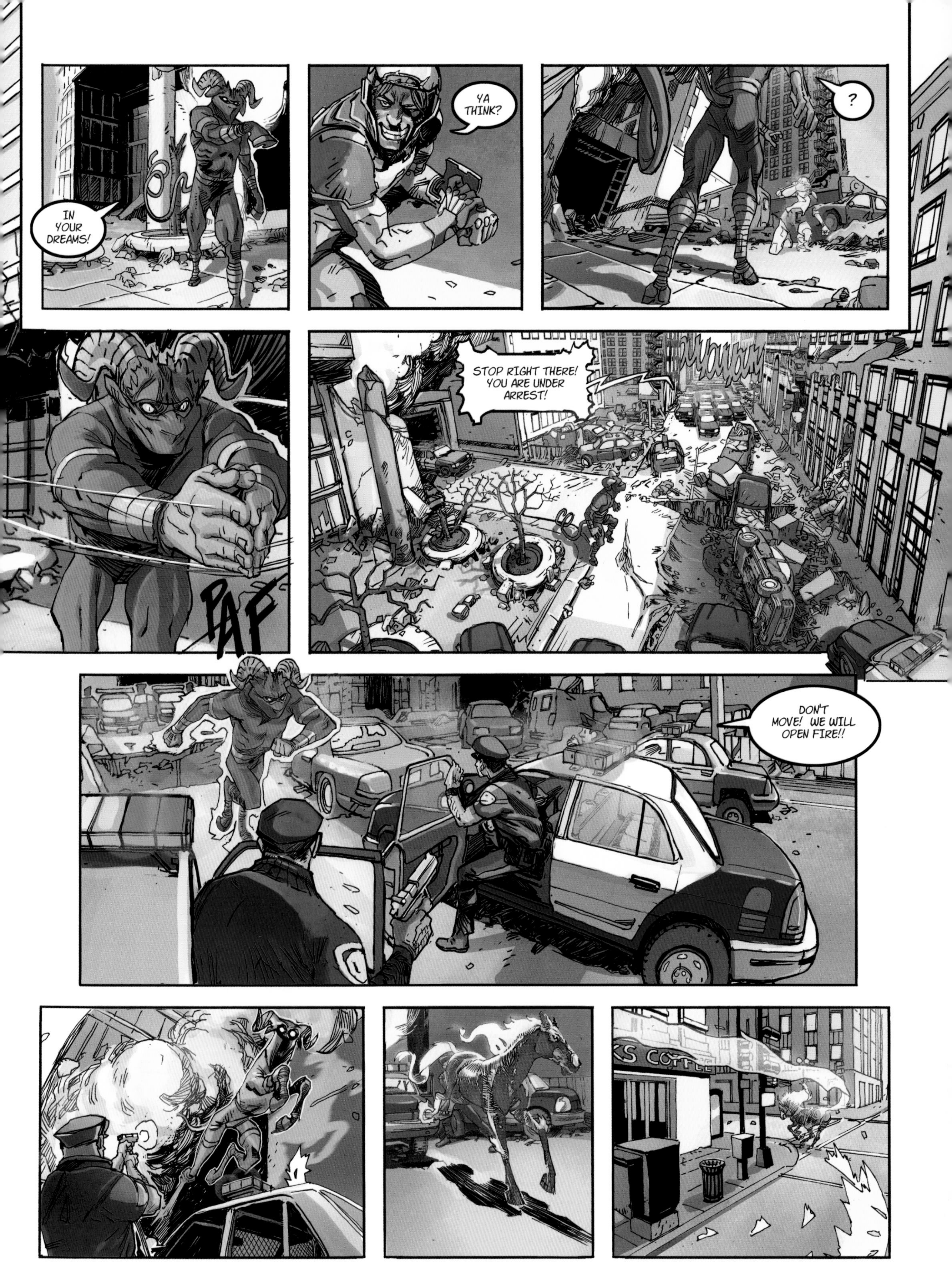
IN YOUR DREAMS!
YA THINK?
?
PAF
STOP RIGHT THERE! YOU ARE UNDER ARREST!
DON'T MOVE! WE WILL OPEN FIRE!!
S COFFE

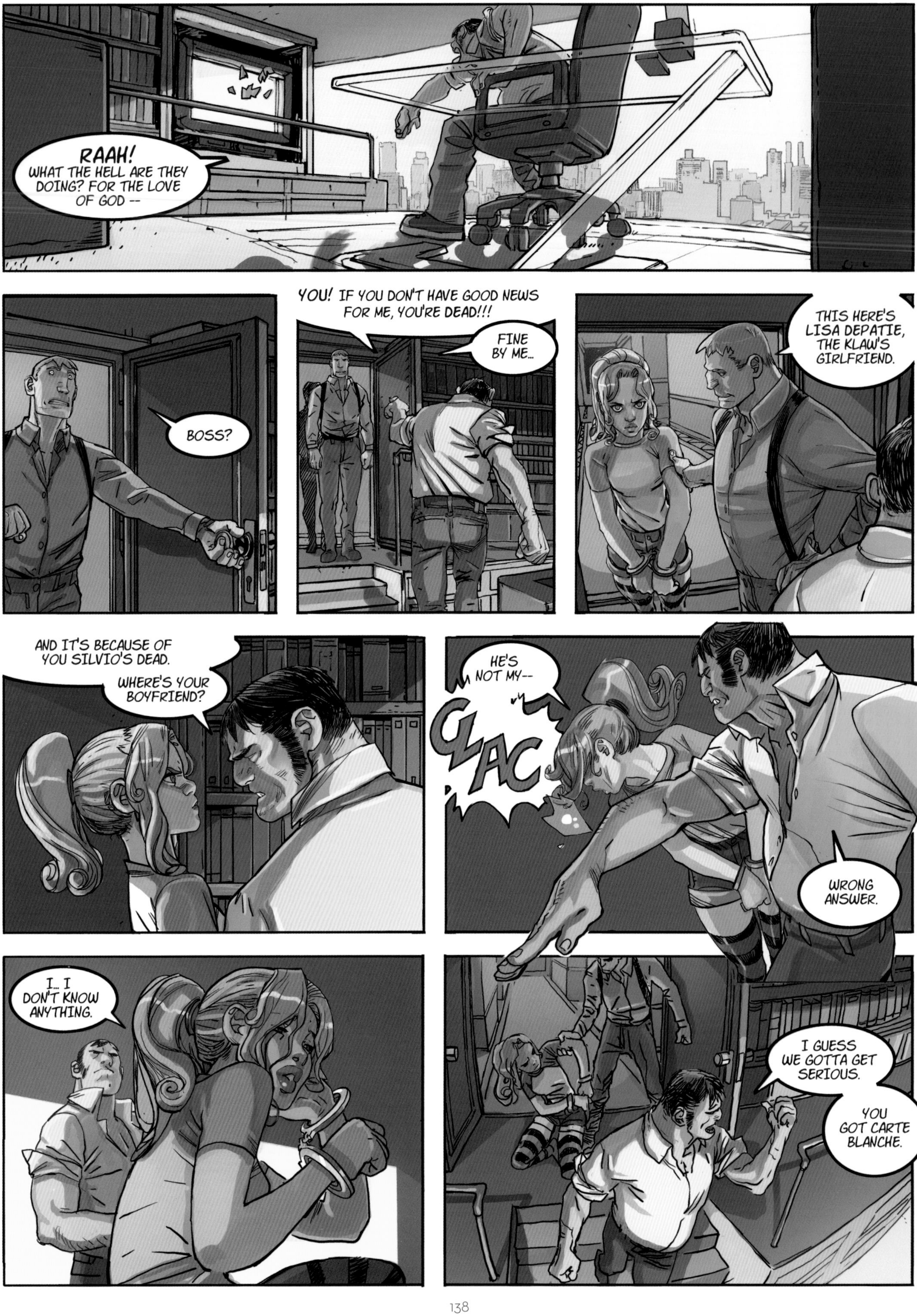
RAAH!
WHAT THE HELL ARE THEY DOING? FOR THE LOVE OF GOD --
BOSS?
YOU! IF YOU DON'T HAVE GOOD NEWS FOR ME, YOU'RE DEAD!!!
FINE BY ME...
THIS HERE'S LISA DEPATIE, THE KLAW'S GIRLFRIEND.
AND IT'S BECAUSE OF YOU SILVIO'S DEAD.
WHERE'S YOUR BOYFRIEND?
HE'S NOT MY--
CLAC
WRONG ANSWER.
I... I DON'T KNOW ANYTHING.
I GUESS WE GOTTA GET SERIOUS.
YOU GOT CARTE BLANCHE.

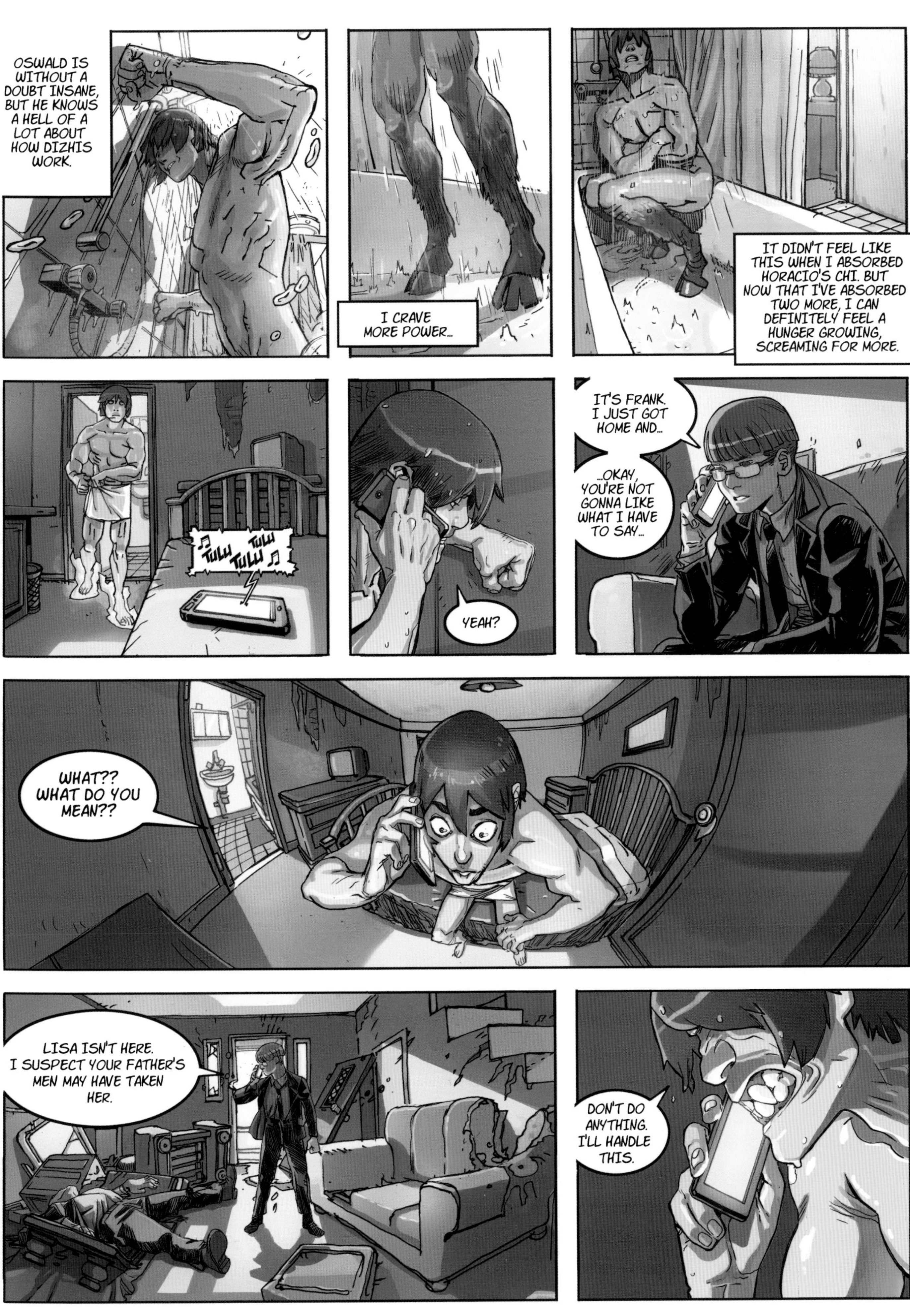

OSWALD IS WITHOUT A DOUBT INSANE, BUT HE KNOWS A HELL OF A LOT ABOUT HOW DIZHIS WORK.
I CRAVE MORE POWER...
IT DIDN'T FEEL LIKE THIS WHEN I ABSORBED HORACIO'S CHI. BUT NOW THAT I'VE ABSORBED TWO MORE, I CAN DEFINITELY FEEL A HUNGER GROWING, SCREAMING FOR MORE.
♫ TULU TULU TULU ♫
YEAH?
IT'S FRANK. I JUST GOT HOME AND...
...OKAY, YOU'RE NOT GONNA LIKE WHAT I HAVE TO SAY...
WHAT?? WHAT DO YOU MEAN??
LISA ISN'T HERE. I SUSPECT YOUR FATHER'S MEN MAY HAVE TAKEN HER.
DON'T DO ANYTHING. I'LL HANDLE THIS.

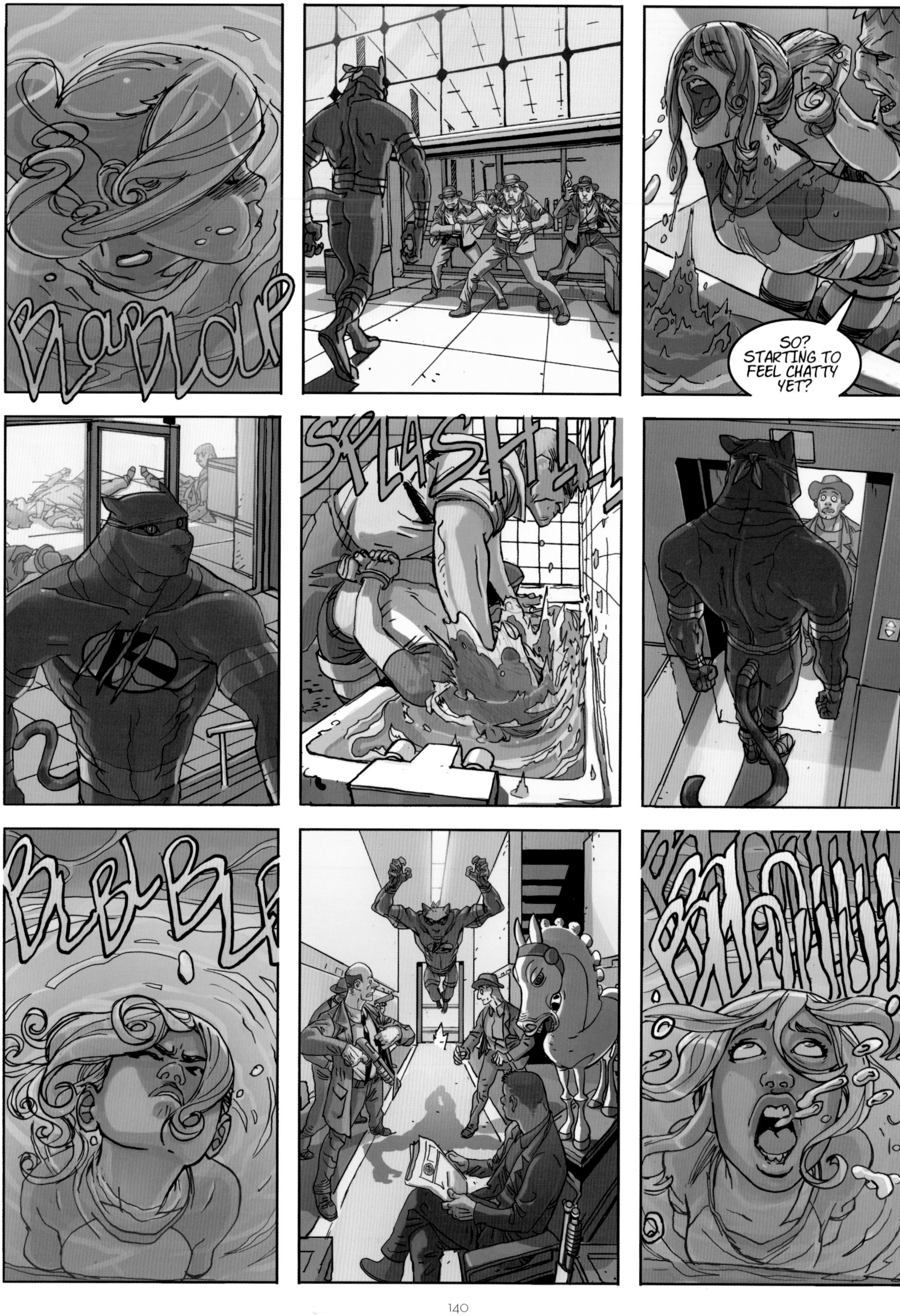
BLOUBLOUP
SO? STARTING TO FEEL CHATTY YET?
SPLASH!!!
BLBLBLE
BLAAAAH!!

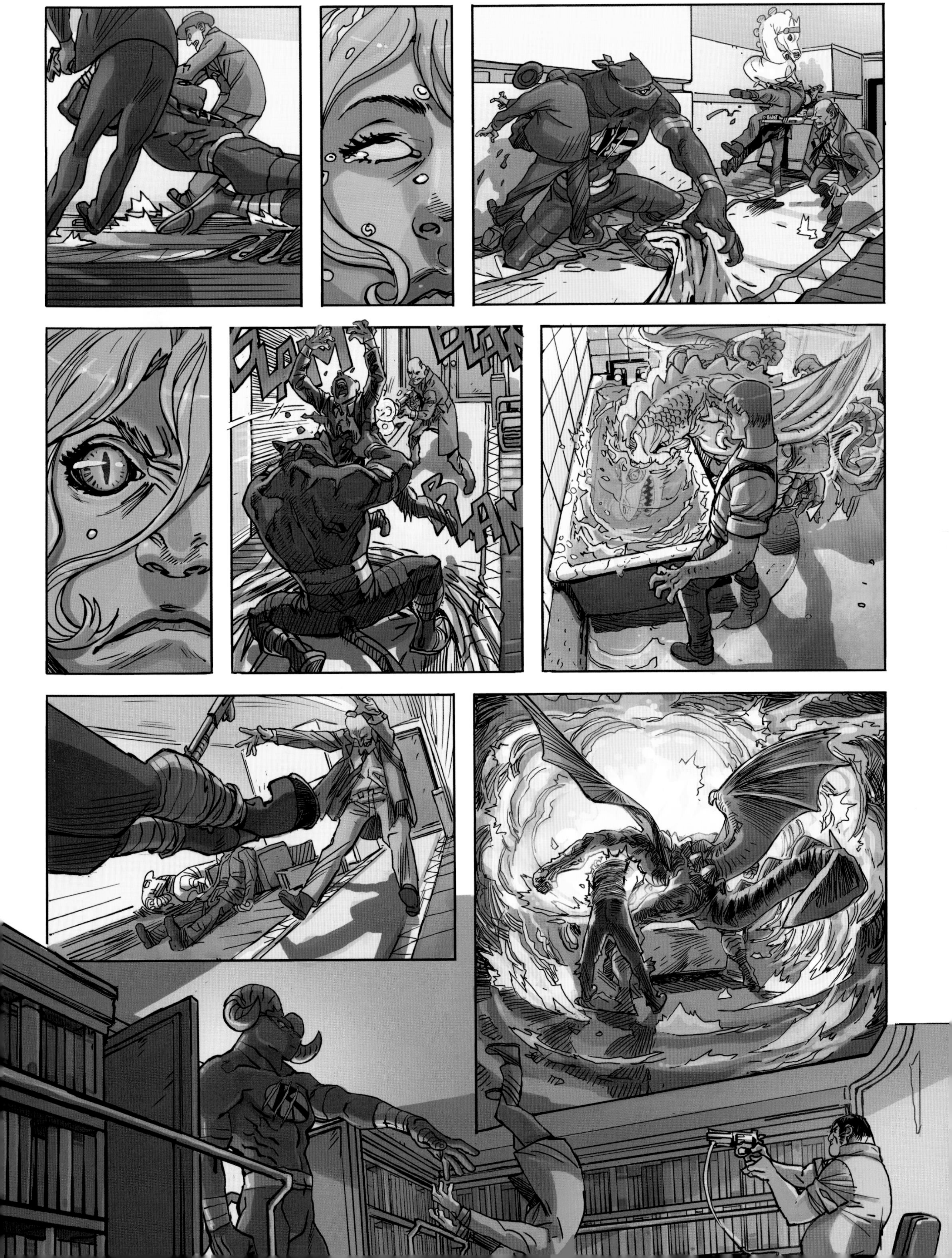

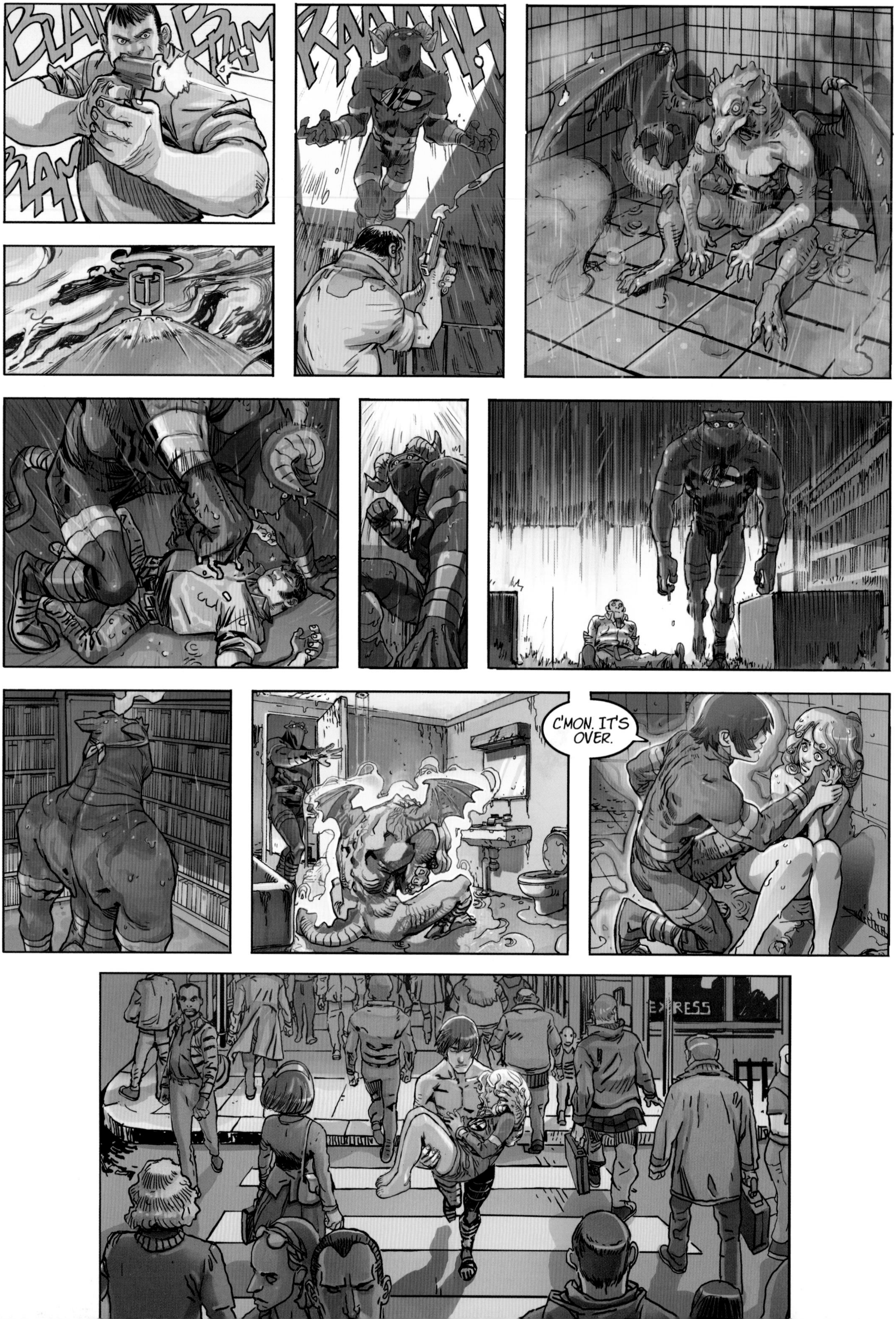
BLAM
BLAM
BLAM
RAAAAH
C'MON. IT'S OVER.
EXPRESS

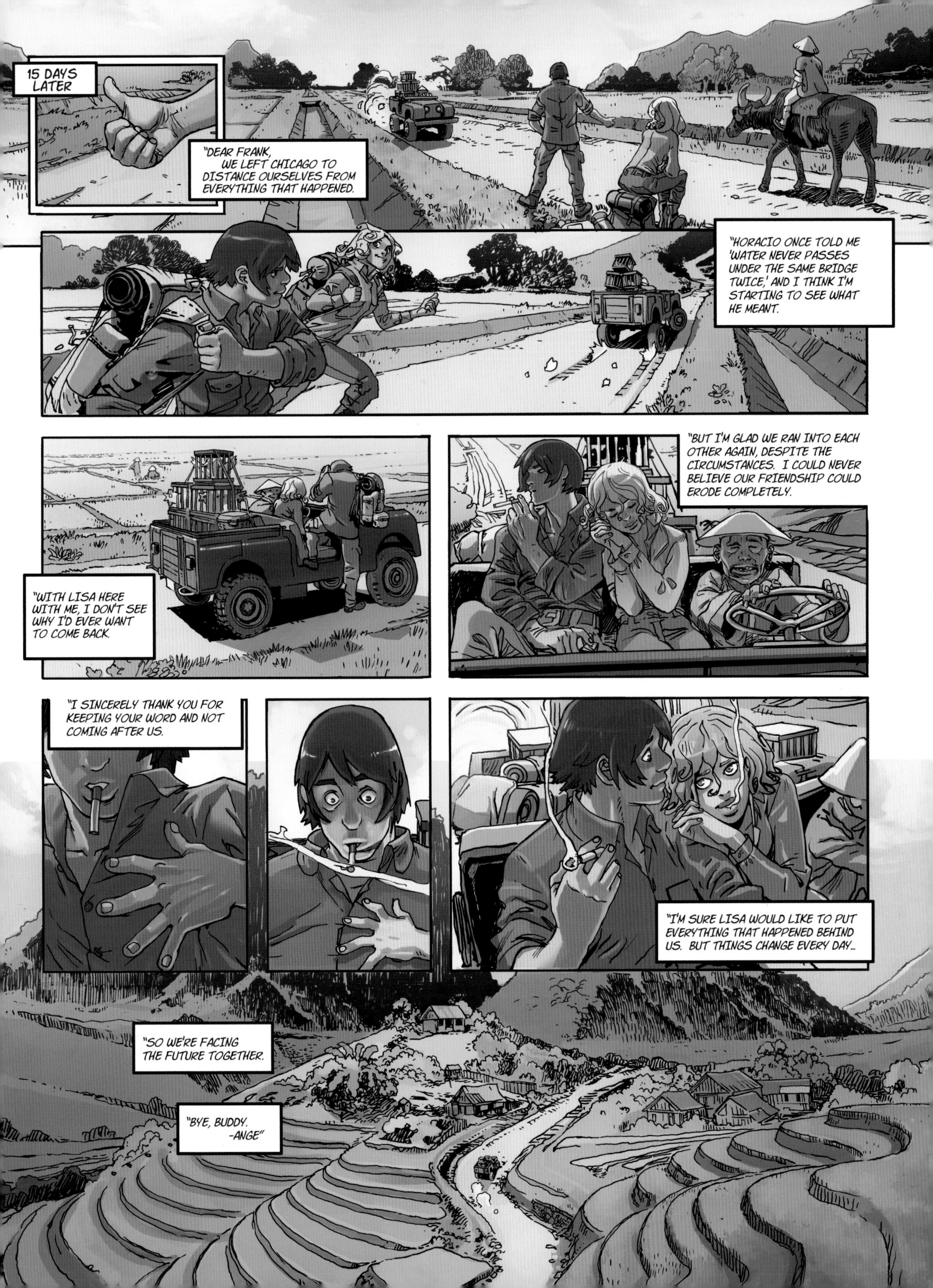
15 DAYS LATER
"DEAR FRANK, WE LEFT CHICAGO TO DISTANCE OURSELVES FROM EVERYTHING THAT HAPPENED.
"HORACIO ONCE TOLD ME 'WATER NEVER PASSES UNDER THE SAME BRIDGE TWICE,' AND I THINK I'M STARTING TO SEE WHAT HE MEANT.
"WITH LISA HERE WITH ME, I DON'T SEE WHY I'D EVER WANT TO COME BACK.
"BUT I'M GLAD WE RAN INTO EACH OTHER AGAIN, DESPITE THE CIRCUMSTANCES. I COULD NEVER BELIEVE OUR FRIENDSHIP COULD ERODE COMPLETELY.
"I SINCERELY THANK YOU FOR KEEPING YOUR WORD AND NOT COMING AFTER US.
"I'M SURE LISA WOULD LIKE TO PUT EVERYTHING THAT HAPPENED BEHIND US. BUT THINGS CHANGE EVERY DAY...
"SO WE'RE FACING THE FUTURE TOGETHER.
"BYE, BUDDY. -ANGE"

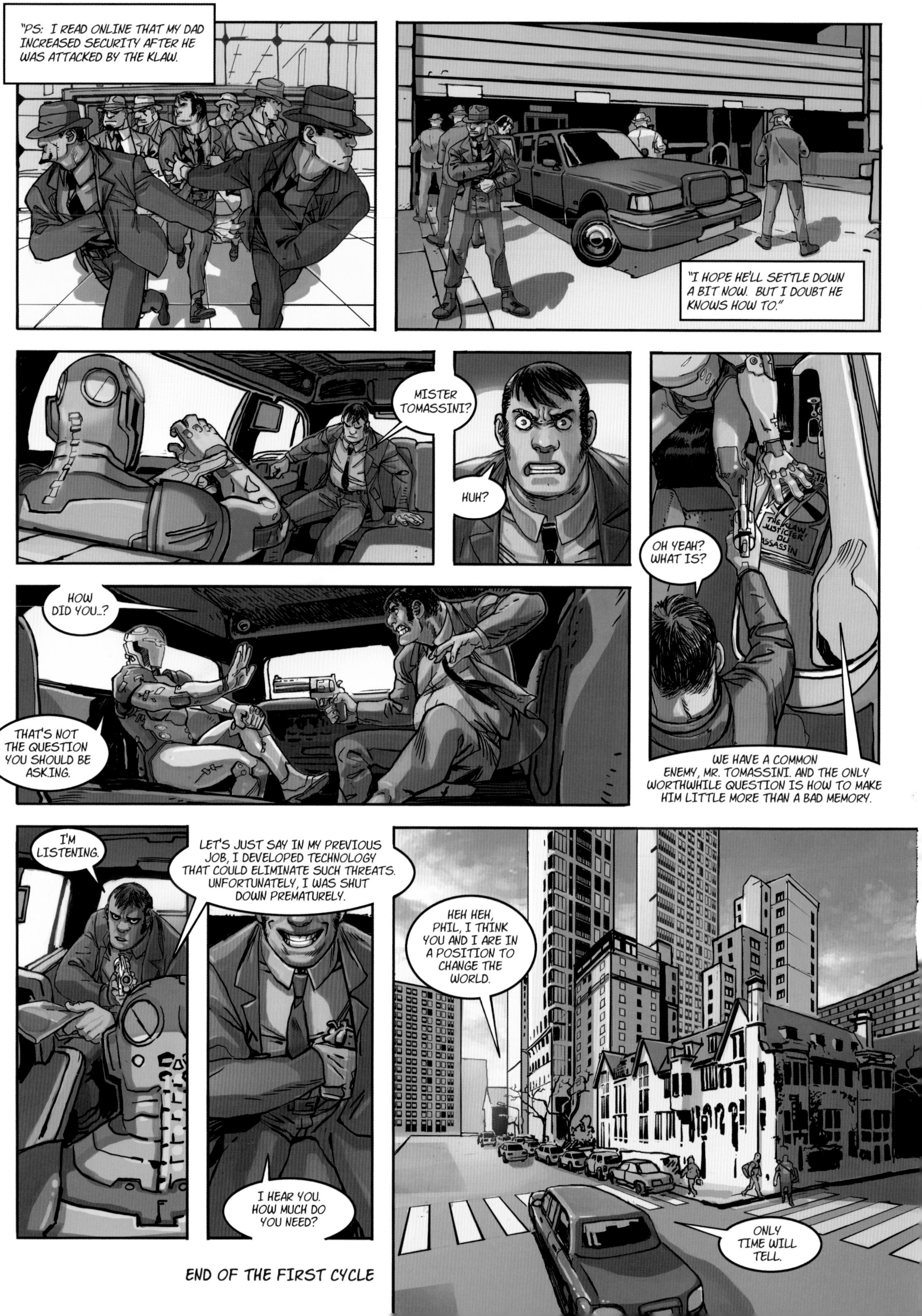
"PS: I READ ONLINE THAT MY DAD INCREASED SECURITY AFTER HE WAS ATTACKED BY THE KLAW.
"I HOPE HE'LL SETTLE DOWN A BIT NOW. BUT I DOUBT HE KNOWS HOW TO."
MISTER TOMASSINI?
HUH?
HOW DID YOU...?
THAT'S NOT THE QUESTION YOU SHOULD BE ASKING.
OH YEAH? WHAT IS?
WE HAVE A COMMON ENEMY, MR. TOMASSINI. AND THE ONLY WORTHWHILE QUESTION IS HOW TO MAKE HIM LITTLE MORE THAN A BAD MEMORY.
I'M LISTENING.
LET'S JUST SAY IN MY PREVIOUS JOB, I DEVELOPED TECHNOLOGY THAT COULD ELIMINATE SUCH THREATS. UNFORTUNATELY, I WAS SHUT DOWN PREMATURELY.
I HEAR YOU. HOW MUCH DO YOU NEED?
HEH HEH, PHIL, I THINK YOU AND I ARE IN A POSITION TO CHANGE THE WORLD.
ONLY TIME WILL TELL.

END OF THE FIRST CYCLE

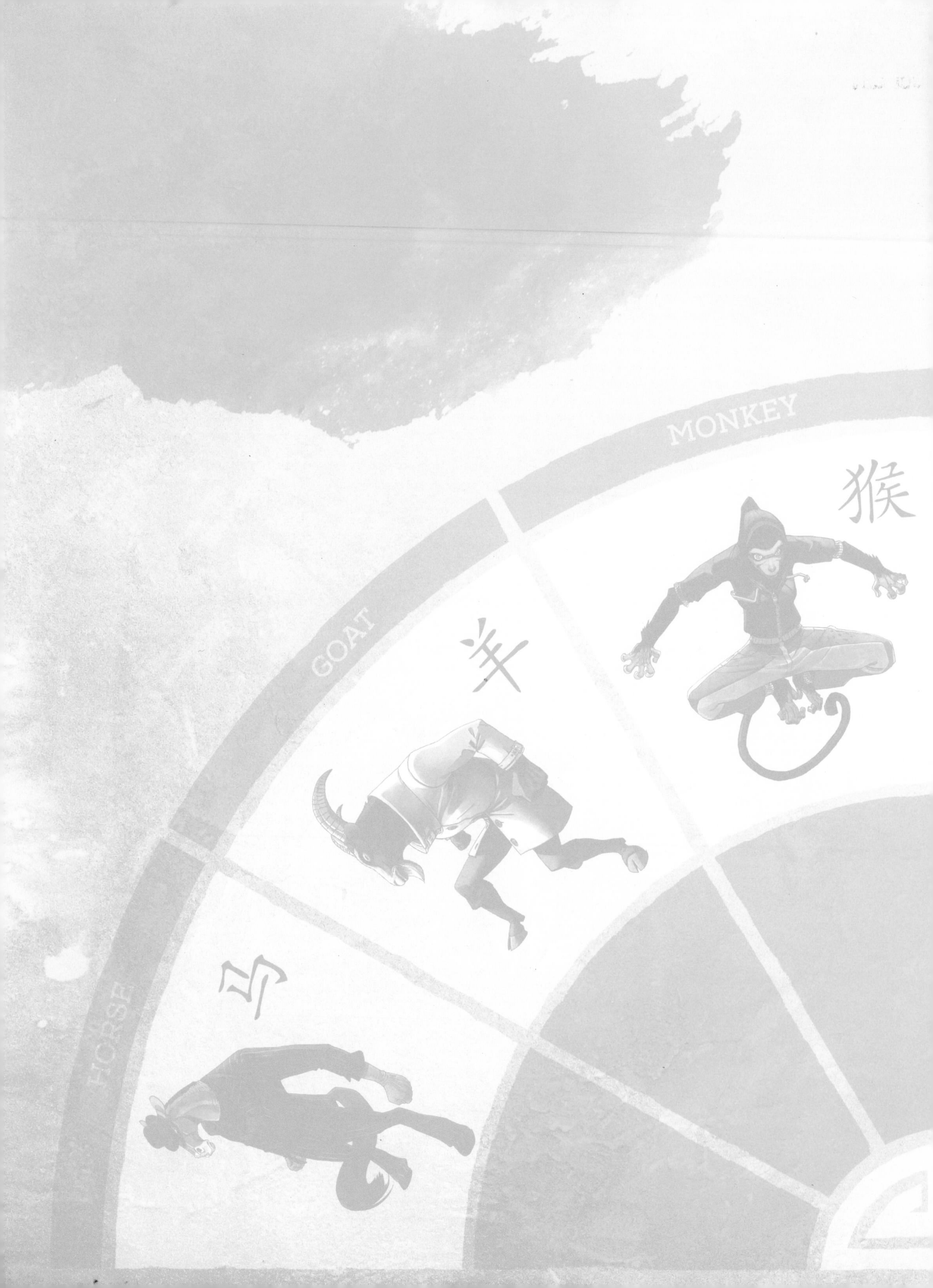
MONKEY
猴
GOAT
羊
HORSE